A young...
A husband...
Stirring times fo...

THE ST...WOOD

Scandals

VOLUME SEVEN

When the debauched Marquis of Sywell won Steepwood
Abbey years ago at cards, it led to the death of the Earl
of Yardley. Now he's caused scandal again by marrying
a girl out of his class – and young enough to be his
granddaughter! After being married only a short time,
the Marchioness has disappeared, leaving no trace of her
whereabouts. There is every expectation that yet more
scandals will emerge, though no one yet knows just
how shocking they will be.

The four villages surrounding the Steepwood Abbey
estate are in turmoil, not only with the dire goings-on at
the Abbey, but also with their own affairs. Each of the
eight volumes in THE STEEPWOOD SCANDALS
contains two full novels that follow the mystery behind
the disappearance of the young woman, and the
individual romances of lovers connected in some way
with the intrigue.

THE STEEPWOOD

Scandals

Regency drama, intrigue, mischief...
and marriage

THE STEEPWOOD
Scandals

Volume 7

Meg Alexander & Nicola Cornick

*M&B™ and M&B™ with the Rose Device
are trademarks of the publisher.*

*Harlequin Mills & Boon Limited, Eton House,
18-24 Paradise Road, Richmond, Surrey TW9 1SR*

First published in Great Britain in 2002

THE STEEPWOOD SCANDALS © Harlequin Books S.A. 2007

Mr Rushford's Honour © Harlequin Books S.A. 2002
An Unlikely Suitor © Harlequin Books S.A. 2002

*Special thanks and acknowledgement are given to
Meg Alexander and Nicola Cornick for their contribution to
The Steepwood Scandals series.*

ISBN: 978 0 263 85501 2

052-0507

*Printed and bound in Spain
by Litografía Rosés S.A., Barcelona*

Mr Rushford's Honour

by

Meg Alexander

After living in southern Spain for many years, **Meg Alexander** now lives in Kent, although having been born in Lancashire, she feels that her roots are in the north of England. Meg's career has encompassed a wide variety of roles, from professional cook to assistant director of a conference centre. She has always been a voracious reader, and loves to write. Other loves include history, cats, gardening, cooking and travel. She has a son and two grandchildren.

Chapter One

Spring 1812

Gina Whitelaw was no beauty—a fact which was not immediately apparent to the watching bystanders who clustered about her coach.

Too short by a full head to be described as willowy, and blessed only with hair of an indeterminate shade of brown, it was difficult to understand the gasp of admiration which greeted her as she stepped into the street.

It was possibly the sheer perfection of her expensive toilette, the dashing bonnet, the beautifully cut redingote which clung so lovingly to her voluptuous curves, or the glimpse of a neatly turned ankle clad in fine leather half-boots.

A passing gentleman noticed none of these things. As she turned her head to speak to her coachman the well-remembered voice stopped him in mid-stride, leaving him feeling as if someone had just dealt him a sharp blow to the solar plexus.

Gina had not seen him. He stepped into the doorway across the street, feasting his eyes upon the face which had haunted him for the past ten years.

She hadn't changed much in all that time. He would have known her anywhere. The brilliant blue gaze was just the same, as was the enchanting smile which curved that generous mouth.

His feelings threatened to overwhelm him. Surely she must sense his closeness. The bond between them had been so strong. Had they not agreed together that they were two halves of one whole? He waited, willing her to reach out to him across the years, but the separation had been too long. The old magic which had made them aware of the presence of each other at a distance had clearly vanished.

She turned away and walked into the house, smiling and chatting to the two girls who accompanied her.

Giles shuddered. Could they be her own? A moment's reflection convinced him that it was impossible. The girls were well-grown teenagers. He looked again at the coach, and recognised the Whitelaw crest emblazoned on the doors. Clearly Gina was still connected with the family, but in what capacity? He was no expert in the finer points of fashion, but the exquisitely dressed creature who stepped down just a moment ago was obviously not a servant. Had Whitelaw made her his mistress? He clenched his fists until the knuckles whitened, miserably aware that he was fully deserving of the agony the notion caused him.

He had left her without a word of explanation, in a foreign country, and at the beck and call of her employers. He could only blame himself if Gina had taken the route followed by many another.

He was only half aware of the buzz of speculation which surrounded him. With the excitement of the new arrival over, the crowd was drifting away. Snatches of their conversation reached his ears.

''Tis high time the old Mansion House was taken,' an elderly woman assured her friend. ''Twill be good for trade to have some new blood in the village.'

'Aye! There will be many as will hope to make their fortune on the back of that young creature's spending.'

'I make no doubt she can afford it,' the first speaker said. 'The place is bought, not rented, so I hear, and at a price that you would not believe.' She named a figure which made her companion gasp. 'The builders are in already,' she continued.

'But who is she? And why come to Abbot Quincey? She looks to me more like a townie than a countrywoman. Them with money prefers the life in Lunnon, especially at her age.'

'Don't you know her? Oh I forgot, you being an in-comer an' all. She'd gone by the time you came to live here. I recognised her at once. 'Tis Gina Westcott, the baker's daughter.'

'Oh my! I thought she was a lady.' The note of disappointment in the second speaker's voice was clear. 'Ain't she the one who ran away to see the world?'

'Some such nonsense!' her friend agreed. 'Looks to me as if she's seen more than the world...' A leer accompanied this remark and brought a chuckle from the other woman.

Giles flushed with anger and moved away before he was tempted into a sharp retort. He turned into the Angel, and early as it was, he ordered a glass of brandy. Then he strolled over to the window and gazed back down the street towards the Mansion House.

What on earth had persuaded Gina to come back to Abbot Quincey? The snide remarks that he had overheard would be the first of many. She would be exposed to every kind of rumour and speculation. No one would call upon her, and she faced a life of bitter loneliness.

He could do nothing for her. Had it not been for his sister's splendid marriage he would be living upon his uncle's charity and the kind invitations of his friends. Sipping his drink, he sighed as he reflected upon the past ten years. Summoned from Italy and Gina's arms, he had returned to Abbot Quincey at his uncle's request in an attempt to save the family fortunes.

It had all been in vain. Hard as he had worked to restore the estate so badly neglected by his charming but feckless father, all had been lost on that dreadful night last year when Gareth Rushford had gambled away the last of his patrimony. Worse had followed when the father whom they loved in spite of his weakness had been crushed to death in a carriage accident.

'Cheer up, old fellow! It can't be as bad as all that!'

Giles turned to find his brother-in-law beside him.

Giles smiled in spite of himself. After an uneasy start he had grown fond of his eldest sister's husband.

'Will you join me, Isham?' He gestured towards his glass.

'I think I'd better if you are about to crush me with some dire news.' Isham signalled to the landlord. 'What is it, Giles? You look as though you've seen a ghost.'

'In a way I have. It is just that…well…I caught a glimpse of someone I used to know.'

'I hope he isn't about to run you through. What have you been up to?'

'It's nothing like that. And it isn't a "he". It's a "she".'

'Oh dear! As bad as that?' Isham began to smile. 'Speak to the lady, Giles. I'm sure she will forgive you…'

'I fear she won't. It is too late for that.' For a minute Giles was tempted to confide in the tall figure beside him. Then he thought better of it. There was Gina's good name to consider. He made an effort to change the subject. 'What are you doing here?' he asked.

'I'm planning to call upon an old friend. The promise was made some time ago.'

'And India isn't with you? She isn't ill, I hope?'

'On the contrary. She is in the best of health, if a little queasy in the mornings… She has been awaiting your return from Bristol for these past ten days or more.'

'We were much delayed.' Giles gave his brother-in-law a rueful smile. 'Mama determined upon a triumphal progress to receive the congratulations of her friends upon Letty's betrothal. I thought we'd never see Abbot Quincey again.' He hesitated. 'Anthony, I didn't mean to stay away so long. I feel I've let you down…about managing the estate, I mean.'

'Nonsense. If you had to be away it was best to go before the spring, and the ladies could not have travelled without an escort. In any case, I was glad you were not here when Henry died.'

Giles gripped his hand in quick sympathy. 'What a brute I am not to have offered you my condolences! That was a bad business. How is his mother now?'

'Lucia is recovering slowly…' Lord Isham gazed into space. Best to let Giles believe that the man the world had regarded as his half-brother had died defending his loved ones from the mob. Only India and Henry's mother knew the truth of it beside himself. Henry, not knowing that he was no blood relative to Isham, had come to the Grange that dreadful night to remove both India and his lordship from his path, believing that he would inherit title, wealth and lands. The mob he led would be used to cloak the murders. By a strange twist of fate he had been killed himself by a single shot fired by one of the Luddites.

'Have the authorities caught the man?' Giles was forced to repeat his question twice.

'What?' Recalled to the present, Isham shook his

head. 'I doubt if they ever will. The crowd was huge and it was dark. Now we are met by a wall of silence.' He glanced at his watch. 'Forgive me, Giles, but I am late. I must present myself at the Mansion House without delay.'

He had not expected his words to produce the effect they did. Giles stiffened and went pale.

'The Mansion House? Why, who...I mean...do you know the people there?'

'Lady Whitelaw has just bought the place. Her husband was one of my closest friends.'

'Great heavens, is her ladyship still alive? When I knew her she was at death's door.'

'When was that?' Isham was clearly puzzled.

'It was ten years ago...in Italy.' Giles forced out the words through stiff lips. 'She was not expected to live beyond the year's end.'

Isham's brow cleared. 'Oh, you are thinking of Whitelaw's first wife. Gina is blooming, as you may see for yourself if you accompany me. She married Whitelaw two years later. Did you not meet her when you were in Italy?'

'Yes...! No...!' Giles was reeling under a second shock that morning. Suddenly, he felt that his high cravat was choking him. If he didn't get away he would betray himself. His little Gina married to a man almost old enough to be her grandfather! It didn't bear thinking of. He made his excuses quickly.

'Another time, perhaps? I must go. Mother and Letty will be waiting. We'll see you at the Grange.'

'I shan't be long. The call is merely to see if Gina

needs help in settling in.' Isham accompanied him
into the street and turned in the direction of the
Mansion House.

Giles felt more confused than ever. If Gina had a
husband why would she need Isham's help? He was
burning to know the answer and cursed himself for a
coward, knowing in his heart that he had been unable
to face her. What must she think of him, if, indeed,
she thought of him at all?

He wasn't proud of his behaviour. She had been
such an open, friendly child, sixteen at the most. And
at twenty how was he himself to know that what had
started as a teasing, laughing friendship would develop so quickly into a passionate love affair.

His thoughts grew sombre. They had been so
young, the pair of them. Perhaps, for her, the pain of
that sudden separation had not struck so deep. There
would have been bewilderment, a few tears, and possibly anger. Then she would have forgotten him. As
he had forgotten her?

His lips twisted in a bitter grimace. Not a day had
passed when she was absent from his thoughts.

On his return to England he had written to her, but
she had not replied. In a Europe plunged once more
into the turmoil of war after the collapse of the Treaty
of Amiens he could not be sure that she had ever
received his letters, or indeed, if she and the Whitelaw
family were still alive. He had no way of finding
them. All his enquiries had been fruitless, and
Napoleon's armies still ravaged the continent of
Europe.

How many nights had he lain awake picturing un-
known horrors? Sometimes he'd imagined her lifeless
corpse beneath a pile of shattered masonry. He'd tried
to close his eyes to a more terrifying fate. Gina might
have been taken alive by an advancing army. He was
under no illusion as to what would have happened
then.

Now he made an effort to recover his composure.
His worst fears had not been realised. Clearly, Gina
was well and happy. For that, at least, he must be
thankful, though he must face the fact that she was
finally lost to him.

Something of the strain he was feeling must have
shown upon his face. His sister noticed it at once.

'Giles, is anything amiss?' she asked quietly.

'You may well ask, Letty!' Mrs Rushford's look of
anxiety gave way to an expression of annoyance. 'My
dear boy, where have you been? I was persuaded that
you had met with an accident. We have been waiting
for you this age. I must hope that I haven't caught a
chill, standing about in this sharp wind.'

'Mother, you should have waited in the coach.'

'We have not been here above a minute,' Letty
assured him. 'Hammonds had the goods we needed.
It took some time to choose.'

Mrs Rushford tossed her head, 'That's as maybe!
It does not take long for a woman of my delicate state
of health to fall victim to an affliction of the lungs.'

'I'm sorry to have kept you waiting. I met Isham
in the town.'

'Was India with him?' Mrs Rushford's petulant expression didn't change. 'Do you tell me that they knew that we were here, and didn't come to greet us?'

'Isham was alone.' Giles handed the ladies into the coach. 'India is waiting at the Grange. She didn't expect us until later in the day.'

'Did I not say that there was no necessity to leave at such a ridiculously early hour this morning? But you would have it, Giles. All this rushing about will do my health no good at all. Had it not been for the invitation from Lady Wells I should not have considered travelling in the winter.'

Letty squeezed her mother's hand. 'But now it is the spring. Besides, you did it for me, and you dealt with Lady Wells so beautifully. In the end she raised no objection to my engagement to Oliver.'

'I should think not indeed. She may consider herself fortunate to have formed a connection with the Ishams. It was far more than she might have hoped for in the marriage of a younger son. The woman is a positive toad-eater! I gave her a sharp set-down or two. Such pretensions! Isham will put her in her place, I make no doubt.'

Letty made haste to change the subject of her fearsome mother-in-law to be.

'How is India? I have missed her so.'

'Why Letty, she is blooming, so I hear, though Isham mentioned that she had been queasy...'

To his astonishment this innocuous piece of information resulted in his gaining his mother's full attention.

'Queasy, you say? Thank heavens for that! Oh,

where is Isham? I must talk to him at once.' Mrs Rushford leaned out of the carriage window and began to scan the street.

'Mother, don't distress yourself. India is not seriously ill.'

'Of course she isn't, you foolish creature! She is probably with child. Oh, drat the man! He is large enough for anyone to see him. Where can he have got to?'

'He is paying a call on Lady Whitelaw,' Giles said stiffly.

'Lady Whitelaw? Who is she? I have not heard the name before…'

'She has taken the old Mansion House…bought it, I believe…'

Mrs Rushford settled back against the leather cushions, her good humour quite restored. 'Splendid! Splendid! I shall call upon her without delay. Does Isham know her well?'

'Her husband is a friend of his.' Giles signalled to the coachman and the carriage rolled away. This was not the time to explain that Lady Whitelaw was the former Gina Westcott, the baker's daughter. Even her title might not be enough to wipe away that taint of trade.

Then he smiled to himself. Isham was more than a match for his snobbish mother-in-law. If he decreed that Lady Whitelaw was a welcome visitor, both she and her husband would be invited to the Grange.

For his own part, the thought filled him with trepidation. How was he to face her? Had his circumstances been different he would have gone away at once, but now, as estate manager, he was tied to the place.

She herself might refuse the invitation when she realised that Isham was married to his sister. On the other hand, she might accept, longing for revenge, and prepared to rejoice in his discomfiture. He lapsed into silence. He would have given much to have heard the result of Isham's interview with Gina.

It would not have comforted him. Gina had welcomed her visitor with every appearance of pleasure. Apparently untroubled by the bustle about her, she hurried towards his lordship holding out both her hands.

'Anthony, you are a genius! How did you find this place?'

'It wasn't difficult,' he teased. 'No one had moved it.' Isham glanced about him. 'Will it suit you, Gina?'

'It is perfect...exactly what I wanted!' The vivid little face was alive with enthusiasm. 'It was good of you to attend to all the details for me. I could never have done it from Scotland. My dear, I hated to ask you when you had so much else to think about.'

'You didn't ask me...I offered,' he said lightly. 'I'm always at your service. You must remember that.'

'How can I forget it? You have done so much for me and the girls.' She laid a sympathetic hand upon his arm. 'I was so sorry to hear of your brother's death.'

'As was I to hear of the death of Whitelaw. He was always a good friend to me.'

'He was one of the kindest people I ever met,' she said simply. 'I was lucky to have known him.'

'He felt the same, my dear. He never tired of singing your praises. I can't think what the family would have done without you. How are the girls?'.

'They are growing fast. I have two young ladies on my hands. Mair will have her Season next year.'

'Great heavens! It doesn't seem possible. I thought that they were still children.'

'They are, in a way, but the young grow up before one knows it.' Gina smiled. 'Enough about our concerns…will you bring your wife to see me soon? We were all so delighted to learn of your marriage.'

The harsh face of her companion softened into an expression of the utmost tenderness. 'I love her dearly, Gina, and now, though it is early days, we may have a child before the year is out.'

He made no attempt to disguise his delight and Gina jumped up and kissed him.

'That is the best news in the world! Now you shall not bring her into Abbot Quincey over these dreadful roads. I shall come to you when it is convenient.' Gina paused. 'Does she know who I am?'

'I haven't discussed your affairs with anyone, but what difference can it make?'

She gave him a speculative look. 'Never forget that I was the daughter of the baker in this village, Anthony. That fact will not sit well with everyone.'

She saw his face darken and made haste to reassure

him. 'You must not be angry with me. You, of all people, would not marry a petty-minded woman, but there are others who will not take so generous a view.'

'Shall you care? I had thought that with this house and your title and...er...'

'The fortune? Well, I won't be mealy-mouthed about it. All that will help, but my antecedents will not be forgotten. I would not put your wife in a difficult position...'

Isham laughed aloud. 'You do not know her yet. If there is one person likely to champion your cause it will be India. She tells me that I am a law unto myself, but the same applies to her.'

'Even so, I feel that you should tell her about my former life. I did run away from here, you know.'

'At fifteen, wasn't it? I've often wondered about that. What made you leave your family? You took a dreadful chance, you know.'

'I wanted to see the world.' Gina was absorbed in straightening the fringe upon her cuff and she didn't look at him. 'I went in search of adventure.' It wasn't the whole truth, but it was as much as she would admit to.

'Well, you certainly found that.' Isham looked at the bent head and wondered. 'Whitelaw told me often of your courage in facing bandits and mutinous seamen. Doesn't anything frighten you?'

'There was no point in being frightened.' She gave him a merry look. 'Much better to learn to use a pistol well and be prepared to use it. It is a powerful persuader in places such as India, especially when one does not speak the language.'

'A telling argument, if ever I heard one!' Isham laughed again. 'Did you find the same in Europe and the Caribbean?'

'I did.' She shared in his amusement and then the laughter faded from her eyes. 'There were the girls to think about,' she said quietly. 'And her ladyship grew worse throughout our travels, though Whitelaw searched unceasingly for a cure. When she died I thought that he would not recover.'

'You were devoted to both of them, I think.'

'I owed them so much. Oh, Anthony, even at fifteen I was not a complete fool. Had I not gone to them as nursemaid to the girls I might have lived a very different life, that is, if I had survived.'

Isham rose to his feet. 'You are a born survivor, Gina. I have no doubt of that. After a brush with bandits a few old tabbies won't distress you with their gossip. Now you will let me know if there is aught that I can do for you?'

'I will.' Gina held out her hand. 'Thank you again, my friend. I'm sure we will be happy here.'

But Isham was still wondering as he walked back to the smithy. Why had Gina returned to Abbot Quincey when she might have settled anywhere in the country?

There was some hidden agenda, he was sure of it, sensing a certain reserve in the normally open manner of his old friend's wife. It wasn't like her, and it troubled him.

Had she returned to her birthplace with the intention of paying off old scores? No, that would be totally out of character. He would not even suspect her of a very human wish to flaunt her good fortune in front of those who might previously have despised her. That was not Gina. He knew her to be cheerful, dependable, and painfully honest. But there was something. He shook his head and went to find his horse.

Meantime, Gina was lost in thought. Her plans were going well, but there was still much to do. She looked up smiling as Mair and Elspeth came to find her.

'Do you like your rooms?' she asked.

Mair settled down beside her, resting her head against Gina's knee. 'Perfection!' she said in a dreamy tone. 'You were so clever to find this place.'

'We have Lord Isham to thank for that,' she told them. 'You have just missed him.'

'Oh, no!' Elspeth was dismayed. Her hero-worship of his lordship had been the cause of much teasing within the family. 'When is he to call again?'

'We are to call upon Lord Isham and his wife,' Gina said firmly. 'Now Elspeth, do not pull a face. It is unbecoming. We are to wish his lordship happy, as you must agree.'

'I thought he would not marry,' Elspeth said ungraciously. 'At least until…'

'Until you were old enough to wed him?' Mair giggled. 'By that time he'd be in his dotage…'

'Really, girls, this will not do! I will not have you

speak so of a family friend. Now we have much to
do. How does cook go on? I told her that our nuncheon should be light today. We shall eat it now.
Then you may get back to your books.'

There was a united cry of despair.

'Must we?' Mair pleaded.

'Indeed you must. Have I not explained so often
the importance of an education?'

'But darling Gina, there is so much time for that.'
Mair held her stepmother's hand against her cheek.
'May we not have a holiday, just for this one day?'

Gina glanced down at the fiery head. 'Sometimes
I despair of you,' she scolded. 'It has taken me a full
ten years to educate myself. Now the task is in your
own hands, if you will but take advantage of it.'

Elspeth took her other hand. 'But you will help us,
Gina, won't you? Suppose we promise to work twice
as hard tomorrow? You can't mean to keep our noses
to the grindstone all the time.'

'I haven't seen much evidence of that,' Gina said
solemnly. Then Mair looked up at her and saw the
laughter in her eyes.

'Why, Elspeth, she doesn't mean a word of it.' She
jumped up, drawing Gina to her feet and grasping her
sister's other hand. 'Time for a war-dance!' she announced.

Whooping and stamping, the two girls drew their
stepmother into a ring, chanting as they moved
around.

'Now we live in Abbot Quincey
All our parties will be princely.'

Gina shuddered. 'That is certainly the worst verse I have ever heard. And which parties are these?'

The girls whirled her even faster.

'Why, those that we give at my come-out,' Mair cried breathlessly. 'Shall we astonish the village, Gina?'

'Nothing is more certain if you go on like this. I doubt if you will have to wait till then. The servants will be persuaded that we have run mad…'

This did not appear to be the case. The butler apparently found nothing untoward in the sight of his young mistress cavorting about the salon with her stepdaughters. Had he not been mindful of the need for a wooden expression he might have permitted himself a smile. As it was he announced that nuncheon was served, remarking only to the housekeeper that Madam seemed to be in the best of spirits.

'And high time too. Madam is allus cheerful, but what a life she's had! Naught but caring for the sick, as far as I can tell.' Mrs Long gave him a speculative look. 'Think you that she'll settle here?'

'Who can tell?' Hanson had long ceased to wonder at the vagaries of his employers. 'Shall you prefer it, Mrs Long?'

'I don't know yet, but there must be more life here than in the wilds of Scotland. Madam will be thinking of finding husbands for the girls within a year or two, and we ain't so far from London.'

'True! I expect that she will open up the London house this year. I'd welcome it, you know. The place was like a morgue when last I saw it.'

'Her ladyship will change all that. Why, she might even find a husband of her own.'

Hanson bent his head in grave agreement. 'The family is out of mourning now. We may expect visits from every fortune-hunter in the country.'

'Then I hope that you will see them off, Mr Hanson.'

'I shall certainly do my best.' With that promise the butler left his confidante and proceeded to his duties.

Finding a husband was far from Gina's mind as she rose from the dining-table.

'Girls, I have a private call to make this afternoon. I shall not be away for long. Will you occupy yourselves?'

'We shall explore the cellars and the attics,' Elspeth promised. 'This house is a perfect maze of secret places.'

Gina nodded. Then she hurried away to change her fashionable walking dress for a plain toilette. She waved aside Hanson's suggestion of the carriage and turned left along the High Street, gazing at the old familiar surroundings with a pang of nostalgia. Abbot Quincey had not changed since her departure all those years ago and she recognised several of the passers-by, but her bonnet hid her face and no one greeted her.

A ten-minute walk brought her to her destination. The old sign was still above the shop and the door was open, but she hesitated by the window. She had rehearsed this moment for so long, but now her courage threatened to desert her.

Her heart was pounding painfully, but she took a few deep breaths. Then she walked into the shop.

'Yes, Madam? May I help you?' The woman behind the counter was an older, plumper version of Gina herself.

'Don't you know me, Mother?' Gina was close to tears.

'Gina?' Eliza Westcott paled as she peered into her daughter's face. 'Is it really you? Oh, my love, I thought that you were lost to us for ever.' She threw out her arms and Gina hurried to her.

'There, don't cry, Mama. I am home again.'

'You wicked, wicked girl!' Mrs Westcott was raining kisses upon her daughter's face. 'I can't think why you left us in the first place. The worry almost killed us.'

'That was foolish, Mama. I wrote to you each month.'

'But from all those outlandish places, Gina. I had never heard of one half of them. You might have been murdered in your bed.'

'But I wasn't. And you knew I was safe in Scotland for these past few years.'

Mrs Westcott sniffed. 'Safe in Scotland, indeed! There's another wild place, or so I hear.'

'The natives are quite friendly.' Gina began to smile. 'Is Father better now?' She had gleaned little from her mother's infrequent letters.

'He is quite stout again, but still so cross with you.'
Mrs Westcott paused. 'When you went away he
blamed himself, you see. He still feels that he did not
do his duty by you.'

'That isn't true, and I shall tell him so. Where is
Father now?'

'He's in the bakery. Come through, my love, and
sit by the fire. I will fetch him for you.'

Gina waited in some trepidation. As the youngest
of the Westcott children she had been the apple of
her father's eye. She could understand his hurt, and
she did not expect immediate forgiveness.

When she looked at the cold face she knew that
she was right. He would not look her fully in the eye.

'Come to honour us with a visit, your ladyship?'
he sneered. 'I thank you for your condescension.'

'I came because I am now free to do so, Father.
As you know, my husband died last year. It has taken
me some time to settle his affairs.'

'So now you are come to queen it in the village?
Well, good luck to you! You won't be needing the
likes of us.'

'I've always needed you,' Gina said quietly. 'I'm
sorry if I caused you hurt.' She went to him and took
his hand. 'Won't you forgive me, Father dear?' She
kissed his hand and raised it to her cheek.

It was too much for the master baker. With a groan
he took his daughter in his arms and muffled his face
against her hair. 'You bad girl! What are we to do
with you?' His cheeks were wet and Gina hugged him
close.

He took some time to recover his composure, but at last he smiled at her.

'Well, Missy, when are you off again on your adventures?'

'Never, I hope! I've taken the Mansion House in the village… The girls are with me, of course.'

George Westcott whistled in amazement. 'You are flying high, my girl. That must have cost you a pretty penny.'

'Whitelaw left me well provided for, Father. Tell me, how are William and Julia?'

'Both well, I'm glad to say.' Westcott's face softened. 'Wait until you see your nieces and nephews. Your brother's little lads are as merry as grigs, and as to the young maids…'

'Don't get him started on the subject, Gina. To hear your father talk you would think that better girls had never been born. If the truth be told they twist him round their little fingers.' Mrs Westcott looked wistful. 'I could wish that you had children of your own, my dear. When you married we hoped… Well, perhaps it was not to be.'

Gina did not reply. This was no time to explain that her marriage had been one of convenience. Dearly as he loved her, Lord Whitelaw had made that clear. Never strong and no longer young, he was well aware that in the natural order of things he would die before her. Caring for her stepdaughters would be a grave responsibility. He had no wish to add to her burdens by leaving her with children of her own.

Gina had understood and she respected his decision, though she'd known it was not the full truth. For Alistair Whitelaw no woman would ever take the place of his beloved first wife. Her own marriage had been based upon trust and affection. She had never resented it, though her own heart had been given long ago.

She thrust aside the painful memories and picked up her bonnet. 'You will come to see me, won't you?'

Mrs Westcott looked at her husband. Then she nodded. 'We'll come in a day or two. Your Uncle Samuel and Aunt Mary are to visit us tomorrow with the children. You won't want a houseful.'

Gina's polite enquiry as to the welfare of her relatives was less than enthusiastic, but her parents noticed nothing amiss. For her own part her father's brother was the last person she wished to see. Now a wealthy grain merchant, she could only be thankful that he was based in London. At some time in the future she would be forced to meet him again. As yet she was not ready to do so.

For the moment another unavoidable meeting filled her mind. Had she made the right decision in coming back to Abbot Quincey? For all she knew Giles might be married and a father. She had not dared to ask about him, fearing she would give herself away. Well, she would cross her bridges when she came to them.

She kissed her parents and walked back to the Mansion House.

Chapter Two

Had she but known it, Giles was at that moment being forced to listen to a long discussion about the latest resident of Abbot Quincey.

Having satisfied herself that her elder daughter was indeed with child, Mrs Rushford proceeded to acquaint herself with all the latest gossip.

'So much has happened since we went to Bristol,' she announced. 'Now, India, you must tell me everything. Who is this Lady Whitelaw? Giles said that Isham went to call on her this morning… She and her husband will be such an asset to the village.'

'Not her husband, Mama. Lady Whitelaw is a widow…'

Giles had stiffened, but his mother did not notice. 'Well, I expect that she will soon make friends. Is she elderly?'

'She must be twenty-six at most.' India smiled.

'And she has taken the Mansion House? She must be well-to-do…' Mrs Rushford gave her son a look of speculation. The widow, though not young, was not yet at her last prayers, and Giles was in need of a wife. If she brought a handsome dowry with her so much the better. 'When are we to meet her?' she enquired.

'Anthony will let us know. I expect that she has much to do, as she only arrived this morning. He promised to give her an open invitation.'

'Then he knows her well?'

'He was a close friend of her husband.' India hesitated. 'You know her yourself, Mama.'

'How can that be? To my knowledge I have never met the Whitelaws.'

'You have met Lady Whitelaw. She was the former Gina Westcott...'

'The baker's daughter?' Mrs Rushford gave a cry of indignation. 'India, you can't be serious! How can you receive a person who was engaged in trade? What of your social position?'

'Mother, those days are gone,' Giles said quietly. 'Westcott himself is a wealthy man and is highly regarded in the neighbourhood.'

'What has that to say to anything?' his mother demanded. 'Much you know about it! India, this is another of your queer starts. I fear you have learned nothing since your marriage. I forbid you to receive her. Isham can know nothing of her background. He has been deceived, which is what I would expect from that sly little madam.'

Giles flushed and was about to speak when he was forestalled.

'Is someone taking my name in vain?' a mild voice enquired.

'Oh, Anthony, there you are, thank heavens! Now will you explain to India that she cannot possibly receive a baker's daughter…this Lady Whitelaw, or whatever she calls herself. I know that this will be a shock to you, but you have been misled. I know that girl, and I would put nothing past her. Lady Whitelaw, forsooth! She was a nursemaid to the family, nothing more.'

'I believe she held that post.' Isham's voice was dangerously quiet, and India closed her eyes. Would her mother never learn? Nothing aroused her husband to anger more quickly than any criticism of his wife.

Mrs Rushford was oblivious of the warning signs. 'Certainly she did, and nothing surprised me more. The girl was fifteen when she ran away from home. Who knows what her life had been before she met the Whitelaws? None of us can be in much doubt, I think. She was always a pert, opinionated miss.'

Isham strolled over to the fireplace. 'You question Lord and Lady Whitelaw's judgement then?' The edge to his voice was lost on Mrs Rushford.

She tossed her head. 'They wouldn't be the first to be taken in by her. She will not have changed. She may claim the title, but I, for one, will be surprised if she has any right to it.'

'Then you must prepare yourself for a shock, Isabel. I was Whitelaw's supporter at their wedding.'

Mrs Rushford stared at him. 'You were? But Anthony, you could not have known about her. How can India receive the daughter of a baker? The scandal will run like wildfire through the Ton. I can't imagine what Lady Wells will have to say.'

'As my wife, India need not concern herself with the opinion of vulgarians. Lady Whitelaw will be received here. I must hope that you will make her welcome.'

Mrs Rushford flushed an unbecoming shade of purple. It was a sharp rebuke, though his lordship had not raised his voice. Her visit to Bristol had caused her to forget just how unpleasant her son-in-law could be when he got on his high ropes. Now he sat down beside his wife and took her hand.

India squeezed it gently and he understood. His lofty manner left him as he turned to her sister.

'So we are to wish you happy, Letty?' His smile transformed the harsh face. 'When is the great day to be?'

'In the summer, Anthony.' Letty was radiant. 'Oliver and I are both so grateful to you. Without your help it could not have come about.'

'Nonsense! Oliver would not have let you go, whatever the difficulties.' Pointedly, he made no reference to the dreaded Lady Wells and Letty did not mention her. Anthony was no hypocrite. If her future mother-in-law had dropped off the face of the planet he would consider it a blessing. She twinkled at him, well aware of his feelings in that respect. Anthony turned back to his wife.

'You are looking better,' he said quietly. 'Has the nausea gone?'

'It is soon over,' she assured him. 'And Lucia has a sovereign remedy. I am to eat a dry biscuit when I wake and drink one of her tisanes.' She blushed a little. 'She says that it will last only for the first few weeks.'

At this moment his stepmother came into the room. Lucia, the dowager Lady Isham, was looking pale and fragile. The loss of her own son had hit her hard, but now she devoted herself to India's welfare.

'Shall you feel able to eat your nuncheon, India?' she asked in her prettily accented English. 'It is so important, my dear one.' She grasped the younger woman's hand and led the way into the dining-room.

Yet it was not India who ignored the food. Giles was too preoccupied to notice what was set before him.

So Gina was a widow? Now, at least, he had no need to picture her in the arms of the elderly Lord Whitelaw. The sense of relief had shaken him to the core, though common-sense persuaded him that it was not much of a comfort. Gina was still beyond his reach. He had nothing to offer her. Had it not been for India's generosity in giving him the management of her estate, he would have been forced to return to a way of life which disgusted him. Since his father's death last summer and the ruin of his family he had been forced to live upon the charity of his friends, accepting invitations to their country houses in the hope that someone would offer him employment.

Napoleon's blockade, the ruin of trade, and a failed harvest had dashed that hope. No one needed an estate manager, however dedicated. Had it not been for India's offer he would have been forced to leave the country and seek his fortune overseas.

Then he took himself to task. He must not be bitter. The Rushford family had survived. India's splendid marriage had seen to that. Soon Letty would be wed to her beloved Oliver. He must be happy for them, ignoring the ache in his own heart.

It would be years before he could think of marriage for himself, though his mother still hoped that he would find a wealthy bride. He would not sell himself. Every instinct revolted at the thought. Perhaps he would never marry, but in time he might recover some of his self-esteem.

His preoccupation didn't go unnoticed. India, surprised by her brother's inattention, looked across at her husband and raised an enquiring eyebrow. Isham smiled, but he gave an imperceptible shake of his head, warning her not to pursue the subject. It was not until later, when she was resting in her room, that he came to her. Sitting beside her on the bed he took her hand and raised it to his lips, kissing her fingers each in turn.

'Well, my love?' he teased. 'Had you not better ask me before you burst with curiosity?'

'You mean about Lady Whitelaw?' she asked artlessly. 'Oh, Anthony, you know that I shall be happy to receive her, or any of your friends...'

'I didn't doubt it, but I wasn't referring to Gina Whitelaw, and well you know it.'

'You still find my face an open book then?' India blushed and then she laughed.

'I do, and It's a lovely face. Now, out with it! You are concerned about your brother, are you not?'

'I can't help it. He is behaving oddly. Have you not noticed? I thought he might have spoken to you.'

Isham was silent as India studied his face.

'He has said something, hasn't he?' she insisted. 'I know that you would not betray a confidence, but Giles is so dear to me. I can't help wondering if something dreadful happened whilst he and Letty were away with Mama.'

Isham laughed aloud. 'Nothing of the sort. Giles is more than capable of dealing with Lady Wells, in the politest possible way, of course. She may be a termagant, but she is no match for him. Besides, are we not much in favour with her ladyship at present, now that Letty is to marry Oliver?'

India shook her head at him. 'Don't try to change the subject, Anthony. You shall not divert me with talk of Letty's wedding.'

His lordship stretched out his long legs and regarded her with a fond smile. 'I didn't expect to do so, my darling.'

'Well then, what else can it be? Mother and Letty have not mentioned anything untoward, but Giles is not himself and it worries me.'

'Now that does concern me.' Isham's smile was gone. 'I won't have it, India!' Swiftly he put his arms about her. 'This should be the happiest of times for us. You are not to worry about Giles, or anything else for that matter. I forbid it! Giles is a man grown, and must be allowed to handle his own affairs. He will not welcome interference in what, I suspect, may be a matter of the heart...'

'Oh, did he say so?' India's frown vanished.

'He did not! And, my clever little witch, you shall not tease me into repeating our conversation. As you say, you and Giles are close. He will tell you if he wishes you to know.'

'Perhaps it was just a lovers' quarrel.' India brightened. 'We had many of those ourselves, if you recall?'

'Shall I ever forget?' His lordship threw his eyes to heaven. 'You left me scarred for life!'

'What nonsense!' India's indignant tone was belied by the sparkle in her eyes. 'You seem to have come about, my lord.'

'Only with difficulty, and much self-mortification.'

As he had hoped, his wife's brow cleared and she began to laugh. 'I haven't seen much sign of that.'

'Then it must have been your kisses which restored me.' He turned her face to his and sought her lips. India submitted willingly, but at last she pushed him away.

'You are a disgrace!' she teased. 'Making love to your own wife in the middle of the afternoon! I never heard of such a thing!'

'You prefer that I made love to someone's else's wife in the middle of the afternoon?'

'Only if you seek further scarring, my dear sir.

Now let us be serious. What are we to do about Giles?'

'Nothing at all, I fear.'

'We might at least find him some diversion. He can't have enjoyed his stay with Lady Wells, although it may be there that he met this mysterious paramour.'

'Quite possibly.' Isham would not be drawn.

'Well, now, at least, he will have some company of his own age. Thomas Newby is visiting Abbot Quincey. He puts up at the Angel. Shall we ask him to stay here?'

'Anything you wish, my dearest.'

A loving smile was his reward. 'He is one of my brother's oldest friends…' India paused 'And then, you know, there is Lady Whitelaw…'

Isham kept his countenance with difficulty. 'You also have plans for her, my love?'

India looked a little conscious. 'It is just that… Oh, don't give me that quizzing look, you odious creature… I thought that she might care to dine with us this week.'

'Together with Giles and Thomas Newby? Matchmaking, India?'

'Not at all,' she said severely. 'I thought merely that she might like to bring the girls, so that we may get to know them.'

'Too kind!' His eyes were twinkling and his tone was so dry that she aimed a playful blow at him. 'I'll leave you to rest, my dear, and to do your plotting in peace.'

Having satisfied himself that India was no longer

so deeply troubled, Isham returned to the salon. There he found Letty and Mrs Rushford absorbed in the details of Letty's trousseau, whilst Giles was anxious to slip away.

'I must return to Abbot Quincey,' Isham announced mendaciously. 'Giles, will you ride in with me?'

His brother-in-law gave him a look of relief. 'I'd be glad to, but I feel that I ought to see the bailiff. There must be matters to attend…'

'Time enough for that,' Isham told him firmly. 'We can discuss them as we go.' He rang the bell to order the horses saddled and brought round.

As they set off Giles turned to him and smiled. 'Thanks for coming to my rescue. For these past few days I have heard of nothing but the latest fashions and the merits of Brussels lace against that of Nottingham. I know nothing of such matters, so it was useless to appeal to me.'

Isham laughed. 'Best make up your mind to it, my dear fellow. For the ladies this will be the main topic of conversation until Letty is wed. Just grin and bear it. A man can do nothing else.'

Giles nodded. 'Is all well with the estate? I'd hoped to try some of the newest farming methods this year. Pray heaven we get a better harvest. These last few years have been a disaster on the land.'

'You've done your best in impossible circum-stances.' Isham did not elaborate. Both he and his companion were aware that Gareth Rushford had been a drain upon the family's resources for more years than his son could remember. 'I like your ideas.

Perhaps you'll give me the benefit of your expertise on some of my other properties?'

Such praise warmed the heart of his companion. Giles was a countryman to the core. He kept abreast of all the latest developments in agriculture, taking note of any innovations which might be of use to him.

Now he flushed with pleasure, but feeling slightly embarrassed he was quick to change the subject.

'You must have much upon your mind,' he said. 'Have you news from London? We were rather out of touch at Bristol.'

Isham frowned. 'The riots in the north have spread, and the Government won't hear of moderation. I voted against the Framebreakers' Bill, but it was passed. Even Byron spoke out against it in his maiden speech, but to no effect.'

'Byron?' Giles looked surprised. 'I always thought him a frippery sort of fellow.'

'So did I, but he was clear that repression was not the answer. ''Can you commit a whole country to their own prisons? Will you erect a gibbet in every field and hang men up like scarecrows?'' he asked. I could only agree with him.'

'Even though Henry was killed by the rioters?'

'Even so. Starving men should not be executed and transported when they try to save their livelihood. The means they chose were violent, but they were in a desperate plight, and the Government ignored them.'

'Byron continues with the struggle?'

'Alas, no! He is lionised everywhere since the publication of his epic poem. The women leave him no time for ought but dalliance.'

'Have you read it?' Giles began to smile.

'I tried,' Isham replied with feeling. 'I must be lacking in sensibility, but these gothic flights of fancy are not to my taste.'

'And India?'

'India cannot understand the fuss about *Childe Harold's Pilgrimage*. For that I must be grateful. Poor William Lamb has lost his wife to the fellow. The scandal has London by the ears.'

'Shall you go up again quite soon?'

'I must appear for the reading of the Catholic Bill. Wellesley resigned on the matter a couple of months ago. He doesn't believe in emancipation.'

Giles looked blank. 'Oh, I thought it was because of the Government's support of the Peninsular war.'

'That too. The last we heard was that Wellington was planning to take Badajoz. Let us hope that he is successful. We need a victory.'

Still discussing the conduct of the war in Spain, the two men rode along until they reached the outskirts of the village. Then Isham changed the subject.

'Your friend Tom Newby puts up at the Angel,' he remarked. 'He sent yesterday to ask for you. We'd be happy to have him stay at the Grange if you care to ask him.'

'Oh, would you? How good you are! He is the best of fellows, and I stayed with him last summer. But...er...will it not be too much for India to have a visitor in the house?'

'It will not!' Isham replied firmly. 'The staff know better than to trouble her with domestic details. They do so at their peril.'

Giles grinned. 'I don't doubt it. Well, then, if you are sure, I'll stop by at the Angel and speak to Tom. He's something of a rattle-pate, but I won't let him tire her.'

'She'll enjoy a change of company.' With this assurance Isham raised a hand in salute and rode off to keep his fictitious appointment. In the event, he turned into his favourite bookshop in search of the latest novels for his wife.

Giles had no difficulty in finding Thomas Newby. That gentleman was seated comfortably in the snug, toasting himself by a roaring fire and addressing a tankard of ale with every appearance of enjoyment.

'There you are, old chap!' Thomas hailed his friend with a beaming smile. 'I made sure you'd look me up as soon as you got back from...Bristol...was it not?'

'It was.' Giles raised a finger to summon the landlord. 'Ever been there, Newby?'

'Not that I recall. A seaport, ain't it, full of slaves and tobacco?' Having given Giles the benefit of his scant knowledge of geography Thomas sought further information. 'Lively, is it and full of pretty wenches?'

'I have no idea,' Giles said drily. 'Young Wells and my sister Letty were the only young company and they had eyes only for each other. An engagement, you see. I spent my time playing cards with the dowagers...'

Thomas whistled in surprise. 'Dangerous! Some of those old biddies spend their lives at cards. They could teach the faro-dealers a thing or two. Did they clean you out?'

Giles gave him a wry grin. 'Unlikely…at a penny a point…!'

Thomas shook his head. 'Dear old chap! How did you stand the excitement?'

'It wasn't easy!' The humour of the situation struck Giles suddenly and both men roared with laughter.

'That's better! You looked a bit down, old fellow.' Thomas was too much of a gentleman to pry into his friend's private affairs. 'How goes the world with you these days? Heard you were managing an estate.'

'It belongs to my sister. By the way, she asks if you would care to stay with us. You'll like her. India is a great gun, and Letty too. India married Isham last December. I expect you heard of it. Do you know him?'

'I know *of* him.' Thomas said carefully. 'Always thought him a bit above my touch.'

'So did I. At first I was against the match, but I was wrong. He's made my sister as happy as a grig. I think him the best of men.'

'That's good enough for me. I'll be happy to accept your invitation.' Thomas rang for the landlord and ordered his bags brought down.

'Fine country this,' he observed as they rode towards the Grange. 'Is it good farming land?'

It was enough to launch Giles into his favourite subject, and Thomas was content. He'd seen from the first that Giles had something on his mind. He had little knowledge of agriculture, but beneath his clowning he was a kindly man.

Over the years he'd been aware of his friend's struggles. He's just had one blow too many, he thought to himself. It's time he had some fun.

With this end in mind he felt it time to make some enquiries.

'Much to do round here?' he asked casually.

'I promise you won't be bored.' Giles smiled. 'We can offer you good fishing. Have you read *The Compleat Angler*?'

'Books ain't much in my line, but I did just glance at it. The old chap, Walton, seemed to know his stuff.'

'He did indeed. His river, the Dove, is further to the north, but there is some good sport here.'

'And Abbot Quincey? I must say, I liked the look of it.'

'Or was it the wenches who took your fancy?'

Thomas took the teasing in good part. 'Give me time! I didn't arrive until yesterday, but bless me if I didn't see three beauties driving through the town this morning.'

'I'm surprised that you didn't stop the coach to introduce yourself.'

'It was going too fast, old son. Gave me no time to pull on my boots.'

'Your man isn't with you then?'

'Gave him the slip in London. If there is one thing guaranteed to take the shine off any expedition it's that old curmudgeon, Stubbins. I'm sure my father makes him dog my heels to keep me on the straight and narrow.'

'Has he had much success?' Giles was laughing openly.

'Not that you'd notice.' Thomas gave him a cheerful grin. 'Still, it don't stop him from trying. That's the trouble with people who've known you since before you were breeched. They won't believe you've left the schoolroom.'

'Won't he worry about your disappearance?'

'Stubbins? Not a chance! That fellow is a human bloodhound. He'll track me down before the week is out.'

'Then you'd best make the most of your freedom whilst you may.'

'I intend to,' Thomas said with feeling. 'Now tell me about Abbot Quincey. Is it a big place?'

'It's the largest of our local villages—more like a small market town.' Giles cast a sly look at his friend. 'For your entertainment we have a corn and cattle market on a Tuesday...'

'Wonderful!'

'We also have an abbey and a vicarage...'

'Too much...!'

'Aha, but we also have a scandal. The Abbey is owned by the Marquis of Sywell...'

'What, that old roué...?'

'The same! Now his young wife has disappeared. She hasn't been seen for months. Rumours have been rife. A favourite is that he murdered her.'

'Wouldn't put it past him.'

'It's more likely that she simply ran away.'

'Sounds a reasonable thing to do. Tell me more…'

'No more is known. We *have* had a murder though.'

Thomas looked startled. 'What lives you lead in the quiet of the countryside! I thought that nothing happened here…'

'This came very close to home. Isham's half-brother was killed some weeks ago in one of the Luddite riots. The mob attacked the Grange.'

Thomas reined in at once. 'My dear chap! Have your wits gone a-wandering? The family won't wish for a guest at such a time. I'll go back to the Angel.'

'No, hear me out!' Giles reined in beside his friend. 'There was something strange about the business. Isham and India have said very little, although they saw the shooting.'

'Not a pleasant thing to remember.'

'No, I agree, but I get the feeling that there was more to it than they'll admit. It's an odd affair, and even Henry's mother, who lives with us, seems not to wish to speak of him. It turns out now that he was no blood kin to Isham, though he thought he was.' Giles paused. 'I wish I could explain. It is the strangest thing, but you'll find no sense of mourning at the Grange.'

'Even after such a tragedy?' Thomas was unconvinced.

'You shall see for yourself. Of course, Isham doesn't plan to entertain in his usual style. He isn't much for convention, nor is India stuffy, but you understand?'

'Perfectly. Got to show respect for the dead, old son.'

'Exactly, but even so, you won't be short of company.' Giles allowed the ghost of a smile to touch his lips. 'I have seven cousins in the neighbourhood, and five of them are girls...'

Thomas brightened at the thought of some feminine company. 'Unattached, I hope?'

'As yet. The younger ones are barely out of the schoolroom, but there, you won't mind that. You'll just about be on their level.'

This gibe caused Thomas to aim a playful blow at his companion, which Giles avoided with ease. Spurring his horse ahead, he took off at a gallop across the flat land leading to the Grange.

As Thomas was about to follow, three riders came up fast behind him. As they swept past he decided to give chase. Bruising horsewomen, he thought to himself, but darned if I'll be beaten by three females.

He was well mounted and he caught them up with ease just as their leader swung round to her right and came to a sudden halt.

'What do you want?' a clear voice called. 'I'm armed, so pray don't think of robbing us.'

Thomas swept off his hat. 'My apologies, ma'am. I didn't mean to frighten you.'

'Nor did you do so.' The lady's hand was hidden in the folds of her riding skirt, but a look at her eyes convinced him that it held a pistol. 'Are you in the habit of chasing females, sir?'

'Only pretty ones,' Thomas answered audaciously.

The lady chuckled. 'I phrased that badly, didn't I? What I meant to ask was why you followed us?'

'Ma'am, your speed was irresistible. I can never turn down a race, can you?'

'Not often. Now, sir, tell me who you are. Are we on your land?'

'No, ma'am, but if it were mine you would be more than welcome. My name is Thomas Newby, and I shall be staying at the Grange with Lord and Lady Isham. Are you a stranger to these parts?'

'No, though I have been away for many years. My name is Gina Whitelaw, and these are my stepdaughters, Mair and Elspeth.'

'Why, you are the ladies who were driving past the Angel earlier today,' Thomas exclaimed with delight. 'You looked so charming. Giles said that I should have stopped your coach to introduce myself.'

'Did he indeed?' Gina permitted herself a faint smile. 'I think he could not have known our names.'

'Why no, but he'll be glad to meet you. Here he comes now...'

Giles had turned his horse and was trotting back towards them with a smile of amusement on his lips. He cast a merry eye at Thomas, promising that gentleman a roasting later on. Then his gaze fell upon the ladies and he reined in sharply, causing his mount to rear at the sudden check.

His efforts to control the animal took him several

minutes, much to Thomas's astonishment. His friend's horsemanship was legendary. Now Giles was making much of the simplest of manoeuvres.

It served. By the time he had stilled his restive mount Giles had schooled his expression to one of polite surprise.

'Lady Whitelaw?' he said stiffly. 'Isham told us that you had returned to Abbot Quincey. I…we…had not expected to find you riding out so soon.' He stole a careful look at Gina's face.

He'd dreamed of this moment for so long, wondering how she would react if ever they should meet again. Now he was baffled. In her look he saw no trace of embarrassment, regret, or the least trace of affection.

She gave him a cheerful smile. 'Giles Rushford! What a pleasure it is to see you again! Girls, do you remember Mr Rushford? We met him in Italy long ago.' She might have been greeting a distant acquaintance.

His own heart was pounding at the sight of his lost love. Lost indeed! This sophisticated, self-possessed young woman bore no resemblance to the loving, innocent girl he'd left so long ago.

Chapter Three

'You know each other?' Thomas beamed with pleasure. 'Good! Giles, will you assure her ladyship that I am not a highwayman?'

'My good sir, I didn't think you were.' Gina gave him a demure look. 'Your face was a study when I threatened you with my pistol.'

'I expect it was, ma'am. For all I knew you might have shot first and asked questions afterwards, perhaps in a fright, you see.'

'Gina is never frightened,' Elspeth told him proudly. 'She killed two men in India, when they came to rob us.'

'I don't doubt it.' Thomas pretended to cower away, much to the delight of both the girls. 'I'm hoping not to make a third. In a fight, your ladyship, I shall wish to have you on my side…'

'And will you be behind me or in front of me, Mr Newby?'

This sally even brought a smile from Giles, though he felt obliged to offer a word of warning.

'I see that you ride without your groom,' he said. 'Is that wise, Lady Whitelaw? You may not have heard of it , but there is some disaffection in the countryside.'

'Luddites?' Gina gave him a measured look. 'I have no plans either to set up a factory or to import the new machinery, Mr Rushford. The frame-breakers have no quarrel with me.'

'Other elements have joined them,' he told her brusquely. 'The riots have often been a cover for robbery and even murder.'

'I thank you for your concern, but, as you see, I am well armed. As for my groom, he rode ahead of us with a message for your sister. I think I see him in the distance...' Gina was smiling, but there was an edge to her tone which left both men with little doubt that she would brook no interference.

She turned her mount as the groom rode up, and bidding the girls to follow she rode off with a final word of farewell.

Thomas gazed after her with an open mouth.

'That's quite a woman,' he said with feeling. 'Did you see her face when you tried to warn her? That one won't stand quietly in harness for any man.'

'I see no merit in being foolhardy,' Giles retorted.

'Perhaps not, but you won't deny her courage. Do you believe that she killed two men?'

'Oh yes! Isham told me something of her history. She and her family travelled widely, as Whitelaw hoped always to find some cure for his first wife's illness. Gina dealt with a Lascar mutiny on board ship and stood up to the Voodoo priests in the Caribbean…'

'Great heavens! How can you think her foolhardy? I should imagine that she will find no difficulties in this country. Perhaps it is no wonder that her husband lets her ride abroad without protection.'

'She has no husband. Gina is a widow,' Giles said shortly. 'Whitelaw died two years ago.'

'Ah, now I understand. The girls are not her own? I thought her too young to be their mother.'

'Gina has no children of her own, I believe.' Giles urged his horse into a trot, clearly anxious to dismiss the subject, but Thomas could not contain his curiosity.

He stole a look at his friend's face.

'You don't like her, do you? Why is that? I thought her a charming little creature…'

'You think all women charming creatures until they let you down. What happened to that stunning bird of paradise who won your heart last year?'

'I ran out of the dibs, old son. Carriages and jewels cost a mint, to say nothing of that pretty little house in Mayfair. When Brande came along with all his shekels I didn't stand a chance.'

'Shall you go up to London for the Season?'

'Not this year. My father has refused to stand for it. Can't say that I'll miss it much. Stale sandwiches and weak lemonade at Almacks', and dodging all those match-making mamas. Of course if I married the old man would stump up, but what a price to pay!'

'You are incorrigible!'

'I know it. But women are funny creatures, aren't

they? They won't rest until they have you by the leg, and then they try to change you, Won't do for me. I plan to remain a bachelor, and you, for one, won't argue with that.'

If this was an invitation to a confidence Giles ignored it. How could he explain that he longed for nothing more than to make Gina his wife?

True, she had changed, but perhaps no more than he himself. Behind the elegance and the casual politeness of a woman of the world there was still the same indomitable spirit. Her smile, the turn of her head and her graceful carriage reminded him so vividly of the days when he had held her to his heart, murmuring endearments and secure in the knowledge that she returned his love.

It all seemed so long ago, and clearly the years of their separation had killed that love once and for all. He could not blame her. He too had changed. At thirty he was no longer a carefree youth prepared to conquer the world for his lady's pleasure. The years of struggle had taken their toll.

He would not, could not, ask her to wait till he might offer her a comfortable future. Gina would marry again, he was sure of it. She was made for love. Why should she waste her youth in vain hopes, even if he should manage to win back her affections. Better to put it out of his mind and pray that when she did re-marry he was not around to witness it.

Gina herself was taking a much more sanguine view of matters. She had been half dreading meeting

Giles again, unsure of her ability to hide her feelings
for him. Now the first hurdle had been overcome and
she was pleased with the result. She had had long
experience in keeping her countenance. What she
could not control was the thudding of her heart. To
her it had seemed deafening. Surely he must have
heard it?

'Gina, you were unkind to Giles,' Elspeth accused.
'Why did you call him Mr Rushford? I thought he
was a friend of ours.'

'He used to be,' Gina said carefully. 'But that was
long ago...'

'But you told us that once a friend, always a
friend,' Elspeth persisted.

'So I did, but times and people change. When we
knew Mr Rushford he was just a boy, and you were
babies. Perhaps he has forgotten the days when you
used to play together.'

'No, he hasn't.' Mair spoke with conviction. 'He
looked so sad. I wanted to make him smile.'

'And you will do so, my dear one.' Gina gathered
her charges to her. 'I have a surprise for you. Lord
and Lady Isham have invited us to dine with them.'

'Oh, Gina, are we to go as well, even though we
are not out?'

'This is just a small family party, my dears, and I
have no fears for you. You know how to behave. It
is so much more sensible to learn how to conduct
yourselves in company before you are thrown head-
long into a London season.'

'Darling Gina!' Both girls hugged her. 'We shall be very good. You'll be proud of us...'

The excitement of being invited to dine at the Grange lasted for the next few days and led to long discussions as to suitable toilettes, and who was likely to be their dinner partners.

'I shall hope to be seated by Mr Newby,' Elspeth announced artlessly. 'Giles is much more handsome, of course, but Mr Newby is my idea of a perfect gentleman.'

This brought cries of amusement from Gina and Mair.

'Don't tell me that Lord Isham is no longer your idol,' Gina teased.

'Well, Mair was right. He is a little old for me. Besides he is married now...'

'For all you know Mr Newby may be married too,' Mair said wickedly.

'Oh, I don't think so. He has not the look of a married person...'

'And what look is that?' Gina was vastly amused.

'Oh, I don't know...perhaps I mean a little staid.'

'Like me?' Gina enquired.

Her companions shouted with glee. 'Not in the least like you,' said Mair.

'Of course not.' Elspeth was quick to support her sister. 'You are no more staid than Mr Newby. Isn't he fun? He makes me laugh so much.'

'I see that he is a paragon of all the virtues. You are quite sure that you were not swayed by his compliments?'

'Of course not!' Elspeth was indignant. 'I know that gentlemen are trained to make pretty speeches. They don't always mean what they say.'

'It might be as well to remember that...' Gina's smile hid an anxious heart. Who had learned better than she to place no faith in pretty speeches?

When Giles had vanished all those years ago the shock had left her reeling. How many times had she relived those final hours together when they had strolled on the terrace of the villa hand in hand, stopping now and then for a passionate kiss as the moon sailed high above the Mediterranean in a cloudless sky. A silver pathway on the mirror-like surface of the sea had seemed to point the way to a lifetime of happiness and love.

The prospect of a few days apart was little to be regarded when they had all their lives ahead of them. With a final, lingering kiss Gina parted from her love with a promise to see him when her employers should return from a brief trip into the countryside.

That trip was soon cut short. With the breaking of the Treaty of Amiens the French were quickly on the move again as Napoleon resumed his dream of conquest. The whole of Italy was thrown into turmoil. The Whitelaws fled back to their villa on the coast and from there to Naples. Refugees had taken almost every berth on the few available ships. Given no choice Sir Alastair had embarked his family on a merchantman bound for the Caribbean.

Gina had suffered agonies of mind, but Giles was nowhere to be found, and in the panic and confusion of those final days in Italy she had no hope of tracing him. She would not believe him a coward who would take care of his own skin, leaving his friends to fend for themselves.

She'd heard that all foreigners had been advised to leave the country, but he must have had time to send a message to the villa.

She could not know it, but Giles had done so. A frantic message from his uncle had warned him to get out of Italy fast before escape became impossible. His father's affairs were in a bad case and Giles was needed at home.

He'd scrawled a few lines before embarking on a vessel bound for Dublin, but it had taken a heavy bribe to persuade his Italian servant to carry his letter to the Whitelaw's home to await Gina's return. *En route* his messenger had had second thoughts. Why should he risk his neck for what could only be some trivial billet-doux? The man tossed the note into some bushes and turned back to the port, thankful to see that Giles had already sailed. His ship was far out in the bay.

Gina's heart was breaking, but she'd been given no time to mourn. The stress of the enforced evacuation from her home had affected Lady Whitelaw's already fragile health. Gina's days were spent in a whirl of caring for the invalid and cherishing her two small charges. Each night her pillow was wet with tears, but by day her expression gave no hint of her anguish.

Now, after all these years, she realised that the experience would stand her in good stead. No one must be allowed to guess that she still loved Giles.

She'd tried to crush that love, telling herself that he was faithless and that his promises were false. She'd even tried to hate him, but such a destructive emotion was alien to her character. Instead, she'd attempted to banish all thought of him from her mind.

Sometimes it worked. Then some remark, some fragment of a song, would bring her memories flooding back, often just as she was beginning to congratulate herself that the pain was growing less. It was in vain.

Then she would throw herself into a flurry of activity, studying the history of each place to which they travelled, noting the customs of the country, attempting to learn the language, and even to record their expeditions with her modest attempts at painting.

After a few years she didn't often permit herself the indulgence of looking back. What was done was done. She could not change it, nor must she waste the rest of her life in vain regrets. Just as the girls developed, so did Gina. Now, at the age of twenty-six, she was no longer the child who had offered her love so freely. She had learned to face reality, and she'd discovered that life was a mixture of triumphs and disappointments. What mattered, she'd decided long ago, was how you faced them.

This philosophy had served her well. She'd had no hesitation in marrying Sir Alastair after the death of his wife. She loved him dearly, though not as she had loved Giles. Sir Alastair was her closest friend, and she'd known how highly he regarded her.

It was not until Lord Isham had married India Rushford that she had news of her lost love. Then she learned that Giles had never taken a bride, although sometimes she had pictured him with children of his own.

Perhaps it was not too late to find happiness the second time around. Giles was living close to Abbot Quincey, her own birthplace. Swiftly she made plans to move there from the Whitelaw estate in Scotland. She had the perfect excuse. Sir Alastair's daughters were growing up. In a year or two she must give each of them a Season, and Abbot Quincey was not too far from London.

She summoned Anthony Isham to her aid. It was he who had found the ideal house in the centre of the village. Next year she would ask him to suggest a suitable place in town.

Meantime her plan of campaign was working well. She'd been undeceived by her former lover's stiff manner. Gina was not lacking in perception and she'd sensed at once that Giles was far from happy. Mair had been right. His eyes were sad and the tracery of lines upon his brow had almost broken her heart. Even so, he was still the handsomest man she had ever seen. The blond hair might have darkened a little, but nothing could alter the wonderful bone structure of his face, and that brilliant blue gaze still had the power to make her tremble.

But Gina knew her man. This would be no matter

of simply resuming a former love affair. Now their roles were reversed.

When they met Gina had been a servant, and worse, the daughter of the local baker in Abbot Quincey. They'd known the difficulties ahead of them. A gentleman would be shunned by society if he married beneath him.

Now Gina had a title and a handsome fortune. That obstacle had been removed, but there was a greater one. The Rushford family had suffered a great reversal of fortune, saved only by India's marriage to Lord Isham. Giles himself had nothing but his position as India's estate manager.

Even if he still loved her, Gina knew that his own pride would make it impossible for him to offer for her. A match with a wealthy bride might be considered desirable by the Ton, but her own heart told her that he would have none of it. That was unless…unless she could persuade him otherwise.

But how was she to do it? The problem exercised her constantly. Certainly she would not throw herself into his arms. Even if he longed to do so, he would not respond. For the time being she must go slowly, treating him in a friendly way as an old acquaintance and giving him no hint that she remembered what had been between them.

Her first opportunity to carry out this plan came at the Ishams' dinner party. Gina had dressed with care in a favourite gown of cream silk crêpe which she had bought in India. It was trimmed with tiny pearls and with it she wore an overdress of lace.

'Gina, you look positively splendid!' cried Mair. 'You are putting us in the shade.'

'Nonsense! You both look charming. Elspeth, would you like to wear my necklace of river pearls? Mair may have this ornament for her hair.'

'Pearls too!' Simple as the jewels were, the girls preened themselves, reconciled to the fact that they were both in the simplest of white dresses.

Gina smiled at them. 'We'll do,' she teased. 'At the very least we won't frighten the horses.'

They were still laughing as they set off for the Grange, but as they drew closer Mair grew silent.

Gina was quick to sense it. 'What is it, darling?' she asked.

'I shan't be able to think of anything to say,' Mair whispered in despair. 'They'll all think me stupid.'

'Not a bit of it! Ask them about themselves. After that you won't need to say another word of your own, but you'll gain the reputation of a brilliant conversationalist.'

'That's an unkind thing to say.' Mair began to laugh. 'I'm sure it isn't true!'

'Try it!' Gina advised. 'The most absorbing topics of interest for most people are their own concerns.'

'Gina, are you what is known as a cynic?' Elspeth enquired.

'No, darling, just a realist.' Gina picked up her wrap as the carriage drew to a halt, and led the way into the house.

As she walked into the salon followed by the girls

there was a hush. Then India came towards her with a welcoming smile.

'I don't propose to treat you as a stranger, Lady Whitelaw,' she said quickly. 'Welcome home to Abbot Quincey. We are all so glad to see you again, are we not, Mama?'

Mrs Rushford had had much to think about in the past few days. If the former Gina Westcott was now as wealthy as Lord Isham had suggested, it would be the height of folly to ruin the chances of her only son with an ill-timed fit of pique. Besides, she dared not snub the girl or attempt to quell her pretensions with Isham's eyes upon her.

She came forward holding out her hands. 'Little Gina!' she said in sentimental tones. 'Who would have thought that you would come back to us as Lady Whitelaw?'

'Not many people, I imagine, ma'am.' Gina affected not to see the outstretched hands. 'May I present Mair and Elspeth to you? They are my step-daughters.'

'Charming…charming…and scarce more than children, Lady Whitelaw…' Mrs Rushford was about to give her views on the unsuitability of allowing young people to dine with their elders, but Gina turned away.

'You will remember my sister, Letty, I think?' India continued.

'Of course. I remember you with pleasure. You were always such a happy child.'

'Letty is even happier now. She has just become engaged to Oliver Wells.'

Gina's felicitations were sincere. As a child growing up in Abbot Quincey she had always liked the Rushford children and their father. They'd been kind to her, unlike their snobbish mother, who'd spoken to her only to administer some sharp rebuke for speaking up too freely when accused of some trivial misdemeanour.

'Anthony you know very well, but this is Mr Thomas Newby, who is our house-guest, and already one of the family.'

Thomas bowed. 'You are too kind. I have already had the pleasure of meeting Lady Whitelaw and her daughters. We met when Giles and I were out riding some few days ago.' He beamed at the girls and won a smile from each of them.

'Giles, you said nothing of this. What a dark horse you are!'

His sister's teasing had no effect on Giles. His formal bow was perfection, but his face was expressionless.

'I see what it is,' India began to laugh. 'Giles fears for his dignity. He knows that you remember him as a grubby lad, forever falling out of trees.'

This brought a smile from the assembled company and Gina turned to the object of their amusement.

'I promise to forget it,' she said lightly. 'There, it is gone, and lost in the mists of time.' She nodded as if to dismiss the subject, and turned back to India.

'I was hoping to offer my condolences to the

Dowager Lady Isham,' she announced. 'Isham has told me that she lost her son. It must have been a great sorrow to her.'

'It hit her very hard,' India agreed. 'Lucia has been very brave, but sometimes she prefers to be alone. Tonight she will dine in her room.'

'I understand.' Gina grew thoughtful. 'For a mother it must be the greatest tragedy in the world. You will give her my good wishes, will you not?'

'So kind, Lady Whitelaw.' Mrs Rushford sat down beside them and heaved a gusty sigh. 'A mother's heart must bleed for her. Should anything happen to my darling Giles I should not want to live. Such a tower of strength as he has been since the loss of my dear husband.' She touched a lace-trimmed handkerchief to her eyes.

'Mama, please don't distress yourself. Did we not promise each other that this was to be a happy occasion? Lady Whitelaw and her daughters will be such an asset to the village.'

'True!' Mrs Rushford gave a brave smile and returned her unsullied handkerchief to her reticule. 'Have you seen your parents yet, my dear?'

'I called at the bakery,' Gina replied in unaffected tones. If it was vulgar to be in trade so be it. She was not ashamed of her background. That, in her eyes, would be an even greater vulgarity. 'My parents are both well, thank you, ma'am.'

'You did not visit the new house? Why, my dear, it is very fine. I declare that I have been hoping this age for an invitation.'

India exchanged a look with her sister, half amused and half irritated by such a bare-faced lie. Mrs Rushford would have considered an invitation from a tradesman as an insult in itself. It would not even have merited a reply.

'You intend to widen your circle of acquaintance, Isabel? A worthy notion...' Isham looked down at his mother-in-law, his dark face alive with amusement.

Mrs Rushford gave him an uncertain glance. Totally devoid of humour herself, she was never sure whether Anthony was being sarcastic or merely funning.

'Naturally,' she replied in a defensive tone. 'We must all move with the times...' In its way this was an admission that the once despised lower classes were beginning to encroach upon the ranks of the aristocracy, but it was a *faux pas* which reduced her companions to silence.

Gina was the first to recover. A lesser woman might have been crushed by the condescending tone of Mrs Rushford's statement, but Gina's lips began to twitch. It was only with an effort that she preserved her countenance, and when she turned to India her eyes were twinkling.

'Lady Isham, I believe that you and your sister attended Mrs Guarding's Academy? Is she still accepting pupils? Mair and Elspeth must finish their education, and I will apply there if you recommend it.'

'Pray don't think of it, Lady Whitelaw.' Mrs Rushford interrupted in an uncompromising tone. 'That woman corrupts young minds. The place should be closed by order of the magistrates. She preaches sedition.'

Lord Isham took a seat beside her with every expectation of enjoyment. 'Strong words, Isabel! Will you not explain?'

'You know my views,' Mrs Rushford retorted. 'She tries to turn her pupils into blue-stockings, filling their heads with nonsense about independence and women's rights. No man wants a pert, opinionated woman to wife.' Her gaze fell upon Gina, who gave her the sweetest of smiles.

'But neither does a sensible man wish for his life-long companion and the mother of his children to be an empty-headed nincompoop,' Giles said hotly.

'Of course not, my dear boy. You misunderstand me. A girl must be trained to be an ornament to society. She must learn to carry herself gracefully, to dress well, to dance, to sing a little, and there can be no objections to lessons in painting and drawing.'

Gina's shoulders were shaking. Her own 'training', such as it was, had been very different, especially as it had included lessons in marksmanship. She had also learnt how to throw a knife. These accomplishments were, however, unlikely to be of use to young ladies brought up in the heart of England.

She raised her head to find that Giles was looking at her. She suspected that, as always, he had read her mind, for his own eyes were dancing. She looked away.

'Mama, we learned those things at Mrs Guarding's

Academy,' Letty protested gently. 'Her teachers were the best that could be found.'

'Some of them, if not others,' her mother said darkly. 'However, I don't propose to indulge in gossip.'

With a valiant effort, India avoided her husband's eye, and also that of Letty, but the tirade wasn't over.

'What, may I ask, is the use of filling a young woman's head with mathematics, and so-called philosophy, which, as I understand it, is simply another name for radical views? It will not help her to run her household or hire and fire her servants.'

'Mrs Guarding seeks merely to teach a girl to use her mind,' India protested. 'The actual subjects do not matter over-much.'

'That's as maybe! That woman has done untold damage. Look at your cousin Hester! She's a constant worry to her parents. And as for that trollop, Desirée Nash, she should be whipped at the cart's tail. Teaching philosophy, Greek and Latin. She'd have taught her pupils more than that if Mrs Guarding hadn't dismissed her.'

India gave a discreet cough to call her mother's attention to the fact that Mair and Elspeth had drifted away from Thomas Newby's side when schooling was mentioned, and were both listening with avid interest to Mrs Rushford's remarks.

It was fortunate that at that moment dinner was announced. With his customary courtesy Isham offered his arm to Mrs Rushford. Thomas Newby escorted India and Giles offered an arm to Gina and Letty.

Gina found herself seated between Giles and Lord Isham. She had not expected it, and was disturbed to be so close to her former love. His hand was inches from her own, and when he reached across her shoulders to help her remove her gauzy scarf his fingers touched the bare flesh of her neck.

Giles started back as if he'd been stung.

'I beg your pardon,' he muttered.

'Not at all,' Gina replied politely. 'It is kind of you to help me. Some of these fashions are well enough in their way, but a scarf is not improved when it falls into the soup.'

It was not the most sophisticated of remarks. Gina felt that she was babbling to hide the fact that her senses were on fire. Her heart was beating wildly, but she was determined not to betray herself. The long-practised self-control came to her aid once more. She turned to Isham.

'What do you think, Anthony? Shall I send the girls to the Academy?'

'By all means. The standard of teaching is high. You won't do better for them.' Isham smiled down at his companion, apparently unaware of the tension in the air. Yet he had felt it from the first. Gina was more on edge than he had ever known her. There was some mystery here.

Chapter Four

'Shall you go up to London for the Season, Lady Whitelaw?' Thomas enquired.

'We've decided to postpone that pleasure until next year, when Mair comes out. Anthony, I hope, will advise us as to a house when the time comes.'

Lord Isham nodded his agreement.

Then Gina was possessed by an imp of mischief. 'Besides,' she said, 'before I go I must learn to waltz…'

'Shocking!' There was a sniff of disapproval from Mrs Rushford. 'Young men careering about a ball-room with ladies in their arms? I must hope that my own girls won't consider it.'

'I'm sorry to hear you say so,' Gina replied solemnly. 'The Prince Regent finds it delightful. In future it will be the rage at all his parties.'

'Which, of course, you will attend, Lady Whitelaw?' There was no mistaking the malicious note in Mrs Rushford's voice.

'Why yes, I believe so, ma'am.' Gina regarded her

questioner with an innocent gaze. 'We are invited to Brighton in September.'

This was enough to reduce Mrs Rushford to silence, and Thomas Newby stepped into the breach.

'When I left town Lady Caroline Lamb was holding waltz parties in the mornings,' he observed to no one in particular. 'It gave me a chance to practice.'

'Truly, can you waltz?' Elspeth was seated beside him, much to her delight. Now she gazed at him with awe.

'I make some kind of a stab at it,' he admitted modestly.

'I don't suppose...I mean...if you came to see us would you show us how it is done?' Elspeth knew that whispering was rude, but she wasn't exactly whispering, was she? She was simply speaking in too low a voice for her words to reach Mrs Rushford's ears.

Thomas replied in the same tone. 'Glad to, Miss Elspeth, if your stepmama don't mind. Got to be up to the mark with the latest fads and fancies, haven't we?'

'Oh, you do understand!' Elspeth gave him a grateful look. 'When one is almost out it is very hard to be treated like a child. Gina doesn't do it, but other people do. I hope she won't insist on sending us to that Academy to finish our education.'

'Well, as I understand it, it isn't a school, Miss Elspeth. It's more like a university for ladies, in a small way, of course.' He smiled. 'It might turn you into a revolutionary.'

Elspeth giggled. 'Are you a revolutionary, Mr Newby?'

'Not I! Don't understand these politician fellows. Always arguing about something, and never getting anything done.' His voice had risen and his words were clearly audible during a pause in the conversation of his fellow guests.

'You are very hard on us, Newby.' Anthony was laughing openly. 'Give us some credit, man. We do try, you know.'

Thomas flushed to the roots of his hair, and he made haste to apologise to his host. 'I didn't mean you, my lord. We know how hard you've worked to ease conditions in the north, and for the machinists here.'

Isham grinned at him. 'So it doesn't all escape you, Mr Newby?'

'I talk to people,' Thomas said vaguely. 'What I know don't come from books, my lord.'

'Many more of us might profit by your example,' Isham replied. 'Sometimes I feel that we foist our ideas on the people, giving them what we think they need, instead of what they want.'

'My dear Anthony! Unlettered louts? Would you have them decide the conduct of the country?' Mrs Rushford could contain herself no longer.

'I thought you believed in a lack of education?' Anthony said mildly. 'Have we not just been discussing the matter?'

'We were speaking of women,' his mother-in-law replied in angry tones.

It was enough to bring India into the conversation with a request to be brought up to date with the London gossip.

'I hope you don't mind,' she said to Gina in a low voice. 'I'll take care to see that nothing untoward reaches the ears of the girls, though Mr Newby will be well aware of the need for discretion in young company.'

She was right. Thomas rose to the occasion. In minutes he had them laughing at the Prince Regent's favourite story.

'Do stop me if you've heard it…' He looked around the table. 'It's the one about the running race.'

'Oh, no! Do tell us!' Elspeth couldn't contain her curiosity, and was rewarded with a look from Mrs Rushford which indicated that young people should be seen and not heard.

'Very well then. This is the story of the fattest man in Brighton. He wagered heavily on himself to win a foot race against the town's best runner.'

'That doesn't sound very sensible…' Gina was smiling as she awaited the outcome of the story.

'He was cunning, ma'am. He made only two conditions. The first was that he should choose the route, and the second was that he should have a ten-yard start. As you can imagine, there were no objections. In fact, he was offered a fifty-yard start, but he didn't take it.'

'The spectators must have thought him mad,' Giles interjected. 'The odds against him winning must have been enormous.'

'They were, but this crafty fellow made a fortune. When the starting pistol was fired he set off down the narrowest streets in Brighton at a jog-trot. His rival came up from behind, but he couldn't pass that vast bulk. Our hero filled the narrow lanes from side to side.'

Even Mrs Rushford was forced to smile. 'Mr Newby, are you acquainted with the Prince?' she asked.

'No, ma'am, my father...er...feels that his fortune would be insufficient to support me in those circles.'

This brought another smile from the assembled company.

'Even so, I'd like to see his palace by the sea,' Thomas admitted. 'I'm told It's like an Oriental seraglio, whatever that is.'

Being well acquainted with the exact meaning of the word, Isham felt it time to step in.

'The Prince refers to his place as a cottage,' he said with some amusement. 'In view of the vast sums lavished on it, it must be the most expensive cottage in the country.'

'Do you like it, Anthony?' Gina was curious.

'It isn't to my taste. I have no quarrel with this fascination for the East and Orientalism. Some of the Prince's treasures are very fine indeed. However, it is difficult to appreciate so many when they fill every room.'

'I hear that he keeps the place at hothouse temperature.' Mrs Rushford was fascinated by this glimpse into the lifestyle of the heir to the throne.

'He does, ma'am, and that, combined with his taste for busy wallpapers and extravagant decoration of every kind, has had a stifling effect on some of his visitors. A lady of my acquaintance described it as "fairly buzzing". It made her feel quite faint.'

'So one must suffer a little if one wishes to hear the Prince sing or conduct the orchestra in his music room?'

'Yes, Gina. You must be prepared for some discomfort when you visit Brighton in September.'

'We shan't mind. I hear he has a pleasant singing voice and reads the poetry of Scott and Southey to perfection. That will please Mair.'

'Your stepdaughter will be in a minority,' Mrs Rushford retorted sharply. 'The Regent is one of the most unpopular men in England with his constant spending, and his disloyalty to his friends, to say nothing of certain other matters.' She glanced significantly at the two young girls. 'As for that poor wife of his…!'

Gina was tempted to ask which wife she had in mind. It was common knowledge that the Prince had gone through some sort of wedding ceremony with his mistress, Mrs Fitzherbert, before his official marriage to the Princess Caroline. His reputation as a bigamist did nothing to enhance his popularity in the country.

'Now, Mama, we know that you champion the Princess's cause, but we must leave the gentlemen to their port…' India rose from the table, anxious to avoid a diatribe about the Regent's treatment of his

wife. She herself imagined that there must be faults
on both sides, but her mother would not hear of it.

In the salon she rang for tea and called Mair and
Elspeth to her. They were favourites with Anthony,
and having met them she could understand it.

Elspeth was short and plump, but Mair, with her
gazelle-like frame, was unlikely ever to reach the
buxom proportions so much admired by society. In
her case it would not matter, India thought to herself.
There was character in that youthful face. Perhaps the
jaw was a little too square, the brow too wide and the
mouth too generous for true beauty, but her Celtic
origins were apparent in the high cheekbones, the
mass of dark hair, and the vivid blue eyes, set off by
a perfect skin.

Elspeth was undeniably her sister, but she had not
yet lost her puppy fat, and in her, at present, one saw
only the energetic schoolgirl.

India began to question them, speaking as she
would to an adult. This she'd found was a subtle form
of flattery, which never failed to please young people.

'Shall you attend the fête at Perceval Hall?' she
asked. 'My aunt would be happy to see you there.
She runs these affairs for charity.'

'We haven't heard of it,' Mair told her shyly.

'Oh, of course not. How foolish of me! I had forgot
that you had but recently arrived in Abbot Quincey.
If you'd like to go I'll ask her to send you an invitation.'

'Oh, would you, Lady Isham?' Elspeth gave her an
earnest look. 'Gina will take us, I feel sure of it. What

happens at the fête? We didn't have them in Scotland.'

'It's an excuse for a party,' India replied. 'There are all kinds of competitions, such as bobbing for apples, and pinning a tail upon a donkey when one is blindfold. There are races too, with prizes.'

'Horse races?' Elspeth glanced at her sister.

'Horse races, sack races, three-legged races, and ordinary running races. You may take your pick. There are trials of strength, and a tug-of-war, and even an archery competition.'

'It sounds such fun,' Elspeth said warmly. 'Gina will love it.' She glanced across at her stepmother, who was deep in conversation with Letty and Mrs Rushford. 'We'll tell her about it later.'

'Well, don't forget to mention the refreshments and the country-dancing…' India looked up as the gentlemen came to join them. A glance sent Isham to rescue Gina from the cross-questioning she was suffering at the hands of Mrs Rushford.

'Thank heavens for that!' Letty sank on to the couch beside her sister. 'Poor Gina! I don't know how she kept her temper. Mama has almost asked her for details of her fortune…'

'We'll have to put a stop to that. What do you say to a game of cards with Mother? It will keep her out of mischief…' A glance of complicity passed between the sisters. Then India made her suggestion.

It was greeted with enthusiasm by Mrs Rushford, who was quick to choose Anthony as her partner. She'd learned from bitter experience that it was almost impossible to beat him and she preferred to have him on her side. Besides, a plan was forming in her mind.

'Lady Whitelaw will like to see the Orangery,' she told Giles in a tone which brooked no argument. 'India and Letty will make up our table.'

'Lady Whitelaw may prefer to join you,' Giles retorted stiffly.

'My dear boy, five people cannot play, and India must undertake a restful occupation. Letty, as you know, is mad for cards...'

This came as news to Letty, who was too startled to reply. She could not look either at India or at Anthony.

'Mrs Rushford is quite right,' Gina was trying not to laugh. 'I believe I mentioned to her that I have no head for cards. I should be most interested to see the Orangery and the gardens. I shall need advice on how to improve my grounds, so perhaps the gentlemen will give me the names of certain plants, and the girls and I will try to remember them.'

Anthony glanced at his wife, who managed to preserve her countenance only with the greatest difficulty. Her mother's plan had been foiled in the most charming way possible. Mrs Rushford had not envisaged the entire party setting forth into the garden.

Giles was furious with her. Her scheming was all too obvious and it filled him with embarrassment. For two pins he would have walked away, but good manners forced him to lead the party through the Orangery and on to the terrace.

He'd planned to take the girls up to the Folly on the hill, but Thomas was ahead of him. Already a favourite with Mair and Elspeth, that gentleman had been challenged to a race and all three were already disappearing into the distance.

In silence he paced beside Gina, but he couldn't look at her.

'Pray go ahead if you wish to join the others,' Gina told him cheerfully. 'I'm afraid that these flimsy evening slippers are not meant for walking.'

'No! I do *not* wish to join the others.' Suddenly Giles longed to tear aside that polished social veneer. 'Must we pretend that we are strangers?'

Gina gave him a sideways look. 'Of course not! Why should you think that? We knew each other as children, and Anthony knows that we met in Italy. Oh, I see! You feel that you should have mentioned to your family that we'd met since my return to Abbot Quincey? That is not so very dreadful. They did not seem to take it amiss...'

'No, I was not referring to that and well you know it.' Giles stopped suddenly and swung round to face her. 'Look at me!' he demanded. 'I can't pretend that we are casual acquaintances...can you?'

'Most certainly I can,' she replied in level tones. 'I'd advise you to do the same.'

Her companion groaned. 'I don't believe that you have forgotten what we once were to each other.'

'I've not forgotten.' With an effort Gina kept her voice steady. 'But it was long ago. I was younger than

Mair is now. At that age one has little experience of the world, and a childish folly is soon forgotten.'

Giles looked as if she had struck him. Until today he'd been resolved that he would never remind her of their love, but his good resolutions had deserted him.

Quickly, he pulled himself together. 'Even so,' he said. 'I feel I owe you an explanation...'

Gina lifted a dismissive hand. 'You owe me nothing...'

'No, please hear me out. I didn't know where to find you. Why didn't you answer my letter?'

'What letter?' she demanded. 'I received no letter.'

Giles stared at her in stupefaction. 'I wrote to you before I sailed...before you came back to the villa. It was to tell you why I'd had to leave so quickly.'

'There was nothing,' she told him.

'Damn the fellow! I paid him well to carry the message.' Giles turned his face away. 'What you must of thought of me?'

'It *was* difficult to understand,' she admitted. 'I hadn't supposed you to be a man who would flee at the first sign of danger, but conditions in Naples were chaotic. Before I knew it we were *en route* to the West Indies.'

'You could have written to me at the Grange,' he said miserably.

'I suppose so, but we were always on the move. It wasn't easy to find a ship prepared to carry mail.' She wouldn't tell him that she'd been too hurt and also too proud to beg him to come back to her.

'I tried to find *you*, you know. I made enquiries at the bakery until your mother became suspicious. I said that Sir Alastair was a friend of mine and I wondered what had happened to him, but I don't think she believed me.'

'She wouldn't have been able to help you. I wrote to my parents when I could, but if they replied their letters never reached me.'

'Oh, Gina, you must have been so lonely.'

'Sometimes, perhaps, but I had the girls, and Sir Alastair and his wife were always good to me.' Gina managed an engaging smile. 'It is difficult to be sad, you know, when one is embroiled in so much action. Distant countries are always full of interest, but they aren't the safest places in the world.'

'I heard something of your exploits from Anthony.'

'Exaggerated, I fear, though I can fire a pistol with some degree of accuracy. Giles, have we not said enough about my affairs? What of you? How do you go on?'

He had been dreading the question, unwilling to admit even to Gina that the fortunes of his family had been saved only by Anthony's marriage to India. The thought still galled him. True, India was happy, but it might so easily have been different. She'd accepted Lord Isham hating him for the part she believed he'd played in the death of her father and the loss of all their property. Only in these last few months had that hatred turned to love.

She'd been prepared to sacrifice herself for his sake, and that of his mother and sister. He could not forget it. Feelings of frustration threatened to overwhelm him. It should have been he who saved the family, and he'd been unable to do so.

It hadn't been for want of trying. Ever since he'd been summoned back from Italy all those years ago he'd been forced to shoulder burdens apparently beyond the capabilities of a young man.

And he'd almost succeeded in turning the Rushford Estate into a paying proposition. He'd worked day and night to bring it round. Their lands were rich and fertile and he'd immersed himself in study of all the latest farming methods, new thinking on the rotation of crops, new strains of various seeds, and all the latest breeds of cattle.

He'd yearned to have the means to buy those implements which would have saved on time and labour, but they were beyond him. Undaunted, he'd been forced to improvise for himself, ignoring the traditional resistance to change so prevalent among all agricultural labourers.

But the drain on his resources had been impossible to halt. Money set aside for improvements had gone to pay the debts of his lovable but feckless father. The end had come last year when, in a night of madness, Gareth Rushford had gambled away the last of his inheritance, losing it to Anthony Isham, and leaving his family destitute.

The shock had been severe. Forced to leave her home, his mother had moved into a small cottage owned by her brother-in-law, Sir James Perceval, taking her daughters with her.

Giles himself had travelled the country looking for employment. It had been in vain. Only now, as India's estate manager, could he see some glimmer of hope for the future. He was realistic enough to know that he had years of struggle ahead of him. Far better to forget his one and only love.

He turned away as they caught up with the others and offered to take them to see a badger sett. Gina declined on the grounds that her slippers were quite soaked through in the long grass. She turned back towards the house, with Thomas Newby as her escort.

'Ma'am, we have been thoughtless.' Gallantly, he offered her his arm. 'I must hope that you will not take a chill.'

'Highly unlikely, Mr Newby. It pains me to admit it, but I enjoy the best of health. Such a trial when it is so much more interesting to be always swooning, or in a state of delicate health.'

'Ma'am, you are making game of me.' Thomas grinned at her. 'You would not care to be in such case, I believe.'

'No, I should not.' Companionably Gina tucked her hand into the crook of his arm. 'There is so much enjoyment in this world. One cannot see it from a sofa.'

'Shall you settle in Abbot Quincey, ma'am?' Thomas felt as though he'd known her all his life.

'I don't know yet, Mr Newby. I must consider the girls. Fortunately we are not so far from London here in Abbot Quincey. I may open the London house this year, or possibly in the spring.'

'You speak of the girls. What of yourself?' As he spoke he wondered if she would regard the question as too personal, but she gave him a friendly smile.

'I never make arrangements too far ahead. That way I am not disturbed if I have to change my plans...'

'Very wise. Oh, Lord!' Thomas had caught sight of a horseman in the distance. 'I hope I won't have to change mine. Here comes Stubbins, if I'm not mistaken...'

'Stubbins?'

'My valet, ma'am, or groom, or whatever you like to name him. In reality, he is a watchdog. My father sets him on me...'

'Leave him to me!' Gina's eyes were dancing. She was prepared to enjoy the coming confrontation.

As the man drew rein beside them she moved even closer to her companion.

'Now how did you find me, Stubbins?' Thomas sounded exasperated.

''T'wern't difficult, Mr Thomas. You left a trail a mile wide.'

'Good gracious, Mr Newby,' Gina simpered. 'Are you fleeing from the law?'

'No, ma'am, this is my valet, Stubbins.'

Gina turned a soulful gaze upon the servant. 'Why, Mr Newby will be so glad to see you. He has been sadly at a loss, have you not, my dear?'

Thomas choked and turned his laughter into a cough. 'I have indeed. Where have you been, you dog?'

Stubbins gave his charge an uncertain look. He'd expected fury, defiance and anything but to find his master escorting a lady who would clearly have gained the approval of Mr Newby, senior.

Now Stubbins sought to rally his forces.

'Beg pardon, Mr Thomas, but you left London without giving me your direction…'

'An oversight,' Thomas asserted stoutly.

'Were you thinking of me, my dear?' Gina draped herself artistically about her companion's person. 'How sweet of you.'

Thomas patted her on the shoulder. 'There, there!' he said. 'I must get you back to the Grange before you catch a chill. Stubbins will ride ahead for us. Lady Whitelaw's feet are wet. She must have hot broth as soon as she arrives.' With a wave of his hand he dismissed the dreaded Stubbins. Then he shouted with laughter.

'Mr Newby, please! You must not let him hear you. I'm sure he has your best interests at heart.'

'Now, ma'am, you shall not preach to me. What a card you are! Stubbins will be convinced that I am trying to fix my interest with you. My father will have the news before the week is out.'

'Oh dear!' Gina looked repentant. 'Shall you mind very much? I'm sorry, but Stubbins looked so…so very disapproving of you. I could not resist the opportunity to tease.'

'Lady Whitelaw, from now on you may consider me your slave. I had not thought to live to see the day when Stubbins could be routed.'

'It was unkind of me. You see, Mr Newby, I am not at all to be trusted. I am inclined to follow impulse.'

'And a most charming impulse, ma'am, if I may say so. I am deeply honoured.'

'Come now, Mr Newby,' Gina spoke in a rallying tone. 'We hear on all sides that you are a confirmed bachelor.'

'Lady Whitelaw, you could change my mind,' came the swift reply.

Apparently Gina did not hear him as she went indoors.

Mrs Rushford looked up eagerly as they returned to the salon. Then her face clouded.

'Where is Giles?' Her tone was sharp. She had expected to see Gina escorted by her son and not by Thomas Newby.

'Why, ma'am, he kindly offered to show the girls a badger sett,' Gina told her smoothly. She'd seen the look of mortification on Mrs Rushford's face, and was aware of the reason for it.

'Such folly! Your girls will take their death of cold to be kept outdoors of an evening. I am surprised that you allowed it, Lady Whitelaw. Sometimes I wonder at Giles…so little regard for other people's health…to say nothing of the proprieties!'

'Why, Isabel, what can you mean?' Lord Isham laid his cards aside. 'I hope you aren't suggesting that Mair and Elspeth are in danger of injuring their reputations by taking a walk with Giles.' He gave his mother-in-law a pleasant smile, but she was quick to notice that it did not reach his eyes.

'Of course not!' she said hastily. 'But Giles is so impulsive. Believe me, Lady Whitelaw, he is all heart. It would not occur to him that he might overtire the girls, in his wish to give them pleasure.'

'I thank you for your concern, but the girls are used to walking. As you see, they have come to no harm...' She looked up as the others returned. 'Did you see the badgers?' she enquired.

'We were too early, Gina. They come out to feed only when it is full dark, so Giles tells us...'

Mrs Rushford was silent. It had occurred to her for once that she must watch her tongue, if Gina was to be persuaded into accepting Giles. It could serve no useful purpose to criticise him in public.

That worthy resolution did not apply to a private talk. She called Giles over to her under the cover of general conversation.

'What are you about?' she hissed. 'Must you pay so much attention to those stupid girls? You should be trying to fix your interest with their stepmother.'

Giles paled so quickly that she was startled. His eyes flashed, and she could see that he was controlling his temper only with an effort.

'Come,' she said more gently. 'I am thinking only of you, my dear. You must not take it amiss. Why should you object to making yourself agreeable to Gina? She has improved so much, as you may see for yourself. Why, one might almost believe that she is one of us.'

Giles was about to turn away. He was seized with the urge to tell her to hold her tongue, but he was incapable of speech. His mother caught at his sleeve.

'Listen to me!' she urged. 'Why must you be so foolish? You won't make the least push to improve your fortunes, even when the chance is there for you. Take care, my boy. If I'm not mistaken your friend Newby will be ahead of you.'

Giles looked at her then, and his mother shrank away. At that moment he looked capable of murder. She knew that she had gone too far, but Giles was too much of the gentleman to vent his anger on her.

'Newby is welcome to try his luck,' he said in a colourless tone. With that he walked back to the others.

Chapter Five

The party broke up almost at once, but not before the girls had whispered a request to Gina.

'May Mr Newby call on us?' Elspeth asked. 'He's promised to show us how to waltz. That's if you have no objection…?'

'None whatever! He can teach me too. We must be in the fashion when we go to Brighton.'

Gina issued her invitation without delay, though she did not mention the reason for it. She'd thought it best to use the excuse of a riding expedition.

'We three are used to riding daily,' she explained. 'But Giles has warned me that it isn't wise to go about without an escort in these difficult times. If the gentlemen would be so kind…?' she looked an appeal at Thomas Newby.

'Glad to, ma'am,' he replied promptly. 'We'd be honoured to escort you, wouldn't we, Giles?'

That gentleman bowed in Gina's direction. 'Under other circumstances it would be a pleasure, ma'am, but I have duties here. I've been away for several weeks, and there is much to do.'

His mother glared at him. 'Nonsense!' she said sharply. 'India has a bailiff, and Anthony will be here. You cannot be indispensable to the place, isn't that so?' She looked at Isham for support.

His Lordship nodded. The situation was beginning to intrigue him. 'I think you should oblige the ladies, Giles. After all, they will not wish to ride all day.'

Giles felt trapped. Everyone seemed to have conspired against him. Now he was left with no alternative but to accept the invitation without giving offence. Still he hesitated. His plans to avoid Gina's company were apparently doomed to failure.

'Do come!' she begged in a low voice. 'The riding is a pretext. Mr Newby has promised to teach the girls to waltz, and they are so excited...'

Giles bowed again. 'It will be a pleasure,' he said without conviction.

'Then shall we say tomorrow...perhaps in the afternoon? We promise not to take up too much of your time.' With that she allowed herself and the girls to be ushered to their carriage, but she was lost in thought as they drove home.

She knew Giles all too well. It was clear that he was determined to avoid her company if possible. Was she being cruel? Perhaps, but her resolution did not falter. He still loved her. She was sure of it. Her offer of casual friendship had been deliberate, as was her untroubled manner when she was by his side.

His efforts to avoid her confirmed what she already

knew. He could not trust himself to pretend that he no longer wanted her. Her attitude had hurt him, but better to hurt him now than to run the risk of rejection if she'd thrown herself into his arms.

She sighed at the folly of men and their foolish pride. Would a woman have thrown away the chance of happiness because of such stupid scruples?

She thought not, but then, women were so much more sensible in these matters. Giles felt that his honour was at stake. He was no fortune-hunter, and unwillingly she respected him for it, but she loved him so.

The solution to her problem seemed no nearer. Giles would not offer for her in his present circumstances.

She might appeal to Anthony for advice, but that would be a mistake. She must not discuss Giles behind his back. If he found out all would be at an end between them. She alone must solve this problem. She longed to think of a way to do so.

Her mouth curved in a wry smile. Why had she fallen in love with such a stiff-necked creature? Her money was enough for both of them, and she too owned estates which needed managing. She knew well enough that she must not mention them. Giles would regard such a suggestion as charity, but of what use were possessions if they stood in the way of happiness? She would never make him see it, so for the present she would take one day at a time.

The following morning brought the promise of rain. 'Will they come, do you suppose?' Elspeth was standing by the window gazing anxiously at the lowering skies.

'Nothing is more certain,' Gina comforted. 'When gentlemen make arrangements they do not break their word.'

'But if it rains Mrs Rushford won't believe that we intend to ride. Must we ride, Gina? May we not spend the time in learning to waltz?'

'No, my dear. If the day is fine we shall ride, if only for a short distance. Would you have me guilty of lying to Lord and Lady Isham?'

'No, I suppose not, but if that stuffy Mrs Rushford had not been so disapproving we might have just had dancing lessons.'

'There will be time enough for that when we get back. Now, Elspeth, you must go back to your books if you are to have a holiday this afternoon. Cheer up, my love, after nuncheon you may forget your studies for the rest of the day.'

'Good. May I wear my new riding habit?'

'Of course.' Gina hid a smile. She guessed that there would be much primping before the girls were ready to greet their visitors.

She herself had much to do. Summoning her cook, she discussed menus for the week. Then she spent some time upon her household accounts. The sound of distant hammering reminded her that the builders were at work. She rose from her desk and made a quick tour of inspection.

The men greeted her with respect. Gina knew what

she wanted. At first they'd had some reservations about working for a female. From long experience they imagined that she would change her mind a dozen times about the alterations to the house. It had come as a surprise to find that her plans were clear. Gina had given her instructions and from then on she did not interfere.

Even so, they were under no illusions. Always polite and charming, Lady Whitelaw's keen eyes examined every detail. No shoddy workmanship would do for her.

After nuncheon Gina went upstairs to change. Her dark green riding habit fitted her to perfection. It was severely plain, but it emphasised her tiny waist and the swelling curves of her bosom.

She studied it in the cheval glass and was satisfied. She had been wise to eschew the fashionable frogging and tassels which were all the rage this year. She had not the height to carry off such decoration. Nothing detracted from the excellent cut of the garment and the clean lines made her look taller.

She had just picked up her charming little hat and was preparing to go downstairs when Hanson knocked at her door.

'Madam, you have company,' he announced.

'So soon? They are early. I did not expect them yet…' Her heart was already beating faster at the thought of seeing Giles again.

But it wasn't Giles and Thomas Newby who awaited her in the salon. Her colour rose as she encountered the knowing look of her father's brother, Samuel Westcott.

He came towards her with both arms outstretched, but Gina moved swiftly, so that the sofa lay between them. She gave him a stiff bow.

'Uncle, I am surprised to see you here,' she said in a cool tone. 'Father is not with you?'

'No, no, my dear, but I bring a message from him. He asks if you will dine at the new house on Thursday.'

'I shall be glad to.' Her manner was uncompromising.

'Well, now, don't you have a kiss for your old uncle?' He had rounded the corner of the sofa and was moving towards her.

'Uncle, you had best sit down. If you touch me you'll regret it...'

His expression changed. 'Too good for us now, my girl? You always were a spiteful little minx...' Instinctively he rubbed the back of his hand.

Gina glanced down and was pleased to see that it bore a scar. 'I thought you might have learned your lesson,' she said pointedly.

He gave her a malicious look. 'Little cat! There was no call for you to bite me as you did.'

'On the contrary, there was every reason. Did you think me too young to understand your pawing and your stroking?'

He sniggered. 'Just affection for a pretty niece. If you took it amiss, why didn't you tell your father?'

'He wouldn't have believed me. My father is a man

of honour. He would not imagine that his brother could behave so ill...'

'Tush! What was it, after all? A kiss or two, a hug...?'

'You disgust me!' she said clearly. 'I have not forgotten how you were always pulling me on to your knee, and sliding your hand beneath my clothing.'

'You have a dirty mind,' he accused. 'I'd be sorry to think that my own girls should think as you do.'

There was no amusement in Gina's laugh. 'Pray don't think me a fool,' she said shortly. 'Even at fifteen I was aware of your intentions. You made them clear enough on the day that I left Abbot Quincey.'

'Namby-pamby miss,' he mocked. Even so, he could not meet her eyes.

Gina watched with interest as a flood of colour suffused his face. Samuel Westcott had always been an ugly man and the years had not been kind to him. Always inclined to excess flesh, now he was positively gross. Pantaloons and waistcoat strained over an enormous belly, and his neckcloth strove in vain to contain his double chins. A small mouth and heavy-lidded eyes almost disappeared in folds of fat.

Now those eyes gave her a vindictive look. Then he turned his head away.

Gina found that she was trembling. It had taken years to wipe out the memory of that dreadful day when he had trapped her in the store-room of the bakery and tried to rape her. She'd fought him off, biting and scratching as she did so, but it was the final straw. Next time she might not be so lucky. Her answer had been to flee as far away as possible.

Now she was praying that the girls would not appear. She rang the bell, intending to ask Hanson to send them out of the house on some pretext or other, but she was too late. Dressed in their most becoming habits, Mair and Elspeth hurried into the room.

'Are they here? Hanson said…' Mair stopped and bobbed a curtsey. 'Oh, I'm sorry, we did not know that you had company.'

'This is my uncle, Samuel Westcott,' Gina said coldly. 'He is just about to leave…'

Both girls stared at her in astonishment. This was not the gentle, friendly Gina they knew.

Samuel Westcott had struggled to his feet, but now he sank back again on to the sofa. 'I'm in no hurry, Gina,' he said smoothly.

She saw with dismay that his tiny eyes were gleaming as they roved over Mair and Elspeth. 'Charming, quite charming!' he announced. 'Tell me, my dears, when do you make your come out?'

'The girls are too young to think of it as yet,' Gina said sharply. 'I'm afraid you will have to excuse us, Uncle, but we have an appointment…'

'Of course.' He struggled to his feet again, but his eyes were fixed on the girls. 'You'll bring the young ladies with you when you come to dine, I hope?'

Gina felt sick. She turned to the girls. 'I have forgot my crop and my handkerchief,' she lied. 'Will you fetch them for me?'

Obediently they went to do her bidding. Then Gina

swung round on her uncle. 'Lay a finger on either
Mair or Elspeth and I will ruin you,' she promised.

'Brave words, little Gina. I think you have forgot.
I'm a man of substance now.'

'It won't be enough to save you. I have influential
friends. I'll make it my business to see that you lose
everything, your home, your business and your reputation.'

'Hoping to sink your teeth into me again?' he
sneered.

'Not this time,' she assured him. 'I have more experience now. My next attack will leave you crip-
pled.'

He was given no opportunity to reply. At that moment the door to the salon opened and Giles and
Thomas Newby were announced.

Giles was at once aware of the tension in the room.
Something had happened to shake Gina out of her
composure, but her visitor was about to take his leave.
As the door closed behind Samuel Westcott he moved
to Gina's side.

'You are very pale,' he observed quietly. 'Has
something happened to upset you?'

'It's nothing.' Gina shook her head. She had never
told Giles the true reason for her flight from Abbot
Quincey. There seemed little point in raking up old
memories.

'Gina, this is me, remember? I thought we were to
be good friends. If you are worried…?'

She decided that a half-truth was better than nothing. 'Well if you must have it, I find my uncle something of a trial. It was a shock to see him here today.'

With commendable tact, Thomas had been studying a picture at the far end of the room. Now he came towards them.

'The rain holds off,' he said cheerfully. 'We shall yet have our ride.'

With an effort Gina recovered her self-control. 'I've promised that it will be short,' she said. 'The girls cannot wait to learn the waltz.'

Thomas grinned as he looked down at his gleaming Hessians. 'I must crave your indulgence, Lady Whitelaw. I ain't no dancing master at the best of times. In these boots I shall prance round like an elephant.'

Gina was forced to smile. 'It was very good of you to offer to teach us, sir. Perhaps if you just gave us the general idea…?'

'That's all you'll get from Thomas!' Troubled by the look in Gina's eyes, Giles made an effort to lighten the atmosphere.

Gina attempted to follow his example. 'And you, Giles? Shall you prance round like an elephant?'

'Don't believe it, ma'am!' Thomas gave her a solemn look, but his eyes were sparkling. 'Giles is one of those aggravating creatures who can carry a tune in his head, and then transfer it to his feet. He'd make his fortune on the stage, I shouldn't wonder.'

'Very droll, Thomas! Will you be my manager?'

'Glad to, old son! Glad to!' With this promise Thomas turned to greet the girls.

Their ride that day was more of a leisurely ramble.
Mair and Elspeth chattered non-stop, quizzing
Thomas about his visits to London, and requesting
anecdotes about the literary lions and other celebri-
ties.

Giles and Gina had fallen a little way behind the
others. 'Mr Newby is very kind,' she observed as she
nodded towards the others. 'He has endless patience
with the girls.'

'He has a heart of gold,' Giles assured her. 'Don't
be fooled by his jokes and his pretence of being afraid
of Stubbins. In a tight corner I'd be glad to have him
by my side.'

Gina smiled. 'It isn't difficult to penetrate below
that light-hearted manner. I like him very much.'

'I'm glad to hear it,' Giles said stiffly. Then he
gestured ahead. 'Shall we catch up with them?'

Gina spurred her horse into a trot. She had no need
to look at her companion's face. She'd heard the note
of jealousy in his voice. She had no doubt that he was
fond of Thomas, but having found her again so recently, he was in despair at the thought of losing her
to a rival.

For a moment she was tempted to reassure him, but
the time was not yet right. Whatever it cost her she
must wait. The stakes were too high for her to lose
the least advantage. Giles must woo and win her for
the second time. She would not make it easy for him.

Was she setting her sights too high? It had been a
gamble to come back to Abbot Quincey in the hope
of regaining his love. In time she might persuade him

to set aside his scruples, but for that to happen he must want her more than anything in the world.

Now an uglier problem troubled her. Would she have returned to the village if she'd known that she and the girls would meet Samuel Westcott? She'd thought herself safe from that creature with his vicious tendencies.

Naturally, she'd made enquiries before leaving Scotland and Anthony had assured her that her uncle was based in London. A successful grain and feed merchant, his visits to his birthplace were said to be infrequent. It was sheer chance which had led him to visit his brother so soon after her return. Hopefully, his stay would be brief.

As they turned for home Giles studied her face again. He was at a loss as to know what to say to her. It was clear that she had no intention of taking him into her confidence, but he longed to comfort her. It was Thomas who broke the silence. He'd been speaking to the girls about their home in Scotland.

'Shall you miss that country?' he asked Gina. 'I hear that it is beautiful.'

'In places it is grand and wild,' she replied, 'but the Whitelaw estates are on the west coast. There we escape the savage winters of the north...'

'Gina says that it is because of the warm Gulf Stream,' Elspeth told him. She was proud to air her knowledge. 'We have grown peaches out of doors...'

'Good farming country?' Thomas was hoping to draw Giles into the conversation.

Gina had recovered her composure. 'We grow an

excellent crop of heather,' she said drily. 'The soil is too poor and thin for us to raise good crops, but our beef is the best in the world.'

'And you should see our Highland cattle, Mr Newby,' Elspeth continued to chatter on. 'They have enormous horns, not like the cows in England.'

'They sound ferocious,' Thomas grinned. 'Did I tell you that I was once chased by a bull?'

'Only because you waved your cloak in front of him.' Giles turned to the others. 'Thomas was inspired by tales of the Spanish matadors. He thought that fighting a bull must be easy.'

'I found out that it wasn't. I must have broken all records to reach the hedge ahead of the beast. I swear I thought he had me. I could feel his breath upon my neck.'

This story was greeted by shouts of laughter, and Gina's good humour was quite restored.

'Giles, you are the expert on good farming methods,' she said quietly. 'I wonder if you would advise me. The Scottish estate is in poor case. My husband, as you know, was never strong. He was unable to oversee the place as he would have wished. Would you think it possible to bring it round? It is a part of the girls inheritance, so it is a matter of some concern to me.'

Giles was interested in spite of his determination to distance himself from Gina.

'I know nothing of conditions in Scotland,' he admitted. 'Mostly what is needed is an injection of capital. One must not throw good money after bad, of course. It's important to decide on the priorities.'

'I understand.' Gina skirted carefully around the question of capital. With the means at her disposal it would not be a problem, but with Giles the mention of money would always be a touchy subject. 'How would I decide on my priorities?'

He gave her a suspicious look. Was she about to offer him some help? That he could not bear.

'Your bailiff will advise you,' he told her abruptly.

'You haven't seen him, Giles. The old man is well on in his seventies, and much opposed to change.'

He smiled then. 'I know the problem. I have the same thing here. Over the years my suggestions have either been agreed to and then ignored, or greeted with dire predictions as to what will happen when one flies in the face of nature.'

'But you *have* made changes, haven't you? Anthony tells me that you have insisted on the use of your new ploughs and seed drills, as well as fertilizers and the correct rotation of crops.'

'You are very well informed,' he said drily.

'I was interested.'

'Really?' Clearly he did not believe her.

'Oh come!' she replied. 'I think that you have forgot that I am country-bred. Anthony lent me a book on Coke of Norfolk. You'll have heard of him, of course?'

'I met him, Gina.' Giles gave up all pretence of indifference. 'The man is a genius. If every farmer could be persuaded to follow his example we could be almost self-sufficient in the matter of food.'

'I can see that that would be important, especially in time of war...'

'It's true. Of course we have the weather to contend with in this country, but there are now new strains of seed which are resistant to both wet ground, and a lack of sunshine, and disease.'

'Is that why you designed your latest seed drill?'

Giles looked his surprise. 'You've heard of that?'

'Of course. Anthony intends to make good use of it. How did you come to invent it?'

'Out of necessity,' he told her briefly. 'The Rushford estate had been run down for years. I couldn't afford to employ much labour. Hand-sowing was out of the question. The drill does the work of several men, but it won't be popular, I fear.'

'You think you may have the same problems as the factory-owners? I mean, won't the local people feel that you are taking the bread out of their mouths, by adding to the unemployment?'

'I couldn't afford to employ them anyway,' he told her. 'With better crops prosperity may return and bread will be cheaper.'

'Prosperity will return in time,' she said warmly. 'Oh, Giles, if only this war were to end... Will Wellington take Badajoz, do you suppose? He is thought to be pushing back the French in Spain.'

'He has done well to date.' Her companion's face grew sombre. 'What a task he had, with his allies fighting among themselves, breaking their promises of men and supplies, and letting him down upon all sides.'

Thomas had ridden on ahead with the girls, but now he came back to them.

'You look as if you are putting the world to rights,' he commented cheerfully. 'Giles, I wonder if we should go into the village before the ladies.' He gestured ahead. 'There seems to be some bustle in the High Street, with people milling about and a lot of shouting.'

'A riot?' Giles asked quickly. 'That's strange…the Luddites operate at night for the most part.'

'I don't know. It don't sound ill-humoured. There's a lot of hallooing and hazzas, and some are waving flags. Still, it might be best to take no chances…'

'Could it be that there is news of a victory?' Without waiting for the others, Gina spurred her horse ahead.

She was right. English tongues had difficulty with pronunciation of the Spanish town of Badajoz, but cheers for Wellington soon convinced her of his victory. She turned to the others with a glowing face.

'Come!' she cried. 'This is a cause for celebration!' She hurried indoors, instructing Hanson to bring up a couple of bottles of her finest burgundy.

As they toasted the Duke's success they shared in the general feeling of elation. Even the girls were allowed a half-glass each, diluted, though it grieved her, with a little water.

Mair twirled about the room, her usual shyness forgotten. 'Oh, I have never felt more like dancing!' she cried. 'Gina, will you play for us?'

Gina laughed. 'A waltz? I don't believe I know a single tune. I've played only for country dancing.'

'It ain't difficult, ma'am. They call it three-four time.' Without the least trace of affectation Thomas began to sing in a pleasant baritone and Gina was quick to follow his lead.

In spite of his claims of clumsiness Thomas was light on his feet and a born teacher. Gina complimented him upon his skill in explaining the steps.

'No trick to it, Lady Whitelaw. I just remember my own difficulties… Now, Giles, if you will take Mair, I shall partner Elspeth.'

Within a half-hour he had them performing very creditably.

'There now,' he assured the girls. 'You'll be more skilled than half the dancers in the room.'

'But what of Gina?' Elspeth protested. 'She has been playing for us and she hasn't had her lesson.'

'Let me play,' said Mair as she moved over to the spinet.

Gina gave up her place with a laughing protest and turned to Thomas Newby. 'I've been watching carefully,' she said. 'I promise not to tread upon your toes.'

Thomas took her in his arms, his hand upon her waist and holding her at a careful distance. In their innocence the girls thought nothing of this close and unusual proximity of their partners, but Gina found it strange.

Thomas smiled at her. 'Relax!' he said. 'You must not hold yourself so stiffly, ma'am. Give yourself to the music.'

Gina tried to obey him, but it was several minutes before she felt at ease. Then suddenly the rhythm became familiar and she almost forgot her partner in the sensation of spinning about the room in a dizzying whirl.

'It feels like flying,' she admitted as the music stopped. 'Mr Newby, you have introduced us to a delightful pastime.'

'Glad you enjoyed it, ma'am, but you must dance with Giles to enjoy it to the full.' He took her hand and led her over to his friend.

This was something that Gina had intended to avoid at all costs, but she could think of no way to refuse. Looking at Giles, she could see that he was equally unwilling, but when Mair began to play he took her in his arms.

Gina felt that her feet were made of lead, and she stumbled over the first few steps, quite unable to follow his lead. She caught her breath. She must not make a fool of herself, but it had been so long, so very long, since he had held her close to his heart.

Everything about him was familiar—the touch of his hand, the faint scent of soap and the outdoors, the power of the arm which encircled her and the knowledge that his lips were a mere few inches from her own.

At length she stole a glance at him, but the handsome face was a mask. It didn't fool her for a moment. To outward appearances Giles was in full control of his emotions, but she was close enough to sense the rapid beating of his heart.

Chapter Six

Gina resumed her seat at the spinet. She would play for the others, but no amount of entreaty could persuade her to dance again.

Thomas remarked on it as he rode back to the Grange with Giles.

'You know Lady Whitelaw better than I,' he said. 'Do you suppose I have offended her?'

'Great heavens, why should you think that?'

'Oh, I don't know. I thought she seemed a little distrait when we arrived today...not quite herself, if you know what I mean.'

'I do, but I can't tell you the reason for it. Perhaps her uncle brought bad news...'

'Possibly. I wondered if she had had second thoughts about my offering to show her the waltz. She did not seem to wish...I mean, she may have found it unpleasant to find herself in the arms of a stranger. I wouldn't upset her for the world.'

'I'm sure that isn't true.' Giles cast a quick look at

his companion. 'Don't allow it to worry you… She holds you in high regard. She told me so herself.'

Thomas brightened. 'Do you say so? I am glad of it.' He rode on in silence for several minutes. Then he returned to the subject.

'There's something I want to ask you,' he said in a low voice. 'Don't take it amiss, old friend, or think that I am prying, but have you a *tendre* for the lady?'

Giles stared at him, and Thomas flushed to the roots of his hair.

'I have a reason for asking,' he explained uncomfortably. 'I mean, I would not wish to offer for her if it should clash with your own intentions towards her.'

'I have no plans to marry,' Giles said in a harsh tone. 'I thought you felt the same.'

'I did…that is, until I met her. She's everything a man could wish for. I hadn't thought to meet any woman with her qualities. She's so full of courage and intelligence. Surely everyone must love her. That smile turns a man's knees to water.'

Privately Giles agreed with him, but he was filled with feelings of despair. Gina might be wealthy, but Newby's family could match that wealth. Thomas could not be considered a fortune-hunter. His father had always made it clear that he wished for nothing more than to see his son safely settled with a suitable bride. Handsome settlements would follow.

'This is a quick decision on your part,' Giles said carefully. 'Are you sure of your feelings for Gina? You've been in love before, or so you tell me.'

'Mere infatuations!' Thomas dismissed his previ-

ous liaisons with a wave of his hand. 'Up to now I
had not thought of marriage. Of course, I may not
stand a chance with her. She may already have plans
in that direction. Do you know if that is so?'

'She hasn't mentioned anyone,' Giles said stiffly.
'Though I doubt if she would discuss such matters
with me.'

'But you are her close friend, are you not? You
always seem to have so much to say to each other.'

'Our conversation has been mostly about farming
practice.' Even as Giles spoke he saw the look of
surprise on his companion's face. Truly, it must seem
odd to be discussing agriculture with such a warm
and loving woman.

'Gina is something of a diplomat,' he continued.
'It's part of the secret of her charm. She is accustomed to speak of others' interests rather than her
own.'

'I see. It doesn't surprise me. I think her the most
agreeable person in the world. How her face lit up
when we heard the news of the victory of Badajoz.'

'Isham will be able to tell us more. He'll have the
news by now, I make no doubt.'

Giles was right. When they reached the Grange
they found Lord Isham in his study, reading a lengthy
missive which had been delivered by special messenger.

'Good news at last!' Isham laid aside the papers.
'Have you heard already?'

'We have…the village is *en fête*. What can you tell
us about the engagement? Was the victory complete?'

'It was. There is a darker side, of course. The Duke was delighted by the bravery of his troops, but then they let him down. Serious looting followed, and the men got out of hand. He wasted no time in restoring order. He was forced to resort to floggings and two men were hanged.'

'For looting?' Thomas was incredulous. 'I thought that it was common in time of war.'

'Not in Wellington's army. He has always insisted that goods requisitioned from the Spaniards should be paid for, which is why we are more popular than the French, who leave the populace with nothing.'

'Even so, it does seem hard when the men have fought so well...'

'His Lordship understands his troops. His army is not made up of gentlemen, you know. On occasion he has referred to them as the ''scum of the earth''. On another he mentioned that he hoped that they would terrify the French, because they certainly terrified him.'

'Yet they follow him without question,' Thomas said in wonder. 'Why is that, my lord?'

'He cares about them in his own way. At times he has turfed his officers out of comfortable billets when they've left their men unfed and without shelter. The troops know him as a hard man, but he is just, and he won't waste lives.' Isham looked at his brother-in-law. 'You are very quiet, Giles. Do you disapprove of Wellington's draconian measures?'

'No! I must suppose he had no choice. It must be difficult to control a drunken rabble.'

'It was. Once they found the stores of wine they drank themselves into oblivion, after raping half the womenfolk. That was one reason for the hangings.' He looked up with a smile as India entered the room. 'Come in, my love. We are just discussing this famous victory.'

'It seems to be a day for news,' she told him. 'The servants have heard that there may be trouble at the Abbey. Yardley has been to see the Marquis. He's thought to believe that Sywell may have killed his wife…'

Isham rose from his desk and took his wife in his arms. 'You must not listen to rumour, India. This is gossip, pure and simple. No one can be sure of what has happened.'

'Then you still believe that she has run away? Oh, Anthony, I do so hope so. Another murder would be more than I can bear.'

Thomas was looking mystified, and India was quick to notice it.

'I do apologise,' she said. 'You cannot have heard the story, but the villagers have thought of nothing else for months.'

'Giles told me that the Marchioness was missing,' Thomas admitted. 'Pray, ma'am, don't distress yourself. Sywell has an evil reputation, and his wife, so I understand, is but a girl. Is it not more likely that she found her life with him intolerable, and decided to go away?'

Lord Isham gave him an appreciative look. 'There,

my love, you see that it is obvious. Would you not have run away yourself?'

'I'd never have married him in the first place,' India said with feeling.

'So you married another ogre instead?' Isham's eyes were twinkling.

'A dear ogre!' India squeezed her husband's hand. 'Shall we dine at home tonight?'

'I believe so, my dearest. Then you may regale Mr Newby with the full story of Sywell's iniquities.' Isham smiled as he looked at his companions. 'It is a favourite topic with my wife,' he explained.

'How can I ignore them?' she protested. 'The man has ruined half the village girls. Now they are left to bring up his children. I beg your pardon, Mr Newby. It is an ugly tale and I should not trouble you with the details.'

'But, ma'am, he cannot still be up to his old tricks? His age must tell on him, I feel.'

'That's true, but how I wish that he would sell the Abbey and move elsewhere. I can't imagine how he manages to run the place. The villagers avoid him, except for Aggie Binns, the laundress, who goes in from time to time. Apart from that he has only a single manservant.'

'Solomon Burneck must be a masochist,' Giles announced with feeling.

'You are right. Not only does he put up with his master's rages, but he must find it difficult to persuade any of the local tradesmen to supply the Abbey. A mountain of debt has ruined one or two of them.'

'A thoroughly undesirable character, ma'am. You would be well rid of him.'

'I think so, but he gives no sign of leaving Abbot Quincey.'

Thomas grinned. 'He could be struck by lightening, Lady Isham.'

'That fate would be too good for him,' India said with feeling, but she was laughing as she left the room.

Isham felt relieved, but he summoned his butler without delay.

'You will call the staff together,' he said firmly. 'I want it clearly understood that Lady Isham is not to be troubled by gossip. Anyone who disobeys my orders will take the consequences.' As always, he did not raise his voice. There was no need. Isham did not make idle threats. He turned to his companions. 'Shall you care to fish tomorrow?' he enquired. 'I can promise you good sport.'

Giles was tempted to protest that he had work to do, but his brother-in-law forestalled him.

'It will give you an opportunity to check the work of the water bailiffs, Giles, and Mr Newby will enjoy it, as I shall myself.'

There seemed little more to say, but Giles was longing to lose himself in the more detailed work of checking the accounts. It was all very well to be invited to fish the river, but it would give him time to think of Gina.

He couldn't dismiss her from his mind, and his conversation with Thomas seemed to have tied his stomach in knots. Why should he have been surprised by Thomas's decision to offer for her? He should have suspected something of the kind.

To be fair, he knew that Thomas had not considered Gina's fortune. His friend had seen only a charming woman, little more than a girl, possessed of wit and a delightful sense of humour. Gina was no fool, and that, allied to her vivid little face and voluptuous figure, had been enough to sweep Thomas Newby off his feet.

For Gina it would be an excellent match, Giles thought miserably. He'd already convinced himself that she would marry again, and Thomas was an eligible suitor. He was of good family, his wealth would match her own, and all other considerations aside, Thomas was a kindly, good-humoured person. His wife would come first in all his dealings. Gina could do far worse.

The thought did not comfort him. It was useless to hope that Gina would refuse his friend. Had she not admitted that she liked him very much? It might be a short step from there to feelings of true affection. When Thomas went upstairs to change Giles turned into his tiny office and busied himself with a new design for his seed drill.

After only a few moments he threw his pen aside in disgust. Inspiration would not come, and after all, what was it? Hardly a scheme to cause a woman's heart to beat a little faster. Gina must think him a dull dog, in spite of her pretence of interest in his inven-

tions. In the blackest of moods he summoned his valet
and went upstairs to dress for dinner.

Gina, as he had suspected, had much upon her
mind. She'd accepted her father's invitation with
much pleasure, though, at the time, she hadn't imagined that her uncle planned to extend his stay in
Abbot Quincey.

Now she was in a quandary. She was tempted to
go alone, claiming that Mair was suffering from a
migraine and that Elspeth had stayed behind to keep
her company. Would she be believed? Unsure, as yet,
of their changing position in society, her parents
might imagine that they were unfit to entertain the
daughters of Sir Alastair Whitelaw. She could not risk
it.

Yet the risks of taking the girls into Samuel
Westcott's company might be even greater. She shook
her head impatiently. Her warnings to her uncle had
been clear. In a family gathering he would not dare
to make advances to the girls, and she would watch
him like a hawk. Even so, she could not feel easy in
her mind.

Two days later, as they set off for the new house,
she looked closely at her charges. It had been a struggle, but Mair and Elspeth were now clothed in the
most modest of garments. The high necks of their
gowns and the long sleeves were perhaps unsuitable
for a dinner engagement, as they had told her.

'Bear with me!' she'd said. 'This is quite different
from your visit to Lord and Lady Isham. I would not
have my parents think that you intended to pull rank.

They are simple people, and they would not take it
kindly.'

It was enough to convince the girls that they must
do as she wished.

That evening she was proud of them. Their curtsey
to her mother and father had been deferential, and
their manners could not be faulted. At dinner she was
careful to make sure that they were seated by her side,
and far from any possible attention from Samuel
Westcott.

That gentleman was surrounded by the members of
his own family. The older girls were married, as was
his eldest son, but George, the youngest, had accompanied his father.

Gina had greeted the young man without enthusiasm, but now she took herself to task. He must not
be blamed for his father's misdemeanours. George
was quiet and polite, but he was quick to address
himself to putting the girls at ease.

Gina looked around the table, marvelling at the fine
array of plate and glass. By dint of hard work her
father had done well, and now he was proud of his
new home.

'Well, Gina, what do you think of it?' he asked
proudly.

'I think it very fine,' she said. She turned then to
her brother and questioned him about his family. He
answered readily enough, but Gina was conscious that
his wife's eyes were resting upon her in no kindly
way. She had no way of knowing that a bitter conversation had ensued earlier that evening.

'So your father is to kill the fatted calf?' The younger Mrs Westcott had complained. 'I don't see why we are to make a fuss, when Gina ran away without a word of explanation.'

'Hold your tongue!' her husband had replied. 'Gina is now Lady Whitelaw. You will treat her with respect.'

'Oh, hoity-toity! I wonder if your sister will do the same?'

It seemed unlikely. The former Miss Westcott eyed her younger sister with undisguised envy.

'Gina, where do you buy your clothes?' she asked. 'I think you did not purchase that gown in Abbot Quincey.'

'I've had it for some time,' Gina told her quietly. 'If you wish I'll give you the name of the woman who made it for me in London.'

'The famous Madame Félice?' her sister jeered. 'Her prices are above my touch.'

'No, she does not dress me. I am not quite in her style. She looks for those who will carry her creations well. I am too short, you see.'

'But you look charmingly,' George Westcott assured her shyly.

'It is kind of you to say so, sir.' Gina turned her attention to her cousin. 'Are you based in London with your father?'

'No, ma'am. I am here to learn the business from your father. My elder brother will take over the London side…'

'And are you happy in Abbot Quincey?'

'I like it here. London is all dirt and noise and bustle. I prefer the country.'

Gina warmed towards him. His father might be anathema to her, but this young man, though shy, was eager to please. She was happy to encourage him, a fact which did not escape her mother's notice.

When the ladies retired she took Gina aside.

'What do you think of your cousin George?' she asked without preamble.

'I like him. Is he living here with you?'

'He is. George has always been a favourite of mine. Had you not gone away, we hoped that in time you and he would make a match of it.'

'First cousins, Mother? Surely that can't be?'

'There is no law against it, Gina, either from Church or State…'

'But it can't be wise. Interbreeding brings such dangers…'

'Not always. I could tell you of many successful marriages between cousins.'

Gina gave her mother a steady look. 'Don't set your heart on it, I beg of you. I would never consider it.'

'Your uncle Samuel will be disappointed. He thinks it best for the family…'

'For *his* family, perhaps, but not for me. I don't intend to marry again just yet, and when I do the choice will be mine alone.'

'Oh, Gina, you haven't changed! Always a hot-head! It can't be right for you to live alone. Don't you want children of your own?'

'In time, perhaps, but not just yet. I have the girls to think of…'

'Take care that you don't wait too long,' her mother warned. 'Youth does not last for ever.'

Gina smiled. 'I'm not at my last prayers, nor am I in my dotage. Trust me, mother dear, I may surprise you yet.'

'Then there is someone…someone who is dear to you?'

Gina seemed not to have heard her mother's last remark. She turned her attention to the girls, to find that George was entertaining them with stories of ghostly happenings at the Abbey and the sighting of mysterious lights in the woods.

'I don't believe a word of it,' Mair said stoutly.

'I do!' Elspeth gave a delicious shiver.

George heard a grunt of displeasure from his father. He was at a loss to understand it, but perhaps he had been wrong to frighten the girls. He stopped in mid-sentence and addressed himself to his hostess.

'I must thank you for an excellent dinner, Aunt. I much enjoyed it.'

'Aye, lad, and you did it justice.' His uncle beamed at him. 'I like to see a good trencherman.'

Gina smiled to herself. Her father had always prided himself on keeping a good table. 'Father, you'll put me to shame,' she teased. 'I must have the recipe for those mushroom fritters and the curd pudding. You'll dine with me next week, I hope?' By that time she hoped that Samuel Westcott would have returned to London, so she did not include him in the invitation.

'We'll see…we'll see! Your fine friends may not care to meet the likes of us…'

'They'll be delighted, Father, but if you prefer we shall make it a family party. George must come too, of course.'

She knew that her father was pleased with the invitation. Society was changing fast, but he was of the older generation. Wealthy as he was, he prided himself on knowing his place. He had no desire to be thought encroaching. With him it was still a touchy subject and he had no wish to risk a snub from any member of the aristocracy.

'You'd like to see the rest of the house, I expect?'

Gina nodded. Good business management and hard work had provided her parents with the means to build this symbol of their success. She was delighted for them.

'I believe I'll take a turn round the garden,' Samuel Westcott said. 'I fancy a pipe of tobacco. George, what do you say?'

George looked startled. His father did not often evince a desire for his company, and he had never smoked. He left his other cousins to their gossip and followed Samuel on to the terrace.

The reason for this private conversation was not far to seek. Samuel rounded on him with a curse.

'Damn your eyes!' he hissed. 'What are you about, my lad?'

George was mystified. 'What is the matter, Father?

Should I not have spoken of the ghosts and the lights in the woods? I thought the girls did not seem frightened, but perhaps I'm wrong.'

'Perhaps I'm wrong,' his father mimicked. 'I'll tell you how wrong you are! Here is your cousin, Gina, with more money than any woman has a right to own, and you must waste your time in talking rubbish to those girls.'

George stared at him, open-mouthed.

'Perhaps you think to fix your interest with one of the Whitelaw girls? I'd advise you to forget that scheme. I know Gina. Neither of them will be allowed to wed the son of a grain merchant, however wealthy.'

'It hadn't entered my head,' George replied with dignity. 'They are little more than schoolchildren.'

'The elder one comes out next year, but that's beside the point. Gina should be your target. She is one of us. There can be no difficulty there. You and she are of an age and she's a cosy armful. Wed her, and you'll keep the money in the family…'

'Why should she consider me? We hardly know each other.'

'What has that to say to anything? Goddammit, boy, can't you make a push in your own interest? She don't appear to have taken you in dislike.'

George gave his father a mulish look. 'I won't do it,' he announced. 'For one thing I'm already promised…'

'Really?' Samuel Westcott's tone grew silky. 'And who, may I ask, is the object of your affections?'

'Ellie works in my uncle's bakery.' George awaited

an explosion, but when it came he was astonished by the virulence of his father's anger.

Samuel seized his arm, thrusting his face up close. Then he began to curse with great fluency.

'I won't listen to this.' George began to walk away.

'Don't turn your back on me, you dog! Will you throw yourself away on some trollop of a servant girl? I suppose you've got her in the family way?'

'Ellie will become my wife,' his son assured him. 'Her family is respectable, and you shall not malign her.'

'Shall not? Who are you to tell me what I shall and shall not do? Let me tell you this, if you defy me, you won't see a penny of my money.'

'I don't want it,' George said simply.

'But you want your job with your uncle, don't you? I need only tell him that I've changed my mind and I want you back in London. As for this wench of yours, I'll think of some excuse to get her turned off without a reference, and that won't be all she'll suffer.'

'No! She is the only breadwinner in her family...'

'Well then, you won't wish to injure her.' Samuel had not expected such resistance from his normally docile son. He decided to change his tactics. 'Gina will wed again, and we all wish her well, I believe. There is naught to say that you cannot make a friend of her...be agreeable, I mean?'

'Nothing at all,' George agreed. 'I like her very much.'

'Well then, why not spend some time with her?

Gina has been away for years. She knows few people here in Abbot Quincey. It would be a kindness to make yourself useful to her. Won't you please your old father in this at least?'

'I'll be glad to, but on one condition. You must give me your word that you won't attempt to injure Ellie.'

'Why, lad, I don't even know the girl. I spoke in haste, but out of concern for your best interests. You know my temper, George.'

'I do. Will you give me your word?'

'Of course. Let us be friends again.' Samuel took out his handkerchief and wiped away a non-existent tear. 'There is nothing like family, my boy.'

Privately, George could only agree, but he made no comment. There was nothing like family indeed. It was only the desire to keep Gina's money in the Westcott family that had caused his father's outburst.

The confrontation had shaken him, but it was the threat to Ellie that worried him most. He knew Samuel Westcott to be a ruthless man and his promise could be worthless. Somehow he must think of a way to keep his beloved safe until he was in a position to wed her. Well, two could indulge in deception.

'Do you believe that Gina will marry again?' he asked innocently.

'There's nothing more certain.' Samuel grew jovial. 'Wed to a man who was old enough to be her father, and widowed for two years? Why, she's ripe for plucking.'

'I doubt she'll lack for suitors. There's something

about her, father, that is not in the common way. I find her charming.' Fear for Ellie's safety had made George cunning. He must give the impression that he was not indifferent to Gina.

'I'm glad you think so.' Samuel was pleased to hear that there was still some hope of persuading George to woo his cousin. His attempt to ride rough-shod over his younger son had not succeeded. Now he must be more subtle.

'Gina has faults, of course. She has always been outspoken and accustomed to having her own way, but a vigorous husband will put an end to all that. What she needs is a babe each year. That will calm her down.' Samuel knocked out his pipe and waddled back into the salon.

There he sank down upon a sofa, closed his eyes and pretended to be dozing. It didn't escape his notice that George had gone at once to Gina's side and was deep in conversation.

Samuel was satisfied. In time the lad would come to see where his best interests lay. As for this wench…this Ellie? Perhaps now was not the time to remove her from the scene. Let George believe his promises. He could afford to wait.

Chapter Seven

'Gina, I do like gentlemen, don't you?' On the journey home, Elspeth was radiant. She had enjoyed her evening.

Gina laughed. 'Why do you say that?'

'Well, they are all so kind. Mr Newby makes us laugh and Mr George Westcott tells such interesting stories…'

'And can you decide between them? I thought that Mr Newby was your latest flirt.'

'I doubt if I'll ever marry,' Elspeth said artlessly. 'I'll never be able to choose.'

'And does Mair feel the same?' Gina glanced at the elder of her charges.

'I'd need to know them better,' Mair said wisely. 'I feel more comfortable with Giles. He seems to me to have a stronger character.'

'Giles is the handsomest of all, but he doesn't laugh so much…' Elspeth continued to chatter on. 'Still, we love him best, don't you?'

'I hadn't thought of comparing him with anyone,'

Gina replied. It was no more than the truth. Giles
alone had touched her heart. Beside him George and
Thomas Newby seemed to her to be no more than
boys. 'But you have known Giles longer. That is
probably the reason.'

Her voice was perfectly steady, but Mair gave her
a long look. There was something slightly fey about
Sir Alastair's eldest daughter. Mair seemed to pick
vibrations from the air.

'Mr Newby has been more than kind,' Gina went
on quickly. 'Without him you would not have learned
to waltz.'

'And he has promised us more lessons,' Elspeth
said with satisfaction. 'Will he come tomorrow, do
you suppose?'

'I imagine that he will wait for an invitation,
Elspeth.'

'Oh, do ask him again. Promise?'

'We must not monopolise the gentlemen. They will
have many other calls upon their time.' Gina was torn
between a longing to see Giles again, and the fear
that if he took her in his arms once more she would
be sure to give herself away.

'But they enjoyed it, Gina. They both said so...'

Gina hesitated. 'Very well,' she said at last. 'You
may have your dancing lessons if the gentlemen
agree, but I must ask something in return...'

'Anything!' they chorused.

'Anything? Well, I shall take you at your word. If
Mrs Guarding has a place for you at the Academy,
will you go there willingly?' She studied the stricken

expression on both faces with a flicker of amusement. 'It's scarce a sentence of execution, my dears.'

'Oh, Gina, must we? You've always taught us up to now...' Mair was never at ease in a new environment.

'I won't say you must, but it would please me. You would learn much which is far beyond my own capabilities. Besides, you would make new friends. We cannot live in isolation here, and some of the other pupils will be of your own age.'

'It *might* be fun, after all.' Elspeth considered the suggestion. 'We'd hear all the village gossip too...'

'That's hardly a reason for attending a place of learning.' Gina's tone was solemn, but her eyes were twinkling. 'Is it a bargain then?'

'It is,' they both agreed, though Mair looked dubious.

Gina patted her shoulder. 'In your case it won't be long, my love. You'll be out of the schoolroom before you know it and it will be a comfort to have friends about you when you make your come-out.'

Mair smiled, and Gina was satisfied. She tried always to reason with the girls, rather than insisting upon unquestioning obedience. To date, the use of that policy had resulted in the happiest of relationships with her stepdaughters.

'And you won't forget to send a message to the Grange?' said the irrepressible Elspeth.

'I shall pay a morning call on Lord and Lady Isham. We must not continue to deceive them as to the true reason for Mr Newby's visits here.'

'But suppose they disapprove?' Mair said quietly.

'I doubt if they will, my dear, and Anthony is master in his home…'

Gina did not pursue the subject. It was not her intention to criticise Mrs Rushford to her charges. On the following morning she ordered her carriage and set off for the Grange.

She was happy to find that India was receiving, and pleased to realise that she was the only visitor on that particular day.

India greeted her warmly. 'Oh,' she cried. 'How good of you to come! Anthony is out riding with Giles and Mr Newby, and Mama and Letty are gone again to Hammonds in the village. I'd like to have gone with them, but Anthony is concerned about my being jolted in the coach.'

Gina sympathised. 'Perhaps It's better to take no chances in these early days, Lady Isham.'

'Please call me India. We are old friends, are we not? I was feeling sadly neglected, but now I'm glad that I didn't insist on going out, otherwise I should have missed you.' India tossed aside her embroidery with a look of relief. 'Don't look at it!' she pleaded. 'I am no hand with a needle.'

'Nor I.' Gina gave her companion a cheerful smile. 'I think it a total waste of time, though it is considered to be a suitable accomplishment for women.'

'You prefer others, so I hear…' India gave her visitor a curious look.

'Rumour abounds, I know, but I have quite given up the practice of marksmanship and the art of murder.' Even as she spoke Gina recollected the recent tragedy at the Grange. 'Oh, I beg your pardon,' she said quickly. 'That was tactless of me.'

When she looked up she found that India was smiling.

'Don't be embarrassed, Gina. I enjoyed your joke. May I offer you a glass of wine? I must not join you, but I am allowed lemonade.'

'Then lemonade for me, India. I find it so refreshing.'

Later, glass in hand, she explained the reason for her visit.

'I have a confession to make to you. I fear it was a base deceit, but Giles and Mr Newby have been teaching the girls to waltz.'

'How dreadful!' India said demurely. 'And here we were, in all innocence, believing that your objective was to ride. I shall take Giles to task!'

'Oh, please don't!' Gina was betrayed into a quick objection. 'It wasn't in the least his fault. I allowed myself to be persuaded by the girls and Mr Newby. Your brother was against it.'

'Was he? That surprises me. He taught both Letty and myself, though my mother does not know it.' India was laughing openly. 'Great heaven, Gina, why should you think we'd mind?'

'I felt I was deceiving you, but we had no wish to offend Mrs Rushford's feelings…'

'Mama will learn to move with the times,' India replied. 'Gina, will you tell me something? You knew Giles in Italy long ago, didn't you?'

Gina's mouth was dry. She could only nod. Was her secret to be discovered after all this time?

'Forgive me! Perhaps I should not ask, but Letty and I have often wondered why he was so changed when he came home. We hardly knew him.'

'In what way had he changed?' Gina found it difficult to speak.

India frowned. 'He was different in that as a boy he was such a cheerful person. Oh, I don't know how to explain it to you. Letty and he and I were close and he was always the leader in our expeditions, full of energy and ideas. And yet…yet when he returned to Abbot Quincey he was not the same. There was a barrier between us…invisible perhaps, but always there. We did not like to question him, but we have always wondered.'

'You love your brother, dearly, don't you?'

'We do.' A tear sparkled upon India's lashes. 'We'd give anything to have him back to his old self, but we don't know how to help him.'

Gina felt the same, but she did not dare to say so. 'You've already done so much,' she insisted. 'Giles is managing your estate. It is the thing he likes best in the world.'

'It's something,' India admitted. 'But he is so proud. It's fortunate that Anthony is such a diplomat. Giles could not bear to live on charity.'

'But, India, that is not the case. Anthony thinks highly of your brother's expertise, and these inventions must change the face of farming in this country.'

'They might, if they were ever patented. Anthony

has offered to back such a project, but Giles won't hear of it.' India looked at her companion's face. 'Tell me about Italy,' she demanded. 'It was there that something happened to my brother.'

Gina froze. She was silent for so long that India grew alarmed.

'My dear, you are so pale. Do you feel quite well?'

With an effort Gina recovered her composure. 'Forgive me! I have tried for so long to forget those dreadful times…'

'How thoughtless of me, Gina. Pray do not speak of them.'

'Yes, I must. It does not help to keep it all inside one's head. When Napoleon attacked conditions in Italy became chaotic. We were staying in the hills behind Naples. We had to get away, but the children were so young, and their mother suffered from a wasting disease. Sir Alastair himself was never strong…'

She paused then, but when she spoke again her voice was bitter.

'I doubt if you would recognise your fellow human beings, India, if you should see them in the grip of panic. We reached Naples with some difficulty. Several times we almost lost our coach and horses to other refugees. Then, at the harbour, we found that most of the boats were already filled, and by young men. It was the young and strong who were able to save themselves. Women and children and the old were trampled underfoot.'

'Oh, do not tell me that Giles took a place which might have been given to a woman.'

'No, Giles had left the week before. Your uncle sent for him in haste, he tells me.'

'But if all the berths were taken how did you manage to get away?'

'There was a vessel sailing for the Caribbean. I boarded as she docked. Then…er…I held the Master at gunpoint until the family was on board.'

'And you sailed with him? Weren't you afraid of being murdered when you were at sea?'

'Not in the least. I kept my pistols by me at all times, and gold was an added inducement to the fellow, with a promise of more when we reached Jamaica.'

India gasped. 'What an experience! You were little more than a child…'

Gina shrugged. 'One is forced to grow up fast when lives are at stake.'

'And…when you last saw Giles in Italy…did you sense anything amiss with him?'

'No. He came to the villa to bid Sir Alastair farewell before we left for the hills. Your brother was unchanged then.' Gina's heart ached as she recalled that final evening of happiness. She and Giles had promised each other that no obstacle would be allowed to stand in their way. The world was their oyster, Giles had said, and she had believed him.

'We…we had expected to see him on our return,' she continued. 'Sir Alastair relied on him so much, you see, but Giles was nowhere to be found. Then we learned that he had taken ship some days before.'

'Do you know why?' India enquired. She had noticed Gina's quivering lips, and her heart went out to her visitor. With Giles gone, the Whitelaw family must have felt abandoned in a foreign country with anarchy and chaos on all sides.

'My lady…India…you need not explain to me. I believe it was some family matter.'

'It was an emergency,' India told her softly. 'My uncle James sent for Giles in haste. He was needed here on the estate. There was a real danger that it would be lost to us without a strong hand at the helm. I won't go into details, but, believe me, it is true.'

'I never believed that Giles would desert us without good cause. Sir Alastair thought so highly of him, India. Giles did mention that he had sent a note of explanation to await our return to the villa, but we did not receive it…'

'That was unfortunate, but you tell me that events moved fast. Giles must have sailed from Naples before that final exodus turned into a rout.' India was silent for a time. 'Perhaps the change in him is caused by guilt. He would not learn of the horror of those final days until he returned to England. He must have wondered what had happened to you. I'm surprised that he didn't try to seek you out.'

India stole a look at Gina's face. She was aware that when Giles and Gina were together there was a certain tension in the air. Perhaps Gina believed him to be heartless.

Gina seemed to read her mind. 'He did, but we did not return to Scotland for some years. My family had no addresses for me… You must not blame him, India, I do not.'

'You are generous, my dear, but your life has not been easy. Shall you be happy here in Abbot Quincey?'

'I intend to be.' Gina's smile transformed her face. 'The girls have agreed to attend Mrs Guarding's Academy. In fact, I am on my way there now, to see if she has places for them.' Her eyes twinkled as she looked at India. 'You may think me indulgent, but I had to strike a bargain.'

'What was that?'

'More dancing lessons, that is, if your brother and Mr Newby will agree?'

'I'll pass on the message,' India promised. 'I think you may rely on them. When are they to present themselves?'

'Perhaps tomorrow, or the next day? I've warned the girls that we must not monopolise their time…'

'You are doing them a favour,' India laughed. 'By day they are not short of occupation, but of an evening we can offer only cards. I wonder…' she hesitated.

'Yes?'

'What do you say to a charity ball at the Assembly Rooms?'

Gina stared. 'Shall you wish to sponsor such an event? You are still in mourning, I believe.'

'It won't be frowned upon if it is intended to raise funds for those ill-used children in the northern mills.

My aunt Elizabeth is used to arrange these functions, but she is in London for her daughter's Season.'

'It's certainly a worthy cause, and I should be glad to help you, India.'

'I hoped you would. Come tomorrow, and we'll make out an invitation list. Would your mother and father care to attend, do you suppose? Mr Westcott has always been so generous in supporting us...'

'Nothing would give them greater pleasure,' Gina assured her warmly. 'They would be honoured...'

She was thoughtful as her carriage rolled away. Anthony could not have chosen a better wife, nor she a better friend. She'd been tempted to confide in India, but for the moment it was best not to give a full account of what had happened in Italy. She had not lied, but neither had she been entirely frank. She was still preoccupied as her carriage reached the outskirts of Steep Abbot.

Looking about her she decided that it hadn't changed in years. It was still the prettiest, if one of the smallest, of the local villages, set as it was beside the River Steep and surrounded by trees.

A request to see Mrs Guarding gained her entry to that lady's presence. Gina found herself under inspection from a pair of sharp blue eyes.

A brief nod was her only acknowledgement for some time, but Gina's tranquil expression did not change.

'Yes, my lady, what can I do for you?' Mrs Guarding said at last.

'My stepdaughters are in need of education,' Gina explained. 'Lord Isham recommended you.'

'Did he?' There was a slight thaw in Mrs Guarding's tone. 'How old are the girls?'

'Fifteen and sixteen, ma'am.'

'I see, and what have you in mind for them? Deportment, needlework, a little painting and sketching, perhaps?'

Gina knew that she was being needled, and she laughed.

'Nothing of the sort, Mrs Guarding. I want them to learn to use their minds. Philosophy and mathematics, that is what I want for them.'

Mrs Guarding gave Gina her full attention. This young woman's remarks were unexpected. It was time to reverse her initial impression. On the surface Lady Whitelaw appeared to be merely a fashionable hostess—a type of woman she despised. Clearly she was wealthy. Beneath the close-fitting spencer there was a glimpse of a fine silk gown. Mrs Guarding might scorn concessions to the latest mode, but even she could appreciate the skilled hand of a master cutter.

'Where have the girls been educated?' she demanded.

'I've taught them myself.' Gina could have laughed aloud at the expression on Mrs Guarding's face. 'Don't worry, ma'am, they are fluent in French and Italian, and they have some Urdu. Their knowledge of geography and history is good, but their skill with the needle leaves much to be desired.'

Mrs Guarding actually laughed aloud. Then she held out her hand. 'We shall deal together, Lady Whitelaw. Send me your girls. I'll give them some Greek and Latin too.'

'Thank you, ma'am,' Gina said meekly. 'Mair is a studious creature, but her younger sister is...er... irrepressible, I fear.'

'That is no bad thing, Lady Whitelaw. I like a child with spirit. It often denotes an acute intelligence. You need have no fear for them when they are in my care.' Mrs Guarding paused. 'You realise, of course, that I am considered a pernicious influence in these parts?'

Gina didn't attempt to deny it. 'So I've heard,' she said drily. 'You don't allow it to worry you, I think.'

'Certainly not. My teachers and I may be considered radical in our thinking, but we have a strict moral code.'

Gina make no comment.

'I have found it necessary to err on the side of morality. Our notions may be rigid, but how else can we counter accusations that education in a woman leads to immorality and grief?'

'That is nonsense!' Gina said briskly. 'I have no patience with such Gothic notions. Rather, one would suppose that a good education would cause a woman to think before she acted.'

Mrs Guarding smiled again. 'Have you never thought of teaching, Lady Whitelaw? I try to instil these ideas into my girls.'

'I'm honoured, Mrs Guarding, but my teaching has

been confined only to my stepdaughters, and to myself of course.'

'That is a pity, ma'am. You are a natural teacher, I suspect. Bring your girls tomorrow then, and we shall make them welcome.'

Gina returned to Abbot Quincey well satisfied with the result of her expedition. Mrs Guarding had made no concessions either to her title or her wealth. Her manner was brusque, and her tone uncompromising, but there could be no doubt that she was a woman of sterling character. Poet, novelist, historian? Yes, she was all of these, as Anthony had suggested, but she was also a dedicated emancipationist. Mair and Elspeth could not be in better hands.

They were still unconvinced but on the following day they set out with her on the journey to Steep Abbot, cheered by the promise of a visit from Giles and Thomas Newby either on that day or the next.

Gina was thoughtful as her coachman turned back towards the Isham estate. Time was passing and the month of May was almost upon them. In September, unless she had persuaded Giles to offer for her, she must go to Brighton for a lengthy stay. It left her only this brief summer to overcome his scruples.

Her conversation with India had confirmed what she suspected. Giles still loved her. His affections were unchanged, but he had given up all hope of winning her. The ruin of their plans had tormented him all these years.

He must have suffered agonies of mind when he learned that she had married. Colour flooded her cheeks. Perhaps he believed that wealth and a title were all she cared for. That might account for his distant manner towards her. Sometimes it verged on rudeness.

She straightened her shoulders. He should know her better than that. If he didn't he was unworthy of her love. She was still the same Gina who had given him her arms, her lips, her heart, all those years ago.

On arrival at the Grange she was shown into the salon, with a promise that Lady Isham would not keep her waiting above a moment or two.

She was turning over the pages of the *Ladies' Diary* when the door behind her opened. Gina rose to her feet and turned round with a smile to find that Giles was standing in the doorway.

In that unguarded moment she had the final answer to her doubts. His smile lit up the room as he came towards her with his hands outstretched. Then memory returned and his hands fell to his sides. He gave her a formal bow.

'I beg your pardon, Gina. I was looking for my sister. I did not expect…I mean…'

'India will be down in a short time. I am to help her with her invitations to the charity ball. We thought of the Assembly Rooms…' Gina's heart was beating fast.

Giles managed a faint smile. 'Such a title dignifies the ballroom at the Angel. What does Anthony say to this?'

'Anthony agrees to anything which will please his wife…' Lord Isham strolled into the room. 'Good morning, Gina. I am in your debt, my dear. India will be glad of your help in planning this event.'

'And I am in yours. Mrs Guarding has agreed to take the girls. I saw her yesterday…'

'What did you think of her?'

'I liked her very much.'

Anthony smiled. 'I guessed her to be a woman after your own heart. How did you persuade the girls?'

Gina looked a little guilty. Then she chuckled. 'Bribery, I fear. I had to promise them extra lessons in the waltz…' She glanced up at Giles. 'I hope that you don't mind. Mr Newby was so quick to offer…'

Giles bowed again, but he felt as if a sword had been twisted in his heart. Would this torment never end? Now he must watch his love again as she danced in Newby's arms. To refuse Gina's invitation would have been impossible without giving offence, especially as Anthony would be sure to override any of his claims to be too busy.

'At what time, ma'am?' he asked stiffly. 'Late afternoon, perhaps?'

Gina nodded and thanked him prettily before she was swept away by India into that lady's boudoir.

Isham sank into a chair and stretched out his long legs. 'Swallowed a poker, have you, Giles?' he teased. 'You are mighty formal with an old friend. Poor Gina! She might as well waltz with a broom handle…'

'Anthony…I have neither the time nor the inclination to give dancing lessons…'

'Really?' The heavy-lidded eyes inspected his face.

'Most men would jump at such an opportunity. All else aside, one could not wish for a better friend than Gina.'

'Believe me, I know her worth,' Giles replied in a low voice. 'Everyone must see it, in fact…' he swallowed a lump in his throat. 'In fact, Newby tells me that he intends to offer for her.'

'Does he, indeed? Will she take him, do you think?'

'I don't know!' Giles turned away in frustration. 'He has everything to recommend him, wealth, a noble family… Why should she refuse?'

'She might not care for him enough to wed him.'

'To date that hasn't been her first consideration,' Giles said bitterly. 'She married Whitelaw, didn't she?'

Isham was tempted into a sharp retort, but he held back the scathing words. He would not hit a man when that man was down, and Giles was suffering. That was all too clear.

'I think that you do not know the full circumstances,' he said quietly. 'Whitelaw offered Gina a marriage of convenience. His wife had died, and he was no longer young. He was concerned about the future of his daughters…'

Giles was startled out of his black mood. 'But…but Gina was so young. Why did she agree?'

'Gina is a realist. She has a head upon her shoulders, as well as a kindly heart. She loved the girls, and she was devoted both to Sir Alastair and his wife.' Isham smiled. 'I think I told you I was his supporter at the wedding?'

'Yes, I remember…'

'Until I met Gina I had misgivings. What do they say: "There is no fool like an old fool"? I thought that my friend might have been seduced by the charms of a young girl. I changed my mind when I met Gina. She justified Sir Alastair's faith in her.'

'Then you are telling me that she was never his wife in the true sense?'

'Sir Alastair was old enough to be her father. His girls, he felt, would be charge enough for her, without adding to her burdens by leaving her with children of her own.'

Giles grew thoughtful. 'Perhaps I have been wrong about her. It was a shock to see her back in Abbot Quincey under such different circumstances.'

'She is still the girl she was,' Isham said quietly. He would not pry, but he was pleased to see that Giles now looked more cheerful.

Meantime Gina was resolved that on this evening in particular, she would refuse to dance. The girls should have the young men to themselves, and she would play for them.

This worthy resolution was put to the test when Mair came over to the spinet and offered to take her place.

Gina waved her away, 'Do you carry on, my dear. I turned my ankle earlier today and it is still quite painful.'

Mair gave her a sideways look. 'You haven't mentioned it before.'

'I had no wish to make a fuss…'

Then Giles was beside her. 'Take my arm,' he said firmly. 'It's but a step out to the terrace. Did you not ask for my advice about your grounds?'

Gina took his arm. She made an unconvincing attempt to hobble, but he stopped her.

'Don't worry!' he said quietly. 'I know that you have no wish to dance with me. I don't blame you, Gina. I owe you an apology.'

He cleared his throat, but Gina did not look at him.

'I have misjudged you,' he went on quickly. 'I had imagined… Oh, Gina, I have been so bitter! I deserve to be horsewhipped.'

She heard the anguish in his voice and it destroyed her. Blindly, she reached out a hand to him.

Then suddenly she was in his arms and he was raining kisses on her brow, her cheeks, her eyes. Lifting her face to his, she offered him her lips.

Chapter Eight

For Gina her lover's passionate embrace wiped away
all the years of loss and longing, but the mouth which
sought her own rested only briefly on her yielding
lips.

Then Giles's hands were upon her shoulders holding her away. 'Forgive me!' he said hoarsely. 'I have
no right to touch you…no right at all.'

Gina stared at him. She could not have been more
shocked if he had struck her.

'Who has a better right?' she asked in amazement.
'Were we not promised to each other? We swore that
we would never change…do you remember?'

'I do. Perhaps we have not changed, but our circumstances are different now…' Giles turned and
took a few paces away from her. 'I have nothing to
offer you, Gina…'

'Have I ever asked for anything? All I ever wanted
was your love. I thought you felt the same.'

There was a long silence. 'We were very young…

perhaps too young to understand that love is not
enough.'

Gina looked up at his set face. The shock of rejection had left her feeling stunned. 'What else is there?'
she asked in wonder. 'We are both free. How many
human beings are offered a second chance of happiness?'

'You don't understand. I am dependent upon India
and Isham for my employment and even the roof over
my head...I could not even offer you a home.'

'I see.' Anger was beginning to overtake despair in
Gina's heart. 'You believe yourself to be some kind
of a remittance man, living upon the charity of others?'

Giles did not reply.

'Do you claim that you give nothing in return?' she
demanded inexorably. 'You must think your brother-
in-law a fool. Would he entrust India's estate to an
incompetent? I think not. Anthony thinks highly of
your skills.'

'That may be true, but it doesn't alter anything. It
may be years before I can make my own way in the
world...'

Their eyes locked and Gina's hopes plummeted. He
would not ask her to wait, and they both knew it.

'You can't think much of my constancy,' she accused.

'I think it is misplaced.' Giles could not trust himself to touch her. 'Sit down, Gina, you must listen to
me... You will marry again...and to someone who
can offer you what I cannot...'

Gina's anger rose. 'How dare you presume to plan my life for me? I won't have it, Giles.' She left his side and began to pace about the terrace. 'In all these years I never thought you a coward. Apparently, I was mistaken…'

'Perhaps you'd care to explain that statement.' Giles had gone pale. Now his anger matched her own.

'How else shall I describe a man who fears the opinion of the world? What is it that troubles you, the gossip, the sly asides, the envy of those who wished to wed a wealthy widow?'

'You dismiss your fortune lightly, Gina.'

'No, I don't. It's there, and it can't be dismissed, but it is no substitute for love. Oh, my dear, what else can be so important to you?'

'I don't fear gossip, Gina, as you seem to think. The opinion of the world is not of the slightest interest to me. If we were to wed my good sense would be applauded. Is it not the ambition of many men to seek their fortune in a splendid marriage? We see it every day. It is not my way…'

'Then it is just your stiff-necked pride? Perhaps I should take a leaf out of your book. I seem to have abandoned my own…'

Giles heard the bitterness in her voice. 'Don't, I beg of you!' he said gently. 'Let us not strip each other of all dignity…'

When she did not answer he came to stand before her. 'I'm sorry that you think ill of me,' he said. 'I would have it otherwise, but it cannot be…' Then he bowed. 'Shall we return to the others?'

He heard a muffled refusal, and sensing that she was close to breaking point he walked away, leaving her to recover her self-control without the irritation of his presence.

Gina stared across the darkening garden. Suddenly everything about her seemed insubstantial and almost dreamlike. The hurt of rejection had wounded her to the heart and the agony was too deep for tears.

Shaken by the violence of their quarrel, she tried to blot out the memory of those bitter words, but the recollection of her own humiliation could not be erased. She had thrown herself at Giles, begging for his love, only to be refused. It had stung her into unforgivable words of reproach, and now, finally, she knew that her long-held plans had come to nothing.

She was unaware that the music had stopped until Thomas came to find her. Statue-like, she was still gazing into space, oblivious of her surroundings.

'Lady Whitelaw?'

Gina did not answer.

'Lady Whitelaw, is something wrong?' Thomas was all concern. 'You have a headache, perhaps? Is there anything I can do?'

Gina shook her head, unaware that the tears had come at last and were pouring down her cheeks unchecked.

'Oh, my dear…Lady Whitelaw…Gina…pray don't distress yourself. Shall I ask Mair to come to you?'

Wordlessly, Gina shook her head. Then somehow Thomas was beside her, with an arm about her shoulders. He drew her to him, resting her head against his chest.

He didn't question her again, waiting patiently until the storm of tears had spent itself.

'You must think me foolish,' she gasped at last. 'Pray don't mention this to the girls. Where are they, by the way?' She looked about her and was relieved to see that she and Thomas were alone.

'Giles wished to show them his new mare,' Thomas assured her. 'He did not mention that you were… unwell… He said merely that you wished for a little air.'

Gina managed a weak smile. 'He was right, Mr Newby. I found it rather stuffy in the salon…'

'We have been thoughtless, ma'am. We take advantage of your good nature in allowing you to play for us for hours at a time.'

'But I have not played so much this evening,' she protested. 'Besides it is a pleasure…'

'Perhaps so, ma'am, but you must take care not to overtire yourself.' He pulled out a large handkerchief and began to dab at her cheeks. 'You do far too much for others. It is not always wise…'

With her nerves stretched to breaking-point Gina didn't know whether to laugh or cry at his solemn expression. It sat oddly on that normally cheerful face with its snub nose, round cheeks and the dusting of freckles.

'Let me ring for your maid, at least,' he begged. 'We shall none of us think it strange if you should care to retire…'

Gina was almost tempted into a sharp retort. She was longing to tell him not to fuss, but she caught herself in time. She must not allow her own exasperation to cloud the fact that Thomas intended only to be kind. It was just that his solicitude threatened to drive her mad.

What was the matter with her? It seemed that she was never satisfied. Giles had rejected her whilst Thomas had made his adoration clear. Now she longed only for both of them to go away. She needed time and solitude to recover her equilibrium.

Thomas continued to pat her hand, but she drew it quickly from his grasp as the others came to join them.

Elspeth was too excited about the new mare to notice anything amiss. 'Oh, Gina, she is beautiful and Giles has called her Star. He says that she has Arab blood... Will you let me ride her sometimes, Giles? She must go like the wind.'

'She does, but she'd be too strong for you, my dear. She's a skittish creature at the best of times...'

'She did seem nervous,' Elspeth admitted. She glanced up at the sky. 'Do you think she can sense a storm?' Even as she spoke they heard the first rumblings of thunder in the distance. The sky had grown livid, but Gina was glad of the darkening light. It would hide her ravaged face.

She rose to her feet as a flash of lightning lit the garden. Then Thomas urged them to go indoors.

'I'm not surprised that you felt the need of air, Lady Whitelaw. The atmosphere is so oppressive...'

Gina gave him a grateful look. He had given her an excuse for her long absence from the others, and Mair had accepted it, though her eyes still rested anxiously on Gina's face.

Then Giles bowed to her. 'Will you excuse us if we get back to the Grange at once,' he said.

'Of course!' Gina's tone was formal. 'If you hurry, you may escape the worst of what I fear will be a deluge.'

As they took their leave of her, Thomas drew her to one side.

'I'll call on you tomorrow, if I may, ma'am.'

Gina managed a faint smile. 'You are always welcome, Mr Newby.'

'I'm glad to hear it.' His face lit up, but he was blushing. 'I shall want to know how you go on, Lady Whitelaw...' For once his easy manner had deserted him, and Giles was aware of it.

On the journey home he asked no questions, dreading what he might hear. Had Thomas seized the opportunity to offer for Gina? They had been alone in the garden for some time. He stole a sideways glance at his friend, but Thomas was preoccupied.

A moment's reflection convinced him that Gina could not have accepted his companion. Thomas would have been unable to contain his joy. Perhaps he had changed his mind.

At length the suspense was too much for him to bear.

'You are very quiet,' he observed. 'Is something wrong?'

Thomas gave him a shy smile. 'Far from it, old son. I've made up my mind, you know. I asked Gina if I might call on her tomorrow. I intend to ask her to be my wife.'

Giles felt that it behoved him to say something…anything…but the words would not come.

'Now *you* are quiet, Giles. Do you disapprove?'

'How could I? We agreed, did we not, that Gina would be sure to marry again? You have so much to offer her.'

'Then you'll wish me luck? I ain't much of a catch, I fear. Gina could do much better, but I think she likes me, and I would look after her.'

'I'm sure of it.' Giles turned his face away, feeling that his expression must be ghastly.

'The dear little creature needs someone to protect her. It ain't much of a life for any woman on her own, and she has the girls to think about.'

His companion muttered something unintelligible, but Thomas was lost in rapture and didn't appear to hear it.

'I expect you think that we haven't known each other long,' Thomas continued. 'But I fell in love with her on that first day when she threatened me with her pistol.' He began to chuckle. 'I don't believe there is another woman in the world with half her character. Don't you agree?'

Giles could only nod.

'I knew it,' Thomas said with conviction. 'You and your family think so highly of her. Believe me, I shall do my best to make her happy if only she will accept me. You need have no worries for her future.'

Giles could listen to no more. Seizing upon the fact that the storm had broken at last and the rain was now pelting down, he spurred his horse into a gallop and raced towards the Grange.

Sleep eluded him that night. Each word of his quarrel with Gina was etched indelibly upon his mind. What must she think of him? She had offered him her love and he had spurned her. The old adage came back to him. What was it they said? 'Hell hath no fury like a woman scorned.' What would she do now?

He was under no illusions. He had killed the flame of love which had burned so brightly in her heart for the long years of their separation.

She had accused him of insufferable pride, but Gina too was proud. She would never forgive him.

Sheer agony of mind kept him tossing upon his bed for hours. What had happened to his resolve never to be alone with her? That had been a fatal mistake. The urge to take her in his arms was uncontrollable.

Ah, but it had been heaven to hold her to his heart again and to seek those yielding lips. But he cursed his own folly. He had succeeded only in hurting her. Whatever he was suffering now, he deserved it. All the torments of hell would not be enough to wipe out the memory of her bitter words. They were burned into his brain.

Had he known it, Gina herself was regretting those words. She would have given anything to unsay them but it was too late. For her too, sleep was out of the question. She paced her room for hours, writhing under the lash of humiliation and self-reproach.

What had happened to the iron self-control on which she prided herself? Love, it seemed, was no respecter of such attributes. As she reached out to Giles she had forgotten all her good resolutions. Heaven knows, she had waited for long enough before seeking out her love again. She could go on waiting, but he had not asked it of her.

So she had struck out at him in despair, calling him a coward, a weakling who could not face the cynical amusement of their world, and accused him of putting his own pride before their happiness.

In her own heart she knew that she was wrong. Honour mattered to Giles above all else. It was one of the reasons why she loved him so. Honour had caused him to promise her marriage all those years ago, though he was heir to the Rushford estate and she merely a servant. Honour had brought him back to England to do his duty by his family, though it must have cost him dear.

Now it was that same honour which prevented him from offering for her. Giles would accept nothing which he had not earned. For him it was a matter of principle. He could not bring himself to live upon his wife's fortune.

She couldn't bemoan the accidents of fate which had left her in her present circumstances. What was money, after all? To Gina it was merely a useful tool, certainly not to be despised as it eased one's path in life. Yet it could buy neither health nor happiness.

Yet for Giles it was an insuperable obstacle, and she could think of no way to persuade him to change his mind.

After a while she grew calmer. She would not be defeated. Had she not been certain of his love she might have given up the struggle, but the memory of his kiss, brief though it was, set her senses aflame. His response had been as fierce as her own.

She pushed the thought of their quarrel from her mind. What was done was done. There was no point in vain regrets. The mistake had been her own. She had intended to keep him guessing for a time, in the hope that he would try to win back her love. Now he was sure of it. She had given herself away, but she treasured the recollection of that moment when she was held once more against his heart. Surely a love like theirs could not be denied for ever. She would think of some way to overcome his scruples.

Perhaps she should have made him a business proposition in the first place. Inventions such as the new seed drill might be patented. Gina herself knew nothing of such matters, but Isham thought them useful and intended to put them into service on his own estates.

Then she remembered. Isham had already suggested such a scheme to Giles, but his brother-in-law had turned it down. Pride again, Gina thought sadly. Giles was only too aware of Isham's generosity. Had it not been for India's splendid marriage, his mother and his sisters would be living in a tiny cottage on the outskirts of Abbot Quincey dependent upon the goodwill of his uncle, Sir James Perceval.

He himself would be penniless, unable to provide for them. Those months when he had scoured the country looking for employment had left deep scars upon his soul.

Gina's heart went out to him. It would take time to heal those scars. Perhaps as he took control of India's estate and brought it into profit, Giles would recover some of his self-esteem. Honour, she realised suddenly, was all he had left at present.

At last she fell into an uneasy sleep, but she was heavy-eyed next morning. When the girls had left for the Academy she started upon her daily tasks, but she found it difficult to give them her full attention.

Did it really matter, she thought wearily, whether they dined on a green goose or a serpent of mutton that evening. Her gaze was abstracted as cook suggested various side dishes such as mushroom fritters, crimped cod, or boiled tongue with turnips. Then there were decisions to be made as to the various merits of an orange soufflé, a Celerata cream, or a basket of pastries.

Gina forced a smile. 'You will have us twice the size we are,' she warned. 'Let us have something light such as a dressed fowl. We might start with white almond soup with asparagus tips. That is a favourite with the girls, and so is your excellent orange soufflé.'

'That won't keep body and soul together, my lady.' Cook was never slow to protest when she was robbed of the chance to show her skills.

'It will be sufficient for this evening. We have no gentlemen to feed today. When we have dinner guests you shall choose the menu yourself.'

Cook was startled. It was unlike her young mistress not to take the keenest interest in every detail of the management of her household. She said as much to Mr Hanson.

'Madam may have her mind on other matters,' her confidante replied in lofty tones. 'Food, Mrs Long, cannot always be her first consideration.'

'Without it we should none of us get far,' came the tart reply. 'If you consider it so unimportant perhaps I should forget the dish of neats' tongues which I had in mind to make for your supper, Mr Hanson.'

The butler hastened to soothe her wounded feelings with the assurance that her culinary skills were match-less. Neats' tongues were, after all, a favourite with him. He went on to point out that it was largely due to the excellence of her cooking that the Whitelaw family was so healthy. None of the ladies suffered from the headaches or the fainting spells so common among the gentry.

'That's as maybe!' Cook replied. She allowed her-self to be mollified by his compliments. 'But Madam ain't herself. Mark my words, she has something on her mind.'

Hanson decided to see for himself. Cook was not a fanciful woman, and she knew her mistress well. If Madam was worried he would do his best to lift the burden from her shoulders.

He tapped gently at the door to Gina's study, and entered to find her gazing into space.

'Shall you wish to see the builder in your usual way, my lady?' he enquired. He had to repeat the question before she became aware of his presence.

'What?'

'The builder, ma'am. Must he give you a progress report?'

Gina stared at him before she replied, almost as if she did not understand the question. Then she pulled herself together.

'No, it won't be necessary. I saw him yesterday and the work is going on well.' She fell silent again.

'Will there be anything else, ma'am,' he pressed. 'Have you orders for me?' Hanson was appalled by his own temerity. In the ordinary way her ladyship was quick to let him know how he could best serve her. It was not up to him to take the initiative, but he persisted.

'Shall you care to ride this morning, my lady?' he asked. 'I could send an order to the stables…' Obviously his mistress was suffering from an attack of the megrims. This happened only rarely, but when it did a long gallop usually restored her to the best of spirits.

'No…! Yes…! I don't know… Tell the groom, I will send word within the hour.'

'Well, Mr Hanson, was I right?' Cook looked at him in triumph.

'I fear you were. Madam is not herself. Let us hope

that she will ride out this morning. For her it is a sovereign remedy for a sad mood.'

Gina was in agreement with him, but there were other claims upon her time. Both she and the girls required replenishments to their wardrobes. Clothing that had been suitable in Scotland would not serve in the softer, warmer climate of Northamptonshire, especially during the summer months. That was, of course, if they were to see the sun at all this year. The last two summers had been disastrous, or so she'd heard.

Idly, she leafed through the pages of *Ackermann's Repository*. India had given her the name of a clever mantua-maker in Northampton, a French refugee, she thought. Even so, she would choose styles, colours and fabrics before she approached the woman.

Gina knew what suited her, and elegance was her aim. She lacked the height to carry off extremes of fashion, such as the famous 'Marie' sleeve which was puffed and ruched with epaulettes, puffed oversleeves and frilled cuffs. In that, she told herself, she would resemble nothing so much as a gaily-coloured mushroom.

Perhaps a plain blue walking-dress in French cambric? And a morning-dress of jaconet muslin, made up to the throat, with sleeves buttoned tightly at the wrists?

She laid the magazine aside, unable to raise even a transitory interest in the coloured plates. She would return to the task later. It would not take her long to decide on the number of round robes she and the girls would require. They could be made in silk or muslin in simple styles and pastel colours.

Evening wear was even less of a problem at the moment. High fashion would be out of place in the country, even when dining with Lord and Lady Isham.

She caught her breath at the thought of returning to the Grange. How could she face Giles again?

For a long desperate moment she was tempted to close the Mansion House and leave for Scotland with the girls. Then common-sense returned. There was nothing to be gained by running away, and much to lose. The girls were settled at the Academy, and Mair, in particular, must be closer to London to make her come-out during the following year.

To flee would be the action of a coward, and cowardice Gina despised above all else. Giles, she knew, would never follow her to Scotland, so she would stay in Abbot Quincey, facing up to whatever the fates might have in store for her.

For the first time the suspicion of a smile touched her lips. Gina was no believer in fate. She had always favoured giving it a strong push. Nor did she sympathise with those who bemoaned a lack of opportunity. Napoleon Bonaparte might be considered a monster by most of her acquaintances, but one of his precepts had stuck in her mind. 'Opportunities?' he had remarked. 'I *make* opportunities.' Gina was fully in agreement with his words.

Well, now she was to be given the chance to put his advice to the test. She rang the bell and ordered her horse saddled and brought round. Her mind was always clearer on a long ride, and the fresh air would do her good.

She was about to go to her room and change from her pale green sacque into riding dress when Hanson reappeared.

'Madam, you have a visitor,' he announced.

Gina frowned. 'I am not receiving this morning, Hanson. You must deny me.'

'Madam, I tried, but the gentleman says that he is expected. It is Mr Thomas Newby.'

'Oh, Lord, I had forgot!' Gina struck her forehead. 'You had best show him in...'

'And your horse, ma'am?'

'I shall still require Beau to be saddled. Mr Newby will not stay long.'

Gina summoned up a smile to greet her visitor. She had not forgotten his kindness on the previous day.

He came towards her looking anxious.

'Have I been importunate, Lady Whitelaw? Your butler said that you were not receiving, and I feared that you were suffering from some malaise. I wished to assure myself that it was not so.'

'Mr Newby, you are very kind, but as you see I am quite well. I gave orders that I was not to be disturbed as I had some matters to attend...' Gina indicated the pile of papers on her desk. 'And then, you know, I am not yet dressed for receiving.' She glanced down at her simple dress.

'You always look beautiful to me,' Thomas said earnestly. 'But I am sorry to have broken in upon your morning's work. Do you find it onerous, ma'am?'

'Why no! I like to keep myself occupied…' Unreasonably Gina was irritated by the note of sympathy in his voice. 'And I am accustomed to dealing with my own affairs…I have done it for so long, you see.'

Thomas shook his head. 'You are so brave, but it must be a strain on you. Ladies have no head for figures, so I understand. Sometimes you must feel the need for help…for a guiding hand perhaps?'

He did not see the flash of anger in her eyes. Gina did not welcome interference, and the only guiding hand which she would tolerate was denied to her. She was almost tempted into a sharp retort, but she bit back the words. Thomas was on dangerous ground, but he meant only to be kind.

'I find that I have a head for figures,' she said mildly. 'Mr Newby, it is good of you to be concerned, but you must not worry about me…'

The next moment Thomas was on his knees beside her chair, endeavouring to seize her hands.

'How can I help it?' he cried. 'Oh, Lady Whitelaw…Gina…I love you with all my heart. I long for nothing more than to share your burdens…to make you happy. That would be my purpose for the rest of my days. Will you marry me?'

Gina was startled into silence. She looked down at the eager face of her companion in shocked surprise, and there was no encouragement in her expression.

'Mr Newby, please get up,' she said at last. 'I am touched by your concern for me, but I fear that it has carried you away. Believe me, I have no thought of marriage at this present time.'

Thomas stayed where he was. 'Tell me at least that I may hope,' he pleaded. 'I'll wait for you for ever, if need be. I mean…until you have given some thought to my proposal. I may not be the cleverest of men, but I can offer you a loving heart.'

'I know that, Mr Newby.' Gently Gina withdrew her hands from his clasp. 'Your heart will be given, in time, to a lady who returns your regard.'

Thomas could not mistake her tone. He rose to his feet. 'As you do not, Lady Whitelaw?'

'I value you as a dear friend,' she said, 'Friendship is important in a marriage, naturally, but there must be something more…'

'You speak of love? But surely that might come in time. I'd do my best to make you love me…'

'Love cannot be forced,' she told him quietly. 'Mr Newby, I have had experience. My late husband was the best of men. He was my closest friend. I have not spoken of this before to anyone, but I want to make you understand. Sir Alastair and I were happy together, but there was something missing… If I were to marry again it would not be on the basis of friendship alone.'

'There are worse things,' he protested.

'True, but there are also better things…' Gina fell silent.

'Is there someone else?' he demanded miserably.

Gina gave him a long look and he blushed to the roots of his hair.

'I beg your pardon,' he said quickly. 'I had no right to ask that question. Will you forgive me?'

'Of course.' Gina smiled at him and held out her hand. 'I intend to ride this morning. Will you go with me, Mr Newby?'

'A pleasure and an honour, ma'am.'

'Then give me a few moments to change my dress. I shall not keep you waiting long.'

She was as good as her word, but they had scarcely left the outskirts of the village before they saw a horseman in the distance, riding towards them at breakneck speed.

'Ain't that Giles? What the devil…? Oh, I beg your pardon, Lady Whitelaw. Didn't mean to swear, but he'll kill both himself and the mare if he don't slow down.'

Giles was upon them before she could reply.

'Turn back!' he ordered sharply. 'I have bad news!' He had eyes only for Gina, and she searched his face in terror. Her first thought was for the girls.

'Mair and Elspeth?' she said faintly. 'Has something happened to them?'

His hand went out to grip her shoulder. 'Nothing like that, Gina, but my news is serious. Spencer Perceval was assassinated yesterday in the House of Commons…'

'The Prime Minister?' Thomas was incredulous. 'Is it a conspiracy?'

'We don't know yet, but we can't discuss it here. When we get back to Abbot Quincey I'll tell you all I know.'

Chapter Nine

Obediently, Gina turned for home. Then Thomas seized her reins.

'Please don't do that,' she said through gritted teeth. 'I can manage Beau myself...'

'But, ma'am, the shock!'

'Mr Newby, I have suffered shock before...' Gina spurred her horse ahead before she uttered words which she would be certain to regret.

Startled by the vehemence of her outburst, Thomas did not attempt to catch up with her. Instead he looked at Giles.

'Never try that again.' Giles shook his head. 'Gina prides herself on her horsemanship. You are lucky she didn't strike you with her crop.'

'Clearly she is overwrought by your news,' Thomas assured him stoutly. 'I'm surprised that she didn't faint upon the spot.'

'Gina?' Giles looked at him in wonder. 'You have much to learn about her, Thomas.'

'I know it,' his friend said sadly. 'I have just this morning offered for her, but she turned me down.'

Giles was seized with an overwhelming feeling of relief. He was ashamed of the sense of exultation which possessed him, and he did his best to conceal it.

'Did she give a reason?' he asked in a casual tone.

'She says that she don't wish to marry again...at least until...until she can give her love.'

He looked so downcast that Giles was moved to pity.

'Don't take it to heart,' he urged. 'Gina has much upon her mind at present, and this latest news must worry all of us.'

'She didn't know of it when she refused me,' Thomas mourned.

'Nevertheless, it is a shocking thing. Perceval was shot in the lobby of the House, with all his friends about him.'

Thomas paled beneath his freckles. 'Will it mean revolution, Giles? I've heard of the French ideas spreading over here. It's barely twenty years since they took to wholesale massacre...'

'Isham doubts it, but he can't be sure. He left for London within the hour to find out what he can. Meantime, I'm enjoined to take good care of the ladies. Shall you wish to return to your home? Your father may be worried.'

'Wouldn't think of it. I have two brothers. They'll take care of my father, if care is needed, but he's a tough old bird, and more than a match for any mob.

He won't take kindly to the thought of a guillotine being set up in the market place of a Yorkshire village.'

'It happened in France,' Giles warned. 'I'm determined to take no chances with our womenfolk.'

'Of course not. I'd be honoured if you will allow me to share the responsibility. Above all, we must not frighten them.'

Giles grimaced. 'My mother is already in strong hysterics. Both India and Letty are likely to have a trying time with her.'

'At least they will comfort each other. Dear little Gina is alone.'

'I think you have forgot her family,' Giles replied with some asperity. 'They live here in the village.'

'Yes, yes! I expect that she will turn to them for protection.'

Much to his surprise, Gina showed no sign of needing protection of any kind. Once inside the Mansion House she drew off her riding gloves and rang for wine before she questioned Giles.

'Can you tell us more?' she asked. 'Was the assassin taken?'

'He was. His name is Bellingham. He is to be tried without delay.'

'Has he confessed his reason for the crime?'

'He has said nothing.'

'That's strange!' Gina mused. 'A fanatic... someone with a cause will usually shout his beliefs to the world at large.'

Thomas stared at her. Instead of indulging in a fit

of the vapours Gina was discussing the murder as a problem to be solved by cool analysis of the facts. Gradually it was being borne in upon him that he didn't know her at all.

She continued in the same vein. 'Do you suppose that he is quite sane?' she asked. 'This may simply be the act of a single madman.'

Giles smiled at her. 'You might be quoting Isham,' he informed her. 'He said as much before he left. Even so, he feels that we should take no chances.'

'Madmen and fanatics?' Thomas was nonplussed. 'Lady Whitelaw, you cannot mean that you have experience with such creatures?'

'Alas, more frequently than I care to recall, Mr Newby. The Indian continent is a hotbed of fanaticism.'

'Oh, my dear ma'am, how very dreadful for you!'

'It was instructive,' she said drily. Then she turned to Giles. 'What would you have me do?'

'For the present you should not ride out too far into the country, and certainly not without an escort. It would be all too easy for some hothead to conceal himself and take a shot at you or the girls.'

He saw the mutinous look about her mouth. He smiled at her again and Gina's heart turned over. That smile, so rarely seen these days, transformed his face, lighting up the room.

'This is not an order, you prickly creature. It's merely a suggestion. Come now, Gina, give me your word! If you won't consider your own safety, I know that you will think about the girls.'

At his coaxing words, Gina's objections vanished.

'You are right,' she admitted in a contrite tone. 'It would be foolish not to take precautions. May I come to visit your sisters this afternoon? India must be worried about her husband's safety in the capital.'

'You'll bring at least one groom?'

'I'll bring two if it will please you.' Unthinking, she held out both her hands to him. 'Am I forgiven for my stubborn ways?'

'Always, my love!' The endearment slipped out before he was aware of it, but Giles did not pay it attention. He continued to hold her hands as he looked deep into her eyes. Neither of them noticed that Thomas had left the room.

'Take care!' Giles whispered. 'Remember, you have given me your word!' He raised her hand to his lips and kissed it briefly. Then he hurried away.

It was not until they had almost reached the Grange that Thomas challenged him.

'You should have told me,' he reproached.

'I've told you all I know.' Giles misunderstood him. 'I didn't hear about the assassination until two hours ago.'

'I'm not referring to that,' Thomas said stiffly. 'I mean…well…had you mentioned that you and Gina…Lady Whitelaw…had a *tendre* for each other I should not have offered for her.'

Giles slowed the mare down to a walking pace. He had never discussed his love for Gina with another soul, but he was not proof against the air of dejection so evident in his friend.

'We knew each other long ago,' he admitted. 'It is ten years since we met in Italy. Gina was little more than a child, and I was a lovesick boy.'

Thomas shook his head. 'She loves you still. I cannot be mistaken. She does not look at me as she looks at you.'

'She is still clinging to a girlish dream.' His friend's tone grew harsh. 'Those can be the most difficult to give up.'

'She is a woman grown.' Thomas was angry. 'Since you met she has been married and widowed, and still she loves only you. Can you dismiss her constancy so lightly?'

'I must. I have naught to offer her.'

'But you will not tell me that you don't return her affection, Giles? I should not believe you. No one can fail to love her.'

Giles gave a muffled groan. 'I need no convincing of that...' He urged his horse into a gallop until they reached the Grange.

Gina herself was feeling much more cheerful. At the first sign of danger, real or imagined, Giles had hastened to her side, clearly concerned about her safety. And he had forgotten his firm resolve to keep her at a distance.

Now she treasured the memory of his smile, his touch and those unnoticed words of endearment which had slipped out unawares.

She ordered a light nuncheon of cold meats and fruit and ate it with much enjoyment.

Dreamily, she held her hand against her cheek, re-living the memory of his kiss. Her lover's defences had crumbled at the first hint of danger to her. She'd been wrong to give way to despair. All was not yet lost.

Then she took herself to task. The danger which she half welcomed had been born of tragedy. She had been thinking only of herself whilst India must be mad with worry about her husband. Isham would take his seat in the House of Lords, just a stone's throw from where the murder had been committed.

Mindful of Giles's warning, Gina ordered her carriage. By now the news of the assassination had spread throughout the village and she could hear iso-lated bursts of cheering.

Quickly she called her household together to ex-plain that they were in no immediate danger.

Cook was unconvinced. She jerked her head to-wards the windows. 'Just listen to 'em, ma'am! They are celebrating the poor man's murder, if you please...'

'Idlers and malcontents!' Gina said firmly. 'They are the ones who run away whenever they are faced down.'

'That's as maybe, my lady. I ain't stirring beyond these walls until the troops arrive.'

'Have I asked you to do so?' Gina's cool gaze re-duced the woman to silence. Then she turned to her outdoor staff. 'You will carry weapons at all times,' she ordered. 'Neame and Fletcher will accompany me

to the Grange this afternoon, and Thomson will
drive.'

'Oh, ma'am, you're never going out?' Cook was
abashed by her own temerity, but she was fond of her
young mistress.

'Indeed I am, but you need have no fears for me.
I am well armed myself...'

Cook screamed and threw her apron over her head.
'You'll be murdered, ma'am, I know it!'

'Not if I can help it!' Gina swept out of the room,
leaving the weeping woman to be sharply reprimanded by Hanson for letting down the household
staff.

''Tis all very well for you,' Cook moaned. 'I ain't
been to these outlandish places with the mistress...'

'If you had you would have no fears for her.'
Hanson was unsympathetic. 'Now pull yourself together, woman. Will you add to Madam's worries?'

His rebuke was unnecessary. Having made her
wishes known to her staff, Gina didn't give Mrs Long
another thought. She regarded hysterics as an unwar-
ranted indulgence on the part of any woman.

She changed out of her riding habit and into a high-
necked gown of French muslin in her favourite blue.
Over it, for warmth, she wore a waist-length jacket
with a high collar and long sleeves in a deeper shade
of blue. Not for the first time she blessed the introduction of this useful garment, known as a spencer.
Then she selected a high-crowned hat in satin straw,
trimmed with matching ribbons. It would crush her
hair-style out of recognition, but that was not of the

slightest moment. She hurried down the staircase, followed by her maid, who was still cramming various small items into a reticule.

'Don't fuss, Betsy!' Gina almost snatched the small bag from her. 'A handkerchief is all I need.'

Without more ado she jumped into her carriage and pulled the check-string.

The journey to the Grange passed without incident, but on arrival Gina was at once aware of the tension in the household.

Letty drew her to one side. 'Mama has upset India,' she whispered. 'She has her in widow's weeds already.'

'Send for the doctor,' Gina advised. 'Perhaps he'd give your mother a sedative.'

'He's on his way,' Letty told her. 'I was worried about India…'

'There is not the slightest need.' India had entered the room. 'I am not so easily overset…except… except that, of course I am worried about Anthony…' Her voice was quite under control.

Gina sat beside her and took her hand. 'Your husband is one of the most sensible men I know. He always looks ahead, my dear India, and on this occasion he is forewarned of possible trouble.'

India's eyes were bright with tears. 'He is my life,' she whispered. 'I could not live without him.'

'And you will not do so. Giles tells me that Anthony believes this crime to be a single act of murder, for what reason we may never know. I suspect the same myself.'

'Then you do not think it the start of an insurrection? Luddites, for example?'

'I doubt it. The frame-breakers have a genuine grievance, as Anthony will have told you, but they are merely trying to protect their livelihood, although it may not be in ways that we commend.'

'But he said...he said that others have infiltrated their movement for purposes of sedition.'

'That may be so, but I have the utmost faith in my fellow-countrymen. They have a strong objection to being used.'

'Oh, how sensible you are!' India smiled through her tears. 'You must think me a veritable watering-pot.'

'I don't think that at all!' Gina pressed her friend's hand. 'All I ask is that you don't meet trouble ahead of time. I've done it so often in the past. Then I've discovered that my worries have been unfounded. In the meantime, I've wasted many unhappy hours in allowing my imagination to dwell upon disaster. Time enough for that if it should happen, and for most of the time it doesn't. Anthony will be back with you before you know it.'

'He said at least a week...' India ventured.

'Quite possibly. I won't make light of this tragedy. The Government must be in disarray, but they will value Anthony's advice.'

India recovered some of her self-possession. 'I expect so. He has been concerned. Oh, I know that he discounts the idea of revolution in this country, but he's aware of the disaffection in the north.'

Gina nodded. She too had heard of the increase in the rioting.

'And then, you know, there is all the unemployment due to Napoleon's blockade. Cotton cannot get through to the towns in Lancashire, and the price of bread is rising constantly.'

'The war will not last for ever,' Gina comforted. 'Wellington is pushing back the French in Spain. When peace comes we shall enjoy prosperity.'

'That may be years away,' India told her sadly. 'Meantime this country is a tinder-box. It needs only a spark to set it aflame.'

'With respect, I think you are mistaken,' Gina replied. 'Take the Prince Regent, for example. He is despised for his extravagance, his bigamy, his mistresses and his treatment of his father and his wife. When he appears in public, he is jeered at and pelted with mud, yet no one attempts to do him serious harm.'

'He is regarded as a buffoon.' Giles had entered the room.

'Oh, no, he isn't that!' India shook her head. 'What the British can't forgive is that he is a patron of the arts. Had he confined his interests to horse-racing and boxing he would have been much more popular.'

'You are very hard on us, Lady Isham.' Thomas smiled down at her. 'Are we then a race of Philistines?'

'I fear you are, Mr Newby. The Prince is suspect because of his passion for orientalism, for design, for luxury, and for exotic foods… These things are not dear to the hearts of people in this country.'

'Especially the latter,' Giles broke in. 'I'm told that the Regent is now so fat that a hoist of some kind is needed to seat him upon his horse.'

Everyone smiled, but Gina felt moved to defend the Prince. 'I cannot but admire his taste in literature,' she protested. 'Is he not an admirer of Miss Austen's novels?'

'Oh, Gina, have you read it?' India's face lit up. 'Anthony has brought me a copy. It's called *Sense and Sensibility*. I'll be glad to lend it to you when I've finished it.'

'I'd like that. Miss Austen is a favourite with many people. They love the humour in her book. It is so subtle.'

'The Prince likes the Waverley novels too,' Thomas objected in gloomy tones. 'I tried one once. Couldn't get past the first page. All ancient history and prosing on as if we were still in the school-room…'

This brought cries of protest from the ladies and resulted in a heated discussion.

Gina glanced at her friend and was satisfied to see that her attempt at diversion had been successful. Some of the colour had returned to India's cheeks and she had lost the haunted look which was so troubling.

As she took her leave, Giles accompanied her to her carriage.

'Have you engagements for tomorrow?' he asked quietly.

Gina gave him a searching look before she answered. 'None that can't be broken,' she replied. 'Why do you ask?'

'I hoped…that is, I wondered if you would be good enough to visit India again. She is a different person in your company. I had not thought she would be so distressed by Isham's absence…'

'It is natural,' Gina comforted. 'And it is partly her condition. Fears can grow out of all proportion unless one gives another direction to one's thoughts.'

'That's true! Unfortunately, my mother adds to India's worries… I could wish that she would pay another visit to her friends…'

'Preferably far from here?' Gina twinkled at him.

'The farther the better!' He gave her an answering smile. 'Anthony can handle her, but my sisters are very much at her mercy.'

'And you?'

'I can't be here all day, Gina. Do say you'll come tomorrow…' He laid his hand upon her arm and Gina jumped as if she had been stung. Even through the fine cloth of her garments his touch had the power to set her senses aflame. Her eyes searched his face for some indication that his resolve was weakening, but Giles appeared to be thinking only of India.

'I'll come,' she promised as she stepped into her carriage.

On the journey back to Abbot Quincey she had much to occupy her mind. She could only rejoice that Giles had dropped his distant manner towards her. Now they were slipping back into the old comradeship which had first attracted them to each other. What had started as friendship had deepened into an overwhelming love. Could it do so again? In time of danger Giles must surely set aside his pride in the basic need to protect her and have her by his side. She prayed that it would be so.

Was she growing selfish? For these past few weeks she had been preoccupied with her own concerns, but now there were others to consider, apart from her own girls. It was a salutary thought.

With a lighter heart she hurried indoors, handing her spencer, her bonnet and her gloves to the waiting maid. If India needed diversion she should have it. Gina looked at her latest acquisition, the poems of Samuel Taylor Coleridge.

She and the girls had read 'The Ancient Mariner' and 'Kubla Khan' until they knew each word by heart. She chuckled to herself. How Mair and Elspeth had shuddered in mock horror as she had declaimed aloud!

Thomas Newby should be made to eat his words when he dismissed the whole of English literature. On the morrow she would make his blood run cold, and India would appreciate the joke.

There was Mrs Rushford to consider, of course. Gina rested her chin upon her hand. She could think of no immediate way of persuading India's mother to curb her foolish tongue. Perhaps the answer was to make some utterly outrageous statement in the hope of drawing her fire.

In the event, she had no need to do so. On the

following day she found the family gathered in the salon at the Grange. Having shaken off the effects of her sedative, Mrs Rushford was in full flow. She broke off to give Gina a sour look.

'I wonder that you dare to venture out, Lady Whitelaw. Had your husband been alive he would have forbidden it, I'm sure...'

'Fortunately, I am my own mistress, ma'am,' Gina said sweetly. 'As you see, I am unharmed.'

'Well, I suppose that you are accustomed to a certain lifestyle. My daughters have been brought up in a different way. They do not go racing about the countryside...'

Gina smiled, but she was aware that Giles had gone pale with anger. He was about to speak, but she shook her head at him. She had no wish to be the cause of a family quarrel.

'You have a letter, my lady.' India's butler held out a silver tray. 'There is also one for Mrs Rushford.'

'From Anthony?' India fell upon her letter with delight. 'Oh, please excuse me, but I must know what he has to say.' She scanned the missive quickly. Then she gave a sigh of relief. 'All is well,' she reported. 'There have been no more attacks. Bellingham is to be tried, but he has said nothing more.'

She looked round, smiling at her friends, but even as she did so the air was rent by a piercing scream.

'Mother, what is it?' Giles was across the room in a couple of strides. 'Are you ill?'

Speechless for once, Mrs Rushford shook her head.

'Then you can't have been listening to India. There seems to be no further danger to your safety…'

Feebly, she waved the piece of paper in her hand. 'Read that!' she gasped.

Five pairs of eyes were upon Giles as he scanned the single sheet. His reaction shocked them all. To everyone's surprise he gave a shout of laughter.

'Do share the joke!' India begged. 'We are all in need of entertainment.'

'And you shall have it!' Giles grinned at them, and then his face grew solemn. 'I am to be adopted,' he announced.

'Oh, Giles, don't gammon us! Won't you tell us what is in the letter?' Letty could not hide her curiosity.

'I've just told you. Mrs Clewes wishes me to take her name. She will then make me her heir.' His eyes were sparkling with amusement and the others refused to take him seriously.

'Wishful thinking, old fellow. Who could be so lucky?'

'It's true!' Mrs Rushford spoke in a hollow tone. 'Oh, my boy, who would have thought it?'

'Certainly not I. I hardly know the woman.'

'And I have never heard of her,' India announced. 'Where did you meet her, Giles?'

'At Bristol. We played cards with Lady Wells and her other cronies…'

'The demon gamblers?' Thomas raised an eyebrow. 'You must have made a great impression, Giles.'

'Giles was very kind to the old ladies,' his mother said with dignity. 'Mrs Clewes is not, perhaps, the type of person one would meet in the best society. She is extremely wealthy, so I understand, but her fortune comes from trade.'

'I liked her,' Giles said simply. 'There is no flummery about her.'

'I'm glad to hear it.' Mrs Rushford beamed upon him. 'My dear, your worries must now be at an end.'

The full import of this remark did not strike Giles at first. Then he became aware of the hush which followed it. He turned to face his mother.

'I hope I misunderstand you, ma'am.' His tone was incredulous. 'You can't possibly be suggesting that I give this offer serious consideration.'

'Consideration?' she snapped. 'Consideration? You should seize this opportunity with both hands. Where else will you come into possession of a fine competence? You will not wed to make your way in life…'

Thomas foresaw the coming storm. Excusing himself, he slipped quietly out of the room. His friend's face had grown dark with anger and he had no desire to witness a serious family quarrel.

Gina made as if to follow him, but Giles stopped her.

'Sit down, Gina!' he ordered. 'This concerns you too. Tell me, shall I accept this offer?'

It was against her own best interests, but Gina did not hesitate. 'You can't!' she said at once. 'You are the last of the Rushfords. You must not give up your name. It would be like selling it.'

'Indeed!' Mrs Rushford was beside herself with rage. 'And who are you, madam, to advise my son? Will you take him yourself and give him heirs?'

Giles took a step towards her, but India intervened. 'Mother, you have gone beyond the bounds of what is permissible,' she said in icy tones. 'Letty and I will take you to your room...'

It was enough to send Isabel Rushford into full hysterics. She screamed, sank to the floor, and began to drum her heels upon the carpet.

Giles took Gina's hand. 'Come into the study,' he said. 'My sisters know how to deal with this.'

'But can't I help?' she asked. 'I have had some experience.'

A grim smile touched his lips. 'I'm sure you have, but this is no case for a bucket of cold water, or a slap across the face. Knowing my mother, the doctor has left a supply of sedatives. The girls will settle her down.'

'I should not have been harsh,' she protested.

'I know it. I was teasing you, but you have every reason to resort to violence. I must apologise for my mother's words...'

'I believe she spoke without thinking,' Gina replied. 'It is understandable that she should consider your best interests as she sees them.'

'At any cost?'

Gina changed the subject. 'Tell me about this Mrs Clewes. Who is she, Giles, and how did you come to meet her?'

'Lady Wells invited us to Bristol when her son and

Letty wished to become engaged. As you can imagine, Oliver and Letty had eyes only for each other. I spent my time in playing cards with the other house guests. Mrs Clewes was one of them.'

'What type of person is she?'

To Gina's surprise, Giles twinkled at her. 'You'd like her. She's an original...'

'In what way?'

'Well, let me see... In the first place she makes no concessions to the present fashions, apart from a fondness for terrifying turbans. In the Grecian style, she informed me, she would resemble nothing so much as a sack of flour, knotted close to the neck.'

'She has a sense of humour then?'

'She has...and it can be withering. Sometimes I was hard put to keep my countenance. She has a way of catching one's eye when something ridiculous strikes her.'

'I can see why you would find her entertaining, but how does she come to be a guest of Lady Wells? Your mother mentioned that the lady's fortune came from trade. Is not Lady Wells a famous snob?'

'It *is* a mystery,' Giles admitted. 'Mrs Clewes may be a family connection of some sort. Lady Wells was forever trying to keep her in her room. Certainly she did not encourage private conversations with this particular guest.'

'But you must have spoken to her yourself.'

'Mrs Clewes and I had a number of assignations,' Giles said darkly.

Gina bridled. 'What age of woman is she?'

'She must be well into her seventies…wid-
owed…and without an heir. I thought she seemed
quite lonely.'

'And what was the purpose of these assignations?'
Gina asked in a casual tone. At least, she hoped that
she sounded casual.

Giles grinned at her. 'Mrs Clewes is fond of a glass
of ''flesh and blood''. It is…er…was not available in
her ladyship's household. I managed to get it for her.'

'Great heavens! What on earth is that?'

'It is a glass of port, well laced with gin. Don't be
tempted to try it, Gina. I did myself. Believe me, it
separates the men from the boys…!' He caught
Gina's eye and they laughed until they were helpless.

'I see now why you are such a favourite with Mrs
Clewes,' she teased.

'It wasn't entirely that.' Giles grew more serious.
'I found her to have a fund of what I can only describe as earthy common-sense. She isn't afraid to
speak her mind.'

'I'm sorry that I won't meet her. What will you do
now?'

'I'll write to her, of course, to thank her for her
offer. If she is a connection of Lady Wells she might
be persuaded to make Oliver her heir.'

Gina gave the suggestion her consideration. 'That
might be best. Oliver is a younger son. He may not
object to taking her name.' She paused. Then she
asked the question that was uppermost in her mind.

'What did you mean when you said that this matter
was of concern to me as well as to you?'

'Did I say that?' Giles looked at her in wonder. 'I needed your opinion, that was all.'

'Not quite all!' Gina was bitterly disappointed, but her expression gave no hint of it. 'There is something else which I should mention to you. Has Mr Newby told you that he offered for me?'

Giles nodded, sick with apprehension. Was she about to tell him that she'd changed her mind and would now accept his friend?

'Then you will know that I refused him. Under the circumstances I think it best if, for the present, you do not bring him to my home again. I'd like to avoid an awkward situation.'

She hoped he would accept the lame excuse, which was only partially true. If Giles persisted in treating her as a stranger she'd be in danger of breaking her heart for a second time, and that, she vowed, must not be allowed to happen. Better not to see him at all than to torture herself with vain hopes.

He made her a formal bow. 'As you wish,' he said. 'We shall not trouble you again.' He paused. 'You need not fear to visit India. We shall not be here.'

Chapter Ten

Giles kept his word to her, much to the disgust of Mair and Elspeth.

'But they promised!' both girls chorused.

Gina found that she was losing patience. 'You are no longer children,' she reproved. 'You must not behave as if some special treat has been denied to you. Both Giles and Mr Newby have been more than kind, but they have other calls upon their time.'

Then she looked at their downcast faces and relented. 'Cheer up!' she said. 'I plan to do more entertaining. You shall come down to dinner with our guests. Meantime we need to think about new gowns for you.' She picked up copies of *The Lady's Magazine* and *Ackermann's Repository* and left them absorbed in studying the latest fashions.

Her visit to India was brief that morning, and she was unsurprised to learn that plans for the subscription ball had been cancelled.

'I can't think it would be right to go ahead in the light of recent events,' India told her. 'Any celebration would be out of place in view of the assassination.'

'I agree, and people are still jittery. Have you more news from London?'

'Not much. There are no new developments, so Anthony tells me. The capital is fairly quiet, but the death of the Prime Minister has led to much rejoicing in the north.'

Gina changed the subject. 'How is Mrs Rushford?' she asked.

India gave her a faint smile. 'Subdued, I fear. She knows when she has gone too far with Giles.'

'Mrs Clewes's offer must have come as a shock to her,' Gina said kindly. 'Your mother had no time to consider the implications.'

'It's good of you to see it in that light, especially as she was so rude to you…'

Gina laughed. 'I often speak out of turn myself. I can't condemn it in others. When does Anthony return?'

'By Sunday at the latest, so he tells me. That wretched creature, Bellingham, is to be tried. If he's found to be insane, Anthony will try to save him, but he doesn't offer much hope.'

India's words were prophetic. When Isham returned a glance at his face told her the result of the trial. She did not question him, knowing that he would not care to distress her, but he spoke to Gina later.

'Is it all over?' she asked.

'Oh yes, justice has been served, or so the authorities would have us believe. Bellingham was tried with indecent haste. The result was a foregone conclusion. He was executed in front of Newgate prison in the midst of ugly scenes. The hangman was pelted by the mob.'

Gina shuddered. 'When will they stop these public executions?' she asked.

'That will come in time. For the present they are regarded as a salutary deterrent. Now let us forget the subject. I am in your debt, my dear, for the way you have supported India. She has come to rely on your good sense.'

'She has a great deal of her own,' Gina assured him.

'That's true, but I worry about her, Gina. Her mother attempts to fill her mind with fears.'

Gina was silent.

'Still the diplomat?' Isham smiled at her. 'Believe me, I don't need your confirmation. I was concerned before I left for London.'

Lost in thought he took a turn around the room. 'I have a little plan,' he said at last. 'Sir James Perceval and his wife are in London for Hester's season. Lady Eleanor is sister to Mrs Rushford. I have an invitation for Letty and her mother to join them. Do you think that it will serve?'

'It's doubtful,' Gina told him. 'Mrs Rushford sees an assassin behind every bush.'

'Then we must convince her otherwise. Bellingham is dead, after all.'

'You might suggest that she spends her time in

choosing Letty's bride-clothes. That is, if…' She paused, but Isham understood her perfectly.

'She shall have a free hand,' he said at once. 'No expense will be too great if she can be persuaded to leave India's side. Will you help me?'

'I'll do my best,' she promised.

She wasted no time in setting about her task. In the event, Mrs Rushford needed little persuasion to undertake a trip to London, armed with rolls of bills in high denominations from her son-in-law and letters of credit drawn upon his bank.

Letty's shy objections were quickly waved aside.

'Are you out of your mind?' her mother demanded angrily. 'Here is Isham prepared to do his duty by you, as indeed he should, and you must make difficulties, you ungrateful girl!'

'I don't mean to be ungrateful, Mama, but shall I really need so much?' Letty thought with horror of the endless lists of proposed purchases drawn up by her mother. 'I mean…Anthony is paying all the expenses of my wedding…'

'And what has that to say to anything? Do you suppose that your brother-in-law can't afford it? Why, Letty, he is rich enough to buy an abbey. Besides, he told me himself that it would be his pleasure…'

Letty was reduced to silence, but she made it her business to seek out Isham in his study and thank him for herself.

'Nonsense!' he said warmly. 'If our roles were reversed would you not do the same for me?'

'That isn't very likely to happen.' Letty was forced to smile.

'Oh, I don't know,' he teased. 'I might invest in some dubious scheme and reduce myself to tramping the open road with India by my side. Do you suppose she would enjoy it?'

'With you, she would be happy anywhere, and under any conditions. You have made her so very happy, Anthony.'

For answer he kissed her cheek. 'Thank you, my dear. I wish the same for you and Oliver. Shall you see him when you are in London?'

Letty's face grew animated. 'Oh, yes. That is one reason why I have agreed...I mean...I don't like to leave India at this present time.'

'Letty, you will be doing me a service. You understand me? I think I need not say more. India must have peace of mind. You will oblige me by staying with your Aunt Eleanor for as long as possible.'

Letty understood him perfectly and she gave him a conspiratorial look.

'You and your mother need not fear the journey,' he continued. 'Giles and Thomas Newby will escort you.'

It was with a good deal of relief that he waved the little party off for London at the end of the following week. Then he ordered his horse brought round and set off for Abbot Quincey.

Gina welcomed him with unaffected pleasure. 'Is all well?' she asked.

'All is very well indeed,' he told her with mock solemnity. 'Today my prayers are answered. Isabel set off for London this very morning, with enough commissions to keep her occupied for weeks.'

Gina laughed aloud. 'Your plan worked then?'

'It did. I wish I could think of another. You don't suppose that she would care to live there permanently? I could take a house for her in some convenient part of the city.'

'You could suggest it,' Gina answered drily. 'She might agree to live with one of her bosom bows for companionship.'

'Are there any such?'

Gina laughed again. 'Now you are being unkind!' she accused.

'Sometimes I feel savage!' Isham said with feeling. 'And now she is at odds with Giles. He and Newby have gone with them, but he doesn't want to stay...' He glanced at Gina's face through half-closed lids, but her expression told her nothing.

'When will you come to see us, Gina? India has missed you these last few days.'

'I was being tactful,' she told him cheerfully. 'Now that you are returned from London, India has no need of anyone else.'

'She values her friends, my dear, and she looks forward to your visits.'

'Then I will come again tomorrow...' Secure in the knowledge that Giles would not return for several days, Gina was happy to agree.

Her resolution not to see him had not weakened,

but she missed him dreadfully. She'd tried to fill the gap by looking up old friends, but she and her childhood playmates had grown too far apart.

Her household duties were quickly undertaken, leaving her time to read, to study, to choose plants for the new orangery, and to consider embellishing her wardrobe. She found that nothing could hold her interest.

More than anything she longed to feel that familiar leap of the heart whenever she saw Giles. Now she dwelt on every detail of that beloved face, loving the way his mobile mouth turned up at the corners when he smiled, the strong line of his jaw and the look in his blue eyes whenever she caught him unawares.

Giles was handsome, certainly, but she'd have loved him if he had been the ugliest man alive. They were soul-mates. If only he'd accept that the bond between them held them both for life.

She pushed the wish away. She had a pile of correspondence to attend to. Her friends in Scotland must not be neglected, but her stay there seemed to have taken place in another existence.

'Mr George Westcott, ma'am.' Hanson ushered her visitor into the room.

Gina turned with a welcoming smile. For the past two weeks her cousin had been her most frequent visitor. She was puzzled. Surely he did not share her parents' hope that she would wed him?

Had he shown any sign of making advances to her, she would have sent him to the rightabout, but George seemed to be content to be her friend.

This morning he seemed troubled.

'Is something wrong?' she asked.

'My father is returned to Abbot Quincey,' he said miserably.

'I see…and you are come to tell me that we shall be one more for dinner this evening?'

It was only with the greatest reluctance that Gina made this offer. Her uncle was not welcome in her home, but not to invite him would give rise to unwelcome comment.

'Not exactly!' George seemed unable to sit still. He rose and began to pace about the room. 'I haven't been honest with you, Gina. Haven't you wondered why I call on you so much?'

'I hoped it was because you enjoyed my company.' Gina prayed that he was not about to make a declaration.

'Well, I do, of course, but you see, I had to come. My father would have made enquiries, and I'm afraid for Ellie.'

Gina saw that he was in great distress. 'You had better tell me all about it,' she said quietly. 'I don't understand you, I'm afraid…'

George sat down then and poured out his story to her. 'It isn't that I don't like you, Gina,' he explained at last. 'But I love Ellie and I want to marry her.'

Gina thought for a moment. She had no doubt that Samuel Westcott would carry out his threat to harm the girl if his son did not obey him.

'It's time for some play-acting, George,' she said. 'This evening you must follow my lead, and remem-

ber, you must not laugh. That would give the game
away...'

George looked mystified. 'I cannot come at your
meaning, cousin...'

'I mean that you must make up to me. I promise
to languish under your ardent gaze. I may even rest
my head upon your shoulder...'

George looked startled. 'Would that not be doing
it too brown?'

'Perhaps. We must keep it within the bounds of
decorum... Are we agreed?'

'It would help to throw my father off the scent,' he
admitted. 'It's the money, you see. He wants to keep
it in the family...'

This bald statement was a severe trial to Gina's
composure, but she kept her countenance.

'I didn't imagine that it was my delightful temper-
ament, or my beautiful blue eyes,' she replied.

George stared at her, uncertain as to whether or not
she was teasing, and Gina groaned to herself. Ellie,
whoever she was, would find George heavy going unless she shared his lack of humour. Even so, she sympathised with him.

It would give her the greatest pleasure in the world
to outwit her unpleasant uncle. He deserved a sharp
set-down. Her only worry was that she might over-
play her hand, but she thought she could judge her
manner to a nicety.

The inclusion of her uncle had made them nine for
dinner. He apologised for upsetting the arrangement

of her table, but she made light of it. In a further blow
to convention she seated George at her right hand.

Her brother exchanged a speaking glance with his
wife, and her sister did the same. The Westcott brothers nodded and smiled at each other. Only Gina's
mother eyed her daughter with some suspicion.

Gina affected not to notice. She kept the conversation light, chattering about her plans for the garden,
and asking for advice from the assembled company.

'I plan a shrubbery, of course,' she said brightly.
'George, what do you think? Shall it be a circuit walk
around the garden walls, in the serpentine style, or
shall I plump for the theatrical? Mr Garrick had twin
theatrical shrubberies in his Thames-side garden at
Hampton House, you know.'

George did *not* know, and it was all too clear, but
he made a manful effort.

'Cousin, I've always admired your taste,' he replied. 'Whatever you decide will be perfection, I am
sure of it.'

'Too kind!' Gina replied in sentimental tones. Apparently without thinking she laid her hand on his and
pressed it warmly. 'When it is finished we shall walk
there. In Horace Walpole's words I plan ''odours beyond those of Araby''. It will be a haven of delight…'

George felt it was time to bring her down to earth.
'What plants will you choose?' he said.

Gina lavished an adoring look upon him. 'I thought
of roses, pinks, honeysuckle and lilac among others.
Are they your favourites too?'

George did not know a honeysuckle from a daffodil, but he did his best. 'I like snowdrops,' he said stoutly.

'Then we shall have those too, and other bulbs, as well as carnations and sunflowers. Oh, I can't wait to order all these treasures.'

'They'll cost you a pretty penny, my dear, but then, I suppose that is not of any concern to you...' Samuel Westcott seemed about to lick his lips. 'Tell me, where are your girls this evening?'

Gina gave him the briefest of looks, but it was enough. 'They are at dancing classes this evening,' she said. She did not miss his dreadful smile.

'Are they not over-young to be allowed out in an evening?' her mother said anxiously. 'You do not fear that they may be in danger?'

Privately, Gina considered that Mair and Elspeth were likely to be in more danger in her uncle's company, but she did not say so. He had a nasty habit of trapping young girls in passageways or hidden corners.

'They are in no danger outside this house.' Her look at her uncle was filled with meaning. 'I sent them in the carriage with two grooms for company...'

Samuel Westcott turned his head away and began to engage his brother in conversation.

'What do you say to this latest stab in the back?' he asked. 'I fear our trade will suffer even more.'

'The declaration of war by our former colonies? It isn't altogether unexpected. They've always resented our blockade of European ports, and they have no love for England.'

'We should have crushed that rebellion when we had the chance.' Samuel replied savagely. 'We should have sent more troops to the Americas. It's beyond belief that we could have been defeated by a rag, tag and bobtail of undisciplined farmers.'

'Yet they had something which our troops had not,' Gina observed. 'They were fighting for their belief in freedom. What was it they said; "No taxation without representation?" That sounded reasonable to me.'

Her uncle gave her a sour look. 'Much you women know about it, Gina! Leave it to those who understand these matters. Now they have invaded Canada. I regard that as the basest treachery. Our war with Napoleon has given them the chance they needed to strike when our backs were turned.'

Gina was about to reply when her mother caught her eye. As Mrs Westcott shook her head, Gina rose from the table.

'We'll leave you to your politics then,' she said as she led the ladies from the room.

Her mother took her to task at once. 'What can you be thinking of?' Mrs Westcott said severely. 'It's so unbecoming to put forward your opinions on matters which are of no concern to females.'

'Wars are of concern to everyone, Mother. Females have husbands and sons who may be called upon to fight. We cannot stick our heads in the sand like ostriches.'

Mrs Westcott sighed. 'You haven't changed, my dear. You were always such a forthright child. It will

not do, you know. Gentlemen do not like it. Take
care, or you will become known as a blue-stocking.'

Gina kissed her mother's cheek. 'Is that such a
dreadful fate?' she teased.

'You may not think so, but I do. Poor George
looked shocked.' She gave her daughter a sideways
glance. 'How do you go on with him?'

'George is a dear. He calls on me quite often,' Gina
told her truthfully. She was well aware that this item
of information would be passed on to both the
Westcott brothers, and she had promised to help
George.

'George looks quite moonstruck,' her sister observed. 'Shall you wed him, Gina?'

'I hardly know him well enough as yet. Besides, I
have no thought of marriage for the present.' Gina's
look was demure. Hopefully, the three ladies would
take it as a sign of interest in her cousin.

'I'm not surprised!' Her brother William's wife
was undeceived. 'Why should you re-marry? You
have money enough for all your needs. Why condemn
yourself to submitting to a husband's wishes, produc-
ing a child each year?'

Mrs Westcott scowled at her daughter-in-law.
'There is such a thing as a woman's duty, Alice.
William would not like to hear you speak so freely.
Besides, Gina would like children of her own. She
told me so herself.'

'That's true,' Gina said with perfect truth. 'But I
must consider carefully. There is no hurry for the moment.'

'You won't be young for ever,' her sister snapped. 'The years will take their toll, as they have done for all of us.'

Gina looked at both Alice and Julia with new eyes. Each of them was close to her in age, but the casual observer would have guessed at a wider gap. Discontent was evident on each face and the reason was not far to seek. They envied her her money and her freedom.

She tried for a lighter touch. Gossip was a favourite topic of conversation in all the Abbey villages.

'Do you hear anything of the Marchioness of Sywell?' she asked.

As she had hoped this brought immediate response from all three of her companions. They vied with each other to bring her up to date with all that had happened at the Abbey since she left.

'You'd be too young to understand the implications when the Earl of Yardley lost the Abbey to Sywell,' Mrs Westcott told her. 'That was the start of the trouble.'

'But I do remember something about it, Mother. We children sang silly songs about it at the time. Did not the Earl of Yardley lose the Abbey in a gambling session? Then he blew his brains out?'

'It was a tragedy, Gina. The Earl had had a serious quarrel with his son. Something about the Viscount's wish to marry a French Catholic, I believe. His father cut him off, but when Lord Rupert was reported killed in Paris the Earl was distraught. He almost drank himself insensible whilst gambling. In the end he lost everything to Sywell, and then he killed himself.' Mrs Westcott shuddered. 'He could not have imagined what we would get in his place.'

'I don't know much about Sywell,' Gina admitted. 'He is not seen in Abbot Quincey…'

'He durst not show his face,' Julia told her. 'For years he and his cronies regarded the village girls as fair game. Orgies were the least of it. He has ruined not only the girls, but also some of the tradesmen. He does not settle his accounts, and no one will deliver to the Abbey now, and none of the villagers will work there.'

'So how does he manage to live?'

'One man has stayed with him. His name is Burneck. He is some kind of valet cum general servant. Occasionally he hires domestics in town, but they don't stay long.'

'And yet the Marquis married?' Gina said in wonder. 'The girl was very young, so I understand…'

'She was little more than a child, my dear. Heaven knows what pressure was brought to bear upon her to cause her to accept that monster. Now she has disappeared.'

'I shouldn't be the least surprised if the Marquis has done away with her,' Alice insisted. 'He's capable of anything.'

'But not of murder, surely?' Gina was shocked.

'Why not? I can't think of a crime which cannot be laid at his door.'

'She may have found her life intolerable. Perhaps she ran away…?'

'Perhaps!' Alice was unwilling to give up her belief in the ultimate perfidy. 'How I wish that the man would sell the Abbey and move elsewhere!'

'The Earl of Yardley has tried to buy back the Abbey,' Mrs Westcott told her. 'It would be a great relief to all of us to have the original family back again.'

'But Sywell will not sell?'

'No, Gina. He takes a perverse pleasure in taunting the Earl.'

'But I thought that Yardley killed himself?'

'The present Earl is a relative. He made his fortune in India and purchased land from his cousin, the Earl of Yardley. With Yardley and Lord Rupert dead, he inherited the title.'

'If Sywell is in debt, he may change his mind.'

'I doubt it. Sywell would cut off his nose to spite his face for the opportunity of doing an injury to one of his erstwhile friends.'

'He sounds delightful!' Gina said drily. 'Let us not lose hope! Someone may decide to remove him from the face of the earth...'

Her remark was made half in jest, but within a week her wish was granted.

Gina was in the garden, leafing through a book of poems by Robert Southey, when her visitors were announced.

Her heart was in a turmoil as Giles strode across the lawn towards her. His visit was unexpected, and she could think of no reason for it, but it was more than welcome. Her good resolutions vanished like snow in summer as she rose to her feet and held out both her hands.

He took them swiftly. 'There's been another murder,' he said without preamble. 'Sywell was found dead this morning.'

'The Marquis? Is this the work of the Luddites, Giles?'

'I doubt it. Sywell was no threat to them. He owned no factories, and had no interest in the introduction of new machinery.'

'How was he killed?'

'Stabbed through the heart, but his valet found no sign of an intruder.'

'I'm not surprised. The Abbey is a warren of passages and hiding places.' Gina thought for a moment. 'It must have been someone who knew the place, and how to reach Sywell's rooms. A casual thief would find that difficult.'

'There's sure to be a serious investigation,' Giles continued. 'The Runners have been summoned, but if I'm not mistaken the Regent will wish his own men to take charge. The murder of a peer of the realm cannot be ignored.'

Thomas Newby intervened. 'I don't see why not,' he objected. 'The fellow was a monster.'

'Even so, the Regent will consider it an unfortunate precedent. Allow the murder of a member of the aristocracy to go unpunished, and our unfortunate Prince may be the next victim. He's one of the most unpopular men in England.'

Neither of his companions was prepared to argue with this statement.

'So many people hated Sywell.' Gina mused. 'One might as well look for a particular straw in a haystack.'

'His widow is a favourite candidate,' Giles told her grimly. 'She will inherit the Abbey…'

'And a mountain of debt,' Gina objected. 'Besides, she hasn't been seen for months…'

'She may not have gone far. If she planned the murder she would lie low, awaiting a suitable opportunity. She would know the Abbey well, you must agree.'

'But women don't often resort to stabbing, Giles. In the first place it requires great physical strength to overpower a man, unless she attacked him whilst he was sleeping. I'm told that the Marchioness was a slender, gentle creature. I doubt if she would be capable of violence.'

'We can't know what her life was like before she left the Marquis. She may have been driven to desperation.'

'That's more than likely,' Thomas agreed. 'We all knew Sywell's reputation, but I agree with Lady Whitelaw. Poison is more of a woman's weapon.'

'Thank you, Mr Newby!' Gina's tone was dry. 'I see that you think highly of us as a sex.'

'I do, ma'am, as you know!' He gave her a look of such blatant adoration that Gina was nonplussed. Irony, she decided, was quite lost on Thomas.

'There must be other suspects,' she suggested. 'The

fathers and brothers of the girls the Marquis ruined must be high on the list, and some of his bastards too will be old enough to take revenge…'

She heard a gasp from Thomas, and guessed correctly that he was unused to such plain speaking from a woman.

'It could be one of Sywell's gambling cronies,' he said hastily. 'He's thought to have ruined many a man and not always by fair means…'

Giles had been silent for some time. 'There is always Burneck himself, of course,' he said at last. 'What better way to hide his guilt than to raise the alarm and set the countryside by the ears…?'

'I can't believe that,' Gina objected. 'Burneck has stayed by his master's side all these years. Why should he resort to murder now?'

'There could be a number of reasons…perhaps a promised legacy withdrawn, or something of that sort.'

'Possibly!' Gina was unconvinced. 'You still think that the Luddites are not to blame?' She had kept up a brave face, but the strain of this latest news was beginning to tell, and she had grown pale. She sat down in the nearest chair and hid her shaking hands within her skirts.

Giles was beside her in an instant. 'My dear, I have been thoughtless,' he said tenderly. 'I should not have troubled you with this dreadful story.'

Gina shook her head. The solicitude in his voice brought her close to tears, but she blinked them away.

'I'm glad you let me know,' she whispered. 'It is

just that… Oh, Giles, there has been so much violence in these past few weeks. First the murder of Isham's half-brother at the Grange, and the riots. Then the assassination of the Prime Minister, and now this… Are we on the verge of revolution? It happened in France not twenty years ago.'

'It couldn't happen here,' Thomas said with conviction.

'Don't be too sure,' she murmured. 'Are we too squeamish a nation to rely on the headsman's axe? We executed our own king, if I recall.'

Giles slipped a comforting arm about her shoulders. 'Do you trust Isham, Gina?'

She nodded wordlessly.

'Then come back to the Grange with us. Talk to him. The Government keeps him up to date with all the latest news. He is convinced that there will be no revolution here. This murder is a local tragedy. He is sure of it.'

Gina allowed herself to be persuaded into visiting the Grange, ostensibly to be reassured by Isham. In reality, she was conscious of a very feminine need to cling to Giles for support. It was ridiculous, she told herself sharply. What had happened to the strong-willed Gina Westcott, with her ability to handle any situation? The character of that iron lady seemed to have changed beyond recognition.

She had expected to find India in a similar state of shock, but to her surprise her friend looked perfectly serene.

India glanced at Gina's troubled face and hurried

to embrace her. 'Come and sit down,' she said gently. 'This murder is a dreadful thing, my dear, but Anthony is convinced that it is the result of some private feud.'

Isham himself confirmed her words. 'There is no talk of general insurrection, Gina, but if you are still worried why not bring the girls and stay with us?'

His wife gave him a smile of thanks. 'That might be best. We have room and to spare now that my mother and Letty are gone to London. Lucia, Anthony's step-mama, went with them.'

Gina recovered some of her composure. 'You are very kind,' she said quietly. 'But I couldn't think of it. I don't know why I've allowed the news of the murder to upset me so. I didn't even know the Marquis, but I seem to be on edge these days.'

Isham could have made a shrewd guess as to the reason but he let it pass. At the sound of carriage wheels he strolled over to the window.

'It seems we have a visitor,' he announced. 'Giles, is this anyone you know?' He was unprepared for his brother-in-law's reaction.

'Great heavens!' Giles had stiffened. 'As I live and breathe! It's Mrs Clewes!'

Chapter Eleven

As their visitor was announced, five pairs of eyes focused upon her in astonishment.

Mrs Clewes was an amazing sight. She was very short and almost as wide as she was tall. In an effort to add inches to her stature she sported an aigrette-topped turban in a particularly violent shade of blue. This clashed in the most painful way with the gown which could be glimpsed beneath her travelling cloak.

It was clear that the lady made no concession to the present fashion for simple Grecian styles. Panniers held out her voluminous skirts, beneath which could be seen an ancient pair of carpet slippers.

At first it seemed unlikely that she would manage to negotiate the doorway, but with the ease born of long practice she turned sideways, swept into the room, and waddled towards the waiting company.

Isham was the first to recover his sang-froid. With his customary courtesy he moved towards his guest.

'Welcome, ma'am!' he bowed. 'It is Mrs Clewes, is it not?'

'It is!' Mrs Clewes was perfectly at ease. 'You'll be Isham, I expect, and Letty's brother-in-law?'

Isham bowed again. 'May I present my wife, and Lady Whitelaw, who is a friend of ours. This is Mr Thomas Newby, and Giles you already know.'

'Aye! He's the lad I've come to find. How do you go on, my dear?'

Giles came towards her then and took her outstretched hands, smiling as he did so.

'Ma'am, I am well,' he said. 'No need to ask how you go on. You are the picture of health...'

'Flatterer! I expect you must be wondering why I'm here?'

'Before you tell us, Mrs Clewes, will you not take a comfortable chair?' Isham led her forward. 'You must have found your journey tiring. Allow me to offer you some refreshment...' He rang the bell.

'I won't deny I'll be glad to take the weight off my feet, my lord.' Mrs Clewes settled herself with a gusty sigh. 'I ain't as young as I used to be.'

'And what is your pleasure, ma'am? Some wine, perhaps?'

It was at this point that Giles intervened. 'Mrs Clewes believes a glass of "flesh and blood" to be the best restorative,' he said solemnly.

'Then "flesh and blood" it is. Tibbs, will you see to it?'

'Certainly, my lord.' Tibbs did not betray his astonishment by the flicker of an eyelid, nor did he need to ask the nature of this tipple. It was a favourite of his own, though to his knowledge it had not been served before in the salon at the Grange.

'Well now, I won't take up your time,' Mrs Clewes announced. 'I came to have a word with Mr Rushford here.'

'A private word, ma'am? If so, may I offer you my study?'

'Not unless Giles insists, my lord. I have a bone to pick with him, you know.'

Giles had suspected something of the kind. Mrs Clewes had greeted him kindly enough, but it was possible that she had been mortally offended by his refusal to take her name.

'You may say anything to me in front of my family,' he told her. 'Believe me, ma'am, when I wrote to you I had no intention of insulting you.'

A crackle of amusement greeted his words. 'It would take a better man than you to do that, my lad.' Mrs Clewes sipped at her drink with great appreciation. 'I didn't expect you to accept. At least, I hoped you wouldn't.'

Giles stared at her.

'Surprised? I can see you are. You passed the test, my dear. Stiff-necked you may be, but you ain't a hypocrite...'

'I'm afraid I don't follow you, ma'am.'

'Dear me! What an innocent it is! Did it not strike you as strange that I should offer to make you my heir when Leah's children have first call upon my purse?'

'You refer to Lady Wells?'

'She is my niece, Giles, though she don't care to acknowledge it. Still, I suppose that we've all got skeletons in the cupboard.'

The thought of regarding Mrs Clewes as a skeleton tried the composure of her listeners sorely, but no one smiled.

'Then why did you make me such an offer, ma'am?'

'Well, I'll tell you. First of all, I ain't accustomed to being treated like a lady, and you was always kind to me. I'm something of a judge of men, but for all I knew you could have had an eye to the main chance.'

Giles stiffened.

'Now, my lad, don't get upon your high ropes! You wouldn't be the first as has tried to take me in.'

'I'm sure that you are not easily deceived, Mrs Clewes...' Giles could not hide his anger.

'No, I'm not, but I had to be sure...'

'For what reason, ma'am?' India was intrigued.

'Why, my dear, this brother of yours has a fortune in his hands, if he would but make use of it.'

'You are mistaken, madam. I have nothing.'

'And whose fault is that, you stubborn creature? It's high time that you set about making use of these inventions of yours. I've spoken to my man of business and he agrees with me.'

'You are interested in farming methods, Mrs Clewes?' Isham was beginning to enjoy himself.

'Not a bit of it, my lord, but I'm interested in making money. Clewes was my third, and he left me comfortable, but I don't turn up my nose when I see the chance of a profit.'

'Your third?' India was bewildered.

'My third husband, My Lady. I've buried three by now. The first two were no fools but Clewes was a ship's chandler at Bristol. He taught me to use my head.'

'I have no doubt of that,' Isham smiled at her. 'How can Giles help you, ma'am?'

'I want him to be my partner. I can afford to back him for a start and then we'll share the profits. The books won't be no trouble to me. I'll see he don't get into queer street.'

Isham forebore to mention that he had already offered to help Giles. He awaited the outcome of this latest suggestion with interest. If he were any judge the redoubtable Mrs Clewes would have her way no matter what the opposition from her unwilling partner.

Incensed, Giles was about to refuse the offer outright. Then, as he looked at the dumpy little figure looking so out of place in the splendid salon he saw that her bright blue eyes were pleading with him.

'Are we not friends?' she said. 'We deal so well together, you and I. We'll be good partners...'

He swallowed his pride. 'You don't understand, I fear, my dear ma'am. There may be no profits. I should not care to be the cause of you suffering heavy losses.'

'Nay, lad, I'm not a fool. I've gone into the matter, and I've brought some papers with me. You'll look at them, at least? Who knows, with the cost of living rising as it does, this may be my chance to enjoy a comfortable old age...'

Mrs Clewes assumed a mournful expression and seemed to shrink into her chair...the picture of an elderly lady on the verge of poverty.

Isham hid a smile. It was a masterful performance. He was beginning to understand why other offers of help had failed. Giles would not accept them on his own behalf, but when asked to be of service to another human being he might yet be persuaded to agree.

'Allow me to send refreshment into the study for you,' he begged. 'You will both wish to study these papers at your leisure.'

Mrs Clewes struggled out of her chair. 'Give me your arm,' she said to Giles. 'If nothing else you can tell me all your news.'

To refuse her would have been out of the question and with a rueful smile Giles led her from the room.

'Good heavens, what a character!' India was stunned. 'Gina, what do you think of her?'

'I think her a very clever woman. If I'm not mistaken she will twist Giles round her little finger.'

'Nothing is more certain,' Isham agreed. 'And high time too. Newby, has Giles said nothing to you about his friendship with Mrs Clewes?'

'He told me that they played cards together.' Thomas was still in a state of shock. 'But they played for pennies. He had no idea at the time that she had a handsome fortune.'

'Perhaps she is not so very wealthy,' India offered. 'She seemed concerned about her future.'

'A subterfuge, my love. You did not see her carriage or her horses. They are the finest that money can buy.'

'And didn't you notice her necklace, India? I've seen rubies such as those in India. They are worth a king's ransom.' Gina was in a torment, hoping against hope that Giles would seize this opportunity so readily offered to him. She would have given much to have heard the discussion taking place at that very moment in the study.

It lasted for more than an hour, but when Mrs Clewes and Giles rejoined them she knew at once that they had reached agreement.

'Then we must celebrate your partnership.' Isham rang for wine, and Mrs Clewes was happy to accept yet another glass of her favourite 'flesh and blood', which appeared to have not the slightest effect upon her.

'Where are you staying, ma'am?' India asked politely.

'I've put up at the Angel, my lady. It seemed the best that the village has to offer.'

'But shall you be comfortable there? You are welcome to stay with us, if you should care to do so.'

'Bless your kind heart, my dear! I shouldn't like to trouble you…'

'Madam, it would be a pleasure.' Isham was at his most gallant. 'We are sadly short of company at present, and Lady Whitelaw has refused us. My wife would welcome a change of conversation. She does not go out at present.'

'Are you increasing, my lady? No signs yet, I see, and the first months are always the worst.'

'You have children of your own, Mrs Clewes?' India had warmed to the old lady.

'I lost my boys in the wars, my dear. One was with Nelson's navy and the other was with Wellington. Your brother ain't unlike my eldest lad.'

This admission told the company much about the unexpected offer to Giles. He came to her then and sat beside her.

'Will you stay with us?' he begged. 'I'll be happy to fetch your things from the Angel.'

'You are too good!' She patted his hand. 'I won't get in the way if you have visitors.'

'You will be our honoured guest,' Isham said at once. He looked up as Tibbs announced nuncheon, and offered Mrs Clewes his arm to lead her into the dining-room.

India smiled at Gina. 'Anthony is much taken with our guest…'

'I'm not surprised,' came the quick reply. 'She's such a good-hearted, straight-talking woman. I should not care to try to hide a secret from her though.' Gina had noticed how the lady's birdlike glance had rested on each of her companions in turn without appearing to do so. She had studied Gina for somewhat longer than the others, but it was some days before she attempted to engage her in private conversation.

The weather had improved, and now all the talk

was of Lady Eleanor's annual fête at Perceval Hall. It was the highlight of the year for the local villagers and all were welcomed with unlimited food and drink.

Gina paid her promised daily visits to the Grange, but she saw little of Giles. She was aware that he and Mrs Clewes had journeyed into Northampton to sign the partnership agreement. Since then the lady had wasted no time. She produced a short list of possible customers and sent Giles off without delay to demonstrate his inventions.

'Missing him?' she enquired one day. She and Gina were alone in the salon.

'I beg your pardon, ma'am?' Gina was startled out of her usual composure.

'I ain't referring to Mr Newby and well you know it, young woman.' Mrs Clewes gave a comfortable chuckle. 'Did you think I hadn't guessed that you're the one for Giles?'

To her own annoyance Gina felt her colour rising. 'You are quite mistaken, Mrs Clewes. Giles Rushford has no thought of me.'

'Bless my soul, Lady Whitelaw, are you blind? He thinks of nothing else, apart from his inventions. When he enters a room he looks for you, and you won't tell me that you don't feel the same. When you are together there is something in the air which cannot be mistaken.'

Gina shook her head. 'I beg your pardon, ma'am but that must be only in your imagination...'

'I ain't got one, Lady Whitelaw. I look only for hard facts...'

'Well, then, the fact is that I haven't exchanged a word with Giles for days.'

'How can you when he ain't here?'

This reasonable statement brought a smile from Gina.

'That's better!' her inquisitor announced. 'You may think I'm a bossy old woman, too fond of interfering, but I have grown to love that young man. I want only what will make him happy, and I think you feel the same. Isn't that so?'

Gina nodded. She could not trust herself to speak. Her lips were quivering and she was very close to tears.

'There now, don't upset yourself.' The older woman patted her hand. 'Give the man time. You've waited for ten years...another week or two won't make much difference.'

'Oh, he should not have told you...' Gina cried in anguish.

'He didn't. There was no need. I saw that there was something wrong when I first met him. It wasn't on the surface, of course. Giles was always the perfect gentleman, but it ain't natural for a man of thirty to be so grave beyond the likes of other men.'

'His life has not been easy,' Gina ventured.

'No more than many another. There was something else. To me it seemed to be a loss of a more serious kind. Giles had had a crushing blow in his youth. I made it my business to discover what had happened.'

'You couldn't have found it easy.'

'I didn't, but I'm a sharp one, Lady Whitelaw. I

pieced it all together. Then, when I met you, I had
the final piece of the puzzle.'

'Ma'am, you are very shrewd,' Gina blinked away
her tears. 'But now you, you know, with this splendid
offer…this partnership of yours…he could have said
something. Until now, he felt that the difference in
our fortunes was too great.'

'Stiff-necked crittur! Don't despair, my dear. All
will be well. He'll come back with more orders than
he can fulfil…'

'You seem very sure of that.'

'Aren't you? When Giles believes in something he
can be persuasive… Besides, he's working now to
prevent me from sinking into a poverty-stricken old
age.'

She gave a hearty laugh, and after a moment Gina
joined her.

'Mrs Clewes, I believe you are what is known as
a card,' she accused.

'Well, my dear, I've had three husbands. Rushing
on like a bull at a gate ain't always the wisest course.
Sometimes it takes a bit more cunning to set a man
to rights.'

'I'll bear that in mind,' Gina promised. On impulse
she kissed her companion gently on the cheek. 'I admire you so much,' she said.

The small gesture of affection succeeded in putting
her companion quite out of countenance.

'Bless me, ma'am, there's no call for you to make
a fuss of me.' For once Mrs Clewes was flustered,

and Gina saw that her eyes were wet. 'You'll turn me into a watering-pot. I ain't used to it.'

'Then you shall grow used to it,' Gina promised. 'Tell me, ma'am, shall you attend the fête at Perceval Hall?'

Mrs Clewes shook her head. 'T'wouldn't be right, my dear. I'd gather a bigger crowd than the coconut shies...' Something in her voice made Gina look a question. To her horror she saw a look of pain in the older woman's eyes.

'You think I don't know what I look like?' her companion challenged. 'Why, 'tis only you and this family who don't regard me as some kind of freak.'

'No one who knows you could possibly think that, my dear ma'am. You could dine with me before the fête, and we could go together...'

It took some persuasion, but when Gina included the rest of the Isham family and Thomas Newby in her invitation Mrs Clewes agreed at last. She beamed as India joined them.

'Well, my lady, what does the doctor have to say to you?' she asked.

'He's pleased, and so am I now the sickness does not trouble me in a morning. It will be a relief to be able to go about again without the need to rush away at times.'

''Tis a trial, my dear, but worth it in the end. When you have your babe you'll forget the discomfort of these months.'

'I'm sure of it. I feel so well at present.'

'I'm glad to hear it, my dear one.' Isham had entered the room, accompanied by Thomas Newby. 'You will be the belle of the fête and carry off all the prizes.'

'I doubt that, Anthony,' India smiled up at her husband. 'But I shall be glad to see so many of my friends again, and most especially Hester... My cousin was always so full of news. I've missed her since she went to London for her Season.'

'Today I hope to prove a worthy substitute, my darling. I too have news. As we expected, the murder of the Marquis is to be investigated by the Prince Regent's men. They are already in the village.'

'Murder!' Mrs Clewes echoed blankly. 'You've had a murder here in Abbot Quincey?'

'My dear ma'am, don't distress yourself. It happened before you arrived here.' Isham was quick to reassure his guest. 'We had no wish to worry you with the story, though I doubt that you will have heard of the victim...the Marquis of Sywell?'

'Oh, I've heard of him, my lord. Show me someone who don't know of his goings-on. We shouldn't speak ill of the dead, I know, but ain't you well rid of him?'

'That is the general opinion, ma'am, but murder cannot be condoned.'

Unrepentant, Mrs Clewes began to chuckle. 'You may be right. We'd be knee deep in corpses otherwise. I can think of a few prime candidates for murder.'

'That's a blood-thirsty statement if ever I heard one.' Giles stood in the doorway grinning cheerfully at the assembled company. 'I must hope that you don't intend to put it into practice, Mrs Clewes?'

'Don't think I ain't considered it at times,' Mrs Clewes beamed at her new-found partner. 'The trouble is I ain't no shot and I can't run fast enough to catch a villain to strangle him...'

'You can't think how relieved I am to hear it.' Giles was laughing openly as he came to her and took her hands, kissing them both in turn.

'Get on with you! You don't believe a word of it! Now how did you fare, my lad? Do we have an order?'

'We have as many as we can handle, ma'am, with others promised for the future...'

There was a general murmur of congratulation as Giles listed his successes. Gina could only marvel at the change in him. His journey had been long that day but he seemed so fresh, so alert, and so alive.

Suddenly she felt unaccountably nervous. With the coming change in his fortunes Giles would be free to offer for her, but would he do so? The uncertainty was unbearable. At the first opportunity she excused herself and left for Abbot Quincey.

On the journey home she took herself to task. Her departure from the Grange had been sudden to the point of rudeness. What must the Ishams think of her? Good manners indicated that she should have stayed to join in the celebrations. Instead, she recalled muttering something about a forgotten appointment. It was a lame excuse, which would not have deceived a child.

She clenched her hands until the nails dug into her palms. She would make amends when she felt calmer. What she needed was time to think.

Her wish seemed unlikely to be granted.

'You have a visitor, Ma'am,' her butler announced as she walked into the hall.

George again? Gina sighed to herself. She had no wish to listen to her cousin's lamentations at that particular moment.

'You should have denied me,' she snapped more sharply than was her wont. 'You knew that I was not at home.'

'I tried, ma'am, but the gentleman would not be denied. He said that you were to be expected within minutes...'

Was George spying on her? Indignantly, Gina stalked into the salon. Then she stopped. It was Giles who came towards her.

'How did you get here?' she whispered. 'I left you at the Grange...'

'You did indeed! Why did you run away, my darling? You must have known that I would wish to speak to you.'

'How could I know that? You've spent these last few weeks in trying to avoid me...' Gina could not hide her hurt and disappointment.

Giles had come towards her with outstretched arms, but now they fell to his sides. 'I can only ask for your forgiveness, Gina. I've been a selfish fool, thinking only of my pride...my honour. Send me away if you must, but believe me when I tell you that I've come to my senses at last.'

'And what has caused this sea-change, sir?' Gina was determined that she would not make the same mistake again. Giles would not find her ready to fall into his arms.

'Long ago I wanted to offer you the world,' he answered sadly. 'I found I couldn't even give you part of it.'

'And what made you think that I wanted the whole world?' she asked coldly. 'Did I ever ask for it?'

'No, you didn't. I know your loving heart. You would have suffered anything with me.'

'There we differ, Giles. You could not put aside your pride for me.'

'Would you have had me do so? I think I could bear anything but your pity and contempt...'

'Contempt?'

'Oh yes, it might have come to that, my dear. How could I live upon your fortune, knowing that I had done nothing to earn a comfortable life?'

Gina kept her eyes fixed firmly on the carpet. 'You must have ridden hard to outpace my cattle, Giles. Will you allow me to offer you refreshment?'

'Damn the refreshment!' he shouted explosively. 'Why do you think I'm here?'

'I haven't the least idea, but I'd be obliged if you would refrain from swearing...'

'You'd make a saint swear, Gina, and I'm no saint.'

'That I can believe. For once we are in complete agreement...' Gina's shoulders were shaking.

'Why you little minx, you are gammoning me!' Without more ado Giles took her in his arms. 'If you weren't so adorable I swear I'd put you across my knee…'

'You could try,' she agreed. 'Have you forgotten my fearsome reputation?'

'I have forgotten nothing…' As his lips found hers the long years of heartbreak faded as if they had never been. The lovers were transported in an instant back to that terrace in Italy where they had vowed eternal love.

When Giles released her at last, Gina clung to him, half laughing and half crying.

'Can this be true?' she whispered. 'I'd almost given up hope that we'd find happiness together…'

'And I! Why do you think I never married, Gina? I hadn't forgotten my vows to you, although it seemed impossible that we should ever meet again.' His mouth came down on hers once more, urgent, demanding and yet filled with tenderness.

'I'd almost decided to go away again…' she told him breathlessly. 'Oh, my darling, would you have let me leave you if you had not had this offer from Mrs Clewes?'

He shook his head. 'Not this time. I would have found some way, even if it had meant asking you to wait… But it was Mrs Clewes who brought me to my senses.'

'She's been a good friend to you…'

'And to you, my love. That morning in the library she gave me a tongue-lashing which I won't forget.

She has a flaying turn of phrase, you know. I felt lucky to escape with a whole skin. I was given a full account of the failings of my character.'

'Perhaps you'd better tell me,' she teased. 'Before I commit myself to a life of misery with a monster.'

His arms tightened about her, and the smile vanished from his lips. 'I wonder that you can be so generous, Gina. I have behaved in a monstrous way, I know. Mrs Clewes left me in no doubt that in refusing offers of help I was thinking only of myself. She left nothing unspecified, and I had no difficulty in recognising the miserable creature she described.'

Gina kissed his cheek. 'It was all said in love, my dear. She is so fond of you. She thinks only of your happiness.'

'I don't deserve either of you,' he said simply. 'Women are amazing creatures. Who would care for an arrogant, stiff-necked fellow, eaten up with pride, and full of self-pity...?'

She raised her fingers to his lips to hush the bitter words. 'No!' she said. 'I won't have that. We both knew you to be an honourable man, and we understood your need for self-respect. Would Mrs Clewes have offered you this partnership if she had not been sure of your honesty? And would I have loved you for so long?'

With a muffled groan he caught her to him again. 'Darling Gina, what can I say to you? If I have failings, you have none.'

Gina chuckled. 'Don't believe it, my dear one. Impulsive, hot-tempered and impatient of convention—

I am all of these things. Shall I go on, or shall we agree that we are fallible human beings?'

He silenced her by raining kisses on her hair, her cheeks, her eyelids and her throat.

'When can we be wed?' he asked. 'Will you keep me waiting, Gina?'

She looked at him with misty eyes. Then she shook her head. 'It shall be whenever you wish, my love.'

With a shout of joy he seized her hand. 'Come back to the Grange with me. Let us share our happiness with the others. Isham will tell me how to get a special licence, though I expect it will be a shock to him…'

To his surprise, this didn't prove to be the case.

'We wondered only what was taking you so long,' Isham observed with twinkling eyes. 'You've been a shocking slow-coach, my dear chap. Gina might have been carried off by half-a-dozen men.'

'And I was one of them.' Thomas came forward to kiss her hand and congratulate his friend, wishing them both all happiness.

He left them then to return within the hour with Mair and Elspeth.

'Mr Newby is so mysterious,' Elspeth cried as she rushed into the room. 'He's promised us a surprise, but he won't tell us what it is.'

'I can guess,' Mair said quietly as she looked at Gina's face. 'You are going to marry Giles?'

'Bless me if the child ain't a witch!' Mrs Clewes

beamed happily at the assembled company. 'How did you guess, my dear?'

Mair blushed. 'I saw the way he looked at Gina when he thought she wasn't watching.'

Giles gave her a bear hug. 'You are a dangerous woman, Mair. Remind me to be more circumspect when I want to keep a secret.'

This brought a ripple of amusement from his companions.

'A secret?' India teased. 'You have been mooning about like a lovesick calf these many months...'

Giles looked disconcerted for a moment. Then he began to smile.

'Families!' he said in mock disgust. 'Gina, what are we to do with them?'

'For a start you might invite us to your wedding,' India suggested. 'When is it to be?'

'As soon as possible,' he told her promptly. 'Gina has promised not to keep me waiting. All we need now is a special licence...'

'But, my dear brother, what of Mama and Letty? You'll wait until they return from London?'

'And when is that to be?' he asked impatiently.

'They plan to be back in time for the fête at Perceval Hall...'

'But that is weeks away...' he protested.

Gina laid a hand upon his arm. 'India is right, my darling. We can't think only of ourselves. Your mother would be heartbroken not to see you wed... Besides, there are matters to attend... I must buy my gown...'

This wasn't strictly true. Gina had no vanity. She would have been happy to be married in her oldest gown, but she guessed that Giles would accept her explanation.

He did so with a rueful sigh. 'Am I to be outvoted then?'

'Always where the ladies are concerned, my dear fellow...' Isham was smiling broadly. 'Take heart! At least you will not need a special licence. There is time for the banns to be called in the usual way.'

Giles did not argue further, but later, when they were alone, he held Gina to his heart, stroking her hair and kissing her hands by turns.

'You are very silent,' she whispered.

'That's because I can't believe that you are to be mine at last. Do dreams come true, my love?'

'Mine have done so, Giles. I never gave up hope completely, even when it seemed that all hope was gone. You are all I want in life...'

He kissed her then with a passion that spoke of years of longing, and Gina clung to him, offering him her heart and soul.

'I wonder if you have any idea how much I love you?' he said at last. 'I swear I'll make you happy, Gina. Nothing and no one shall ever harm you from now on.'

'Is that a challenge to fate?' Laughing, she threw her arms about his neck. 'Perhaps I should have my fortune told. Do you fear dark forces in my future?'

'Nothing shall ever injure you, my darling...'

'Of course it won't,' she said with happy certainty. 'I have no enemies, my dear.'

Chapter Twelve

Gina spent the following weeks in a daze of happiness. She seemed to be living in another world, where every sense was heightened. Suddenly, she felt like a girl again, for the sensation was familiar from those long-ago days when she and Giles had first fallen in love.

Now she could look forward to daily visits from her lover, smiling at his protestations that every hour spent away from her was like a lifetime. They dined together, walked in the gardens talking eagerly, and learned to know each other again as they renewed their vows of love.

Then he came to her one day, his face alight with joy.

'Mother and Letty have returned,' he said. 'Now, my dearest, we can decide upon our wedding day.' His mouth came down on hers in a passionate kiss.

'Would all your family care to dine here at the Mansion House?' she asked a little breathlessly.

'India and Isham hope that you will dine with them.

She plans to give a small party for you, your mother
and father and your brother and sister, as well as Mair
and Elspeth. Do say you agree! It would give her so
much pleasure.'

'How can I refuse? She is so kind, and my parents
will be delighted.'

It was no more than the truth. After their initial
disappointment when they heard that her cousin was
not to be her choice, George and Eliza Westcott had
rejoiced in Gina's happiness.

'This is a surprise to us, my dear child, but I can't
fault young Rushford,' her father had admitted. 'He's
twice the man his father was, and his life has not been
easy. It was pitiful to see all his efforts go for naught
when Gareth Rushford was alive.'

'Now, Father, don't rake up old scandals,' Eliza
Westcott begged. 'We've always liked Giles. He was
such a merry lad and full of mischief, though there
was no harm in him. I never found him other than
polite. He'll make you happy, Gina, I am sure of it.'

They said as much to Giles, welcoming him as one
of the family without the least trace of self-
consciousness. George Westcott was his own man. He
had done well in business and though he was aware
of the social gulf between the aristocracy and those
in trade, he sensed that times were changing. His wife
was not so sure.

When Gina arrived with the invitation to dine with
Lord and Lady Isham she met with some resistance
from her mother.

'I don't know,' Eliza looked uncomfortable.

'We've been taught to keep our place, and to look up to our betters, not to dine with them.'

'Mother, please! How can you speak of "your betters"? Lord and Lady Isham are human beings like ourselves...no better and no worse... You knew India as a girl. How can you think that she has changed?'

'She's married to Lord Isham now...'

Gina laughed. 'So that is what is worrying you? Believe me, he is nothing like you might imagine. His boon companion at the moment is Mrs Clewes, the widow of a ship's chandler.'

This won a reluctant smile from Mrs Westcott. 'That may be so, but I can't abide that Rushford woman. She never exchanges a civil word with me.'

'I think you'll find she has changed.' Gina gave her mother a wicked look. 'Now I am her dearest Gina, a paragon of all the virtues...'

'Then she doesn't know you, love,' George Westcott chuckled. 'Come wife, your own daughter has a title now. You cannot let her down.'

It was enough to stifle all objections, and later that week, although claiming that she felt like Daniel about to enter the lion's den, Eliza Westcott accompanied her family to the Grange.

Her fears were soon allayed. Isham's easy greeting soon set his visitors at their ease, and Letty and India were their usual charming selves, insisting that Mrs Westcott sat between them.

'You shall not stand on ceremony, ma'am,' India said prettily. 'You've known us all our lives. May I make you known to our dear Lucia, the Dowager Lady Isham?'

Mrs Westcott nodded shyly.

'And here is Mrs Clewes, a friend of ours, as is Mr Newby. My mother you know already as a neighbour.'

'How pleased you must be to have dear Gina home again,' Mrs Rushford gushed. 'And now to hear this happy news! I declare that I am over the moon about it...'

Eliza viewed the speaker with a sardonic eye. She was under no illusions. Gina's fortune had brought about this startling change in Mrs Rushford. Without it the woman would not have given her the time of day.

Mrs Rushford noticed nothing amiss. 'Two of my children to be wed this year!' she continued in sentimental tones. 'I hope that you won't consider a double wedding, Gina? A bride's day should be hers alone.'

'We haven't decided yet,' Gina said truthfully.

'Well, time enough, my dear. You will wish to go to London for your bride-clothes. If you wish it I will give you an introduction to Madame Félice... She has provided Letty's trousseau.'

Gina laughed. 'I thank you, ma'am, but I think not. I am not quite her style...'

'Perhaps not!' Mrs Rushford subjected her future daughter-in-law to a searching inspection. 'Letty is, after all, a beauty...not that you do not always look charmingly, Gina, though you might consider something a little more modish.'

Gina hid a smile. Mrs Rushford's penchant for extravagant trimmings was well known. She could see no virtue in understated elegance. It had escaped her notice that Gina's shawl of the finest Norwich silk had cost the best part of fifty guineas.

'Well, Mama, at least you and Letty are prepared for all occasions.' India hastened to divert her mother's attention from Gina. She had caught her friend's eye and she realised that Gina was struggling to keep her countenance. 'I never saw so many packages in my life...'

'The shopping was tiring,' Mrs Rushford admitted grandly. 'You must blame Isham, my dear India. He insisted that Letty must have the best of everything.'

Letty shot an anxious glance at her brother-in-law. 'But not *quite* so much of everything,' she said in a low voice. 'Oh, Anthony, I am so sorry. I couldn't stop her. We shall be forever in your debt.'

Isham drew her into the window embrasure. 'Not nearly so much as I am in yours, Letty. Your mother was filling India's head with foolish fancies. Had you not taken her away I should have been forced to speak severely. That would have upset my darling wife.'

'India looks so much better now. Gina's company has been good for her, I think.'

'That's true! And now, with the two weddings to occupy your mother's mind, India will get some peace. When does Oliver arrive?'

'In time for the fête at Perceval Hall, I hope.' Letty

was radiant at the prospect of seeing her betrothed
again. 'When I wrote I warned him of the date, so I
expect him by Thursday at the latest. The fête is on
the eighteenth, is it not?'

'It is. That is Friday of next week. I had best rally
the troops. Lady Eleanor will be hoping for a good
attendance…'

Mrs Rushford caught his last words. She leaned
back in her chair with a gracious smile. 'My sister's
gatherings are *always* well attended,' she announced.
'One is often surprised by some of the guests, but
times are changing, as we all know, and the villagers
enjoy the opportunity to mingle with their betters.'
She leaned towards the Westcotts and for an awful
moment India feared another gaffe. She was saved
when dinner was announced.

Local gossip would prove to be the safest subject
at the dinner table, she decided, but none of her guests
could throw any further light upon the mysterious
murder of the Marquis.

'But what of the Prince's men?' Gina was puzzled.
'Have they discovered nothing?'

'Not yet, so I understand.' Isham turned to Mr
Westcott. 'What is your opinion, sir?'

'I won't speculate, my lord. The facts are few, it
seems, in spite of the enquiries made throughout the
village. Burneck, the single remaining servant at
Steepwood Abbey, is thought to know far more than
he'll admit. Pressure may be brought to bear on
him… Otherwise he'll keep his secret.'

'Truth will out!' Mrs Clewes said cheerfully. 'I confess I'd like to know before I leave for Bristol…'

There was a general outcry.

'Ma'am, you don't think of leaving us yet?' India was dismayed. 'Won't you attend the fête?'

'I'd love to,' Mrs Clewes said promptly. 'But it's my feet, my dear. I ain't in the way of being able to walk about so much.'

'Then you shan't do so, my dear ma'am.' Isham grinned at her. 'If you'll accept the offer of a bath-chair I shall challenge you to a duel at the coconut shies…'

'Done! What is your wager, sir?'

'If you lose we hold you prisoner here for the rest of the summer…' He gave her a conspiratorial wink.

'Bless me, my lord, you'll have me ruined with this life of luxury.' Mrs Clewes beamed her pleasure at the invitation. 'I'll be naught but a parasite…'

'No, ma'am, I have ulterior motives. Giles tells me that you like a game of cards. With Mrs Rushford we shall make up a useful foursome…' Isham gave her a long look, and Mrs Clewes was quick to understand. With her support India would have some protection from her mother's gloomy prognostications.

'I play for pennies, sir, but there, you won't mind that. Besides, I don't intend to lose the wager…if this fine weather holds, which I make no doubt it will.'

She was right, and on the following Friday the entire party joined the queue of carriages at the entrance to Perceval Hall.

Mrs Rushford was in the best of humours. The long wait did not trouble her in the least as she nodded and smiled at her acquaintances.

'July is just the best of months for a function of this kind,' she said approvingly. 'With the Season over, so many of our friends are returned to the country. I declare, we shall never be at home. Since the announcement of your betrothal appeared in the London papers, Giles, we've had kind messages and invitations by every post.'

The villagers too were pressing close to the open carriage, offering their good wishes to the future bridegroom. India glanced at him and then at her sister.

'Dear Giles!' she said softly. 'He looks as radiant as any bride. Is it not wonderful?'

Letty pressed her hand, but her gaze was fixed on Oliver. 'We are all so lucky, India. A year ago we could not have imagined that we should be here, within weeks of our marriages to those we love so much.'

India looked at the sea of faces that surrounded her. 'Your weddings will be well attended, love. The news has spread like wildfire since the first of the banns was called.'

'I can't believe it yet,' Letty's eyes were dreamy. 'Oh, look! There is Gina with the girls…'

Giles was out of the carriage in an instant, though the procession was already beginning to move. Minutes later he handed Gina down, tucking her hand beneath his arm.

'Let me make you known to my aunt and uncle, my darling…' He glanced back to see his mother deep in conversation with one of her bosom bows.

Mrs Rushford had prepared her story carefully, stressing Gina's title, hinting at her fortune, and glossing over the previous background and unfortunate antecedents of her future daughter-in-law.

'Mother will be fully occupied for the day,' he predicted as they approached Sir James and Lady Perceval. 'Later we'll slip away somewhere on our own.'

Gina looked up at him with laughing eyes. 'And what of Mair and Elspeth?' she asked. 'I have certain responsibilities, my dear.'

'Nonsense!' he said fondly. 'Look at them! They have already found their friends…'

It was true. Mair and Elspeth were surrounded by a group of girls, many of whom attended Mrs Guarding's Academy, and included the Vicar's younger daughters, Frederica and Henrietta.

Gina was welcomed kindly by Sir James and Lady Perceval.

'Shall you care to attend the running races?' Lady Eleanor enquired. 'They are always well supported, and the Vicar will present the prizes…'

Gina and Giles strolled off in company with their host and hostess and for the next hour they were fully occupied in clapping home the various contestants. There was keen competition among the villagers for the chance to win a new smock for the men, and lengths of material and ribbons for the girls.

Giles looked round as the smell of roasting meat drifted across the lawns.

'I'm starving,' he announced 'Will the ox be ready, Aunt?'

'I hope so, Giles. The fire was lit at first light yesterday. Gina must be hungry too. Will you take her over to the tables?' She turned to Gina. 'In the ordinary way we should dine *en famille*, my dear, but today is open house, and all are welcome to as much as they can eat and drink. We don't stand on ceremony.'

Gina looked at the milling crowds. 'You are generous, ma'am.' She twinkled at her hostess. 'Your guests appear to be taking full advantage.'

'I'm glad of it,' her ladyship said simply. 'Times have been hard for everyone in these past years and we have felt so helpless. This is the least that we can do... Now off you go, and enjoy yourselves...'

'Your aunt feels strongly for the local people,' Gina observed as they strolled away. 'My mother and father have the highest praise for her.'

'She deserves it, Gina. Had Steepwood Abbey not have been lost to the Marquis, it would have been the Earl of Yardley who looked to the welfare of the villagers. Now those duties have fallen upon my aunts and both my uncles.'

'I'm glad that your uncle William is to marry us,' she told him shyly. 'Are you happy with this notion of a double wedding?'

For answer he slipped an arm about her waist and held her close. 'Can you doubt it? I'd have agreed to anything, my love, just so long as you become my bride.'

Gina blushed. 'People are looking at us, Giles.'

'Let them look!' He helped her to a generous portion of roast meat. 'I think we need not stay for long. No one will miss us in this crush if we slip away.'

'First I must find the girls and let them know. They will wonder if we are nowhere to be found.'

'Will they?' he teased. 'You forget, my darling, Mair and Elspeth are almost women grown, and Mair, in particular, soon found out our secret.'

'Even so, I don't wish to desert them.' Gina looked about her. 'I don't see them anywhere, do you?'

'Were they not with Frederica? She is with her sister, over there. Shall I ask for them?'

As he moved over to speak to the girls, Gina followed him.

'Why, Mr Rushford, we all went to see the hermit's grotto in the grounds,' Frederica told him. 'Mr Westcott sent us back to find some of our friends. He felt that they would like to see it...'

Gina's blood turned to ice in her veins. 'Mr Westcott? Are you speaking of my father?'

She knew the answer before the girls replied. 'No, ma'am,' Henrietta said politely. 'It was Mr Samuel Westcott who mentioned the grotto to us...'

'There now, you have no further need to worry...' Giles turned to Gina, only to find that her face was deathly pale.

'Where...where is this grotto?' she choked out.

'Why, ma'am, it is along that path...' The girls
were startled by the urgency in Gina's voice.

'Giles, will you get my father?' Gina threw the
words at him as she sped away. She was ploughing
through mire on leaden feet, unable to gain speed.
Pray heaven that she was not too late. Ignoring the
stitch in her side, she hurried on, until the shell-lined
grotto came into view.

Now common-sense returned. She slowed, approaching the grotto from the side. Hopefully, nothing
untoward had happened. Peering into the gloom, all
she could see was the vast bulk of her uncle. He
seemed to be pleading with Elspeth.

'Were you hoping to see the hermit?' he asked. 'He
won't appear if there are two of you.'

'I don't believe that there is a hermit,' Elspeth told
him scornfully. 'How would he live here in the winter? This place is cold and damp.'

'Then fetch Gina,' he suggested. 'She will tell you
the truth of it. Mair and I will wait for you...'

'I think not!' Gina stepped into the cavern. 'Mair,
you and Elspeth must return to others...'

'But, Gina, this place is fascinating,' Elspeth stared
at her. 'Just look at all the shells! It must have taken
years to build them into the walls...'

'Do as I say!' Gina's voice was verging on hys-
teria. The girls did not argue further. They hurried
away.

Samuel Westcott turned towards her, his small eyes
alive with malice. 'Gina to the rescue?' he jeered.
'You'll do instead, my dear.'

Gina faced him squarely. 'I warned you, uncle,' she said quietly. 'This time you have gone too far...'

He laughed in her face. 'For showing the girls a grotto? It seems innocent enough to me...'

Gina stood her ground. 'I know you all too well,' she replied. 'You were trying to get rid of Elspeth. What would have happened had I not arrived?'

'Shall I show you, Gina?' He waddled towards her then, his fat hands reaching out for her. 'Are you to be wed? I'll have you first, you vixen.' Then he was upon her, tearing at her gown. 'I've waited long enough for this...'

Gina screamed as he ripped her bodice open to the waist. His hands were everywhere, fondling her breasts, sliding over her hips, and tugging at her skirts.

'Don't fight me!' he said thickly. 'You know it's what you want. How long is it since a man has bedded you?'

Gina didn't answer him. With a sigh she let herself grow limp within his grasp. To struggle would be useless. He was much too strong for her, but she might outwit him with guile.

'Fainted, have you?' he grunted. 'Pity! I wanted you to know exactly what I'm going to do to you...'

Gina thought quickly. Her thin kid slippers were too soft to hurt him if she kicked out, and he was holding her too close for her to raise a knee and sink it into that amorphous mass of flesh.

He shook her roughly, and when she didn't respond

he loosened his grip just enough for Gina to bend her arm. Then she drove her elbow into his stomach.

He doubled up with a gasp. He was standing between her and the narrow entrance to the grotto, but when she tried to push past him, his hand shot out and gripped her waist. Gina bent her head and tried to bite him, but he wound his fingers into her hair and pulled until the pain was unbearable.

'Still up to your old tricks, my girl? I've owed you something for these many years. Now It's time to pay…'

'Let me go!' she cried. 'Giles is following me…'

'Giles is following me!' he mimicked. 'He ain't here yet, my dear. Thought you'd trick me, didn't you, by making up to George? But I know you, you bitch! George ain't good enough for you. Will Rushford want my leavings…?'

Her situation was hopeless, but Gina fought him tooth and nail, clawing at his face and drawing blood.

With a curse he slapped her hard across the head, knocking her to the ground. Then he threw himself upon her, fumbling at her skirts.

Gina writhed beneath him, but she felt that she was suffocating. Nausea overcame her at the smell of his stale sweat, but the lascivious mouth came ever closer to her own.

Then, suddenly, the weight was gone and she heard a crash as her uncle was thrown bodily across the floor of the cave to land against the stone wall.

Giles was upon him in an instant, his hands around the bull neck. He hadn't uttered a word and somehow

his silence was more terrible than any shouts of outrage.

Gina watched in horror as Samuel Westcott's feet
began to drum upon the ground.

'No!' she cried. 'Don't kill him! He isn't worth a
hanging!'

Giles seemed not to have heard her as she struggled
painfully to her feet.

'Let him go, I beg of you!' Her hands were upon
her lover's shoulders, but he didn't look at her.

Then she was gently set aside, as her father took
her place. By exerting all his strength he broke the
death grip which Giles had upon his brother.

'Gina is right,' he said quietly. 'This animal isn't
worth a hanging. He won't trouble you again. I'll
make sure of that.' He looked in disgust at the cow-
ering man upon the ground.

'Get out!' he said in icy tones. 'You are no kin of
mine. Show your face in Abbot Quincey ever again
and I'll destroy you. Don't forget that I own most of
your London business...'

With a speed surprising in so large a man, Samuel
Westcott scuttled away.

Gina was shaking uncontrollably. Only the fact that
Giles was holding her enabled her to stand upright.

'Come out into the light,' he urged gently. 'Shall I
carry you, my love?'

'Just give me a moment,' she whispered. 'I shall
be perfectly all right.' Weakly, she tried to draw together the edges of her gown, which was ripped from

bodice to hemline. 'It's ruined!' she said inconsequentially. Then she burst into tears.

'My dear child!' Her father was still deeply shocked. 'Let me take you home... You need to rest...'

'Sir, with respect, I will take Gina home. If you'd be good enough to find the girls and follow us...?'

'No!' Gina wiped away her tears. 'No one must ever know what has happened here. Let the girls stay... I want to change before I see them.'

'Then I'll come with you to the Mansion House,' her father said firmly. 'I have much to say to you...' His eyes were so sad that Gina reached out to him.

'How much did you hear?' she asked.

'Enough to know the answers to much that has puzzled me for years. Why did you not tell me, Gina?'

'I couldn't!' she confessed. 'He is your own brother. Would you have believed me?'

'I no longer have a brother,' he said sternly. 'Was this why you ran away from us, my dear?'

She nodded, but she could not trust herself to give him the details of those far-off attempts upon her virtue.

'I've been a fool,' George Westcott said. 'The truth has been staring me in the face for years. Other incidents have been reported to me. I didn't believe any of the complaints, putting them down to envy and illwill.'

'It's over now,' she comforted. 'You know the truth about him. He will not face you ever again.'

Gina turned to Giles. 'Will you take me home, my darling?'

Wordlessly, he put his arm about her and held her close, burying his face in her hair.

'I might have been too late,' he whispered. 'When you were most in need of me I wasn't there... Oh, my dear, why did you decide to confront your uncle on your own?'

'I didn't think,' she told him frankly. 'When I heard that he was alone with Mair and Elspeth I forgot the danger. I'd fought him off before, you know.'

Giles held her away from him and looked down at the vivid little face.

'What am I to do with you, my love? Will you still be battling on when we are old and grey, forgetting that you have a husband to take care of you?'

'I doubt that I shall forget my husband...' Gina raised her face to his, reaching up to trace the outlines of his mobile mouth with her fingertips. 'You are dearer to me than life itself...'

He kissed her then, and the world was lost to them as they pledged their love in a passionate embrace.

Gina released herself at last, and, blushing, she looked round for her father. Discreetly, George Westcott had disappeared.

'We had best go before we are discovered.' Gina managed a faint smile. 'I am in no fit state to greet the world at present.'

Giles grinned at her. 'Fear not! Our friends will think only that my passion got the better of me...'

'Why, Giles, that would cause a scandal!'

'And shall you care, my love? What happened to the woman who had no regard for conventions?'

'I intend to change when we are married,' she said demurely.

'God forbid!' Giles looked at her in mock horror. 'What shall I do for entertainment...?'

'I'm sure you'll think of something...' With a wicked smile Gina whisked away from him and slipped through the entrance to the grotto.

As Gina had hoped, no breath of scandal was ever attached to the sudden departure of Samuel Westcott from Abbot Quincey. He'd given pressure of business as his excuse, and this was generally accepted. George gave a sigh of relief and announced his intention to marry Ellie without delay, since Gina was already spoken for and his father could no longer pressure him.

Gina herself had soon recovered from her ordeal. As her wedding day approached she was fully occupied in making arrangements for Mair and Elspeth to stay with India for the duration of her honeymoon.

'Are you quite sure?' she asked anxiously. 'The girls would be happy to visit their relations in Scotland.'

'Oh, let us have them,' India begged. 'It is such fun to have the young about the place...'

'But you say that about the old, my dear. What of Mrs Clewes?'

'Gina, she is a boon! My mother is now fully occupied. Mrs Clewes is a marvel. Mama has not even interfered in the arrangements for your wedding...'

'Still playing cards?' Gina twinkled at her friend.

'That, and gossip, my dear. Anthony is off on some mysterious errand at this very moment. He won't get through the doorway before they pounce on him...'

There was much truth in her remarks, but Lord Isham was looking thoughtful as he entered the room.

'Anthony, what is it?' India's eyes searched her husband's face. 'Do you bring us news?'

'I do.' Isham sat down by her and took her hand. 'I'm sure it will delight you. I hear that there is now a real possibility that the Earl of Yardley will regain possession of the Abbey.'

There was a general murmur of approval.

'Is it certain?' Giles said doubtfully. 'I thought there was at present no visible owner...'

'It won't happen overnight,' Isham agreed. 'But, as you know, Yardley was in the process of negotiating to buy it back from Sywell, though the sale was not confirmed before the Marquis died.'

'But what of the Marchioness? Suppose she reappears?' India looked concerned.

'Yardley has considered that possibility. If his lands are returned to him and she returns he has promised that she will be cared for, both financially and in every other way.'

'How like him!' India's face was alight with pleasure. 'Oh, my dear, just think what it will mean to the local people to have Yardley back again! How soon shall we be certain?'

'Not before November, I imagine. There are the legalities to consider, and these matters take time. Representations have been made to the authorities.'

Isham saw that Mrs Clewes was looking puzzled. 'Ma'am?'

'I was just wondering, My Lord...who is the Earl of Yardley? I have not heard of him...'

Mrs Rushford gave a gusty sigh. 'My dear Madam, the Earls of Yardley were the greatest landowners in this district. They have owned Steepwood Abbey for generations, that is, until some twenty years ago, when the place was gambled away to Sywell.'

'All of it?' Thomas Newby was incredulous. 'The Earl could not have been in his right mind...'

'He wasn't!' Giles said bluntly. 'Mother, you know the story better than any of us. Won't you explain?'

Delighted to be the centre of attention, Isabel Rushford settled back in her chair. 'It started with a scandal,' she said with relish. 'Viscount Angmering, Yardley's eldest son, returned from his Grand Tour with some young French aristocrat. The Earl refused his consent to the marriage because the girl was a Catholic. When Angmering refused to give her up his father threw him off.'

Mrs Clewes pursed her lips in disapproval. 'I'd have stood by my child no matter what he'd done,' she announced.

'And so would I!' India said warmly. 'Up to and including murder!'

'Women!' Isham shook his head at them but he was smiling. 'Isabel, will you go on?'

'Well, the news came from France that Angmering had been killed in a bread riot. His father was distraught, blaming himself for banishing his heir. The Earl went up to town and started drinking. Somehow he found himself in Sywell's company at one of the gambling clubs. That night he lost everything at the tables—the Abbey, his lands, the house in town and his estates in the north of England. Then he shot himself...'

India looked at her mother in concern. Mrs Rushford was pale and trembling. Her story was all too close to home. To a lesser extent Gareth Rushford had done the same.

Isham offered her a glass of wine, but she waved it away, determined to continue her story. 'Thomas Cleeve is the present Earl. He inherited after the death of the Earl and Viscount Angmering. He's tried for years to buy back Steepwood Abbey.'

'He's wealthy, then?' Mrs Clewes was fascinated.

'He made his fortune in India, so I understand. I never heard scandal of him. What a boon it would be to have the family back at Steepwood Abbey...'

'Most certainly.' Isham looked round at the assembled company. 'Yardley takes his responsibilities seriously. Already he has paid off monies owed to the local tradesmen, but we must be patient. Now it has been discovered that Sywell gained the Abbey by murdering the old Earl, rather than honourably, if all goes well the present Earl's heritage will be restored to him before the year's end.'

'And then?' Giles questioned.

'Why, then the local people may look forward to better times. There will be work for all. Yardley intends to restore the Abbey and improve his lands. He speaks of repairing the workers' cottages, hedging, ditching, rotation of crops, and general profitability.'

Giles did not attempt to hide his pleasure. 'And the tenant farmers on his land? Are they to get some help?'

'With your assistance, Giles. The Earl is hoping to see you soon. He intends to make full use of your inventions.'

'Then we must invite him to our wedding.' Gina's smile was radiant. 'Will he come, do you suppose?'

'I don't doubt it, Gina.'

Isabel Rushford touched a handkerchief to her eyes. 'Just two more days and my children will be gone from me,' she mourned. 'What it is to be old and lonely…!'

'You will be much in need of company,' Isham agreed. 'What do you say to a trip to Brighton with Mrs Clewes? Many of your bosom bows will be there for the Prince's stay. He will be happy to make your acquaintance…'

Mrs Rushford brightened at once. 'Do you say that we shall be received at the Pavillion by the Prince himself? That is something I have dreamed of. We shall meet the highest in the land…and the shops…! Oh, my dears, if my health will stand it, I shall be happy to undertake the journey.' Then she bethought herself of her proposed companion. 'Mrs Clewes may not wish to go…' she said sadly.

'Whyever not?' the lady replied. Earlier she had been primed by Isham, who assured her that the Prince was anxious to make her acquaintance. Isham was on safe ground. He had already entertained the Prince with stories of the redoubtable widow from Bristol, and he knew that Mrs Clewes was quite in the Regent's style.

'Then if you insist…!' Mrs Rushford allowed herself to be persuaded into undertaking an extravagant holiday at her son-in-law's expense.

'This is such a happy time for all of us,' she said brightly.

That sentiment was echoed in many a heart.

On the day of the wedding the sun shone upon both brides. They arrived together at the church in Abbot Quincey, with Letty upon Isham's arm and Gina with her father.

The crowds overflowed into the churchyard, commenting with awed approval upon the gowns, the bonnets, the flowers, and the handsome appearance of the guests.

Gina was unaware of it. She had dressed with care that morning in an elegant gown of finest ivory silk beneath a tunic of spider lace in the same shade. A tiny head-dress sat upon her shining hair, trimmed only with a few pearls.

She would never outshine the beautiful Letty, and she had no intention of doing so. The girl beside her was a vision of loveliness in her bridal gown, but the onlookers could not decide which of the two looked the happier.

For Gina there was only Giles, waiting for her at the altar steps. She looked long into his eyes, and saw there a man restored to love and life, waiting to claim her as his bride.

When they made their vows she found that she was trembling, but he gave her hand a reassuring squeeze, and she smiled up at him with misty eyes.

The rest of the day had a dreamlike quality and later she had little recollection of the celebrations, the sumptuous wedding breakfast at Perceval Hall, and the congratulations of her friends.

Giles stole her away at last, laughing as he hurried her to the waiting carriage.

'I thought we'd never get away,' he said, as he slipped his arm about her waist. 'Now I can kiss you as I've longed to do all day, my darling wife.'

Gina lifted her face to his. 'Is it really true?' she asked in wonder. 'I can't believe that we are wed at last.'

'Why, Mrs Rushford, I am deeply shocked! Here we are, about to live together for the next fifty years or so, and you doubt that we are wed?'

Gina hid her face in his coat. She was blushing deeply. 'Don't tease!' she whispered. 'Giles, I have not told you this before, but I have never been a wife in the true sense.'

He looked down at her and his eyes were filled with tenderness. 'I guessed as much, my dear one. You

have never lost that look of innocence you had when
I first met you.'

'Then I did not deceive you?'

'Never, Gina!' His lips found hers in a lingering
kiss, and Gina forgot the wasted years in an overwhelming sense of rapture. She threw her arms about
his neck, murmuring inarticulate words.

His heart beat strongly against her own and she
revelled in the old familiar sensation of his closeness,
his strength, and the delicious feeling of being pro-
tected from all harm.

'I love you so,' she whispered.

'Then show me!' he demanded as he nibbled gently
at her ear.

Gina threw all decorum to the winds as she cupped
his face within her hands and drew it down to hers.
She teased him then with feather-light caresses, tracing the curve of his eyebrows with her fingertips,
dropping kisses upon his eyelids, and finally seeking
his mouth.

The strength of his response left her breathless, but
she looked at him with perfect trust. 'I want you, my
love,' she said. 'When you make me your wife in
truth, my happiness will be complete.'

Giles kissed her again, and in that kiss there was
the promise of a lifetime of devotion.

*   *   *   *   *

An Unlikely Suitor
by
Nicola Cornick

Nicola Cornick is passionate about many things: her country cottage and its garden, her two small cats, her husband and her writing, though not necessarily in that order! She has always been fascinated by history, both as her chosen subject at university and subsequently as an engrossing hobby. She works as a university administrator and finds her writing the perfect antidote to the demands of life in a busy office.

Chapter One

September 1812

'Just how many pairs of gloves does a lady need, Lavender?' Caroline Brabant asked her sister-in-law.

The two of them were sitting in the library at Hewly Manor, a long elegant room lined with walnut bookshelves that the Admiral, Lavender's father, had stocked with all manner of fascinating collections from his travels abroad. Caroline was reclining on the sofa and Lavender had just finished reading aloud to her from *Sense and Sensibility,* a novel of manners and morals that they were both enjoying.

Lavender looked up from the book. Caroline's query sounded idle but Lavender knew that she seldom asked pointless questions. Nor, being a lady of quality, did Caroline need Lavender's advice on matters of elegance. There had to be another reason for the question…

'I am not sure, Caro,' she began carefully. 'Three or four, perhaps? A best and second best pair and a pair for evenings—'

Caroline sighed and put aside her magazine. 'Hammonds the drapers must find you quite their best customer then,' she observed gently, 'for by my calculations, you have bought no less than six pairs of gloves in the last quarter alone!'

Lavender avoided her eyes. Caroline was disconcertingly shrewd.

'If not gloves then bonnets, scarves or materials...' Caroline was saying now. 'Have all your clothes worn out at the same time, Lavender?'

Lavender jumped up and crossed to the library window. Dusk was falling across Hewly Manor gardens and it was time to light the candles. She kept her back to Caroline and tried to speak casually.

'You know how it may be, Caro...' She was proud of the lightness of her tone. 'Sometimes everything seems to need replacing at once! Now that it is autumn again I find I have a need for some new items, warmer clothes to suit the weather—' She broke off, aware that she was starting to ramble and sure that she could feel Caroline's intent gaze riveted on the back of her head. Usually she was delighted to have Caroline's companionship and felt that her brother Lewis could not have made a better match. Usually, but not today. Not when Caroline was in the kind of mood to press her on her new-found interest in drapery.

'I think I shall take a walk before dark,' she said hastily, feeling the need to escape Caroline's shrewd eye. 'I have the headache and a brisk stroll around the gardens may help...'

Caroline picked up the needlework that lay beside her on the rose brocade sofa. 'Very well. I shall not offer to accompany you, for I find I tire so easily these days.' She tilted her head to consider the baby clothes that she was embroidering with such enviable skill. 'I believe I shall be in need of some more thread tomorrow. Perhaps you would be so good as to walk into Abbot Quincey and purchase some for me, Lavender?'

Lavender shot her a suspicious look, but Caroline's face was serene as she bent over her work. Now that she was increasing, there was an air of contentment about her that Lavender thought was even more marked than in the first days of her marriage to Lewis. Unfortunately for Lavender, Caroline's pregnancy had affected neither the quickness of her mind nor her powers of observation.

Lavender closed the library door softly behind her. She could hear a bell ringing in the depths of the house as Caroline called for the candles to be lit, and a housemaid scurried out of the servants' quarters, dropped Lavender a curtsey and gave her a smile, before hastening to do the mistress's bidding.

Lavender had been quick to see that all the servants liked Caroline. There was such an air of peace about Hewly these days, though Caroline joked that all that would be ruined once the baby was born.

Lavender went to fetch her coat and boots from the garden room. The house was spick and span, though giving the impression of being a little frayed at the edges. There was little spare money for refurbishment, for Lewis was ploughing it all back into the estate in order to repair the neglect of the last few years. Lavender did not mind—she found Hewly's worn elegance comforting and tasteful, and besides, she knew that whilst they were still in mourning for her father it would not be appropriate to begin a major restoration. Lewis had hinted that they might go up to Town the following autumn, but Lavender hoped that they would not. She had endured one tedious London Season four years before and had no wish to be bored by another. Yet it did raise the spectre of her future, for now that Lewis was married and with a family on the way she did not wish to hang on his coat-tails. Neither he nor Caroline would ever give the impression that she was an unwelcome third, but even so…

Lavender went out of the front door and paused for a moment on the gravel path, trying to decide which way to go. Before her, the formal parterre led to the walled gardens and beyond that to the orchard. She could see the moon rising through the branches of the apple trees. She drew on one of the many pairs of gloves that Caroline had referred to, and started to walk along the path.

Perhaps, Lavender thought as she walked, she could become one of those redoubtable maiden aunts upon whom every family depended. As Lewis and Caroline's brood expanded she could be an additional nursery nurse and governess, indispensable to servants and family alike. Everyone would remark on how good she was with the children and how they doted on her. As she grew older she could become eccentric, buy herself a cottage and keep cats. She would have her painting and her botany…

Lavender's pace slowed. The truth was that the thought left her with a hollow feeling somewhere inside her. She had every intention of being a devoted aunt to Lewis and Caroline's children, but what if she wished for a family of her own? She was unhappily aware that at three and twenty she was well past marriageable age and that she had never met a man who made her pulse race. Well, if she were honest, she had met one, and that was the root of the whole trouble…

She reached the orchard and stopped for a moment whilst the wind snatched the fallen leaves from the path and whirled them around her. The sky was a clear, dark blue and it promised to be a chilly night. It was September, one of Lavender's favourite months, but already she could feel the year turning, echoing her own feeling of passing time.

On impulse she let herself out through the door in the wall and found herself in the cobbled street that led from the Manor down to the Steep River, past the Guarding Academy. She had not intended to walk far, but now that darkness was falling a sudden inclination took her down to the water, along the Abbey wall and to the edge of the woods. In the daylight Lavender wandered far and wide with no concerns for distance or safety but it was not so sensible to do so at night. She had heard that there were poachers in the woods, and whilst she thought they would not hurt her, it was best not to be seen. Lavender shivered a little in the sharp breeze. She had seen and heard plenty of odd things in the time that she had lived in Steep Abbot, but she never told a soul...

She passed the Guarding Academy and smiled a little as she heard the faint sound of singing on the air. Tonight must be choir practice. The music followed her down to the river, where it was lost amongst the noise of the tumbling water. The moon was a silver disc on the rippling surface and the wind hummed in the trees.

There was a short cut along the edge of the woods back to the Manor gardens, a little path that was bordered on one side by a stone wall and had the whispering trees on the other. It was only a step back to the Hewly estate, but for some reason Lavender felt unexpectedly nervous. Telling herself that it was hunger and not fear that rumbled in her stomach, she stepped out boldly.

She had gone only four paces when she almost stumbled over a large sack that was lying at the side of the path. She looked around hastily, but there was no one in sight. The shadows were thick beneath the trees and the leaves rustled. She could still hear the sound of the river running, for it was only a few yards behind her.

Gooseflesh crept along Lavender's skin. She could not decide what to do. She could retrace her steps and go home the way she had come, or she could pass by, pretending that she had noticed nothing. That was surely better than opening the sack and discovering some choice piece of game that a poacher was about to reclaim. Then she thought she heard a sound from inside the bag and in spite of her better judgement, she bent down. She had just stretched her hand towards it, when the whole sack shifted of its own accord, as though possessed. Lavender let out an involuntary scream.

Immediately there was a step behind her on the path and before she could even stand up, someone grabbed her arm and spun her round.

Lavender found herself in the rough embrace of someone who clearly wished to prevent her from screaming again. One of his arms was tight about her

waist and the coarse material of his coat scored her
cheek. He was very tall. And broad. Her hands were
pressed against his chest and she was conscious of
the hard muscle beneath her fingers and the steady
beat of his heart.

Curiously this discovery led Lavender to become
acutely aware of the information her senses were pro-
viding. She could hear the rustle of the trees mingled
with her assailant's breathing, feel the cold touch of
the breeze and the warmth of his skin as he bent his
head and his cheek brushed her hair. And he smelled
wonderful, a mixture of cold air and the faint tang
of citrus. It was this last impression that somehow
weakened her and she felt her legs tremble and his
arm tighten about her in response.

'Mr Hammond!'

Lavender could not have said how she knew his
identity but she had no doubts at all, and the words
were out before she even had time to think. She
pushed a little shakily against the man's chest and he
let go of her at once, stepping back so that he was
facing her, a few steps away.

'Miss Brabant!' Barnabas Hammond's voice was
as slow and thoughtful as she remembered, but
warmed now by an amusement that Lavender felt
was surely out of place. She had always liked the
way that Barney spoke, with perfect courtesy but no
hint of deference. His father was always obsequious
towards his upper-class clients in the draper's shop,

and Lavender found this grated on her, particularly when she had seen his dismissive scorn towards the poorer customers. She had observed that Barney always treated everybody in exactly the same way and had liked him for it.

Now, however, she felt oddly at a loss, as though the clear definition of their relationship had somehow been blurred. He was a shopkeeper's son and she was an admiral's daughter, and with the shop counter between them she had allowed herself to dream a little. He might always speak to everyone in the same manner, but there was a decided hint of warmth when he addressed her, an admiration in his eyes that had made her heart beat a little faster. Then he had been so kind to her when her father had died. He scarcely knew her and yet his words of comfort had been so perceptive.

Caroline was right—she had been calling in at the draper's shop more often of late, contriving an order of ribbons here, a pair of gloves there. She blushed to think of it now. She had thought... But here her thoughts became at the best confused. Was she a snob, aware of her status and the relative inferiority of his, or was she above such things, scornful of those whose lives were ruled by rank and privilege? Whatever the case, she had never met Barnabas Hammond in a situation such as this and it made her feel strangely vulnerable.

The odd effect he had on her caused her voice to

come out with decidedly squeaky overtones when
she would have preferred to sound authoritative.

'Mr Hammond, what do you mean by creeping
around in the dark—and with *this*—' She gestured
with her foot towards the offending sack. It seemed
obvious that he had been poaching and worse, that
his quarry was still alive.

'I would have thought better of you!' she finished
with self-righteous indignation.

'Would you?' Barney Hammond sounded surprised and amused. 'Naturally, I am flattered, Miss
Brabant, but why should you?'

Lavender frowned slightly. She could not see his
expression properly, for it was almost full dark now
and besides, he was possessed of a face that was
inscrutable at the best of times. She had heard the
maids giggling over Barney Hammond, remarking on
his good looks and athletic physique, and whilst
Lavender would have said that he was in no way
classically handsome, she was aware that there was
definitely something about him. It was a something
that made her feel quite hot and bothered when she
dwelt on it and it had even led Caroline once to remark, completely dispassionately, that she could see
why all the village girls were wild for him.

Lavender tried to concentrate, aware that such
thoughts were making matters worse rather than better. She knew that it would be best to make her excuses and leave, but Barney was waiting politely for

her response and she felt it would be rude simply to walk away.

'I did not imagine that you would stoop to poaching,' she said coldly, indicating the sack again. It had not moved again but she knew she had not imagined it. 'And to take your prey without killing it cleanly— that is rank cruelty!'

This time she heard him laugh. 'Oh, so you think I am a poacher, Miss Brabant? I see!' The warmth in his tone had slid into teasing and Lavender was even more confused. Not only was this inappropriate, it suggested that he was completely heartless!

'What else am I supposed to think?' she countered angrily, wondering why the timbre of his voice was so attractive when his words were so much the opposite. 'I heard a noise from the sack—and I saw it move! And why else would you be out after dark—'

She watched in amazement as Barney crouched down on the path and loosened the string at the neck of the sack. Suddenly she did not want to see whatever poor, maimed creature was inside.

'I pray you, put it out of its misery quickly,' she said hastily, looking the other way. 'How can you be so unkind—'

'Putting them out of their misery was precisely what my father intended,' Barney said dryly. 'I fear that you have jumped to the wrong conclusions, Miss Brabant.'

Lavender heard a tiny mewing sound and looked

round sharply. Barney was easing something gently
out of the sack, something soft, fluffy and with very
sharp claws. Lavender saw him wince as the kitten
sank teeth and claws simultaneously into his hand.

'Oh, there are two of them!'

'Yes, and not precisely grateful for my clemency!'

Lavender stepped closer and Barney opened his
fist to reveal the two tiny bodies. They were shivering a little, peering round with huge-eyed apprehension. Lavender put a hand out and tentatively stroked
one tiny head.

'Oh, how adorable! But—' She looked up suddenly into his face. 'The sack—you were going to
drown them in the river?'

'My father intended them for such a fate,' Barney
corrected her. He was stroking the kittens with gentle
fingers and Lavender could hear their ecstatic purrs.
'Their mother was a stray and he did not wish to
encourage her, but my sister Ellen had grown much
attached to the kittens and begged me to find them
a good home. So I offered to take them away and
my father assumed I would get rid of them.'

Lavender shivered. 'But what were you intending
to do with them? Has someone offered to take them
in?'

For the first time, Barney looked a little shifty.
'Not exactly. There is an old byre just up the path
and I was intending to make a nest for them there
and leave them overnight. I was just collecting bed-

ding for them when you stumbled upon the sack!
Then tomorrow, if I could, I hoped to persuade someone to give them a home...'

Lavender raised her eyebrows. 'That does not
sound a very good plan! They might stray away and
they can scarce be expected to catch their own food,
you know!'

'I brought some scraps of food and some milk with
me,' Barney said, his voice completely expressionless.

Lavender found herself trying not to laugh. It
seemed ridiculous that this man had been devoting
himself so wholeheartedly to the welfare of such tiny
kittens. Yet the little creatures evidently liked him,
for they had subsided into blissful balls of fluff under
the stroking of his hands. Lavender found her mind
making a sudden and unexpected leap from the fate
of the kittens to the caress of Barney's fingers, and
felt herself turn hot all over.

'Do you have any butter with you?' she asked,
somewhat at random. 'If you butter their paws they
will be too busy washing them to think of straying.'

Barney looked crestfallen. 'I did not think of that.
Do you truly think they might lose themselves in the
wood?'

'Cats are homing creatures,' Lavender explained,
glad to be able to speak with authority, 'and they
might try to find their way back to you. But they are
so far from Abbot Quincey they could never make

the journey! Why, they might fall in the river, or become exhausted, or be eaten—'

'Miss Brabant, pray do not distress yourself.' Barney sounded amused and rueful at the same time. 'I am sure they need suffer no such injury—'

'Well, but you cannot know that!' Lavender said indignantly. She took a deep breath. 'I have just the idea—I will take them back to Hewly with me and they may have a home there.' The suggestion seemed to come from nowhere, and startled her almost as much as it seemed to surprise Barney. He stared at her through the dark.

'You will? But—'

'We are forever having problems with mice at the Manor,' Lavender said, improvising hastily in order not to appear too sentimental. 'The kittens will be the very thing to deal with them.'

Barney looked at her. It hardly needed pointing out that the kittens were scarcely bigger than mice themselves.

'They will grow,' Lavender said defensively, as though he had spoken aloud. 'With a little care—'

She put out a hand for the sack, but Barney picked it up and slipped the cats back inside.

'It is very kind of you,' he said slowly. 'If you are certain—'

'Of course! And then you may tell your sister that they have gone to a good home!'

Barney looked at her inscrutably. 'And what will you tell your brother and sister-in-law?'

'Why, that I found the kittens in a sack on the path, just as I did! It would not do to lie, and they know me well enough to know I would not just leave them there!'

Barney swung the sack up. 'I will escort you back to the Manor then, Miss Brabant.'

'There is no need! And if anyone should see you—' Lavender broke off, aware that he might misinterpret her words. She did not wish him to think that she thought herself above his company.

Barney gave her a look, but he did not speak, merely standing back to allow her to precede him along the path. It seemed that her objections had been overruled. Lavender opened her mouth to protest, then closed it again.

They went a little way in silence, then Barney said suddenly, 'So you truly thought me a poacher, Miss Brabant?'

Lavender found herself on the defensive. 'Well, I was not to know! Why else would a man go creeping about the woods in the dark?'

'There could be any number of reasons, I imagine,' Barney said surprisingly. 'I am disappointed that you hold so low an opinion of me, Miss Brabant! I hoped you might think better of me than that!'

The last thing Lavender had expected was to find herself apologising. 'Well, I am truly sorry, but you must allow me some justification. Besides, you made matters considerably worse by manhandling me—' She broke off again. Perhaps it was not wise to remind him of that either. There was a pause.

'Yes, I beg your pardon.' She thought she could detect amusement in his tone again. 'I believe that was purely instinctive, but I apologise for upsetting you.'

Lavender had no intention of admitting that she had been disturbed rather than upset. His proximity and his touch had quite set her senses awry and she was still trembling slightly with the same strange awareness.

They had reached the gap in the wall where the path to Hewly gardens cut across the fields, and she turned to him.

'It would be better if you did not come any further, Mr Hammond. If anyone sees you they will know there is more to my tale than meets the eye.' She took the sack from him. 'Please assure your sister that I will take care of her kittens. Now I'll bid you goodnight.'

Barney stood back and gave her a half-bow, executed as neatly as any of the gentleman of society whom she had met. He then spoiled the effect by giving her a grin, his teeth flashing very white in the moonlight.

'Goodnight, then, Miss Brabant. And thank you.'

He had already melted into the dark as Lavender

turned away to hurry across the fields to home. She
found herself wanting to turn and watch him go,
which impulse both puzzled and annoyed her.
Grasping the kittens to her, she let herself in at the
garden gate and steadfastly refused to look back.
There was no doubt that Barney Hammond had disturbed her. He had disturbed her very much indeed.

'I cannot believe that you have managed to foist
two repellent strays upon this household, Lavender,'
Lewis Brabant said testily, as he disentangled one of
the kittens from his trouser leg at breakfast the following morning. The little creature, a bundle of gin-
ger fluff, hung on tenaciously. Lewis put his newspaper down and picked it up with a gentleness that
belied his words. The kitten started to purr immediately and Lewis pulled a face.

'See how she likes you,' Caroline offered with a
smile. She was feeding the other kitten on her lap
and it was eating ferociously. 'Poor little scraps—I
believe they are half starved!'

Lewis made a noise indicative of disgust. 'Well,
they had best start to earn their keep! The kitchen
will be the best place for them, not the drawing-
room!'

'Yes, my dear,' Caroline said soothingly. She gave
him a winning smile. 'They will surely be warm and
well fed if we keep them indoors!' Her smile broad-

ened. 'You cannot cozen me—I know you think them delightful.'

Lewis gave a non-committal grunt and got up from the breakfast table. He bent to kiss his wife. 'I shall be in the estate room if you need me. If I find any mice, I shall know what to do!'

Caroline was still smiling as she watched him out of the room. She turned to her sister-in-law. 'I do believe your new pets are a success, Lavender! Lewis is quite smitten!'

Lavender raised her eyebrows. She knew that her brother's disapproval was partly feigned but she had been hard pressed to explain her rescue of the kittens in a convincing fashion. To go out for a walk and return with two new pets in a sack was somewhat singular, especially as she was claiming simply to have found them.

'Is it not strange,' Caroline was musing now, 'that the kittens were wrapped in a sack from Hammond's store? The sort of sacking used to bind up reels of material and the like? I wonder if they have lost them? Perhaps we should ask, for they may wish for them back—'

Lavender jumped, spilling some of her hot chocolate. She had not thought of that.

'Was it one of Hammond's sacks? I did not notice,' she said, as casually as she was able.

'Which reminds me,' Caroline continued, 'that you promised to go to Abbot Quincey for some purchases for me today. Some embroidery thread, and I find I need some ribbons as well. I have made a list. Is that still convenient, Lavender?'

Lavender sighed. It was unfortunate that Caroline should have a commission for her today of all days. She did not wish for a walk this morning and she certainly did not want to go into Abbot Quincey and into Hammonds drapers shop. Having paid the shop too many visits in the past month, she now felt a distinct inclination to stay away from Barnabas Hammond, a need to avoid all those puzzling and disturbing feelings that he had brought to the surface. She had tossed and turned for a good hour before she had fallen asleep the previous night, and most of her thoughts had centred on Barney Hammond.

She realised that Caroline was watching her with bright hazel eyes, and that she had not yet replied.

'It is perfectly convenient, Caro,' she said hastily. She pushed away her plate of ham and eggs. Suddenly she did not feel so hungry.

'I must send a message to Lady Perceval as well,' Caroline said. 'Now, where did I leave the writing box? In the library? I have become so tiresomely forgetful of late…'

Lavender smiled. 'Nanny Pryor says that that happens to ladies who are increasing!'

Caroline looked offended. 'What arrant nonsense!'

'Then why are you wearing your thimble for breakfast, Caro?'

Caroline looked down at her finger and tutted. 'Gracious! I could have sworn that I left that in my sewing bag!' She caught Lavender's eye and smiled reluctantly. 'Very well, you have proved your point! Now, what was it that I was looking for?'

'The writing paper.' Lavender got up hastily. 'I will fetch it for you, Caro! I do not wish you to become lost on your way to the library!'

Chapter Two

The walk into Abbot Quincey was one that
Lavender knew particularly well and normally she
enjoyed it immensely. She loved the sound of the
wind in the tall trees, the shadow patterns of the
clouds as they raced across the fields and the sting
of the fresh air in her face. Her walks always gave
her ample time to think about her painting and her
reading and any number of other delightful and intellectual pursuits that had always filled her time until
now. But this morning—Lavender paused to tie the
ribbons of her bonnet more firmly under her chin, for
the wind was tugging the brim—she was aware of
feeling decidedly out of sorts. In fact, she admitted
to herself, it was worse than that. She felt blue-
devilled.

Her mother, the Honourable Lavinia Brabant, had
always maintained that a lady had no excuse for idle-
ness or boredom. An informed and educated mind

would always provide resources for solitude, and if that failed one should just remind oneself of the good fortune that had placed one in such an enviable position in life. Lavender felt very strongly that her mama had been quite right and would not approve of her daughter's current indisposition.

Lavender sighed. She knew that some of her restlessness sprang from the thoughts she had been having the previous day about her place at Hewly and her future plans. She felt unsettled, unfulfilled. Something was missing…

She went first to the church and laid some fresh flowers from the Hewly gardens on the grave of her father, Admiral Brabant. The graveside, in a quiet corner of the churchyard under a spreading oak, was peaceful and somehow comforting. Lavender sat down on a wooden seat nearby and rested her chin on her hand. Perhaps her father could help her sort her thoughts into some kind of order. He had always been a stickler for method and regulation during his lifetime.

It occurred to her that he had left her a considerable sum of money, and that that would enable her to leave Hewly if she so desired and to set up in a respectable house elsewhere. She could engage a companion—certainly she could afford to engage several—and if she were to find someone as amenable as Caroline, she would count herself lucky. Perhaps Lady Perceval could help her, for that matron was so well connected and well informed that she would know of any suitable persons seeking employment. The idea held some appeal but it also held some drawbacks. Lavender acknowledged that she liked living at Hewly and she liked the Abbey villages, and indeed, no one was trying to drive her away. Lewis and Caroline would no doubt be mortified if they even suspected her thoughts. She sighed again. Her musings did not seem to be getting her very far.

Lavender looked at the neat mound of her father's grave. She could imagine him addressing her, puffing out his chest in the imposing manner in which he used to lecture to his sailors: 'Action, not inaction is the solution to any crisis. Cease this foolish woolgathering, my girl, and get about your business!'

With a faint smile, Lavender got to her feet and picked up the basket.

She could always marry. The thought popped into her head as she was walking back around the church and heard the clock strike the hour. She had always been accustomed to thinking of herself as at her last prayers, but Caroline was nine and twenty, a good five years older than she. Perhaps there was a chance—although not much a chance of finding a husband as good as her brother.

Lavender considered the idea idly as she walked into the town. Her bridegroom would need to be an intelligent man who would appreciate a bluestocking

wife and enjoy discussing weighty matters with her.
He would encourage her sketching and her writing
and would have plenty of interests of his own. He
would not be at all the sort of man to want a pretty
ninnyhammer, for she was well aware that her looks
were no more than ordinary. He would need to be
possessed of a reasonable competence, to live in the
country and to shun the society pursuits that she had
so detested when she had visited London. Lavender
started to laugh at her own absurdity, but the thought
persisted. As for age, well, she was prepared to accept an older man, for he was likely to have more
sense, and as for looks… Here, with startling clarity,
the face of Barnabas Hammond appeared before her
eyes.

All Lavender's recent good humour vanished. She
shook her head a little sharply to dispel the image
but it was too late. She felt cross-grained and irritable
and for two pins she would tell Caroline to run her
own errands in future. She walked up the main street
of Abbot Quincey positively scowling, and arrived
in front of the draper's shop.

Hammonds General Store in Abbot Quincey was
not as imposing as Arthur Hammond's emporium in
Northampton, but it served a small town very well.
Now that the seasons were turning, Mr Hammond
had draped winter fustian and twilled cashmere about
the door, and huge bolts of the cloth were stacked
on shelves inside. Arthur Hammond himself was be-

hind the counter and was encouraging the doctor's wife to feel the quality of the nankeen that he had spread out over the top. He was a big man, florid and full of bonhomie. As ever, he was smart in a tailed coat and old-fashioned knee breeches, with a waistcoat straining over his ample stomach. He always dressed like a gentleman.

'All our materials are purchased in London, of course,' Lavender heard him say, in the oily tone that she so detested, 'and you will not find a better quality of cloth anywhere, ma'am...'

He broke off when he saw Lavender and hurried to greet her, which set her teeth on edge even more. She noticed that Barney came forward unobtrusively from the shadows to smooth over his father's defection and flatter Mrs Pettifer into making the purchase. Lavender felt awkward. She had no wish for Hammond to snub the doctor's wife just because she was from Hewly Manor and Hammond always curried favour with his noble clients. Besides, she was only buying ribbons and thread.

Lavender's transaction was almost completed when Barney emerged from the stock-room carrying a trestle table obviously intended for the display of some new goods. He gave Lavender a slight nod as he passed, but did not even speak to her. She knew that he was working and did not have time for idle chatter, but nevertheless Lavender felt slightly crushed, and was annoyed with herself for feeling so.

She put her purse away, thanked Mr Hammond for his help, and made for the door.

It opened before she got there, to admit two girls whom Lavender recognised as the daughters of a farmer over towards Abbot Giles. Both had dark curly hair, and open, laughing faces. They were giggling together as they came into the shop, and edged over to the table where Barney was now arranging winter bonnets on the hat stands. Lavender paused to watch. Her first thought was how incongruous it was to see a man of Barney's calibre working on ladies bonnets. Her second thought was how much she disliked the giggling, pouting girls, who were now looking flirtatiously at Barney from under their lashes and asking him questions that were punctuated frequently by coy laughter.

As she stood in the doorway, Arthur Hammond bustled up, clearly unamused by all the banter. He berated Barney for his lack of skill with the display, cowed the girls with one sharp glance, and set to rearranging the bonnets, flitting here and there like a preening bird. It seemed to Lavender that whilst the son and heir had no disposition towards drapery, the father was obviously in his element. She went out into the street, wondering for the first time whether Mr Hammond found it frustrating that his eldest son had not inherited his talent as a merchant. She knew that Hammond was immensely successful, for as well as the emporium in Northampton he had a string of other shops in the county, and it was clearly his life's work. Barney, on the other hand, looked as though he would be much more at home in some other occupation.

She walked down the main street, past the bakery and the Angel inn. The sun was bright and Lavender had just decided to take her sketchbook out to do some drawing that afternoon, when there was a step behind her and a breathless voice called:

'Miss Brabant!'

She turned to see Ellen Hammond panting up the road behind her, face flushed with exertion. Hammond's daughter was about fifteen, and had inherited the dark looks that gave Barney his enigmatic air. Lavender thought that Ellen would probably be a beauty, but the girl showed no signs of being aware of it. She was smiling with unaffected pleasure.

'Oh, Miss Brabant, please excuse me! Barney— my brother—told me that you had given the kittens a good home and I so wished to thank you!'

Lavender smiled at her. 'I was happy to be of help, Miss Hammond! They are the most adorable creatures, are they not? You must come over to Hewly sometime and see how they progress!'

Ellen's face flushed pink. 'Oh! May I indeed? You are so kind, Miss Brabant!' Her expression crumpled. 'Father was going to drown them, you know! Of all the cruel things! But Barney is so kind and said that he would save them but that I was not to tell—'

'That's enough, Ellen. I am sure that Miss Brabant has other business to attend to in town!'

Neither of them had noticed Barney Hammond come round the side of the Angel inn. His hands were in his pockets and he looked relaxed enough, but his dark eyes were watchful. Ellen flushed at the implied rebuke and dropped a little curtsey. 'Excuse me, Miss Brabant,' she murmured. 'I did not intend to presume.'

Barney gave Lavender a slight bow and took his sister's arm. They turned away up the street together. Lavender, watching them go, was astonished to discover that she suddenly felt very angry. She was not sure if it was Barney Hammond's high-handed action in interrupting the conversation that had annoyed her, or the implication that Ellen should not push herself on her notice. Either way, she was not going to let the injustice pass.

'Mr Hammond!'

Barney and Ellen had only gone five paces and both stopped at the imperious tone. Anxious not to add to the impression of upper-class hauteur, Lavender added politely: 'Mr Hammond. I should like to speak to you, if you please!'

She saw Barney hesitate, before he bent and spoke softly to Ellen and the girl scooted off up the road on her own. Barney turned back to Lavender and came forward courteously. His expression showed nothing but polite enquiry, but Lavender wondered what he was thinking behind that inscrutable façade.

'Miss Brabant?'

Lavender was feeling nervous. She cleared her throat and fixed him with a stern look. 'Mr Hammond, there was no need to reprimand your sister. She was doing no harm. She is a charming girl.'

Barney's civil expression did not waver. He met her look with an equally straight one of his own.

'Miss Brabant, I am sure that you mean well, but I do beg you not to encourage Ellen. Your kind attentions would be sufficient to turn her head, and that would only lead her to wish for more than she could have.'

There was a long moment whilst their eyes met and held and Lavender had the strangest feeling that he was not simply referring to Ellen's situation. Her eyes narrowed in a frown, but before she could speak, Barney had sketched a bow and walked away.

Lavender's heart was thudding. She watched his tall figure catch Ellen up, saw them exchange a few words, then Barney took her hand and together they strolled up the road, swinging their linked hands as they walked. Lavender felt the foolish tears prickle her eyes. She need scarcely have worried that Ellen would have been hurt by Barney's reproach. The sign of family unity contradicted that firmly. She was the one left feeling heart-sore. There was no doubt that she had been warned off, and for a misplaced act of kindness too. Yet she could not help but believe that there was more to it than that.

Lavender burned with embarrassment to think that Barney might have been addressing his words directly to her. Suppose he imagined that she was developing some sort of *tendre* for him and was trying to advise her that her feelings were inappropriate. It was true that she had imagined that there was some warmth in his manner towards her and had liked it. And last night, when they had met in the wood… A wave of mortification swept over her as she remembered how distracted she had been by the warmth of his touch and the hardness of his body against hers. She was glowering fiercely by the time she reached the end of the street. She had liked and admired Barney Hammond, she told herself angrily, but that was entirely at an end. She doubted that she would ever speak to him again.

Lavender had always found sketching to be soothing for a troubled mind. During her father's last illness she had derived great comfort from her drawing, and had even tentatively started work on a pictorial catalogue of the flora of the Steepwood Abbey woodlands. She was meticulously accurate in her sketches and thought that the work had some merit, although she did not dare hope that it would be good enough for publication. Now, however, her work offered just the solace that Lavender needed, and after luncheon she set off with her sketchbook and crayons, and went into the forest.

It was a beautiful day. The sunlight ran in dappled rivulets beneath the trees and the canopy was alive with the sound of birds, the loud laughing call of the green woodpecker and the chatter of the jay. The leaves were starting to fall and were crunchy beneath her feet and between their crisp covering the mushrooms pushed up. She spread her rug on a bank and sketched a few of the most colourful ones: the amethyst deceiver, with its vivid violet blue cap, and the verdigris toadstool that nestled in the grassy clearings. Gradually the fresh air and the peace had their desired effect and Lavender started to feel better. She drew a clump of wood vetch whose tendrils were clamped around a nearby tree stump. She knelt down to fix the detail of the purple-veined flowers and the fat, black seed pods, and it was only when she got up again that she saw that her skirt was streaked with earth and green with grass stains. The sun was lower now and she knew she had been out for several hours. She studied the sketch; it was good, the proportions were correct and the detail accurate, and she was happy to add it to her portfolio. Perhaps she would even show Caroline what she had done, for her sister-in-law was a keen amateur botanist.

Lavender packed up her bag, dusted her skirt down, and fixed her bonnet more securely on her

head, retying the ribbons. Her hair was coming down
and escaping from under the bonnet's brim—long,
straight strands of very fine fair hair that got caught
on the breeze. Her cousin Julia had told her often
that she was plain and Lavender knew that it was
true that she seldom took care of her appearance, but
just lately she had thought that her deep blue eyes
were a little bit pretty and her figure quite good...
Finding by some strange coincidence that her
thoughts were drifting from her own appearance to
that of Barnabas Hammond, Lavender hastily started
to plan the next drawing for her catalogue.

She was walking along, weighing the rival merits
of Caper Spurge and Mountain Melick Grass—neither of them colourful, but both an important part of
the botanical record—when she heard the strangest
sound and paused to listen. It was not a woodland
noise at all—not a sound with which she was very
familiar and certainly not one she expected to hear
in Steepwood. It was the unmistakable sound of steel
on steel.

Edging forward, Lavender crept down a path that
was closely bordered by scrub and the pressing trees.
It was not a path she had taken before, but she knew
she was walking in the direction of Steepwood Lawn
and was not afraid she would become lost. She was
more afraid of being seen, but curiosity held her in
a strong grip and she picked her way silently and
with care. Within a hundred yards the forest fell

back, revealing a sweep of green turf that was ideal for a duel and it was here that the contest was taking place. Lavender crept as close as she dared, staying in the cover of the trees. She took refuge behind one broad trunk and peeped round.

She had seen very few fencing matches, for it was not an activity of which most gently bred females had much experience. Years before, Lewis and Andrew had staged mock fights in the courtyard at Hewly, but Andrew was always too indolent to take them seriously and Lewis had won very quickly. Lavender could tell that this was no such match. She knew that the two men fighting here were doing so for pleasure rather than in earnest, for she could see the buttons on their foils, but she could also tell that they were taking it very seriously. Both were skilled swordsmen and fought with strength and determination, giving no quarter.

Lavender leant a little closer. One of the men was a complete stranger to her, a fair-haired giant who moved more slowly than his opponent but had the benefit of strength and reach. The other was only a few inches shorter, dark, lithe, muscular... Lavender gave a little squeak and clapped her hand over her mouth. There was no mistake—it had to be Barnabas Hammond.

It was fortunate that the noise of the contest drowned out Lavender's involuntary gasp, for the last thing that she wanted was to be discovered. She stood, both hands pressed against the tree trunk, and stared. A ridiculous image of Barney as she had seen him that very morning floated before her eyes, a vision of him arranging hats on a trestle table. It was absurd. That man and this could surely not be the same—yet when the movement of the fight brought him round so that she could see his face again, Lavender knew there could be no mistake. Forgetting concealment, she simply stood and watched.

He moved with a speed and strength that held Lavender spellbound. There was something utterly compelling about his confidence and skill. Her avid gaze took in the way his sweat-damp shirt clung to the lines of his shoulders and back, and moved on with mesmerised attention to his close-fitting buckskins and bare feet. His shirt was open at the throat, revealing the strong, brown column of his neck, and the sun glinted on the tawny strands in his hair and turned his skin to a deep bronze. When he finally succeeded in disarming his opponent with a move that sent the other man's foil flying through the air, he threw back his head and laughed.

'A fine match! You get better, James, I swear you do!'

Lavender watched as the fair man retrieved his foil from the bushes and threw himself down on the grass. He was laughing too. 'I rue the day I ever crossed swords with you, Barney! I would challenge you to another round for my revenge, but I am prom-

ised to a party at Jaffrey House and dare not be late!'
He sat up, grinning, and started to pull on his boots.
'You do not know how fortunate you are to be spared
such things, old fellow! If it were not for the beautiful blue eyes of a certain Miss Sheldon, I doubt I
could stomach it!' He sighed. 'But she is the most
angelic creature...'

'Spare me.' Lavender saw Barney grin. 'Last time
I saw you, it was a certain Lady Georgiana Cutler
who had taken your fancy!'

'I know!' The fair-haired man got to his feet. He
shook his head. 'I am fickle! But Lady Georgiana
could not hold a candle to Miss Sheldon—'

'Take your languishings off elsewhere,' Barney
advised, picking up his foil. 'I shall take me to the
shop and work at my books whilst you are carous-
ing!'

'Life is damnably unfair!' The other man grinned,
clapping him on the back. 'You to your studies and
me to my fortune-hunting! Ah well. I'll see you in
Northampton, no doubt.'

They shook hands and Lavender watched him
walk off in the direction of Jaffrey House, both foils
tucked under his arm. She stayed quite still, watching, as Barney pulled his boots on and started to walk
slowly across the greensward towards the trees. His
head was bent and the dark hair had fallen across his
forehead. He smoothed it back with an absent-

minded gesture. Lavender could hear him whistling under his breath, a lilting tune that hung on the air.

She froze where she stood as he passed close by. Of all the odd things she had seen in Steepwood, this had to be amongst the strangest. That Barney Hammond should be such a superlative swordsman was extraordinary, since she could not imagine that fencing was amongst the pursuits that he had learned as a boy. Then there was his friendship with a gentleman who was clearly staying at Jaffrey House, the home of the Earl of Yardley. Lavender had heard that a party was staying at the house and if the Brabants had not been in mourning, they would have been invited to join them. She frowned. It was very odd. But perhaps she was simply being snobbish— again—in expecting Barney to conform to her expectations. He really was a most mysterious man...

At that moment, craning to get a last glimpse of him before he entered the trees, Lavender took a step forward. There was a deafening snap by her left ankle, something tugged hard at her skirts, and she tumbled over in the grass. The tree canopy spun above her head and her bonnet went bouncing away across the clearing, leaving her sprawled in a heap with her petticoats around her knees and a sharp pain in her left leg. She sat up a little unsteadily and bent to inspect the damage.

There was a rusty iron trap snapped shut around her skirts, its teeth grinning at her in an evil parody

of a smile. Lavender felt a little faint as she realised
how close she had come to stepping on it. Another
few inches and it would have been her leg between
those metal jaws, her bones broken without a doubt.
She had seen traps before, man-traps and spring-guns
and leg-breakers like this one set to catch poachers,
but she had had no idea that she might stumble on
such a thing in Steep Wood. She could not imagine
who would have set such a trap.

Worse was to come. From her position prone in
the grass she could no longer see Barney, but it
seemed impossible that he had not heard the trap
going off or the alarm call of the birds as they scattered into the tops of the trees at the sudden noise.
Panicking, Lavender tried to get to her feet, then sat
down again in a hurry when the weight of the trap
made her over-balance. She could not prise it open
and it was too heavy for her to pick up, though she
would definitely have made a run for it, trap and all,
if she could have done so. She could now hear foot-
steps, coming closer, and she knew they had to be-
long to Barney. She closed her eyes in an agony of
mortification.

There was a step in the grass beside her, then
Barney's voice said, 'Miss Brabant! What in God's
name—'

Lavender opened her eyes. The wind was ruffling
his thick dark hair as he stared down at her from
what seemed a great height. He had a casual shooting

jacket slung over his shoulder, and at close quarters she could see that his buckskins fitted like a second skin and his shirt was still clinging to his muscular torso. Feeling hot and very peculiar, Lavender closed her eyes again.

She was not sure what was the most embarrassing aspect of her current situation. Perhaps it was being found in such an undignified tumble by such an attractive man, or perhaps the fact that he would guess she had been spying on him was even more embarrassing. She kept her eyes closed and hoped he would go away.

He did not. Lavender reluctantly opened her eyes again.

She saw his gaze go to the cut in her leg, and tweaked her skirts down as best she could, but not before he had seen the tell-tale trickle of blood. He frowned and went down on one knee beside her in the grass.

'You are injured! Have you fallen and hurt yourself—'

The trap was all but covered by Lavender's skirts. She gestured towards it. 'As you can see, sir, I have had an accident.'

Barney's gaze went from her reddening face to the rusty trap. He bit his lip. Lavender would have sworn that he was about to laugh.

'Oh dear. I see. Presumably it is too heavy for you to hobble home?'

Lavender's face reddened even more, this time with fury. 'Your amusement is misplaced, sir! It is not remotely funny that people go around setting traps strong enough to break a man's leg! If you cannot find anything more constructive to say, perhaps you should leave me to deal with it as best I may!'

'I'm sorry.' Barney spoke gently. 'Take comfort from the fact that it did not in fact break any bones. Although,' his gaze turned back to her ankle, which Lavender was trying to hide under her skirts, 'I did think that you had sustained a graze...'

'It is nothing!' Lavender snapped. She did not think that she was spoilt but she felt she was entitled to feel a little sorry for herself. The refusal of this man to sympathise with her predicament was infuriating. Barney was still kneeling by her side and she wished that he would just go away.

'My sister Ellen was caught in a man-trap in these woods once,' he said conversationally. 'She was not as fortunate as you, Miss Brabant. She fell into the pit and pierced her arm on a spike. She bears the scar to this day.'

Lavender was silenced. Suddenly the tears of shock and self-pity were not far away. She sniffed and turned her head away so that he would not see.

'I am sorry,' she said, a little stiffly, 'but who would do such a thing—'

'The Marquis of Sywell, I imagine.' Barney had

picked up the trap and was attempting unsuccessfully to open it. 'He used to derive much pleasure from maiming and killing—man or beast, it did not matter. This is an old trap of his, I am sure.' He looked at her. 'I am sorry, but I cannot move it. You will have to take off your skirt.'

He spoke in such a matter-of-fact tone that at first Lavender did not register the sense of his words. Then she did and forgot her tears in her outrage. She glared at him. 'How can you be so nonsensical, Mr Hammond! I shall do no such thing!'

Barney grinned. 'Come now, Miss Brabant, this is no time to be missish! I had thought you had more sense than most ladies of your class, but it seems I was wrong!' He stood up. 'Have no concern for my feelings! I have three sisters and shall not be shocked!'

Lavender stared, open-mouthed. It had not occurred to her that he was about to watch.

'But Mr Hammond, you must go away!'

'Miss Brabant,' Barney gave her a quizzical smile, 'if I am to help you, I must stay.'

Lavender tried to struggle to her feet and stumbled as the weight of the trap bore her down again. Immediately, Barney's arm was about her waist. She could feel the warmth of his hand through the cotton of her dress.

'Let me assist you—'

'No!' Lavender almost yelped with fright at his touch. 'Go away! I can manage perfectly well!'

She realised that she did indeed sound like one of the hen-witted society girls that she so despised. Barney was laughing at her, a twinkle deep in those dark eyes.

'If I let you go you will fall over. Now, pray be sensible, Miss Brabant. You will either need to remove the skirt or at the very least, rip off the offending piece—'

'Thank you,' Lavender said, knowing that she sounded sulky. 'I had worked that out for myself! If you will stand a little off, Mr Hammond, I shall do what is necessary!'

Barney gave her another grin and let her go very gently. Once Lavender had found her balance she discovered that she could manage perfectly well, and was even able to hop into the shelter of a nearby oak, dragging the trap behind her. Having checked suspiciously that Barney was being as good as his word and had turned his back, she slipped her skirt off, her fingers clumsy in their haste. Once she was free of it, it was a relatively simple matter to tear off the strip that was caught, and rearrange the rest about her as decently as possible. When she had finished, she decided that she looked almost respectable, if a little odd. The left-hand side of the skirt was a little lop-sided at the hem, showing a couple of inches of petticoat and an entirely improper glimpse of ankle, but it could have been so much worse. Her leg was sore and stiff from the cut, but she was tolerably certain that she could manage to limp home.

Barney was whistling again, the lilting tune that she had heard earlier. As she came out of the shade of the trees he turned to look at her, and Lavender's heart did a little skip at his long, slow scrutiny.

'Can you manage to walk home, Miss Brabant, or shall I carry you?' he asked. 'I saw that you had a nasty cut to your leg.'

'I can manage, I thank you,' Lavender said, feeling quite weak at the thought of Barney picking her up in his arms.

'Then I shall carry your bag rather than your person,' Barney said, stooping to pick up the bag with Lavender's sketches and crayons. 'I should not like to outrage your sensibilities any further.'

'There is no need to accompany me at all,' Lavender argued, her temper decidedly scratchy by now. 'And whilst we are settling our differences, Mr Hammond, I must ask you not to make patronising assumptions about me! I am no feather-brained girl to fall into a swoon just because I have a small accident! If it comes to that, *you* are very different inside your father's shop from out of it, but you do not hear me making ill-bred observations!'

There was a taut silence, but for a wood pigeon cooing in the branches above their heads. Then Barney gave a slight nod. His gaze was very steady.

'Very well, Miss Brabant. I accept your reproof—
if you will accept my escort back home.'

Lavender shrugged with an ill grace. She went
ahead of him to the path, trying not to limp too obviously as she struggled with brambles and the grasping stems of dog rose that seemed determined to rip
the rest of her skirt from her. She was beginning to
wish that she had never let curiosity get the better of
her when she had heard the fencing match.

Pride could only get her so far. Eventually they
came to a place where a fallen tree had blocked the
path, and she was obliged to accept Barney's hand
to help her over it. After that he walked by her side,
kicking a stray branch from her path and holding
back the straggling stems of rose and bindweed
whenever they threatened to catch on her clothes.
Lavender tried to repress the treacherous feeling of
warmth that this engendered, but it was impossible
not to feel more in charity with him for such gallantry. Then, when they had been walking in silence
for about five minutes, he said, 'I infer from your
remark about my being a different person outside the
shop that you saw the fencing match, Miss Brabant?'

Lavender stole a quick look at his face and
blushed.

'I am sorry… It is not that I was watching, but the
noise of the contest attracted my notice and I stopped
to see what was happening—'

'I see.' She thought Barney sounded as though he saw rather too much. 'No doubt you were surprised?'

'Well, I…' Lavender struggled to think of a way of expressing her feelings without sounding rude. 'I suppose I was. It was not something that I expected you…' She broke off. 'That is, you seemed very proficient—' She stopped again. Now she had given away that she had been watching long enough to make a judgement.

'Thank you.' Barney was smiling at her. 'No doubt it must seem odd to you, but I have been fencing since I was a boy. James Oliver, my opponent a few moments back, was also my first adversary. I met him and a few of his aristocratic playmates when I was about eleven, and walking in the forest.' He shot her a look. 'They taunted me, the poor village boy, and I was so angry that I challenged James to a fight. Imagine my dismay when he suggested we should fight with swords, like gentlemen rather than peasants, as he put it!'

Lavender could not help smiling at his droll tone. 'What happened?'

The laughter lines around Barney's eyes deepened. 'Well, no doubt I was a little unorthodox in my style, but I discovered that I had a natural bent for fencing! I beat James easily and then he and his friends did not crow so loud! And since then he has sworn he will beat me one day, but he has yet to do so!'

'He seems a better friend to you now than he must

have been then,' Lavender ventured, for one of the things that had struck her about the two men was their easy camaraderie.

Barney laughed. 'Oh, he learned respect! No, James is a good fellow at heart and I have counted him a friend for many years now.' He hesitated. 'All the same, Miss Brabant, I should be grateful if you told no one that you witnessed our match.'

Lavender stopped, taken aback. 'Of course, if you wish it! But is this some strange kind of reverse snobbery that prompts you not to acknowledge your aristocratic friends, Mr Hammond?'

She could have bitten her tongue out as soon as she had spoken, for she knew she did not know him well enough to ask such a personal and challenging question. Whilst Lavender had little time for the commonplaces and evasions of polite society, she did at least feel that she always spoke with courtesy. This time, however, she had been lured by the unusual nature of their conversation into asking a rather direct question. She saw Barney raise his eyebrows at her plain speaking, but he did not seem in any way taken aback and he answered her without prevarication.

'Not at all. The truth is that I prefer not to tell anyone. Were my father to know I fear he would take shameless advantage.'

Lavender turned aside and started walking again. She felt a little embarrassed. She knew exactly what he meant. Arthur Hammond was such a social climber that he would be beside himself with excitement to discover that Barney had such upper-class friends. No doubt he would use the fact to push himself on their notice and ruin the comfortable companionship that existed.

'Have you kept it a secret for all these years, then?' she asked, unable to prevent her curiosity surfacing again.

'Oh, it is but one of many secrets!' Barney said easily. Lavender saw a hint of amusement in his eyes as he watched her. 'In general terms, Miss Brabant, I find it easier not to tell people things!'

Lavender struggled to equate this with what she thought she knew of him. It was true that most of it had been based on assumption and conjecture, about the shop, about his father, about his life... Just as he had apparently seen her as a spoilt society miss, she had imagined him to be the son of a solid merchant family, destined inevitably to take over the business one day. Now, suddenly, all her ideas were in a spin.

They had reached the stile at the edge of the wood and paused whilst still under the shadows of the trees. The sun was slanting through the leaves in blinding shafts. Lavender put up a hand to shade her eyes.

'Thank you for carrying my portfolio. I am sure I can manage from here back to Hewly—'

'At the least, let me help you over the stile,' Barney murmured. Before Lavender could either accept or decline, he had swept her up in his arms and deposited her on the other side, ruffled and indignant. She grabbed hold of him to steady herself. The material of his shirt was soft beneath her fingers and once again, Lavender could feel the warmth and the hardness of the muscle beneath. She positively jumped away from him.

'Really, sir—'

'Miss Brabant? Surely you did not wish to risk further injury to your ankle?'

Barney handed her the portfolio. 'Will you show me your drawings one day? I should be most interested…'

Lavender looked at him suspiciously but he seemed quite in earnest. 'If you would truly care to see them—'

Barney flashed her a smile. 'Thank you. I will leave you here, Miss Brabant, if you are sure that you can manage alone. And take care when you are walking in the forest. You can never be sure what you might find.'

Lavender felt the colour come into her cheeks again. His gaze was very steady and in a second, mortification overcame her. He had made no direct reference to her spying on the fencing match that afternoon, but suddenly her guilty conscience was too much and she was sure that he *knew*—knew that it was not the first time she had watched him. Some two months previously she had been wandering

through the woods where the river ran, and had seen
Barney in the pool beneath the trees. He had been
swimming strongly and the water had streamed over
his bare brown shoulders and down his back, and
Lavender had wanted to strip down to her shift and
join him in the water there and then... A huge wash
of guilty colour swept into her face, and she turned
and ran from him, regardless of her torn skirt, the
pain in her leg, and the amazed expression she knew
must be on his face as he watched her run away.

Chapter Three

'Lavender, you have had a Friday face for at least the past week!' Caroline observed to her sister-in-law, ten days later. 'I declare, you are making me miserable, and I was in the greatest good spirits until this morning! Whatever can be the matter with you?'

Lavender refused to look up from her book. She did not want to face Caroline's shrewd questioning at the moment. They were sitting in the drawing-room, Caroline embroidering and Lavender half-heartedly reading *Sense and Sensibility*. She was dismally aware that she was not enjoying herself—and had not done so ever since her disastrous encounter with Barney Hammond in the wood.

The scratch on her leg had healed quickly, but her feelings were still sore. She was uncomfortably aware that she had made a complete cake of herself. It had been undignified enough to have been caught in the man-trap but she had made matters infinitely worse for herself by running away in so melodramatic a fashion.

'It is nothing of consequence,' she muttered, knowing she sounded ungracious. 'I am sorry if my poor spirits are lowering to yours. I shall go into the library.'

She made to get up, but Caroline put out a hand to stay her.

'Do not sulk! I was only teasing.' She patted the sofa beside her and Lavender sat down reluctantly. 'In fact I have the best of news! You know that Lewis is to go to Northampton on business for a few days?'

Lavender nodded.

'Well, by great good chance I have just had a letter from Lady Anne Covingham this morning. The family are at Riding Park for a se'nnight from Friday, and urge us to join them. It will be the very thing! We may stay at the Park and visit in Northampton, and be as merry as grigs!'

Lavender fidgeted uneasily. 'I am not sure,' she said doubtfully. 'I do not feel inclined for company at the moment, Caro—'

Caroline opened her eyes wide. 'Upon my word, you are very retiring at present! I know you did not enjoy your London Season, but you are perfectly at ease in good company and the Covinghams are not so high in the instep to put one in dislike! Why, they have always treated me with friendship even when I worked for them!' Her face changed. 'But I shall not force you to go if you do not wish it. If you will not be comfortable, dearest Lavender, you must stay here—'

Lavender shook her head. The thought of staying at Hewly on her own seemed even worse than that of going away. Impatient with herself, she smiled at her sister-in-law.

'I'm sorry, Caro. Take no notice of me, I am in a fit of the megrims at the moment! A change of scene is just what I need.'

'Capital!' Caroline smiled. 'I shall write to Anne directly. You will see, Lavender—it shall be just the thing!'

Their first evening at Riding Park was a comfortable one. The house party was small and consisted only of themselves, Lady Anne Covingham and her husband Lord Freddie, and the youngest Covingham daughter, Frances. Frances was eighteen and a lively brunette, and Lavender eyed her with caution. She had met girls like Frances Covingham during her London Season, and was miserably aware that she had nothing in common with them.

Lady Anne was exactly as Caroline had promised. Small, dark and vivacious, she possessed a warmth of manner that immediately made Lavender feel at home. Lord Freddie was equally charming and they all seemed utterly delighted to see Caroline again, and to get to know her new family. Miss Covingham in particular was thrilled to see her old governess and fell on Caroline's neck with tears of joy.

They dined *en famille* the first night, with no ostentatious display of plate or silver, though Lady Anne was at pains to explain that this was not out of a lack of respect for their visitors, but simply because they considered Caroline so much a part of the family. She explained that there was to be a dinner and ball in a few days, but in the meantime they preferred the house party to be informal. As though to underline this fact, the gentlemen did not linger over their port, but rejoined the ladies quickly for tea in the drawing-room, where Miss Covingham played a number of Schubert pieces. She performed prettily and with competence and Lavender, who had never been musical, felt her fragile spirits sink again. She was glad that no one asked her to play, for after Frances's skill she knew she would have sounded like an elephant clattering over the keys.

When Frances had finished, she came over to the window-seat and sat down next to Lavender with a smile. Lavender smiled back, a little hesitantly.

'You play very well, Miss Covingham! You must have a natural talent for music!'

Frances laughed, her big brown eyes sparkling. 'Truth to tell,' she confided, 'the credit for my playing should go to Miss Whiston—Mrs Brabant, that is. I was a terrible pupil and though I shall never be truly talented, Mrs Brabant persisted until I was at least no embarrassment!' She smiled across at Caroline, who was deep in conversation with Lady Anne. 'Oh, it was a sad day for me when Miss Whiston left us, for she was the greatest good friend to us all!'

'You must have missed her a lot,' Lavender ventured.

Frances gave her a dazzling smile. 'Oh, prodigiously! My two sisters were already married, you see, and I was very lonely! But we always fought over who should have Miss Whiston, for we were all most attached to her! When she married, my sister Louisa wanted Miss Whiston to go with her as her companion, you know, but Harriet and I could not bear to spare her! And Miss Whiston said that it would be better for Louisa and Cheverton to have some time on their own.' She frowned. 'Louisa is volatile, you know, and she and Cheverton were forever arguing! But they rub along tolerably well together now and have two delightful babies, so I suppose they must have settled their differences!'

Lavender blinked slightly at this insight into the Cheverton marriage. 'And your other sister, Miss Covingham—Harriet, is it? You said that she is married as well?'

Her sisters' marriages were evidently a perennially interesting topic with Frances, who wriggled slightly on the window-seat as she settled down for a really good gossip.

'Oh yes, Miss Brabant, Harriet is married to Lord John Farley—Stapleton's heir, you know. But I fear they do not suit.' Her round face took on a doleful expression. She leaned closer to Lavender and dropped her voice to a whisper. 'Mama and Papa were not at all happy about the match, you know, but Harri is headstrong and threatened to elope! Well, she nearly set the house by the ears! Mama was in a fit of the vapours and Papa was storming around and threatening to horsewhip the fellow, until Miss Whiston made everyone calm. She spoke to Harriet, you know, but she could not persuade her! I was listening at the door, and heard Miss Whiston— Mrs Brabant—tell Harri that Farley was a womaniser who would make her unhappy, but Harri was hot for him and would not listen!' Frances shrugged her plump white shoulders philosophically. 'So in the end Papa gave his consent and they were married and now,' she dropped her voice confidentially, 'he keeps a mistress quite openly and Harri is as miserable as sin!'

She sat back and opened her eyes very wide. 'Now what do you think of that, Miss Brabant!'

'I am sorry for your sister,' Lavender said truthfully. 'It must be a dreadful thing to love a man who does not care as much for you.'

'Oh, Harri fancied herself in love with him,'

Frances said, assuming a world-weary air that seemed far in advance of her years, 'but it was all a nonsense! Why, now she has a *tendre* for another gentleman, and is thinking of running off with him—' She broke off, seeing that both Caroline and her mother were eavesdropping, and bit her lip. 'Anyway, I should not gossip so! But Harri has caused me no end of trouble,' she added gloomily, 'because I was to have my come-out this year, but with all the fuss over Harri's wedding, Mama thought it best to wait until I was older and more sensible! She says that the three of us are headstrong and flighty but I would never be so foolish!'

Lavender laughed. She was finding it impossible to dislike Frances Covingham. On the one hand she epitomised everything that Lavender had always thought she had an aversion to in young ladies. She was dark and modish, and had no interest in scholarship and a fascination with fashion and gossip that Lavender found quite tedious. On the other hand, she was clearly a sweet-natured girl and Caroline had obviously worked hard to instil in her a set of values that went beyond the money and consequence granted by her position. Lavender realised that Frances's uncomplicated warmth and friendliness were a far cry from the haughty snobbery that she had encountered during her London Season.

Frances smoothed her skirts. 'Forgive me, Miss Brabant. I am such a sad rattle! Tell me about yourself, and about Hewly Manor. It sounds a delightful place…'

'Oh, I am a poor subject of conversation,' Lavender said hastily, 'but I am always happy to talk of Hewly! It is a beautiful house and I love to wander in the grounds and the countryside—'

'By yourself?' Frances looked struck halfway between incredulity and respect. 'Only fancy!'

'Oh yes, for there is no danger in the woods and lanes—'

Lavender broke off, remembering that sometimes one met with the unexpected in Steep Wood.

'Fancy!' Miss Covingham repeated vaguely. 'Indeed, it sounds delightfully pastoral!' Her brow wrinkled. 'You will be sorry to leave Hewly when you marry then, Miss Brabant!'

Lavender frowned slightly at what seemed to be a *non sequitur*. 'Oh! But there is no likelihood of that, Miss Covingham! I am well past my last prayers and do not intend to marry!'

It seemed she had uttered the unthinkable. Frances gave a little shriek and caught her arm. 'Oh, Miss Brabant!' Frances said breathlessly. 'But that is impossible! Of course you must marry!'

Lavender raised her eyebrows, smiling. 'Indeed! Must I? Why so, Miss Covingham?'

'Well…' Frances seemed quite taken aback at the challenge. Lavender waited confidently for her to say that all girls should hunt themselves a husband, but when Frances finally replied it literally took Lavender's breath away.

'Because you are so pretty!' her new-found friend declared triumphantly. 'Oh Miss Brabant, it would be such a waste otherwise!'

Later, when Frances had said goodnight with many professions of friendship and had promised to show her the estate the following day, Lavender lay in her vast bed and looked up at the scarlet drapes that hung above her head. It was foolish for a woman of sense to be so moved by a compliment, and yet when Frances had declared how pretty she was, Lavender had almost asked her if she was sure. Perhaps it was true. Her hair was, after all, a very attractive silver gilt colour—not the fashionable golden blonde of the London beauties, perhaps, but still quite nice. And she had often been told that her deep lavender blue eyes were her best feature… Smiling slightly, she fell asleep and dreamed, rather improbably, of ribbons and lace, and gowns of rose crêpe and lavender to match her eyes.

The following day was fair and whilst Lewis went off into Northampton to see his man of business, the ladies took a carriage and drove about the estate. Riding Park was a very fine house, an Elizabethan mansion in red brick, with rolling parkland and a beautiful lake. Lavender was particularly taken with the hunting-lodge, which stood between the walled gardens and the park, and Frances gleefully told her that it was haunted by the ghost of the first owner, Sir Thomas Gleason, who was supposed to walk from the Lodge to the house on stormy nights.

'They say he was a philanthropist who bemoans the fact that the money he left in trust for the poor was stolen by the rich,' Frances confided, her eyes huge. 'He walks with his steeple hat under one arm, and wears a ruff, doublet and hose! What do you think of that, Miss Brabant! I declare I should faint with fright were I to see him!'

'They do say that Hewly is haunted,' Caroline put in, from her seat opposite the girls. 'The Grey Lady, is it not, Lavender? I have never seen her, but they say she stalks the house when there is about to be a death in the family.'

Frances shivered enjoyably. 'Oh, how Gothic! Poor, desperate creature that she must be!'

Caroline and Lavender exchanged a smile.

'Frances is the dearest creature, is she not?' Caroline said later, when, having dressed for dinner she came along to see how Lavender was progressing. 'I was so hoping that the two of you would be friends. For although you have scarcely an interest in common, I dare swear you think her the sweetest girl!'

Lavender was spending longer in front of the mirror than was customary, for she was trying out a new hairstyle, one that involved a bandeau of pale green to match her dress. It also entailed a complicated procedure of curling her hair into ringlets and gathering them up on one side of her head. The suggestion had quite taken her maid by surprise and consequently had thrown her into a fluster until Caroline had appeared and had the good sense to call Frances's own maid to help. The result was rather pleasing, Lavender thought, as she turned this way and that to admire her reflection.

'Oh, Frances is a lovely girl,' she agreed heartily, gathering up her bag and fan. 'She has promised to help me dress for the ball on Friday night. And we are to go shopping together in Northampton tomorrow, Caro. Is this not fun!'

And she totally failed to see Caroline's expression of amused surprise as she swept out of the room on the way down to dinner.

The whole party drove into Northampton on the following day. Although Lavender had been to the town several times before, this was the first time that she had approached from the west, over the river and up Black Lion Hill into the Marefair. As they grew near, the whole town was spread out before them and they all agreed it to be a very fine sight indeed. On such a sunny day the jumble of roofs shone in the light and the stone gleamed warm.

They drove past St Peter's Church, and into the

Horsemarket, and Lady Anne requested that the coach set them down in Mercers Row.

Lavender leant forward to look at the passing shops and houses. 'The buildings are very fine, are they not? I do so wish I could come into the town again just to walk round and admire the architecture! A sight-seeing tour of the churches would be great fun, for I know I have read that they are all very splendid…'

Frances, who had been discussing with her mother the rival merits of several dressmakers' shops, broke off, looking horrified. 'A tour of the churches…' She caught Lady Anne's eye and recovered herself. 'Well, if you wish it, dearest Lavender, I shall be happy to accompany you.'

Lavender smiled at her. 'You are very noble, Frances, but I should not put you to so much trouble! I know that ancient monuments are not to everyone's taste!'

Frances looked relieved. 'Well, I'll own that it is not a great interest of mine, but I do assure you, Lavender, that I should be very pleased to go with you!' She brightened. 'Indeed, I could act as guide myself! I remember that St Sepulchre's church is one of a very few in the country with a round tower.' She screwed her face up. 'It dates from the…thirteenth century! There! Mrs Brabant! Are you not proud of me!' And she dissolved into irresistible giggles at the looks of frank amazement on everyone's faces. 'Oh dear, I shall never be a blue-stocking, but I can still surprise you all!'

They dismounted from the carriage at the Bear inn, and swiftly went their separate ways. Lord Freddie wanted to visit the gunsmith's and Lewis arranged to meet him there after he had consulted his man of business. Meanwhile Frances and Lady Anne needed to call in at the drapers to pick a few final necessities for the ball. Frances also wanted to visit the milliners, the haberdashers, the linen-drapers and the perfumiers, but Lady Anne shook her head decisively over this last and said that *poudre subtil* was not appropriate for young girls. Frances was not squashed and caught Lavender's arm, eagerly encouraging her to look in the window of the first of many drapers' shops.

'Oh Lavender, look at that bonnet! Now which would be most becoming, the red or the green?'

Lavender looked at her thoughtfully. 'I do believe the green would suit your colouring best, Frances. The red is pretty, but the green matches your eyes.'

Frances seemed much struck by this. 'I do believe you are right, Lavender! You have good taste! Well, we shall see!' She rummaged in her reticule. 'I fear I have little of my allowance left, but there may be just enough… But I will not choose just yet, for there are so many other shops to see!'

Lavender, who had not intended making any purchases, found that under Frances's encouragement it was easy to buy a very pretty spencer tippet and a fur muff for winter. She watched with amusement as Frances swept through each shop, collecting ostrich feathers, silk gloves and embroidered handkerchiefs with complete abandonment. Finally, when Frances had declared her interest in a Turkish turban, Lavender was forced to intervene and point out that it made her look too matronly.

'I do not know how you may be so sparing, Lavender,' Frances complained, looking from her own pile of purchases to Lavender's modest parcel. 'Why, you should be stocking up with all the necessaries for a tolerable winter! Surely the best shops in Abbot Quincey cannot match your choice here!'

Lavender turned away and pretended to examine a blue scarf. 'We have the best draper's imaginable in Abbot's Quincey,' she said lightly. 'Arthur Hammond himself—'

'Hammonds!' Frances squeaked excitedly. 'I had all but forgot! We cannot go back without a visit to his emporium!'

Lavender hung back, suddenly wishing she had not been prompted to mention the name. She did not wish to risk a visit to Arthur Hammond's shop, although it was scarcely likely that Barney would be there.

'But we have plenty of purchases already, Frances!' she said hastily. 'You will be bankrupting yourself with any more!'

Frances brushed this aside. 'What nonsense!' She hurried across to the counter, where Lady Anne was buying some embroidered muslin. 'Mama, I know we are due back any moment, but may we just call in at Hammonds on the way? Oh please... They have the very best goods...'

The shop assistant serving Lady Anne gave Frances a glare at the mention of such a rival, but Lady Anne seemed nothing loath.

'Very well, my love,' she said, 'but only for a moment or the gentlemen will set off home without us!'

Lavender made her way over to Caroline, who was resting on a chair in an alcove whilst she waited for the others.

'Does it suit you to go on to another shop, dearest Caro?' Lavender asked anxiously. 'You are sure you are not too tired? If you wish to go back to the inn I will gladly come with you...'

Caroline gave her a searching look. 'I am very well, I thank you, Lavender, but I appreciate your concern. Do I gather from your reluctance that Frances has suggested we visit Hammonds? If *you* do not wish to go there and buy some more gloves, I shall come with *you* back to the inn...'

Lavender blushed. She was not at all sure how her sister-in-law had guessed that she had an aversion to Hammonds at present, nor was she going to ask.

'Oh no, I am very happy to go there,' she said

airily. 'I was only concerned that you should not tire yourself—'

'Very thoughtful, my love,' Caroline said with a smile, 'and I am sure that Mr Hammond will not be in Northampton today—'

Lavender shot out of the shop before Caroline could humiliate her further and before Frances should start asking awkward questions. The chill air on the street served to cool her red face a little. She reflected ruefully that Caroline was obviously some kind of clairvoyant, for she could swear that she had not mentioned Hammonds and in particular Mr Barney Hammond for at least ten days. Even when she had returned ignominiously from her accident in the wood, she had managed to skate adroitly over the fact that it was Barney who had found her there and escorted her home. She stared fiercely at a gold shawl in the shop window and told herself that she was being foolish. There should be no particular reason for her to avoid Barney Hammond, nor to seek him out, for that matter. She should just behave naturally.

Even so, when they reached the doorway of Hammond's Emporium, she was most reluctant to go in. It did not improve the situation that the first person they saw was Arthur Hammond himself, who looked first surprised and then unctuously satisfied to see them. He rushed forward, almost knocking over an elderly lady in his hurry to greet them.

'Ladies! How charming to see you! How may I be of assistance?'

It seemed that in very short order, every sales assistant in the shop was scurrying round to measure and cut—lace for Caroline, sarcenet for Lady Anne, stockings for Frances, which Hammond passed to her with a roguish smile. All the other customers, with their flannel petticoats and ribbons, were obliged to wait, whilst Hammond rubbed his hands and said how honoured he was to have such noble visitors, until Lavender left the shop in very disgust.

She stood on the pavement and gazed at the apothecary's shop next door whilst a feeling of relief crept through her that Barney had not been present. Then a voice said, 'How do you do, Miss Brabant? It is an unexpected pleasure to see you here in Northampton.'

Barnabas Hammond was standing before her in a coat of blue superfine, buff pantaloons and a pair of boots that Lavender suspected owed more to Hobys of London than the admittedly excellent shoemakers of Northampton. The coat fitted his broad shoulders without one superfluous wrinkle, and suited his tall figure to perfection. Lavender found herself staring and tried to stop, but seemed unable to do so. His dark hair was worn a little long and curled thickly over the collar of his jacket. He looked freshly shaved and smelled very faintly and deliciously of eau-de-cologne. Yet none of that was what really compelled her attention. Lavender puzzled, and came to the conclusion that it was somehow Barney's containment that was so attractive, the impression of raw power captured and held under control, but barely. He was not cut out to play the society fop, polished and perfumed. He was too physical a man for that. His appearance conjured up a dangerous vision, the image of him in the pool, the brown, muscular body, the water sliding over him... Or during the fencing match, his shirt sticking to his body as he moved with skill and grace...

Lavender swallowed hard and tried to summon up a polite social smile. The streets of Northampton were in no way an appropriate place for such wayward thoughts.

'Mr Hammond! How do you do, sir?'

'I am well, thank you.' There was the implication of a smile in Barney's voice. He did not say anything else, but watched her with those very dark eyes that always made Lavender feel strangely self-conscious. She could feel it now, feel her already shaky social skills slipping away from her. All she could think of was that she had made a complete fool of herself the last time they had met, and now she was set fair to do the same again. Her gaze fixed desperately on the parcel in his arms.

'You have been shopping, I see,' she said, with what she knew to be ghastly archness. 'Have you bought anything interesting?'

'I have been to the apothecary's shop for some remedies for my mother,' Barney said with a smile. 'I was in there when I saw you. She always gives me a commission, for she swears by Dr Anderson's Scotts Pills and Vegetable Syrup of de Velnos!'

'What maladies do they cure?' Lavender asked, fascinated by the slow amusement in his voice and the warmth in those dark eyes. Barney smiled and her heart gave a little skip.

'Just about everything, I believe!' he said cheerfully. 'Certainly my mama suffers from just about every disease known to man! She has a copy of *Solomon's Guide to Health* at home, Miss Brabant, and looks up every ailment in it! It gives her great pleasure to decide what she will suffer from next!'

Lavender giggled and tried to turn it into a cough. 'Oh dear. You do not sound very sympathetic, sir…'

'No.' The amusement died from Barney's face. 'Your pardon. I should not make a joke of it. Truth to tell, the apothecary's business has always fascinated me. Whilst there are any number of false remedies for sale, and some positively dangerous, I believe, there are some chemists and pharmacists who do the most interesting work. I should like—' He broke off, turning slightly away. 'I beg your pardon, Miss Brabant. I can become most tedious on the subject!'

Lavender opened her mouth to contradict him, but in that moment they were joined by the gentleman

whom Lavender had last seen pitting his fencing skill
so unsuccessfully against Barney that day in the forest. He was tall and fair, and at close quarters
Lavender could see that he had a twinkle in his blue
eyes and a humorous set to his mouth. Barney performed the introductions very smoothly.

'Miss Brabant, this is Mr James Oliver, a friend
of mine. Jamie, this is Miss Lavender Brabant.'

Mr Oliver bowed. 'Delighted to meet you, Miss
Brabant. I believe you must be another of the inhab-
itants of the Abbey villages? I rather think I recognise the name—'

Lavender was just explaining where Hewly fitted
in when the rest of her party spilled out of the doorway, chattering excitedly about their purchases. They
broke off when they saw that Lavender had company.

'Mr Hammond! What a pleasant surprise!'
Caroline smiled at Barney and held out her hand.
'What brings you to Northampton, sir?'

'I am here on business,' Barney said, achieving an
elegant bow over her hand. 'How do you do, ma'am?
Ladies…'

Introductions were effected. James Oliver mentioned that they were going to the booksellers to collect tickets for a concert that night and they all fell
into step as Lady Anne invited the gentlemen to escort them back to the Bear inn on their way.

Whilst James chatted to Frances, Lady Anne and

Caroline engaged Barney in conversation. Lavender felt secretly chagrined. In a contrary fashion, she had been hoping he would walk beside her.

'Do you find much to amuse you in Northampton, Mr Hammond?' Lady Anne enquired. 'It is only a small town but it seems quite lively!'

Barney gave her his slow smile and Lavender was almost sure she saw Lady Anne blink under its impact. It seemed that no one was immune.

'There is certainly plenty to see and do, ma'am!' Barney was saying. 'Tonight we are promised for a concert at the guildhall, as James mentioned. It was a choice between the recital and a performer of magical illusions, but I prefer the music because I am forever trying to work out how the magic tricks are done! It ruins one's enjoyment!'

'You must be a scientific gentleman, Mr Hammond,' Lady Anne said, with a smile. 'For my part I am always fascinated by such sleight of hand and never pause to question how it comes about!'

They reached the Bear and found the gentlemen already waiting for them in the parlour. Whilst they all shook hands, Lady Anne seemed struck with a good idea.

'Mr Hammond, Mr Oliver, are you already engaged for Friday night? If not you must come to our ball! No, positively you must! It would be delightful!'

Lavender felt rather than saw Barney glance across

quickly at her. It seemed obvious to her that he was torn between a polite lie and a reluctant acceptance. Her heart sank as she decided his natural inclination would be to avoid the ball on her account.

'Well, ma'am, you are most kind...' Barney began, 'but I do not think—'

'Oh, come now, old fellow,' James interposed, with a lazy smile at Frances, 'don't disappoint the ladies!'

'Oh, please say you will come!' Frances had turned quite pink as she added her heartfelt pleas and received a quelling look from her mother for her pains. Lavender did not dare look at Barney again. Part of her wanted him to accept and the other half was ready to sink with embarrassment.

'For my part, I should be delighted, ma'am,' Mr Oliver said quickly, 'and I am sure that Barney will be able to drag himself away from business if he tries hard enough!'

'That's settled then,' Anne Covingham said briskly, but with a warm smile. 'We shall look forward to seeing you at Riding Park on Friday night. I will send someone over with cards for you.'

Farewells were said and the gentlemen went off in the direction of Lacey's booksellers. Frances positively bounced over to Lavender's side. 'Oh Lavender, you lucky creature to know Mr Hammond already! Is he not the most charming man! And so prodigiously attractive...'

Lavender raised her eyebrows. She had thought that it was James Oliver who had been commanding most of Frances's attention and found that she felt more than a little jealous of her new friend's interest in Barney Hammond. For surely Barney *was* prodigiously attractive but she did not wish everyone to think so. Frances was rattling on.

'And Mr Oliver! I declare we are so fortunate to meet not one but two delightful gentlemen!'

'Here, on the other hand, is an encounter less enjoyable,' Caroline said dryly. She put a hand on Lavender's arm. 'Don't look now, my love, but I see your cousin Julia is in town!'

Lavender turned to peer out of the window. A smart travelling coach had pulled up in the yard and was disgorging its occupants. The gentleman was quite elderly, greying and distinguished, but hanging on his arm was a younger woman whom Lavender recognised with a sinking heart.

'Oh no, Caro, I fear you are right! It *is* cousin Julia!'

The vision was dressed in vivid blue, in a robe trailing acres of lace and surely more suitable for the boudoir than the town. A matching blue hat framed a face of pink and white perfection with huge blue eyes. Ringlets of guinea gold blew in the breeze.

The perfection was marred somewhat by a heavy frown, and even from inside the parlour, Lavender could hear her cousin's hectoring voice as she harangued a servant.

'What do you mean, the private parlour is occupied? Tell them to go elsewhere! We are far more important—'

'Who is *that?*' Frances Covingham whispered in Lavender's ear, staring hard. 'Why, she looks like a demi-rep!'

Anne Covingham, catching the edge of this whisper, shot her daughter a furious look. 'Frances, come away from the window—'

'I fear it is too late for escape,' Caroline said sepulchrally. 'They are coming this way—'

There was a step in the passage and the door swung open. Julia's china blue eyes swept over them all and she let out a little shriek.

'Lud! Caroline? Lavender! Lewis...'

Caroline had already stepped forward, with a mixture of resignation and courtesy, to greet the new arrivals.

'Julia! How do you do? This is a...surprise...'

'She is a distant cousin of ours,' Lavender whispered to Frances. 'Mrs Chessford—'

'Oh, I have heard of her!' Frances's eyes were bright with amusement. 'Mama calls her a bird of paradise masquerading as—'

'Delighted to meet you, Mrs Chessford,' Anne Covingham said hastily, stepping forward, hand outstretched. 'We have all heard such a great deal about you! I believe that you were hoping for a private parlour? By great good chance we were just leaving…'

The others all gathered their purchases together hurriedly. Lavender thought that Julia looked quite torn, on the one hand thanking Lady Anne graciously for her kindness and on the other evidently annoyed to be denied such august company.

'I shall call on you at Riding Park to express my obligation,' she gushed, grasping Lord Freddie warmly by the hand. 'It is so delightful to have some acquaintance in the locality!'

Lavender thought she saw Anne Covingham blench. She shepherded them all out to the carriages in short order and soon they were rattling back to Riding Park.

'The worst of it,' Caroline said gloomily, speaking for them all, 'is that Julia *will* call at the Park and will be impossibly difficult to shake off! I should not say it, but she is like a nasty rash—all over one and inducing unpleasant humours!' And they all collapsed into laughter.

Chapter Four

'This is all very dull,' Julia Chessford whispered in Lavender's ear. 'I had expected far better! This is just country neighbours of the Covinghams and not a coronet amongst them!'

They were sitting in the ballroom at Riding Park, watching a few couples circle the floor in a stately minuet. Up on the wooden minstrels' gallery a string quartet was playing and around the room the buzz of conversation was rising as the guests arrived and the servants circulated with a very fine champagne.

Lavender gave her cousin a look of comprehensive dislike. She had just been thinking the occasion very pleasant, and felt that Julia was more than fortunate to have been invited in the first place.

After the encounter at the inn, Julia had positively forced herself on their notice. She had taken advantage by calling every day, had proclaimed a fulsome fondness for Caroline and Lavender which the latter found quite nauseous, and had contrived to invite herself to the ball without so much as an 'if you please.'

Julia had grown up at Hewly as Admiral Brabant's ward and Lavender had known from the start that she was a sly, devious girl who would wheedle her way into company simply for what she could gain. Julia had been secretly betrothed to Lewis when they had both been in their green days, but she had thrown Lewis over for his elder brother Andrew, only to elope with Andrew's best friend instead. They had not heard from her again until her husband was dead and his fortune frittered away, then Julia had come to Hewly to try to extract money from her guardian and had used the excuse of the Admiral's last illness to foist herself on them once again. For a time Lavender had feared that Lewis would succumb to Julia's charm again, and had been relieved as well as delighted when Lewis's choice had rested on Caroline instead. Julia had left Hewly under a cloud when her attempts to blackmail the Admiral had been exposed, and for the best part of a year they had not heard from her. And now here she was again, like a bad penny…

'I am amazed at Lady Anne permitting her daughter to associate with tradesmen,' Julia continued, a sneer in her voice as she nodded across the ballroom at Frances Covingham, who was dancing the cotillion with Barney Hammond. Lavender felt the twin irri-

tations of a stab of jealousy and a rush of dislike for
Julia, and shifted uncomfortably on her rout chair.
Barney had not asked her to dance yet—if he was
going to ask at all—and it did not help that he appeared very popular with Lady Anne's female guests.
Lavender thought that Barney looked very striking in
his evening clothes. More than that, he moved with
an unconscious confidence and easy grace that made
him look quite at home.

'I suppose he dresses like a gentleman,' Julia said,
echoing Lavender's thoughts, 'but that is only to be
expected when one's father is a draper! Extraordinary! Northampton merchants in the Covinghams'
ballroom! It takes more than a fortune to wash away
the smell of the shop!'

'Well, of course, you would know that, Julia!'
Lavender said, pricked into retaliation by Julia's niggling. She knew it was childish, but since Julia's own
father had been in trade she thought her snobbery the
outside of enough.

Julia, however, had a hide as thick as an elephant.
'Well, I suppose the Covingham chit may be hanging
out for a fortune and Hammond could probably buy
up everyone in the room! But what is that to the
purpose when he has no breeding? The Covinghams
may not be high in the instep but surely they would
never permit their daughter to marry into trade!'

'I think you are jumping to extraordinary conclusions, Julia,' Lavender said coldly. 'Miss Covingham

has danced but once with Mr Hammond and looks in no danger of eloping! Besides, she has danced twice with Mr Oliver and even you must admit he is a very eligible *parti!*'

'Yes.' Julia's blue eyes narrowed thoughtfully. 'I confess I could develop a *tendre* there myself, for Mr Oliver is very good-looking and has all the connections that Mr Hammond lacks! He is a sad flirt, however, and faithless as the day is long!'

Lavender's lips twitched. Once again she felt the pot was calling the kettle black, for Julia's lack of fidelity was breathtaking.

Julia was still watching Frances and Barney Hammond as they danced the cotillion.

'Of course, the inclination to bolt does run in the Covingham family! Harriet Covingham threatened to run off with John Farley and now the *on dit* is that she is about to run away with her latest lover—'

Lavender sighed and fidgeted, wishing that either some gentleman would take pity on her and ask her to dance, or Caroline would return from her coze with Anne Covingham and rescue her. It was particularly galling that she had had no offers to dance, for she had thought she was quite in looks this evening. Frances had helped her choose her most flattering gown, a lavender silk of simple but stylish design, and she had arranged her hair in an elegant Grecian knot. She had felt reasonably happy with her appearance until Julia had arrived, tiny and stun-

ningly beautiful in soft rose pink, her hair a mass of
golden curls. Julia had allowed her blue gaze to linger on Lavender with a certain degree of pity and
her cousin had felt her warm glow of confidence
shrivel a little. And now the gentlemen did not ask
her to dance...

'Would you care to dance, Lavender?'

Julia smirked as Lewis Brabant bowed in front of
his sister. 'Lud, dancing with your own brother now,
Lavender! How slow!'

Lewis gave his cousin a look of disdain. 'Your
servant, Julia. I see that Lord Leverstoke has taken
refuge in the card room! I am surprised you could
not persuade him to dance with you!'

Julia flushed a little. She was evidently sensitive
about her elderly beau, whom Lavender had heard
was still married to someone else. Lewis gave
Lavender his arm and turned smartly away.

'We do not have to dance,' he said with a smile,
as they drew away from Julia, 'but Caro suggested I
bring you over to her anyway. It is a pity that Lady
Anne's manners are so good that she felt obliged to
invite Julia tonight! Our cousin is clearly as much of
an encroaching mushroom as ever!'

Lavender giggled. 'You are ungallant, Lewis!' she
chided. 'Lord Leverstoke seems to dote on her!'

Lewis shrugged his broad shoulders. 'Leverstoke
always had poor judgement! And he has no money
either, so I do not anticipate Julia wasting her time

on him for long! Someone younger and richer would be more to her taste!'

Lavender's glance slid away to Barney Hammond, who had finished his dance with Frances and was being introduced to another blushing débutante by Anne Covingham. The sight made Lavender feel sadly out of sorts. Turning her shoulder, she took a seat by Caroline, and Lewis strolled off to fetch them some more champagne.

Her sister-in-law welcomed her warmly. 'We thought we should rescue you, my love, for you looked as glum as a wet Tuesday! Who does Julia have her knife into this time?'

Lavender smiled and felt a little better. 'I fear she was being cruel about poor Mr Hammond! Of all the hypocrites, when her own father made his fortune from trade!'

'I can see you feel very strongly about it!' Caroline observed, raising her brows. Lavender realised that she had probably given away more than she intended. She blushed and tried to moderate her tone.

'Well, it is all so unfair, Caro! Mr Hammond has a pleasing address, and just because his father is a draper…'

'Yes,' Caroline smoothed the skirts of her amber gown, 'it is unfair. I should know, for I spent many years being slighted as an upper servant!' She smiled at Lavender. 'That is why the Covinghams are such particular friends, for they never made me feel in any way inferior. But it is a sad fact that most of society is not so generous! I deplore the gradations of snobbery but I see them all around me!'

Lavender slumped a little. She did not know why she felt the difficulty of Barney Hammond's position so keenly, but Julia's words had made her burn with fury. And it was not even as though Barney had pushed himself on their notice as Julia herself had done. Lavender told herself that she hated Julia's conceit, but at the back of her mind was a little voice that asked her if she was any better. She remembered her encounter with Barney that first night in the wood, and how she had thought his conversation impertinent. Had that not been because she was so sure of their relative positions as draper's son and admiral's daughter? And yet there was nothing so clear-cut about her feelings for him now…

Lavender squeezed her fan so tightly that two of the struts splintered. She pushed it into her bag, feeling even more annoyed.

'Of course,' Caroline continued, as Lewis came back to them with the refreshments, 'there is another reason that Julia dislikes Mr Hammond!'

Lewis handed her a glass of champagne and looked enquiring. 'Pray divulge it, my dear,' he said with a grin, sitting down beside them, 'for both Lavender and I are now on the edge of our chairs!'

'Well…' Caroline said. She sat forward a little, her eyes sparkling. 'I do believe that our cousin took Mr

Hammond in dislike after he…' she paused, 'after he rejected her advances!'

Lewis raised his eyebrows quizzically. Lavender drew a sharp breath.

'Oh Caro, no! Say she did not make a set at him!'

Caroline shrugged. 'Why not? She would scarce be the first lady to try!'

'Do you have any evidence for this theory, my love,' Lewis said lazily, 'or is it just scurrilous gossip on your part?'

Caroline looked hurt. 'Now Lewis… You know I do not gossip!' She bent a little closer to them. 'No, we were in Hammond's shop one day, and Mr Barnabas Hammond was dealing with Julia's requests for ribbons and bows, when suddenly I heard her remark that he was a fine figure of a man and a good advertisement for his father's tailoring!' Caroline's eyes twinkled. 'Well, I knew I was not supposed to be party to the conversation, but at that I leant closer!'

'I am sure you did…' Lewis murmured dryly.

Lavender patted her sister-in-law's hand. 'Take no notice of him! I want to hear what happened—'

'I am sure you do!' Lewis said ironically. Both girls glared at him.

'If you wish to spoil the story, pray stand further off, my dear!' Caroline said severely to her husband. She turned back to Lavender. 'Well, then Julia said that she had a particular commission for him, and would he care to come out to Hewly to consult with her privately! I do not think that *that* could be misconstrued!'

Lavender stared at her, her eyes huge. 'Caro! And Mr Hammond—'

Caroline started to laugh. 'I will never forget this bit! Barnabas Hammond said that he was grateful for her attention, but he was sorry, his father always dealt with the older ladies! I do not believe Julia ever forgave him! After that she always made me run the errands to the drapers!'

Lavender gave a snort of laughter. Even Lewis was hastily trying to repress a guffaw. There was something exquisitely pleasurable about Julia, who had made all their lives miserable with her high-handed ways and niggling remarks, receiving the set down that she so richly deserved.

'Oh dear, how dreadful!' she said, wiping the tears of laughter from her eyes. 'And truly, we should not laugh, but...' Her shoulders shook as she tried to get her mirth under control.

'Well,' Lewis said, 'I shall look on Hammond with even more kindness in future! I always thought him a man of great good sense, and here we have the proof!'

A half hour later, Lavender had just resigned herself to the fact that she would be sitting amongst the chaperones all evening, when James Oliver approached to ask her to partner him in the set of country dances that was just forming. After that, Lavender was besieged with partners, as though the company had only been waiting for one gentleman to approach her before they all rushed in. She was a good dancer and acquitted herself well, and found the social dialogue required on such occasions quite undemanding. One could not really strike up a proper conversation, for the steps of the dance were forever separating the partners, but Lavender reflected that this was perhaps all to the good. She had heard quite enough about Mr Henshaw's pack of gun dogs and she was not terribly interested in Mr Salton's new curricle. She remembered that her chaperone during the London Season had told her that a lady should always appear to find a gentleman's conversation fascinating, but Lavender thought this so much nonsense. She had quickly seen that a gentleman was treated as though he was even more charming if he had the good fortune to be an Earl or a Duke.

Mr Salton was still holding forth about the brilliance of his team when Lavender saw Barney Hammond approaching them across the ballroom. It had not escaped her notice that he had danced twice already with Miss Covingham and that the irrepressible Frances had been very reluctant to lose his company.

Barney bowed very formally to her, but there was a smile in his eyes.

'Miss Brabant, I have been hoping against hope that you would still be free to grant me the supper dance? I would be honoured.'

Lavender was about to agree, when Mr Salton cleared his throat meaningfully. 'Don't think that would be quite the thing, old chap. After all, there is an order of precedence at these events, don't you know, and for you to lead in Miss Brabant...' He let the sentence hang with just the faintest implication of a sneer.

Lavender saw Barney flush as the insult struck home, saw the flash of pure fury in his eyes before he fought down his anger and gave the younger man a bland smile.

'Thank you for your advice, old fellow.' There was more than a little sarcasm in his own voice now. 'I was, however, addressing Miss Brabant...'

He turned back to Lavender and for a second she saw the hint of uncertainty in his face, before he squared his shoulders as though preparing to receive a set down. That brief moment when she saw his vulnerability gave her the strangest feeling inside.

'Thank you, Mr Hammond,' she said a little tremulously. 'I should be delighted to dance with you.'

The music had already struck up. Barney offered her his arm and led her into the nearest set.

'Thank you for your kindness, Miss Brabant,' he murmured, as they took their place in the dance. 'It was most generous in you—'

Lavender had recovered herself and could not bear to hear him sound so humble. 'I am neither generous nor kind, Mr Hammond,' she said crisply, 'except in general terms, of course. I *wished* to dance with you!'

For a moment Barney looked startled by such a frank admission, then he rallied.

'Well, in that case—'

'And pray do not thank me again,' Lavender finished, thinking that she may as well be hanged for a sheep as a lamb, 'for I did nothing but consult my own inclination! There! We may be comfortable again!'

Barney's face was grave, shadowed. It seemed that he could not shake off Mr Salton's insults so lightly. 'Do you not judge as the rest of the world then, Miss Brabant, on rank and consequence and such matters?'

'So much nonsense!' Lavender said, knowing she sounded just like her late papa, the Admiral. 'A fine thing it would be for me to apply society's rules when I am one of those it most disapproves of, for valuing books above looks!'

Barney's expression lightened as he laughed. 'And where do accomplishment and intellect rate in the eyes of the world, Miss Brabant?'

'Why, almost nowhere, I believe! Accomplishment in a female is quite a good thing as long as it is restricted to drawing prettily and playing well, but it cannot compensate for good looks!'

'You are an outspoken critic,' Barney said slowly.

'Of society's rules? Well, they are so foolish and fickle they deserve my derision!' Lavender smiled at him. There was still a small frown between his eyes but it melted as his gaze met hers and something warmer took its place. Lavender suddenly felt unaccountably hot. She fell silent, pretending that she was concentrating on the steps of the dance.

Dancing with Barney was more disturbing than she had anticipated; the touch of his hand stirred memories of their encounter in the wood, and once again, his proximity had a wholly disconcerting effect on her. Lavender was used to being in control of her emotions and she found this weakness deeply unsettling.

'Perhaps we should conform to convention and speak of more commonplace matters, Mr Hammond?' she said, a little at random. 'Are you enjoying the ball?'

'Yes, indeed. The Covinghams are very pleasant people,' Barney said promptly. 'Your friend, Miss Covingham, is a delightful girl, is she not?'

Lavender felt the same sinking feeling that she remembered from the parties and balls of her London Season. Just as soon as she had thought she had found a pleasant gentleman with whom to converse in a sensible fashion, it seemed that he only wished to discuss her prettier companions. That it was Barney Hammond talking to her this time only seemed to make matters worse.

'Oh, Frances is the kindest creature imaginable,' she said, trying to keep her tone light, 'and a true friend to me since we first arrived here!'

'She tells me that she is much in awe of you,' Barney said, with a smile. 'She said that she wishes she were even half as accomplished, though given your recent remarks, you may not rate that a compliment!'

Lavender smiled. 'Well, I know Frances would never deal in Spanish coin, so I am grateful that she at least values my attainments! But then with Caro as her governess, it is no surprise that she sees the value of useful accomplishments!'

The final flourish of the music swept them into their respective bow and curtsey, and it was then time to go into supper. Caroline waved at them across the room.

'Do you wish to take supper with us?' she asked, slipping her hand through Lavender's arm. 'The most diverting thing—I have just been talking to the odious Mr Salton! He was chatting pleasantly until I said that I had worked for the Covingham family, upon which he started, bowed slightly and said that he had mistaken me for a friend of the family! He then walked off—'

'And I almost ran him through!' Lewis finished, somewhat grimly. 'Insufferable young puppy!'

'Anne tells me that he has just inherited his uncle's estate and is all puffed up with his own conse-

quence!' Caroline said. 'Never mind. Let us talk on
more agreeable topics!'

They chatted pleasantly about Northampton, its
entertainments and amusements, until supper was
ended and Barney excused himself to dance with another of Anne Covingham's protégées.

'Mr Hammond is very popular tonight,' Caroline
observed idly, 'and most confident in this setting. He
is a most unusual young man. Do you not think so,
Lavender?'

'Oh, he is very pleasant,' Lavender agreed
brightly, hoping she did not sound as though she
were trying too hard to sound careless.

'Damned with faint praise!' Caroline said, but
there was a twinkle in her eye.

It was towards the end of the ball that Lavender
had the misfortune of bumping into the graceless Mr
Salton again. She had gone upstairs to fetch a wrap
for Caroline and had paused in the Long Gallery to
admire some of the Covingham portraits on the way
back. There was a very fine likeness of Lady Anne
as a young girl, a flattering portrait of Lord Freddie,
and beside it a small picture of a gentleman in a gilt
frame. Lavender had almost passed it by, for it was
in a dark corner, but something caught her eye. She
stepped a little closer.

The gentleman in the picture was young and dark,
with an inscrutable expression that seemed strangely
familiar. Lavender was just puzzling over where she

had seen him before when she heard a footstep beside her and someone's arm insinuated itself about her waist. Lavender turned sharply to confront Mr Salton's flushed face and recoiled from the stench of wine on his breath.

'Miss Brabant! Loitering with intent, ma'am?'

Lavender tried to step back, but he held her firmly.

'I have no notion what you mean, sir!' she said, with distaste. 'Kindly leave me alone!'

Mr Salton leered meaningfully. 'No need to play coy, ma'am! I know that you were waiting for me!'

He leant forward clumsily and Lavender realised belatedly and with horror that he was about to try and kiss her. She turned her head sharply and felt him press his wet lips to her neck rather than her mouth. She shuddered.

'Mr Salton! You forget yourself! Unhand me at once!' She wanted to sound authoritative but was aware that instead she sounded breathless with outrage and surprise. She struggled, kicking his shins as hard as she could in her ball slippers, and slapping his grasping hands aside with her fan. The treatment was probably not painful but it was effective. Mr Salton's already flushed face turned a deeper red and he yelped with fury, grabbing Lavender's wrist.

'You little vixen! You'll pay for that—'

'Can I be of service, Miss Brabant? Mrs Brabant sent me to find you—she was somewhat concerned that you had been gone for some time...'

Lavender closed her eyes for an agonised moment.
The measured tones could only be those of Barney
Hammond, who seemed to be making a habit of res-
cuing her these days. Her face burned with a mixture
of embarrassment and fury to have been found in
such an undignified situation. Nor was Mr Salton
helping the case, for he was evidently so inebriated
that he could barely grasp what was happening and
was still holding on to her wrist. She saw Barney's
dark eyes narrow murderously as he took in Mr
Salton's drunken state and the fact that he was still
gripping her arm. As she tried to free herself, Barney
said silkily, 'Unhand the lady, Salton. You are making a nuisance of yourself.'

Mr Salton's hand dropped away from Lavender as
he turned unsteadily to face his new adversary.
'Don't presume to tell me what to do, Hammond,'
he sneered. 'What can the jumped up son of a draper
possibly know about polite society—'

Barney's face was expressionless. 'My antecedents
have nothing to do with your bad manners, Salton.
Stand aside.'

Mr Salton stepped back and took a wild swing at
Barney. The blow failed to connect since he was so
drunk he could barely see straight. Lavender drew a
sharp breath. For a moment, Barney looked so dangerous that she was certain he was about to hit Salton
and she was sure that his aim would be considerably
more direct. Then Barney paused, put one hand on

Salton's shoulder and simply pushed the younger man. The drink did the rest. Salton staggered, cannoned off the edge of the window embrasure, and slumped quietly on the floor. Lavender pressed both hands to her mouth.

'Oh no! How dreadful!'

'But infinitely better than it might have been.' Barney's face was still expressionless.

He took a couple of steps towards her. 'I hope that you are not hurt, Miss Brabant?'

All Lavender's mortification came flooding back. 'Not in the least, sir. Thank you for your prompt intervention. I am sorry that it was necessary.'

'So am I,' Barney said a little grimly. 'If you will loiter in poorly lit corridors, Miss Brabant—'

Lavender, suffering from shock and embarrassment, reacted strongly to the injustice of this. It had not occurred to her that any of the blame might attach to her. 'I merely paused to take a look at the portraits, sir! I cannot see that that gives Mr Salton the right to think that he may force his attentions on me!'

'Not the right, but the opportunity,' Barney said, with an expressive lift of his dark brows. 'You seem to be forever wandering into trouble, do you not, Miss Brabant? Walking in the forest at night, getting caught in traps during the day, facilitating the attentions of a drunken womaniser—'

Lavender flushed with fury. She took an impulsive

step forward. 'How dare you, sir! Your observations on my conduct are discourteous—'

She found that her anger had propelled her far closer to him than she had intended, and that an acute physical awareness of him suddenly overcame her. The words dried in her throat and she stared up into the dark eyes that were suddenly so close to her own. She saw the moment when his own expression changed, focusing more intently on her, setting her heart racing. He took a step towards her, the final step. They were very close now. Lavender could not tear her gaze away from him.

Barney's hand was already on her arm when there was the sound of a step along the stone corridor and they broke apart, the moment shattered.

Caroline's voice said, 'There you are! I had quite given up on my wrap—' She broke off as her gaze fell on the recumbent form of Mr Salton. 'Oh dear, I see—your handiwork, Mr Hammond?'

Lavender heard Barney take a deep breath. 'I can claim little credit, I fear, ma'am,' he said. 'The gentleman was so inebriated he could barely stand.'

Caroline tutted. 'Well, let us leave him here until Lord Freddie's servants throw him out! Mr Hammond, would you be so good as to escort us back to the ballroom?'

'Gladly, ma'am.' Barney stepped back with scrupulous courtesy to allow Lavender to precede him.

She was very aware that he was avoiding looking directly at her. His expression was quite blank.

'I think I shall retire,' she said quickly. 'I have no taste for further dancing. Good night, Mr Hammond. Good night, Caro.'

She sped away before Caroline could demur, hurried along the corridor to her room, and threw herself on the bed, lying back and staring at the canopy. Her heart was still beating quickly, the residual excitement still fizzing in her blood.

Another second, and she knew Barney Hammond would have kissed her. She had wanted him to, ached for him to take her in his arms. She was still trembling at the thought, could still feel the touch of his hand and see the concentrated look in those dark eyes... Lavender rolled over, pressing her hot face into the pillow. The same heat had infused her blood when she had seen Barney at the pool in the forest. He was as prodigiously attractive as Frances Covingham had said, and she could not deny it.

She lay there breathing in the sweet scent of lavender from the sheets and listening to the faint sound of music from the ballroom below. What was happening to her? It was one thing to admire a personable man, or to be drawn to the conversation of a man of sense and integrity. It was quite another to feel such passion, both physical and intellectual. She had never experienced the like of it before and it was utterly perplexing. Lavender lay still, conjuring up the memory of Barney's touch, his voice. She shivered. She knew she was in danger of losing her heart and it was a frightening thought. For all her brave words against snobbery, she knew that such an unequal match could never be.

'Oh Lavender, I swear I have lost my heart and it can never be!' Frances Covingham was shredding a tiny white handkerchief between her fingers and was obliged to borrow Lavender's considerably larger one to wipe away her tears. 'Mama has warned me—gently, but warned me nonetheless—that he is too old and quite ineligible! I feel so desolate I think I shall cast myself into the lake!'

Frances accompanied the words with a look over her shoulder at the Riding Park lake, which glittered placidly in the midday sun. It was the afternoon following the ball and the two girls were sitting on a bench that was prettily positioned under some weeping willow. A family of ducks fluttered and splashed in the shallows. It was a tranquil scene, but Frances was far from calm. She had positively dragged Lavender away from the rest of the party in order to unburden her heart to her and Lavender felt ill equipped for the role of confidant.

Lavender had not slept particularly well, for her dreams had been snatched and full of images of Barney Hammond. Unlike Frances, who managed to look desolate but pretty, Lavender knew that she simply looked wan. And now, to hear Frances speaking of her tender feelings for Barney almost broke her heart.

'I have never met such an interesting and personable man,' Frances lamented, another tear rolling down her cheek. 'Last night—it must have been after you had retired, dearest Lavender—we sat and talked for hours! I felt so warm and so comfortable and so *happy*—'

She gave a miserable sniff.

'Perhaps your mama might relent,' Lavender said, feeling like a traitor, though whether to herself or to her friend she was not quite sure. 'Although, Frances, I must allow that Lady Anne is in the right of it. Your grandfather was a Duke and you are very eligible, whereas he—'

'I do not see that he is at all ineligible!' Frances disputed hotly. 'He has air and address and besides, his family is as good as mine!'

Lavender frowned, wondering if she had missed something. Frances seemed so distressed that she did not wish to add to her misery, but she could not agree.

'And now this morning Mama tells me that I must not see him again,' Frances finished, 'for she says that I am too young to form a lasting attachment and he has a reputation as a flirt—'

Lavender looked at her in astonishment. Whatever the charges that could be levelled at Barney

Hammond, this was not one of them. 'A flirt! Surely not! I have never observed Mr Hammond behave in such a way!'

Frances's green eyes opened very wide. 'Mr Hammond! Well, of course Mr Hammond is not a flirt! But I have heard that Mr Oliver has a reputation for it, although with me,' she blushed, 'he was the perfect soul of propriety even when I wished him not to be!'

Lavender frowned again. Her head was beginning to ache a little. The sun seemed very bright.

'I beg your pardon, Frances, but is it Mr Oliver for whom you have formed this attachment rather than Mr Hammond? I thought—' She broke off, deciding that there was no point in confusing the issue further. Frances was already looking at her with eyes wide with incredulity.

'Of course it is Mr Oliver! Who else? Really, Lavender, have you not been listening to a word I was saying?'

'No doubt it was very vexatious of me,' Lavender agreed meekly, 'but I was confused. After all, you had danced several times with Mr Hammond—'

'Yes, and Mr Potts and that odious Mr Salton! What is that to the purpose, pray? I sat and talked to Mr Oliver—James…' She blushed again, 'for hours, and he was so charming and kind to me! But Mama says that he is a hardened flirt and that she will not have another of her daughters making a foolish match and so…' she gave a little sob '…I am not to see him again!'

She held the soaking handkerchief forlornly in her hand, and Lavender rummaged in her reticule and produced a second one. 'There! How fortunate that I should have two! But pray do not cry any more, Frances, for it makes your nose quite pink! What if Mr Oliver were to call to pay his compliments and you are sitting out here with eyes and nose as red as a white rabbit?'

Lavender felt quite heartless as she spoke, but this was undoubtedly the best way to calm Frances, who was much struck by the idea of looking ugly. She wiped her eyes for a final time and took a deep breath.

'I suppose you are right. A melancholy air—without the tears—might be the very thing!'

'Precisely!' Lavender spoke bracingly. 'I am truly sorry that you needs must suffer for your sister's indiscretions, Frances, but perhaps Lady Anne will relent if she sees you behave in a sensible way! And if Mr Oliver is also steadfast in his affections—well, who knows…?'

Frances grasped her hand. 'Lavender, will you carry a letter to Mr Oliver for me? You could give it to Mr Hammond, for they are friends, after all, and Mr Hammond could pass a note on…'

Lavender's heart sank. Evidently Frances's idea of sensible behaviour and her own were poles apart.

'I do not think that a very good idea, Frances! Only think what would happen if your mama discovered you in a clandestine correspondence—'

'Oh please!' Frances's big green eyes pleaded with her. 'A letter can do no harm! Why, Mama should commend my industry, for she knows I hate writing letters!'

Lavender wriggled uncomfortably. She hated having to play a discouraging role, but she knew it was a bad idea to encourage Frances's hopes.

'I do not think that your mama would see it that way, Frances! And truly, it is not a very good idea!'

Lavender broke off. It was difficult to counsel sense to Frances when the idea actually held some appeal. To be the courier for Frances's letters to James Oliver, and have an excuse to see Barney Hammond again without having to buy another unnecessary pair of gloves... Lavender shook her head sharply. She knew that now she was just being foolish. If James Oliver was not an acceptable suitor for the granddaughter of a Duke, Barney Hammond was even less so for an Admiral's daughter. Besides, Frances did at least have some grounds for believing her feelings reciprocated. Lavender gazed at the sparkling lake and reflected miserably that she had no such basis for believing that Barney liked her. He had been courteous, kind even, and she had imagined that he might have wanted to kiss her, but that was all it was—imagination. And it was high time she accepted the truth.

Chapter Five

They left Riding Park two days later, sped on their way by good wishes and promises to visit from all the Covingham family. Frances had hugged Lavender and sworn that she would write, despite reminding her that she was the very worst correspondent in the whole world. The Covinghams planned to stay another two to three weeks in the country before making their way to London for the Little Season, and Frances was torn between high delight at the thought of her début in society and continued melancholy over her feelings for Mr Oliver.

The carriage was comfortable and Caroline dozed a little as they made slow progress along the narrow lanes. Lavender stared out of the window, and Lewis read one of the books that he had stopped to collect in Northampton. He had also picked up a parcel for Barney Hammond whilst he was there, for the bookseller, knowing that the Brabants were from Steep Abbot, had asked if they would undertake the delivery. Lavender wished that Lewis had refused but her brother, ever obliging, had cheerfully taken the commission.

Lavender looked at the parcel for Barney and, despite herself, wondered what it contained. Perhaps it was another medical dictionary for his mother, or some work of fiction for his sister. She remembered his references to his studies and wondered suddenly if these were academic books, and whether this was another of Barney's secrets. Perhaps he read Byron of an evening, seated in the drawing-room of the fine house that the Hammonds owned in Abbot Quincey. She tried to imagine it—for a moment she actually tried to place herself there, before the fire, with her botanical sketches and her works of scientific reference. Then her imagination fixed upon her sharing a fireside with Arthur Hammond, and her mind shuddered at the picture. Decidedly that would not do. Whichever fortunate young lady ended up as Barney's choice, she would have to love him a great deal to tolerate such a father-in-law.

Lavender looked out across the fields. The hedges and trees were fading from red and gold to the bare brown of winter. She usually loved the turning of the year, but just at the moment it made her feel sad. She looked up to see that Lewis had put down his book and was regarding her solemnly.

'What is it, sis? You look blue-devilled!'

Lavender smiled at the childhood appellation. 'I suppose it is just the loss of company. I had not expected to get pleasure from our visit to Riding Park, yet I had a prodigiously enjoyable time of it!'

Lewis nodded. 'Yes, it was most agreeable. And now we are thrown back on our own company—'

'Well, it will suffice!' Lavender suddenly felt more cheerful. 'I shall enjoy seeing Hewly again and besides, if we are short of company we may always invite Julia to stay—'

They laughed together.

'You may mock,' Caroline said sleepily, uncurling from her corner, 'but I heard her say that she would call! And she is still a sort of cousin, for all her misdemeanours!'

They started to discuss the ball.

'It is strange, is it not,' Caroline said, as the carriage rattled along, picking up speed now, 'how a man so pushing as Arthur Hammond should have produced a son as charming as Barney. One would think that he would not have it in him!'

Her words stirred a memory in Lavender's mind, a picture of herself taking tea with Nanny Pryor in the cottage on the estate where her old nurse had moved in her retirement. It had been two years ago, or perhaps three. They had been chatting and Lavender had idly said to the nurse that the Hammonds all had very distinctive dark good looks,

apart from Arthur Hammond, who was fair and
florid. And Nanny Pryor had poured the tea into the
flowered china cups and had said that the Hammonds
had all been fair in the male line until Arthur
Hammond's grandfather had married a Spanish girl,
and that Barney Hammond had inherited his looks
from his mother. Lavender could remember the
pursed look on Nanny Pryor's face, the prim expression that always preceded a major piece of gossip.
Then, sure enough, the nurse had said that Barney
was really Hammond's nephew and not his son at
all…

'I had heard that Barney is not Hammond's real
son—' Lavender said thoughtfully, breaking off at
the look of astonishment on the faces of Lewis and
Caroline. 'At least, that is the rumour,' she added, a
little hesitantly, 'but I have no notion if it is true…'

Lewis was frowning. 'I have never heard that tale,
Lavender. Where did you get it from?'

'Nanny Pryor told me,' Lavender said, blushing to
be repeating gossip. 'She said that Eliza Hammond
was Barney's mother, making Arthur Hammond his
uncle, not his father. No one knew who his real father
was, but there are those who say that it was the
Marquis of Sywell…'

Lewis whistled. 'Well, there are enough of
Sywell's brats about the county, it's true! What became of Eliza Hammond herself?'

'She died in childbirth and never spoke the name

of her lover,' Lavender said. 'At least that is what Nanny Pryor said. Apparently the Hammonds took the child as their own and never spoke of it again. I had almost forgot the tale until just now.'

Caroline raised her eyebrows. 'It's an intriguing story! It would certainly explain why Hammond treats Barney as a type of glorified shop manager rather than a true son!'

The others looked at her enquiringly. 'Well,' Caroline pointed out, 'have you never observed that Hammond has sent his second son—his eldest son, if the tale is true—away to university whilst poor Barney is expected to work in the shop? Hammond has been so successful and is such a social climber, that he grooms his children as ladies and gentlemen! The boys have a tutor and the girls a governess, and he clearly feels the shop not good enough for them. What man would not, having achieved what he has done? And this gives him the best of both worlds, for whilst they may inherit his fortune, Barney will be there to carry on the business!'

Lavender turned to look out of the window. She did not wish her face to betray her. She had given little thought to the old tale before, for the Abbey villages were always full of gossip, but now it made her wonder—and it made her burn with indignation for Barney. She could not see why he should be made to suffer twice over, once for being illegitimate, and a second time because he was obliged to do Hammond's bidding to earn his keep. That would explain why he kept so much a secret from his family, the adoptive relatives with whom he did not quite fit.

'I cannot see that it would be much advantage to be another of Sywell's by-blows,' Lewis was saying. 'Unlikely that a man would inherit any good looks or charm from that quarter!'

'Do you think that they will ever discover who murdered the Marquis?' Caroline asked idly, with a little shiver. 'Ugh! It gives me the horrors to think of someone creeping about that old barn of an Abbey intent on murder!'

Lavender turned away again. This was one conversation that she certainly did not intend to join, for it pricked her conscience. There were certain things that she knew, things she had seen, that the Lord Lieutenant who was investigating the Marquis's murder would be very interested to know. But she could never tell...

'I do declare we are become as good gossips as anyone in the kingdom,' Caroline said, on a yawn. 'It must be the Covinghams' influence! Lord, I am tired, though! I am glad we are nearly home!'

The coach had almost reached Steep Abbott now. Lavender sat back and watched the trees of Steep Wood press in on the road. In the distance she could see the curve of the river. It was familiar and beautiful, and it did a little to assuage the ache in her heart. There was no doubt, though, that the remedy for her indisposition lay in her own hands. She would have to avoid Barney Hammond, at least until this foolish *tendre* she had developed had faded away. Then she might be able to treat him with equanimity. Now she had no such chance.

The following day saw Lavender walking into Abbot Quincey, in direct contradiction of what she knew to be her own best interests. Lewis had originally intended to take the gig out and drive round the estate, visiting Abbot Quincey afterwards to deliver Barney's books and make a number of other calls. However, the tenant of Hewlton, a farm some three miles away, had called on Lewis urgently to discuss the problem of a fallen tree that had breached the estate wall. The two men were closeted in Lewis's study and Caroline had suggested gently that Lavender might like to visit the Percevals—and hand over the books on the way.

Lavender had wanted to refuse but could not think of an adequate excuse. Part of her wanted to confide her feelings in Caroline anyway, but the other part was in such a turmoil that she knew not what she might say. In the end she had agreed, and had taken the package of books and an offering of apples from the Newton Wonder tree for Lady Perceval.

Barney was serving in the shop when she went in, and was just handing a parcel over to an elderly lady, coming around the counter to hold the door for her with a word and a smile. Lavender dodged behind a bolt of nankeen in order to avoid Arthur Hammond, who had not yet seen her. She waited until Barney was back behind the counter, then popped out from behind the roll of material and leaned across the work top. 'Mr Hammond!' she hissed.

Barney raised his eyebrows, looking faintly amused. 'Miss Brabant? Is something amiss?'

Lavender frowned at him. 'Pray lean closer, sir!'

Barney obligingly bent forward. 'Yes, Miss Brabant?'

'I have some books for you,' Lavender whispered. 'I thought you might not wish your father to see—'

Barney glanced over his shoulder at Arthur Hammond, who was draping a roll of sarsenet around a pillar and humming under his breath.

'Books from Northampton?' Barney whispered. Lavender nodded, though she was not really concentrating on his words. She noticed that his eyes were very dark brown indeed, with a ring of black around the iris. His eyelashes were incredibly thick and black, and his hair looked so soft and silky…

'Miss Brabant!' Barney said sharply, and Lavender jumped, blushing.

'Yes?'

Barney looked faintly exasperated. 'I will unroll a bolt of cambric on the counter. Slide the books beneath.'

Lavender scrabbled in her basket, gave Arthur Hammond a quick glance to ensure that he was not watching, and slid the package beneath the material.

'Thank you!' Barney gave her his heart-shaking smile. He looked over her shoulder and the smile faded. 'Not to your taste, Miss Brabant?' he asked, suddenly formal. 'Perhaps the sarsenet? There is an elegant display over by the pillar...'

Lavender sensed rather than saw Arthur Hammond standing directly behind them. She turned and threw him a dazzling smile.

'Mr Hammond! We were so very impressed by your emporium in Northampton, sir! Lady Anne Covingham was saying that it is the finest store in the whole town...' She edged towards the door, still talking, and saw to her relief that Barney had eased the books under the counter and out of sight. Arthur Hammond was preening himself and basking in her flattery, and he saw her out of the door with many fulsome compliments and thanks, totally failing to notice that Lavender had bought nothing at all.

She walked rapidly away from the shop and only paused to draw breath when she reached the Angel inn. She reflected that she was not really cut out for deception, even so simple a deception as this. It made her wonder why Barney had to hide his academic pursuits from his father, but she supposed that if Arthur Hammond was determined that his adopted son should concentrate his attentions on the shop, he might be incensed to think that Barney was distracted by other interests.

Lavender slowed her pace and paused to adjust her bonnet. It was a sunny day, but rather more humid than of late. She had forgotten her parasol again, despite Caroline's reminder.

There was the sound of running feet and Lavender turned to see Ellen Hammond hurrying down the road towards her, as she had done the day after Lavender had taken the kittens in.

'Miss Brabant!' Ellen was out of breath. 'Barney asked me to give you a message. He thanks you for bringing his books and asks if it would be possible for you to do so again when his next delivery arrives.' She blushed. 'Our father, you know, is most disapproving of Barney's studies—'

'I understand,' Lavender said quickly, wondering just what it was that Barney could be studying so secretly. She was torn, for on the one hand there was something appealing about being drawn into a conspiracy with him, even over a matter as inconsequential as some secret books. On the other, she knew it was a foolish indulgence, tempting because it would lead to further meetings... But Ellen was looking at her with such entreaty and it was impossible to resist.

'Please tell your brother that I should be only too happy if he wishes his books to be sent to Hewly,' Lavender said.

Ellen gave her a radiant smile. 'Oh thank you, Miss Brabant! You are so kind!'

They walked a little way down the road together, Ellen confiding artlessly about how hard Barney had to work and how he sometimes studied late into the night, poring over his books by candlelight. In return, Lavender told her that the kittens were growing fast on a diet of kitchen scraps provided by the indulgent servants, and that they were too lazy to catch the mice that scratched in the barn outside. She and Ellen parted company, the best of good friends, at the entrance to Perceval Hall, and Lavender watched the girl skip away up the road back into the town. Her own step was slower. There was no doubt that it would have been wiser for her to refuse Barney's request, leave well alone, avoid him... Unfortunately her own heart was now engaged and common sense had nothing to do with it.

The next consignment of books arrived ten days later. Lavender had spent the afternoon with Caroline in the garden, where her sister-in-law was advising Belton, the gardener, on the restoration project. It was Lewis and Caroline's intention to re-create the gardens of a hundred years before, when Hewly had been part of the Perceval estate. Then, as Belton never ceased to remind them, the Hewly Manor gardens had been considered amongst the finest in Northamptonshire.

It was another hot day and the sun was low as Lavender trailed back inside. She had been in the kitchen garden, where the damson, walnut and green-gage trees had provided some shade against the unseasonably hot sun. Although she had been speaking knowledgeably of fruit trees and cold frames with Caroline and Belton, most of Lavender's mind had been preoccupied with thoughts of how and when she would contact Barney. It was Sunday on the morrow and although they might all meet up at Abbot Quincey church, she could scarcely attend with a parcel of books tucked under her arm.

The stone-flagged hallway of the Manor was cool in comparison with outside, and so dark that Lavender at first failed to see the figure waiting patiently at the bottom of the stairs. She jumped as he stepped forward, and she saw with a little leap of the heart that it was Barney Hammond himself.

'Miss Brabant!' Barney came forward quickly, sketching her a bow. 'Forgive me for troubling you, ma'am. I was at pains to deliver your order as soon as it was ready.'

He held out a parcel that was wrapped in brown paper and tied with a ribbon. Lavender took it automatically, looking a little confused.

'My order?' she echoed. 'But I did not—'

Barney shot her a warning glance. One of the maids was polishing the banisters, dusting assiduously as she edged ever closer to them.

'Oh, that order!' Lavender said, hoping she did not sound too hen-witted. 'How kind you are, Mr Hammond! I was not expecting it so soon!'

'Would you care to open it to see if the goods are of the appropriate quality?'

Lavender unwrapped the package hesitantly. It was a shawl, silky as gossamer and blue to match her eyes. She looked from it to Barney and saw that he was smiling.

'It is beautiful! But—'

'I wondered, perhaps,' Barney said quickly, 'whether you had anything to return to me, Miss Brabant? You mentioned that there was a fault in the cambric you purchased—'

'Oh, indeed!' Lavender said, catching his meaning. She had been puzzled by the delivery of the shawl but now saw that it was just a useful excuse. 'By chance, I was only examining that today, sir. It is indeed a pity, but I believe the consignment must be returned to you.'

'I am happy to wait if you would care to hand it back,' Barney said. 'However, if it is not convenient, perhaps…later?'

Lavender paused. Rosie was giving the banisters such a polish that Lavender feared they might wear away. She knew she could dismiss the maid so that she could talk to Barney freely, but that would only cause further speculation in the servants' hall. She could not really invite him into the drawing-room either, for that simply did not happen when the draper was delivering an order. She bit her lip. She did not like the feelings of snobbery that the whole situation engendered. In fact, it seemed all wrong for Barney to be waiting on her like this.

'If you would be good enough to call some other time, sir... I need to fetch the material and package it up, and would not care to keep you waiting...'

'I would be happy to return later,' Barney said meaningfully. 'After dinner? Perhaps we could meet as we have done before, Miss Brabant...'

Lavender walked with him to the door and watched him stroll away across the gravel sweep. She knew she had not misunderstood him. He would be waiting for her later in the woods—and she would certainly be there.

When Lavender slipped out of the gate that led from Hewly gardens to the wood that night, Barney was already standing in the shadows beneath the trees. It was just getting dark and the sky was a clear, dark blue, with the leafy outlines of the trees imprinted against it in black. Barney came forward to hold the gate open for her. Lavender could hear the brook running in the background and the wind in the trees, smell the faint, fresh scent of the forest. It was a beautiful evening.

They fell into step with each other without speaking, turning along the path that skirted the edge of the wood. Last year's leaves crunched underfoot. Lavender felt the excitement and the secrecy and the darkness stir in her blood. It was a heady mixture. She wanted to take Barney's hand and run through the wood until she was breathless.

'You have the parcel?' Barney whispered.

'Yes,' Lavender held out the brown paper package to him. 'I have also brought the shawl, as I thought—'

'That was a present,' Barney said. 'For your help, Miss Brabant.' His tone brooked no argument.

'Oh!' Lavender smiled a little diffidently. She had never received a gift from a gentleman and was not certain if she should accept. 'Well—' she tried to sound businesslike '—I have your books here! A heavy package this time! What are all these volumes that you are buying, Mr Hammond?'

Barney hesitated. 'They are works on medicine, Miss Brabant. The Northampton bookseller orders them for me from London.'

Lavender was intrigued. 'Are you then studying to be a doctor?'

Barney laughed. 'No, not that! I study pharmacy, Miss Brabant; the uses of medicaments and chemical preparations for alleviating illness. That is why I was forever in the apothecary's shop in Northampton, and why I have all these books sent to me.' He tapped the parcel under his arm. 'I am hoping that this is the new London *Pharmacopoeia,* for I have been waiting for it a while.'

'How long have you been studying these works?' Lavender enquired.

'Oh, for ever! I have some old books on botany and the healing properties of herbs…' Barney smiled. 'That was what first caught my interest, and I have always wanted to learn more of medicines and compounds.'

'Do you wish to dispense medicines—to be an apothecary yourself?'

Barney laughed again at that. 'I would rather be a pharmacist! It is the development of new cures that interests me rather than the prescribing of them! But,' his voice fell, 'I am entirely self-taught, as you may imagine, and though I have been in correspondence for a while now with a London pharmacist, it will be a long time before I can put my plans into effect! One day I aim to establish myself as a member of the Royal Pharmaceutical Society, but—'

He broke off to resume, carefully, 'Well, there is the drapery business, and my father has other ideas…' He stopped again. 'Forgive me, Miss Brabant! You have been more than kind in taking delivery of the books for me but I have no wish to bore you with my plans…'

'It is not boring,' Lavender said warmly, 'and indeed you must already know of my own interest in botany! I should be fascinated to see your old books…'

'You may borrow them if you wish,' Barney said, with a smile. 'Yes, I had not forgotten that you had been sketching the plants that day when I found you caught in the trap! And in fact I often go out collecting roots, bark and leaves, for some of my preparations. Playing truant from the shop all the time, I fear!'

'So that is why you are forever wandering in the wood—' Lavender started but stopped again hastily as she realised this was a conversational path she did not necessarily wish to follow. All her thoughts seemed to lead inevitably back to seeing him at the pool in the forest and she did not wish to speak about that. 'I thought that most cures were from plants growing in the New World rather than our own woodlands,' she said, quickly. 'Ipecac from Brazil, for instance.'

Barney slanted her a look. 'You are very well informed, Miss Brabant! Yes, it is true that a lot of our medicines were brought back by explorers and traders, but that is not to say that we cannot find our own remedies!'

'People have used herbs for generations, I suppose,' Lavender said thoughtfully. 'Nanny Pryor has a tincture she swears is sovereign against fever!'

'Exactly. I heard recently of an apothecary in Shropshire who cured dropsy with a preparation made from foxglove leaves.' Barney frowned. 'I imagine one must be careful, however. Many of these plants have poisonous effects if taken too liberally!'

'You would not wish to poison the population of Abbot Quincey in the interests of science!' Lavender said, with a giggle. 'Has anyone offered to take your preparations yet, Mr Hammond?'

'No, indeed, for I keep my work a secret!' Barney was laughing now. 'And so I cannot claim any success at all, for I have no notion whether or not they work!'

They laughed together. 'I suppose it is not just plant extracts that the apothecaries put in their mixtures,' Lavender said, after a moment. 'Do they not also use animals for their medicine? Oil of goat and grease of dog...'

'Now you are making it sound like a witch's spell,' Barney commented. 'Though it is true that some of the old remedies recommend such ingredients! I once sat by the river for hours trying to trap a heron to make a medicine that required heron's grease, but—' he shook his head '—so fastidious was I that when I netted one I was obliged to let it go at once! I could not hurt the poor creature!'

'Not even for the advancement of your science?'

'Not even for that, Miss Brabant!' Barney smiled down at her. 'Perhaps I lack the ruthlessness to be a success!'

'Success at any cost is not necessarily a victory,'

Lavender said, the smile still in her voice, 'and I cannot believe heron's grease to be truly efficacious, although I know Nanny Pryor swears by goose grease for a bad chest!'

They had reached the end of the Hewly boundary wall, having walked further than Lavender had intended. She hesitated. It had been so easy—and so pleasant—to walk with Barney in the moonlight, and the conversation had been so enjoyable that she had not wished it to end. This was strong enchantment indeed, seeing the other, more academic side to the man of action, sharing his secrets... She was aware of a strong disinclination to go back inside just yet.

'Miss Brabant...' Barney was leaning against the wall, looking at her. 'Speaking of walks in the forest, there is something that I would wish to ask you. It has been troubling me for some time, I confess.'

Lavender made a gesture of surprise. 'Then ask, sir...'

Barney hesitated. He seemed suddenly at a loss, choosing his words carefully. 'It was last June, and I had been out in the wood in the evening, collecting some plants. I was returning by the pool in the river, when I saw you down by the bank.'

Lavender stared at him. She felt suddenly cold. The breeze stirred the leaves and trickled down her spine, making her shiver.

'You were digging something out of the ground with a little trowel,' Barney continued, his gaze now

riveted on her pale face. 'I believe it was the trowel
you use for extracting your plant specimens. I could
not see exactly what you were digging up, but it
seemed to me that it was a bundle of clothes and in
the moonlight they looked dark and stained... You
picked them up and carried them off in the direction
of home, Miss Brabant. And you were acting very
furtively, looking behind you and keeping in the
shadows. I confess it made me curious.' He straightened up. 'Particularly curious, since it was the day
after the Marquis of Sywell had been found murdered...'

Lavender turned away sharply and gazed out
across the darkening gardens. Ever since it had happened, she had been afraid of this. She had imagined
herself alone that night, for she had seen no one on
her hurried journey to the pool in the river. She had,
as Barney had said, kept in the dark shadows and
checked that no one was following her. Yet he had
seen her, and for four months he had said nothing...
Until now...

'Well, Miss Brabant?' Barney's voice broke into
her thoughts. His tone was still low, but there was
an insistent note in it. 'Am I mistaken in thinking
there was a link between the murder and your strange
and secretive actions? What explanation can you provide?'

'I...' Lavender cleared her throat. She did not want
to lie to him, and just at the moment her mind was

a total blank anyway. She could invent no story to cover what he had seen. 'It is true that I was there,' she said weakly, 'but I cannot explain to you—'

Barney shifted slightly. 'Truly? Well, if not to me then surely you could explain to the authorities investigating the case? I understand they have made precious little progress in their enquiries and might appreciate some help...'

Lavender swung round on him. 'You would not do that—'

'Would I not?' Barney raised his eyebrows. 'It's true that I had as little time for Sywell as any other man would, but murder...' He shook his head. 'Some might say that he deserved it—'

'He did deserve it!' Lavender burst out. 'You know as well as I that the man was evil—a mad, cruel despotic creature who would rape and beat and abuse indiscriminately! We are well rid of him!'

Barney sighed. 'I cannot dispute your words, but... For the sake of all those who do not sleep easy in their beds for fear of another attack—and for those on whom suspicion may fall... Miss Brabant, you must speak out!'

'I cannot!' Lavender turned away again, clenching her fists. 'I *will* not! It is not fair—'

Barney took a step closer. 'Then at least tell me who you are protecting—'

'No! I will tell nothing—'

'Is it your brother?'

Lavender swung round on him with incredulity. 'Lewis? What on earth could he have to do with this?'

Barney pulled an expressive face. 'Who knows? There are any number of candidates for the role of Sywell's murderer, are there not, Miss Brabant? The servants he abused, the villagers he ruined, the husbands he cuckolded... For all I know, Sywell might have cheated your father out of his estate after the Admiral had been struck down, and when your brother discovered it he could have threatened Sywell, and...' Barney broke off, shrugging. 'He is as good a contender as any!'

'It's nonsense!' Lavender said. Her voice was shaking now. She pressed both hands against the rough stone of the estate wall. 'You would never spread such a tale—'

'No, I would not do such a thing,' Barney conceded. 'But you must see that your actions are most suspicious, Miss Brabant! If anyone were to know...'

'It only requires for you to keep quiet!' Lavender moved closer to him, her eyes fixed on his face. 'No one else saw me—nobody knows—'

'Can you be sure of that, Miss Brabant?' Barney's tone was expressionless. 'You did not even know that I was there!'

Lavender put a hand on his arm. 'I am sure! And if I keep your secrets, surely you will keep mine!'

There was a sharp silence. Barney stared down at

her. It was too dark now to see his face, but when he spoke, Lavender thought he sounded almost amused.

'Oh Miss Brabant, what is this? Blackmail? You equate my secret studies with your desire to protect a murderer?' He stepped back, making a repudiating gesture with his hands. 'Tell, then! I'll wager it will not cause half the stir as when I tell the Lord Lieutenant that you are covering up for a murderer!'

Lavender grabbed his arm again. 'Please! You will not do that!'

'Are you concerned for yourself or for someone else?' Barney asked roughly.

'It is not like that!' Lavender screwed her face up, trying to think of a way to explain without giving away all of her secrets. 'It is just that it would cause so much trouble and misery! And no one regrets Sywell's death—'

'It is hardly your place to decide whether or not someone should be punished!' Barney said, sounding really angry now. 'You must care a great deal for him—'

'Not in the way that you mean!' Lavender faced him out. 'But I would do anything to prevent this coming out! Please—'

'Just what are you offering, Miss Brabant?' Barney's tone was suddenly smooth. 'Do you wish to stick with your blackmail, or revert to bribery instead? Your choice!'

Lavender glared at him. 'It was not my intention to bribe or blackmail! You know that!'

Barney laughed derisively. 'Do I? It seems, Miss Brabant, that I do not know you quite as well as I had imagined! But that can be remedied...'

At the last moment, and with utter amazement, Lavender realised that he was about to kiss her. She felt totally confused. She had been so wrapped up in defending herself from his accusations that it had never occurred to her that she might need to protect herself from another, more dangerous, approach. And although she had thought he was going to kiss her at the Covinghams' Ball, it had not happened and she had not really imagined that it would. She had thought of it with a little shiver of pleasure, as a forbidden extravagance. But now...

Yet for all her frightened realisation, she did not draw back from him. She felt his arm slide about her waist, pulling her against him. His hands were mercilessly hard on her slender frame, holding her still, but when his lips touched hers they were gentle, undermining her defences completely. Lavender felt her bones melt, resistance turning to response.

She had had very little experience of men, and the suitors she had met during her London season had soon bored her. Certainly she had no experience of the kind of physical awareness that Barney could evoke in her, the awareness that had been building throughout their encounter. She had never even imagined it.

When Barney let her go, the sensual excitement was still fizzing through her blood like wine. For a moment she could remember nothing of where she was, and felt disappointed and deprived that he had let her go. She put out a hand towards him and he caught it in his, pressing a kiss on the back before letting it go.

'No...' His voice was low, husky. 'Lavender, we must not. It is my fault and I am sorry—'

Lavender wanted to throw herself into his arms then and persuade him to change his mind, but Barney was already withdrawing from her, stepping back more deeply into the shadows under the trees. 'I must go. Forgive me...'

Lavender understood what he meant. She was Admiral Brabant's daughter and could not be for him, but in that moment between them, it had not mattered. This time she did not run from him, but turned and walked away slowly, deliberately. And she did not look back.

Chapter Six

Lavender lay on her back in the grass beneath the apple trees, staring through the branches at the pale blue sky. She had discarded her straw bonnet and her hair was loose about her shoulders. Instead of wearing one of her plain gowns, she had chosen a dress of dimity in pink and white stripes that was at least five years old. It was one of the ones that Julia had told her was unmodish and far too young for her, and Lavender had thrust it to the back of the wardrobe despite the fact that she liked its light, fresh colours. Now, as she lay in the orchard and contemplated the world from a different angle, Lavender wondered how she could have been so foolish as to have taken Julia's advice.

It was another Indian summer day and everyone spoke of the weather breaking with a thunderstorm. Scattered in the grass about Lavender were her crayons and drawing paper, a half-finished sketch of

Field Scabious, and her book, *Sense and Sensibility.* Lavender had started by trying to draw, found it too much effort in the heat, and had rolled over on to her stomach to read the book. As she had devoured the story of Elinor and Marianne, she had reflected that ten days ago she had compared herself to the sensible elder sister, whereas now she was set fair to throw her bonnet over the windmill like the younger one.

How had such a transformation come about? Lavender watched dreamily as the little white clouds floated across the sky. Perhaps it had been on its way for a while, or perhaps it was a sudden change. She could not be sure. After her Season in London there had been so much unhappiness—the death of her mother was followed so swiftly by that of her elder brother, and then her father's long illness... And throughout it all, Julia had been there like a sticky burr, pricking Lavender's confidence and undermining the younger girl in her own home. It was only when Lewis had come home and had married Caroline that a measure of contentment had returned.

And now...Lavender wriggled a little, a small smile curving the corners of her mouth. Now there was Barney Hammond. She had thought that he liked her and now she knew it to be true. No matter that they had quarrelled over her clumsy attempts to persuade him to keep her secret; she knew she could put that right if only she explained the whole to him.

Lavender had thought long and often about their encounter in the wood two nights before, and the memory of their kiss warmed her far more than the sun that was now beating down from a near-cloudless sky. Barney's arms about her had been reassuring and exciting at one and the same time, a promise of things to come, a remedy for unhappiness. She understood his reluctance, the thought that he was not good enough for her, and she wanted to repudiate it with all her strength. He was a fine man and she had finally come to realise that his parentage, his trade, their relative situations counted as nothing if they were truly meant for each other. She would find him and tell him so…

The warmth was soporific. Lavender's ears were full of the drowsy buzzing of the bees and she slept until the sun started to go down and the cool breeze of evening took its place. Then, shivering a little, she opened her eyes and realised that the reason she was cold was that a shadow had fallen across her. It moved, and the late afternoon sun lapped about her again.

'They said that I would find you here.'

Lavender narrowed her eyes against the reddening glare of the sun. Suddenly all she could think of was that her hair was a tumbled mess and her dress had deep creases where she had squashed it whilst reading her book. Her last coherent thought before she fell asleep had been that she would seek out Barney to tell him how she felt; his appearance at this point, before she had had time to think about her approach, was decidedly not a part of the plan.

Lavender sat up and started to pick the dried grass out of her hair. She could feel Barney's dark gaze appraising her, moving over her face and figure with an intentness that brought the colour into her already flushed face. He sat down on a nearby tree stump.

'You look very pretty today. The pink suits you.'

They were not the polished words of a society gallant but they made Lavender blush harder all the same. 'Thank you, sir. Are you... Did you wish to see me?'

'I did.' Barney looked ill at ease. His tone was suddenly formal. 'I wanted to apologise for my conduct the other night, Miss Brabant. I fear I must have given you a disgust of me—'

'Oh no!' Lavender could not help the involuntary interruption, for secretly she had hoped he would repeat his conduct plenty of times. 'Mr Hammond—'

'Please hear me out.' Barney's face was expressionless. 'Miss Brabant, I behaved towards you as no gentleman should do—'

'Please!' Lavender scrambled to her feet. 'Do not say any more, Mr Hammond!'

She realised that Barney had interpreted her embarrassment as ladylike shrinking when in fact it was simply that she did not wish to hear him humble himself. Before she could correct this false impression, he stood up.

'Yes, having said my piece I should leave you. But I would like to thank you, Miss Brabant, for your kindness in encouraging my work. I will not forget it.' He put a hand into his pocket and took out a small book. 'You mentioned that you would like to see the old books on botany that I had in my possession. This is one of them, and no use to me as I do not read the Latin script! I should be honoured if you would accept it.'

'Oh!' Lavender took the little book, feeling the smooth old leather binding beneath her fingers. 'You cannot give me this! It must be of great value—'

Barney shrugged easily. 'I inherited it from my mother but as I said, I cannot read it. I would rather it went to someone who would treasure it.' He raised an eyebrow. 'A parting gift, Miss Brabant.'

He sketched a bow and made to turn away. The tears pricked in Lavender's throat. She understood that this was a permanent farewell. What he was really saying to her was that they could not meet again—it was foolish and inappropriate to indulge in a relationship that could never lead to more. A few days before she might have agreed with him, but now she could not let him go so tamely. She thought quickly.

'Mr Hammond, if we are not to…meet again, there

is something I wish to tell you. Would you do me the honour of listening?'

Barney paused. Lavender could feel his reluctance, but she was depending on his innate good manners. Surely he would not refuse to hear her out? She held her breath.

'Very well, Miss Brabant,' Barney said unwillingly, 'but I must be gone shortly.'

Lavender gave him a smile of relief. 'Of course. Thank you! There is a bench over there beneath the trees. Shall we—'

They walked to the stone bench at the top of the orchard. Barney helped her to a seat first, then sat down an irreproachable three feet away. He did not look at her directly, but fixed his gaze a little sternly on the topiary figures that lined the path in the rose garden below. Lavender cleared her throat.

'The last time we met,' she said carefully, 'you reproached me for keeping secrets, sir. Since we will not speak like this again, there is something that I would wish you to know.'

Barney's gaze came back from the topiary and fixed on her face.

'Yes, Miss Brabant?'

'It concerns the night you saw me by the pool in the forest,' Lavender said. She took a deep breath. 'You were not mistaken, Mr Hammond. You did indeed see me dig up a bundle of clothes from a hole beneath the river bank. I brought them home and burned them on the kitchen fire.' She looked sideways at him, trying to read his face. Barney was watching her closely, but he said not one word. Somehow this seemed to make it more difficult. Lavender swallowed hard.

'It was the second time in two days that I had been to the pool,' she said slowly. 'I had been there the previous night, the night of the Marquis of Sywell's death, although I knew that not at the time. I was waiting for a night-flowering plant to bloom.' She paused, distracted. 'It was the Enchanter's Nightshade, you know, and I had heard that it opened in the moonlight, but I think it must be only a tale, for certainly I did not see it—'

'So what did you see instead?'

Barney's quietly worded question brought Lavender back to the point.

'Oh! Yes, of course. I saw a figure come down to the pool, wash himself in the water and bury something under the bank. I thought... I could not be sure...' She looked up and met his gaze. 'I could not really tell who it was.'

Barney's eyes had narrowed thoughtfully. 'But you suspect someone. I can tell—'

Lavender shivered, although the sun was still warm. She wrapped her arms about herself. 'Yes, I do suspect, but I cannot be sure. All I saw was a man's figure, though I thought I recognised him. I was mightily puzzled by what I was seeing. It was full dark, and the clothes just looked like a pile of rags. Naturally, I wondered what he was doing! But the next day I heard the tale of the Marquis's murder and I suddenly thought…'

'You thought you had seen the murderer? And you went back to the pool a second time to see what you could find?'

'I did.' Lavender pulled a face. 'Foolish of me. I should have left well alone, but curiosity…' She shrugged. 'I found the clothes hidden under the bank and they were all over blood, and so I thought that whoever it was that I had seen must have killed the Marquis that night.'

Barney was shaking his head. 'Why did you take the clothing away? And burn it! That makes you seem guilty yourself—'

'I know!' Lavender sighed. 'I sat there for what seemed like hours with the bloodstained clothes in my hands, and I thought of what would happen if I told anyone what I had seen.' She made a slight gesture. 'Oh, I did not keep quiet for scandal's sake, or anything like that, but I could not be sure of who I had seen that night and I did not want to accuse an innocent man.' She shook her head. 'I knew then that I could not tell anything of what I had seen.'

Barney shifted a little on the bench. 'But why did you burn his clothing? Why not just leave it there?'

'I was afraid that someone might stumble across it! Many people use the pool—' Lavender broke off, remembering that she had seen Barney himself swim there. 'I did not think the matter through very well,' she added hastily, 'for once the clothes were burned and gone, it suddenly occurred to me that their owner might return to retrieve them and find them missing! And I can scarce reassure him—'

Barney smiled. 'And so your deception began to catch you out! Lavender, it is clear that you know who the murderer is, or at the very least, who it was you saw that night. I would wager that you are partly keeping quiet to protect him, for all that you pretend you do not know his identity! It must be someone for whom you have a great deal of respect. Will you tell me who it was?'

Lavender shook her head. Barney's observation was perceptive, for she did indeed have a very clear suspicion of who the murderer was and she held him in the highest esteem, but even so…

'It would not be right,' she said uneasily. 'I have no wish to accuse an innocent man and I cannot be sure.' She pulled a stem of the long grass through her fingers. 'Last time we spoke of this, Mr Hammond, you told me that it was not my decision to make. Well, I have taken that right, but now you may denounce me if you wish!'

There was silence but for the soft, repetitive coo of the white doves on the Manor roof. After a long moment, Barney said, 'Why did you tell me, Miss Brabant?'

Lavender looked away from that observant regard. The truth was that it was because she loved him and could not bear him to think ill of her. The first she could not say, but perhaps the second…

'I wanted to tell you the truth,' she said, avoiding his gaze by watching the swing of the weathervane on the stables. 'I could not bear for you to believe I was protecting someone for all the wrong reasons. Nor, if I am not to see you again, could I bear you to carry away a poor opinion of me—'

'I'll not do that.' For a moment Barney's hand covered hers on the warm stone of the seat. Lavender's pulse leaped. She looked into his eyes and saw the dizzying combination of love and wanting that dried her throat and made her heart race, but in that moment it was gone and Barney was speaking again, deliberately expressionless.

'Thank you for telling me. I shall keep your secret, Miss Brabant.' Their eyes met, Barney's lightened by a faint smile. 'I shall have to trust your judgement that you are doing the right thing in keeping quiet.' He shrugged. 'Well, so be it. It has been an honour to know you, Miss Brabant, but now I must go.'

Lavender watched his tall figure walk between the trees, down the topiary path and round the side of the house to the stable yard. A few minutes later he rode out onto the drive, raising a casual hand in thanks and farewell to the groom. Lavender thought of his instinctive authority and the easy courtesy he had with all men, and raged inwardly at the barriers of birth and class that stood against him. He had recognised them himself and had bowed to the inevitable by repudiating her. And because he had done it with such grace, he had made it impossible for Lavender to oppose him.

By the time that darkness fell, the threatened thunderstorm was upon them. After dinner they sat in the library with the curtains drawn and the candles lit, and listened to the rain hurling itself against the window panes and the thunder rumbling ever closer. Lavender had abandoned the precise prose of *Sense and Sensibility* in favour of something more dashing and had plucked *Marmion* from the library shelves. Caroline was sewing and discussing developments in the American War with Lewis, who was reading them the latest dispatches as recorded in the newspaper.

'The truth is that the Americans have a navy as good, if not better, than our own,' Lewis said dryly, as he turned a page. 'I know it is hard for the Lords of the Admiralty to accept it, but those of us who served in a more humble capacity could see the change coming for many a year!' He shook his head. 'I fear that they may be in for a sharp shock!'

Lavender let her book fall to her lap and stared thoughtfully at the candles. She had fully expected to suffer a reversal of spirits after her meeting with

Barney, but was surprised to find that she felt quite buoyant. It was as though she had not really accepted that they could not be together and expected the situation to resolve itself, and soon. She did not question this rash assumption, but sat feeling content as she listened to the murmur of Lewis and Caroline's conversation, and the thunder overhead.

It was hardly a night for visitors and they all jumped when the bell sounded, harsh in the quiet house. Caroline folded her needlework into a tidy square and got to her feet.

'Gracious, who can that be calling in the middle of a storm? I know that the Covinghams said that they might call, but surely not now! Lewis—'

The door opened to admit Kimber, the butler. He bowed. 'Captain Brabant, a gentleman by the name of Sir Thomas Kenton is without. He is marooned by the storm and has stopped to seek shelter here.'

Lewis strolled out into the hall, Caroline and Lavender at his heels. An elderly gentleman was standing there, leaning on a gold-topped cane and dripping water on to the floor from his great coat. A huge flash of lightning lit the house, dimming the candlelight.

The gentleman brightened when he saw them, smiling gently and blinking with myopic blue eyes. He was frail and looked to Lavender like an elderly scholar who had unaccountably wandered out on the worst night of the year.

'Captain Brabant, sir?' The gentleman bowed to
Lewis. 'Sir Thomas Kenton, at your service.
Ladies…' He bowed again with old-fashioned courtesy to Lavender and Caroline, before turning back
to Lewis.

'I apologise for this intrusion, sir, but I am a trav-
eller in dire need of help and stumbled on your house
through sheer good chance. Can you furnish me with
the direction of the nearest inn? One of my carriage
horses has gone lame and I fear I will not make
home, for all that it is only ten miles—'

Lewis smiled. 'I could direct you, sir, but would
not dream of turning you out into such a night as
this! You must stay here, at least until the storm
abates. My head groom will see to the stabling of
your horses.'

Sir Thomas looked worried and relieved at the
same time. 'Oh indeed, I could not thus impose on
your hospitality—'

'No imposition, sir,' Caroline said now, coming
forward and taking his arm. 'Kimber, pray take Sir
Thomas's coat. Sir Thomas, will you take a glass of
wine with us? Please join us in the library, and tell
us how you come to be benighted in such a storm!'

They went back into the room, Caroline installing
Sir Thomas in an armchair beside the fire, and fetch-
ing a glass of Madeira for him herself. In the light,
Lavender could see that their guest was indeed frail,
with a thatch of hair that was entirely white and a

face as wrinkled as a walnut. Yet when he smiled he had the sweetest of expressions and a slow, warm smile that seemed strangely familiar. Lavender racked her brains, but the resemblance remained elusive.

Sir Thomas was warming his hands before the fire and reminiscing. 'I do believe it is over thirty years since I was at Hewly, or perhaps more? I forget… But it was in the days before your father bought the Manor, Captain, for I believe it was part of the Perceval estate?'

'It was indeed, sir.' Lewis smiled. 'Yet I do also believe we have met before, at one of the garden parties at Perceval Hall? It was many years ago, but you had brought a kite, your own invention, and flew it from the lawn!'

Sir Thomas looked delighted. 'Why, so I did! Yes, I recall—you were that solemn child who asked so many questions! You had an elder brother, a bucolic boy who preferred the animals, and a little sister—a pretty, fairy child with silver gilt hair…'

'I expect that that was Julia,' Lavender said.

Caroline gave her an exasperated look. 'I rather think that Sir Thomas is referring to you, Lavender!'

Sir Thomas nodded enthusiastically. 'I remember it all now! The kite became stuck in a tree and one of the Perceval children climbed up to free it and fell out and feared he had broken his leg…' He shook his head. 'Ah, fine days, fine days!'

'You were quite the inventor, sir!' Lewis said. 'I remember my father saying that you had designed the most excellent miniature battleship and that the Admiralty should have developed a full-size one!'

'Ah well,' Sir Thomas finished his wine and beamed at Caroline as she replenished his glass. 'Those days are long gone, I fear! Yet still, I have my books. I do not go into company much these days.'

'Your family?' Lavender ventured, and was sorry to see Sir Thomas shake his head sadly.

'All gone, my dear! My younger son died a long time ago, wild and foolish boy that he was.' A shadow chased away his smile. 'He had my enquiring spirit, I fear, and was forever off on mad starts! He wanted to study medicine and we quarrelled bitterly over it, for I did not see it as the work of a gentleman.' Sir Thomas shook his head again. 'Well, I was a stiff-necked old bigot in those days, but John went off abroad and fell ill with a fever and I never saw him again…'

There was a silence, but for the crackling of the fire. 'It is not good for a man to outlive his sons,' Sir Thomas said eventually. 'It makes him old to have no family about him.' He roused himself and gave them all his gentle smile. 'It is good to see new life breathed into this house, at any rate! Tell me of your plans, Mrs Brabant!'

They spent a convivial couple of hours discussing

the restoration of the house and garden, before Caroline gently pressed Sir Thomas to accept their hospitality for the night. As the rain was still drumming on the roof he took little persuasion, and presently requested a book to take up to his room with him.

'I can see I am spoilt for choice,' he said, browsing along the library shelves, and pausing to consider Plato's *Republic*. He picked it up, then put it back and took up *The Iliad* with a fond smile. 'Too martial for my time of life, perhaps... Something more soothing would be in order, I believe. Architecture, or horticulture...'

'I have a splendid book on botany here,' Lavender said, passing him the slender volume that Barney had given her earlier. 'You might not wish for the exertion of reading in Latin tonight, sir, but it is well worth the trouble! It is full of the most fascinating—'

She stopped as she saw the expression on Sir Thomas's face, a mixture of puzzlement and suspicion. He was weighing the little book in the palm of his hand and staring at it as though he had seen a ghost. He ran a hand through his thick thatch of white hair.

'Oh, but surely... This is the one that we ... I thought—'

He looked from Lavender to the book, then turned a few pages.

'No mistaking…' She heard him mutter. 'The very one! And at the start—'

He turned back to the title page. 'I thought so!'

They all looked at him in confusion. 'Sir Thomas?' Caroline questioned.

Sir Thomas was holding the book up triumphantly so that the light fell on the title page. 'The arms of Kenton!' He declared. 'I thought so! This was one of my most prized works, but John borrowed it from me and I never saw it again! Of all the odd coincidences! But—' his brow furrowed '—how came it into your possession, my dear?'

'It was a present from a friend,' Lavender said hastily, seeing that Lewis and Caroline were watching her curiously. 'I saw the coat of arms, but did not know its provenance. It is of no consequence. If the book is yours, sir, then you must have it back.'

Sir Thomas looked appalled. 'My dear, I would not dream of depriving you! Your friend must surely have come by it quite honestly!' He pushed it into her hands. 'Pray keep it!'

'Oh no!' Lavender handed it back, suddenly quite desperate. 'Sir—'

'I am sure the mystery can be easily solved,' Lewis said, unwittingly making matters worse for his sister. 'Lavender, where did this come from?'

Lavender frowned at him. 'It was just a gift! Lewis, pray do not concern yourself—'

Lewis frowned in his turn. 'You are being confoundedly mysterious about this, Lavender! A gift from whom?'

'From Mr Hammond!' Lavender said, blushing. She had not wanted to confess it, for it seemed too personal to admit that Barney had been giving her presents. She tried to remember what he had said about the book's origins. 'Perhaps he bought it from the bookseller in Northampton! I cannot recall—'

'No one is suggesting that he stole it!' Caroline said mildly. 'We shall ask Mr Hammond how he came by it, and the mystery shall be solved!' She turned to Sir Thomas, who was still turning the book over in his hands. 'In the meantime, dear sir, as it is an old friend, I pray you rediscover it with pleasure! Now, is there anything else we can do for your comfort?'

Sir Thomas reassured her that he was very well served, and the party went up to bed shortly after. The storm was still rumbling in the distance, and Lavender lay awake for a while, puzzling over the botany book and its origin. Sir Thomas had said that his son had borrowed the book originally, but where it had been since, and why it had come into Barney Hammond's hands, was a complete mystery. She could remember now that Barney had told her he had inherited the book from his mother and that he could not understand the Latin text. Lavender wondered if Eliza Hammond had been able to read Latin and frowned over the mystery.

Lavender turned over and thumped the pillow into a more comfortable shape. It was cool and comforting under her cheek. It seemed too soon to seek Barney out again when he had specifically told her that they could no longer meet. Yet now she knew she would have to tell him about Sir Thomas, and ask him how a book with the arms of Kenton had ever come to be in his possession.

The following morning was overcast but warm, as though the thunderstorm had failed to lift the humidity that hung over the countryside like a blanket. Caroline sighed and claimed that her clothes were already sticking to her and that the heat made her feel indisposed. Lavender resolved to take refuge in the woods with her sketching paper until she had decided when she dared to approach Barney again.

They were still at breakfast when they heard the sound of a carriage on the drive and the knocker sound a moment later. Fluting female tones wafted on the air. Caroline and Lavender exchanged a look.

'More visitors!' Caroline said, with a lift of her brows. 'How diverting! Here we are going along with our own company all this time, then suddenly—'

'That sounds like—' Lavender began, then the breakfast-room door swung open, and Julia Chessford stood on the threshold, exquisitely bridal in a cream satin dress and matching lace-adorned cape.

'My dears!' She held her arms wide and for a dreadful moment Lavender wondered if she were about to embrace them all. 'I promised that I would visit, did I not, and here I am!'

Lavender noticed that Lewis seemed to be having trouble keeping his face straight. 'So you did, Julia,' he murmured, 'but I am not at all sure that we believed you!'

Given that Mrs Chessford had left the Manor under something of a cloud previously, it seemed odd to Lavender that she had had the impertinence to return and expect a welcome. It was also unfortunate that Sir Thomas Kenton was an unwitting spectator to the scene, since it made it impossible for Lewis to suggest that his cousin turn round and depart the house directly. In short order, therefore, Julia had drawn a chair up to the breakfast table and had prettily requested that the maid bring her some food: 'Eggs buttered just as I like them, Rosie, and a cup of chocolate—not too sweet, not too bitter...'

Caroline caught Lavender's eye and grimaced at her. Her lips formed the words 'pockets to let.' Lavender nodded slightly. They both suspected that it could not be a fondness for their company that had led Mrs Chessford to take refuge at Hewly, but the fact that she was an inveterate gambler and was probably without a feather to fly. Lavender sighed and

toyed with her food. Julia's arrival had acted to sup-
press the appetite and much else too. Just now she
was expressing naïve surprise that Lewis and
Caroline had yet to redecorate the house, which had
been shabby even when she had last been there. She
then turned her most dazzling smile on Sir Thomas,
and quizzed the unsuspecting baronet about his estate
and fortune. Sir Thomas answered her with the same
mild courtesy that he had shown previously, evidently having little suspicion that he was being sized
up as a potential husband.

'Is she not shameless!' Caroline said later, having
grabbed Lavender's arm and practically dragged her
from the breakfast-room. She wiped the tears of
laughter from her eyes. 'I suspect that Julia has lost
her beau and that poor Sir Thomas is being considered as a replacement!'

Lavender's shoulders shook. 'No doubt she would
think him ideal—elderly, rich and childless! Oh dear,
Caro—should we have left the poor gentleman alone
with her? They will be betrothed ere breakfast is
over!'

Sir Thomas, however, proved surprisingly resilient
to Julia's charms. When they ventured back into the
room they found him in the middle of a discourse on
agricultural improvements at Kenton, and he explained that his charming companion had been asking him about his interests. Julia was hiding her
yawns behind one white hand and angling for a visit

to Kenton Hall, but in vain. Sir Thomas promised to send her a tract on land reform, thanked Caroline gravely for her hospitality and stated that he must be on his way home. He kissed Lavender's hand with old-fashioned gallantry.

'Thank you for the loan of your botanical book, my dear,' he said with a twinkle in his eye. 'I enjoyed rediscovering such a treasure! Now it is yours and I hope it brings you pleasure! And if you wish to study the rest of my library, you shall be very welcome at Kenton Hall!'

Julia pouted as the door closed behind him. 'What a prosy old bore! And what a waste! Why, I declare, that estate is worth ten thousand a year and it will all go to some distant nephew on Sir Thomas's death! Lud, if I could attach his interest—'

'I should concentrate on the distant nephew, Julia,' Caroline advised, sitting down and pouring herself another cup of chocolate from the pot. 'He will be younger and may be more susceptible to your charms! I fear Sir Thomas is only interested in his land and his books—a shame, but you could never compete with Plato!'

Julia brightened. 'Oh, a capital idea, Caro! I shall make enquiries! Now, how do the two of you plan to entertain me today?'

Caroline tried and failed to look apologetic. 'I fear the heat makes me feel quite enervated, Julia, so I shall be resting in my room! Lavender?'

Lavender smiled. 'I am working on my botanical collection today, cousin Julia! If you wish to accompany me into the wood, you are very welcome!'

Julia gave a little shudder. 'Lud, how unpleasant! The heat and the flies…' Her blue eyes sharpened spitefully. 'It amazes me that you are still devoting yourself to that boring old study, Lavender! Still, when a lady has no prospect of marriage and family, I suppose it is good to have a hobby! I shall drive into Abbot Quincey, I think, and call on the Percevals. I have no doubt they will be delighted to see me again!'

Lavender and Caroline exchanged a look. Both remembered that when Julia had last tried calling on their aristocratic neighbours, most of them were unaccountably from home.

'Just as you wish, Julia,' Caroline murmured. She turned to Lavender. 'Do not tire yourself out walking, my love. This heat is very intense. And be careful where you go. I know you think the forest is safe, but I have had enough strange experiences in there to make me know that it is anything but!'

Chapter Seven

It was a hot afternoon. Lavender struggled across the meadow with her portfolio of sketches clutched under one arm and her skirts held up in the other hand. She could feel the material of her dress sticking to her back in the sunshine and wished that she had worn something lighter. One did not expect such warmth in early October.

She had spent the morning drawing plants for her collection and now, by mid-afternoon, felt sleepy and ill-disposed to do any more work. On the other hand she felt disinclined to return to the Manor, where Julia was no doubt well settled in by now and busy stirring up trouble.

She wandered towards the river, drawn by the cool sound of the water playing over the stones. Here under the trees it was shady, but the air was still humid. Lavender propped her portfolio against a tree trunk and made her way towards Steepwood Pool. She was feeling a strong desire to plunge into the water fully clothed, but her natural modesty prevented her from swimming there, no matter how refreshing it might be. She decided that she would make do with bathing her hands and face, and she unfastened the buttons at the neck of her gown so that she could feel the breeze against her hot skin.

As she drew near to the water, Lavender could see that the pool was already occupied. Someone else had had the same idea as she, only they had no qualms about stripping off for a quick dip in the water. She knew that she should not linger, but she stood watching for a split second, a second too long.

As she hesitated, she saw the figure reach the bank and pull himself out of the water. It was Barney Hammond. There was no mistaking that broad, well-made figure, the dark hair glistening now with droplets of water. He was naked from the waist up, barefoot, and his soaking trousers clung to his muscular legs. Lavender saw him raise his hands to rub the water from his face, and she caught her breath as the hazy light burnished his skin from golden to deep bronze. Her heart was racing and a peculiar excitement lit her blood, the same feeling as when he had kissed her that time, an undercurrent of sensuous pleasure. Lavender stared, and Barney raised his head and looked directly at her.

In that moment Lavender was suddenly reminded of all the respectable reasons why she should not lurk in the forest spying on semi-naked men. She turned away hastily and started to walk back to pick up her portfolio, but even as she retreated she was aware that he was following her. Her skirts were long and the forest floor strewn with branches and brambles to trap the unwary. Barney reached her in what seemed to Lavender only half a dozen easy strides, caught her arm and pulled her round to face him with negligent ease.

'Miss Brabant!' He did not even sound out of breath. 'Why are you running away?'

It was more a challenge than a question. Lavender raised her chin.

'I was *walking* away, sir, because I had understood that you did not wish to meet with me any more and besides,' she could not help herself from looking at him pointedly, 'you are scarce in a fit state to greet a lady!'

Barney glanced down at the breeches that were still moulded to his thighs and grinned.

'You have not let that weigh with you before, ma'am, on the other occasions when you have watched me in the forest or at the pool!'

Lavender opened her mouth to deny it and closed it again. The colour flooded into her face. She could hardly deny that she had seen him fencing with James Oliver, and as for the rest... She had always suspected that he knew she had seen him at the pool before. And it was so undignified for a lady to be caught spying.

'I… I beg your pardon, sir,' she managed to force out. 'It was never my intention to…to deliberately watch you—'

Barney raised his eyebrows in a gesture that conveyed disbelief more clearly than any words.

'Indeed?' he drawled. 'Well, if you were only intending to take a swim yourself, why do you not do so?' He gestured behind him. 'There is plenty of room for two!'

Lavender's eyes opened wide. 'Oh, I could not! It would not be seemly—'

'Less seemly than to watch in secret?' Barney questioned. He was smiling slightly. 'You have an odd idea of proper behaviour, Miss Brabant!'

Lavender bit her lip. It seemed he was not going to let her off lightly. 'I told you that it was an accident, sir—'

'Oh, so you did—'

'One meets many people and sees many things in the forest!' Lavender burst out, stung by his sarcasm.

Barney grinned, his teeth very white in his dark face. He leant one hand against the trunk of the nearest tree. Lavender fixed her gaze on the distant stands of oak and ash. She knew he was watching her but she could not look him in the eye. She certainly did not want to look lower, where his bare torso still gleamed with stray drops of water, or lower even than that where his damp trousers outlined his body with all the explicit beauty of a classical statue.

'I must go,' she said. 'It is too hot to be wandering out here—'

It was true. The air around them seemed to shimmer with a heavy, sensual heat.

'I see that you had already started to unfasten your dress,' Barney said expressionlessly, his gaze lingering on the hollow in Lavender's throat, where she knew a frantic pulse was now beating. 'Are you sure that I cannot tempt you into the pool?'

Lavender felt suffocated. What she wanted and what she knew she should do were now drifting ever farther apart. She cleared her throat. 'No, truly, I should go—'

Her words sounded weak even to her own ears and Barney ignored them, straightening up and stepping closer to her.

'Then at least take off your straw bonnet. There is no direct sunlight here and it would be far more pleasant for you to feel the air on your face...'

He put out a hand and took hold of the end of one of her ribbons, pulling gently until the bow unravelled. Lavender could feel the bonnet slipping back and tumbling to the ground. It was true—there was the very slightest of breezes that day, and it was warm on her hot face.

She had tied her hair in a plait that morning and pinned it up, and now she saw Barney's hand move again and the sunlight glinted on the golden heads of the pins as he methodically pulled them out. She could feel his fingers in her hair, feel the slippery weight of it gather and start to fall about her shoulders. Neither of them said anything.

Barney gathered a handful of the silver gilt threads and let them slip between his fingers. 'That's better. I wanted to see it like this again. You looked so beautiful yesterday lying in the grass with your hair spread about you—'

'You should not…' Lavender's words came out as a whisper. She was trembling all over, afraid that her legs were about to give way. She knew her breathing was quick and shallow and she could not tear her gaze away from him for fear—and fascination—of what he would do next.

Barney brushed the long strands of hair away from her neck, his fingers just grazing her skin where the collar of her dress was open. When he started to undo the tiny pearl buttons down the bodice, Lavender felt her trembling increase. Her throat was dry but her skin felt flushed and sticky with sweat. She felt light-headed and more than a little faint, and she could think of nothing but that she wished Barney would kiss her, and that there was the most intolerable ache inside her and that she would do anything she could to appease it.

There was a look of intense concentration on Barney's face as his hand drifted lower, undoing an-

other button, a second, a third... His gaze fell to
where the edge of Lavender's white lawn shift was
now visible, with the slight curve of her breasts
above.

Lavender made a slight noise, half-gasp, half-
moan, and put a hand out, but whether to stop the
progress of his fingers or to help him, she did not
know. In the event he captured her hand and returned
it to her side, the same look of distilled concentration
on his face. Her back was against a tree; she felt its
rough bark against her palms as she steadied herself.
Barney had unfastened the buttons almost to her
waist now and was sliding the material of her bodice
over her shoulders so that the dress crumpled to her
feet and she stood in her shift alone. Lavender, who
had ten minutes before contemplated and rejected the
idea of stripping down to just such a state of undress
for her swim in the pool, shivered convulsively at
what she was discovering.

She longed to touch him. The proximity of that
hard, tanned body to hers was almost too much to
bear, and she reached for him again, gasping with
relief this time as he pulled her into his arms.

His voice was so soft she could hardly hear it. 'Oh,
Lavender... I have so wanted this...'

Lavender wanted it too. As his mouth took hers at
last she closed her eyes, abandoning herself to touch
and taste.

The kiss was almost violent with pent-up emotion.

Lavender's lips parted, responding wildly to the demand of his. Sensuality flared between them, a scalding tide in Lavender's blood. She pressed closer to him, running her hands over the muscles of his bare back and revelling in the groan she wrung from him with her caress. His skin was smooth and cool, still slightly damp from the water. Barney kissed her again, fiercely, hungrily, tilting her chin up so his mouth could plunder the sweetness of hers. His lips moved to the corner of her mouth, then to the sweet hollow of her throat, then down... Lavender arched against him, in an agony of wanting until she felt his fingers cup her breasts through the thin shift, felt him push the material aside and lower his head to take one sensitive tip in his mouth. A dart of exquisite pleasure shot through her. His stubble grazed her exposed skin and she gasped aloud.

They tumbled down into the grasses and lay there, winded, adrift with desire, and only inches apart.

Lavender opened her eyes. She was lying on her back staring up at the pattern of green leaves against a pale blue sky. Barney was propped on his elbow beside her, still watching her with that intent, concentrated desire. She could see the tiny, golden hairs on his forearm, and put out one finger and ran it along his arm. He was warm to touch and smelled of sunshine and fresh air. Barney smiled, a slow, lazy smile that made her quiver. He pulled her back into his arms, sliding one hand inside her unlaced shift,

his fingers teasing her breasts again. Lavender's head
fell back, her hair spread about her.

'Kiss me again…'

She heard Barney laugh. His voice was very
husky. 'Are you sure that's what you want,
Lavender?' He leant over her, kissing the soft skin
of her breasts. 'More than this…'

Lavender's voice caught on a sigh as she closed
her eyes. 'Oh…'

He was kissing her again, they were tangled in
each other's arms, blind to all else, deaf to intrusion.
It was only when a heron rose flapping mightily from
the pond and scared all the other birds out of the
trees, that Lavender stirred and pulled a little away.

'Barney? Was someone there?'

The mood was broken. They sat up. They could
see no one between the ranks of dark trees, but
Lavender shivered a little. Her gaze went to her dis-
ordered clothing and she drew her shift together with
shaking fingers. Her mind was numb—she could not
regret what she had done, nor even think about it
clearly. All she knew was that she had wanted
Barney to make love to her, wanted it to the exclu-
sion of all else, but that now the moment had gone.

The air was still hot and heavy, humming with
bees, but now it felt more like the prelude to another
thunderstorm. Lavender picked up her dress and
struggled to do up all the little buttons.

Barney had been watching her, his expression inscrutable. Now he got up and came across to her. She knew he could see how much she was still trembling, how her hands shook on the buttons.

'Here, let me.' He spoke quietly, buttoning them up with as much swift efficiency as he had used in unfastening them. He finished and stood back a pace.

'Lavender—'

Lavender suddenly realised that she was about to cry. She did not know why, only that her throat was closed with tears that threatened to spill over.

'Please, don't—'

'Sweetheart...' Barney ignored her plea and the stiffness of her body to take her in his arms, and after a moment she relaxed. He spoke into her hair.

'Lavender, after the last time I kissed you I swore to myself that it would not happen again.' He held her a little away from him, touching one hand gently to her cheek. 'I apologised then, but I was not sorry and nor am I now. Given a choice...' He shook his head slowly. 'But there is no choice. We cannot meet again.'

Lavender looked up, her drenched lavender-blue eyes suddenly furious. 'You are scarcely gallant in your rejection! After all that has just happened between us—'

Barney let go of her. 'You know it is not like that... I could wish for nothing more than you, but it cannot be.' A look of exasperation came over his features. 'Oh Lavender, be sensible! There cannot be anything between us—'

'It is a little late in the day for that!' Lavender lifted her chin defiantly. 'I wish you had not stopped—at least then you might act as a gentleman ought!'

There was a closed look on Barney's face. 'I am no gentleman and you know that that is precisely the problem! I have nothing to offer you, Lavender! I wish it were otherwise, but it is not!'

Lavender came close to him, resting both hands against his bare chest. 'But you want me—you know it…'

There was a tight, strained look on Barney's face. 'It is not that simple—'

'Why not?' A huge knot of jealousy had formed in Lavender's chest. She banged her clenched fist against his arm. 'Why with all those other girls— village girls to be tumbled as you please—and not me?'

Barney caught her wrist. 'In the first place, there were no other girls! And in the second, even had there been, you are not like them!'

Lavender was silenced by his first statement, rather than by the obvious truth of the second. She stared. 'No other girls? What—never?'

'No.'

'But surely…' Lavender hesitated. 'They are forever throwing themselves at you! And…and it was clear that you knew what you were about…'

She saw Barney smile as he bent to retrieve her bonnet from the long grass. 'I am flattered that you should think so! In fact I think we were both about to find out for the first time!' He shot her a look. 'What do you take me for, Lavender? Yes, it is true that I have had offers, but why should I avail myself of them?'

Lavender frowned. 'I just… I suppose I thought… It is the way of the world!'

Barney shrugged. 'That may be so, but it is not my way.' A shade of colour stole into his face. 'I wanted to wait until I had found something better, and the irony is that I have now found it, but I cannot take it!' He looked at her angrily. 'This is pointless! I am sorry, but it cannot be. Now, please excuse me. I must go.'

Lavender put out a hand to stop him, but he shook her off and turned away.

'No, Lavender! Do not, I beg you, try my self-control any further!'

Lavender watched him walk firmly away from her, back to the edge of the pond where he retrieved his shirt and pulled it on. He did not look her way again. Presently, when he had put his boots back on and picked up his jacket, she saw him walk back towards the path that led to Abbot Quincey. He did not spare her another glance, merely walking, head bent, and resolutely avoiding her gaze. She watched him until he disappeared through the trees, then she started to walk slowly back in the direction of Hewly. Her portfolio was still propped against the tree where she had left it, what seemed like hours before.

She picked it up and wandered back towards the house, still trying to sort out her thoughts and feelings. She felt warm and dazed, happy and sad, all mixed up together. She knew now that she loved Barney deeply and, from all the things that he had said, she was certain he loved her too. He had claimed himself to be no gentleman but as far as Lavender could see, his reticence to press his suit was for very chivalrous reasons. He felt that he had nothing to offer her and whilst she, dazzled and bewildered by her emotions, might consider that she would be happy living in a cottage with him, he was evidently thinking of what was due to an Admiral's daughter, a lady descended from two very distinguished families.

Lavender smiled a little to herself, swinging her bonnet by its ribbons. The material point was surely that Barney cared for her, and since that was the case, she would persuade him to change his mind. She had not the least notion how she would accomplish this, but she was very determined. She knew she would prevail. She was so wrapped up with her newly discovered emotions that not even Julia's sharp asides could trouble her, and she spent the rest of the day floating around the house with a faint smile on her lips and a dreamy look in her eyes.

It was still early the following morning when there was a tumultuous rapping at the door followed by the sound of a decided altercation in the hall outside. Kimber trod into the room looking very slightly ruffled.

'Excuse me, Captain Brabant. There is a person here demanding to see you. He says that it is very urgent. I have taken the liberty of showing him into your library, sir. It is Mr Arthur Hammond—'

Lavender turned her head sharply, dropping her piece of toast on to the floor where it was immediately attacked by one of the kittens. Her reaction was not lost on Julia, whose blue eyes sharpened with interest. Lewis put down his napkin with a look of resignation and got to his feet.

'Very well, Kimber, thank you. We seem to be plagued with early morning visits at the moment! Ladies—' He dropped a kiss on Caroline's head '—pray excuse me!'

'Whatever can that be all about!' Caroline said, pouring herself another cup of tea. 'Arthur Hammond, and so early in the morning! I am sure that we have paid all our bills most promptly!'

Julia's big blue eyes moved from Caroline's face to Lavender's flushed one. 'I may be mistaken,' she said with a hint of malice, 'but I believe that Cousin

Lavender may know the answer to that one! Lavender? What do you have to say, my dear?'

Lavender knew that she was blushing even more. She hated Julia's spiteful ways. 'I fear I have no notion what you mean, Cousin Julia,' she said with as much composure as she could muster. 'The matter is no doubt being resolved between my brother and Mr Hammond as we speak—'

It seemed, however, that she had spoken too soon. Despite the fact that the study was across the hall and that both doors were doubtless closed, the sound of a voice raised in strident emotion, could now be heard.

'Captain Brabant, if you wish your sister's good name to be bandied about the villages like a common strumpet—'

Caroline stood up, gently putting the other kitten down on the carpet. She cleared her throat. 'Well, I think I shall rest for a little. I feel fatigued again this morning. Lavender, will you come up with me and read to me?'

They were too late to escape, however. As they went out into the hall, Arthur Hammond's voice, even louder and disastrously clear even from behind the study door, could be heard bellowing, 'The rumours are all over the village, sir! Either they announce their engagement immediately or Miss Brabant is ruined!'

Caroline shot Lavender a quick glance and moved

closer to her side as the study door opened and Lewis propelled Hammond out into the hall, evidently intending to throw him out of the house. Behind them, Julia stood in the breakfast-room doorway, her face registering excitement and spite. Lavender felt sick.

Hammond had not stopped talking even whilst he was being manhandled towards the door. His voice had sunk a little now, become ingratiating.

'Come now, it is not so bad a match, Captain! Your little sister may have the breeding but my boy has the money! Or at least he could have if I chose to be generous, and with such a match I could be more than that—'

Lewis's voice interrupted him, cold and cutting.

'Mr Hammond, I do not think that that is in the least pertinent to the situation! I shall speak to no one but your son about this! If he wishes to come here and explain why he has compromised my sister's good name—'

'My son knows nothing of this!' Hammond sounded pugnacious. His embroidered waistcoat swelled alarmingly. 'It is I who have come here, as a good father should, to try to save the reputations of my son and your sister, Captain Brabant! Your refusal to discuss the matter seriously—'

'Believe me, Hammond, I take the matter very seriously indeed!' There was a glitter in Lewis's eye and his mouth was drawn into a tight line, suggesting a temper barely held under control. Lavender saw his gaze sweep over them, lingering with contempt on Julia's avid little face. 'However, I will discuss this only with your son, and certainly not within earshot of my guests and my servants!'

'Very commendable, Captain,' Hammond sneered. 'Your servants are at this very moment discussing the gossip they have already heard in Abbot Quincey—'

'Doubtless,' Lewis said coldly. ''I must ask you to leave now, Hammond. At the moment there is nothing further for us to consider. Kimber, show the gentleman out!'

Hammond looked somewhat nonplussed. Kimber, his face as wooden as a church pew, held the front door open.

'Good day, sir,' he said, in sepulchral tones.

Hammond, still blustering, was expelled on to the gravel sweep before the front door. Inside the hall there was a charged silence.

'Lavender,' Lewis said, very politely, 'I wonder if you would be so good as to join me in the study?'

Caroline suddenly woke up to the fact that Julia was lapping the scene up. 'Julia!' She grabbed their cousin's arm. 'Would you care to give me your opinion on the new red damask for the dining-room? You are such an arbiter of taste!' And she positively hauled a reluctant Mrs Chessford away.

Lewis stood aside courteously for his sister to precede him into the study. Lavender's heart was beating light and fast. She so seldom saw Lewis angry, for he had the most equable nature, but when his temper was really aroused it could be fearsome. Since he had returned from sea the previous year, they had built up a strong friendship and she could not bear to lose his good opinion. She locked her hands together to still their trembling, and eyed him nervously. Lewis strolled over to the window.

'Do sit down, Lavender. Or remain standing, if you prefer.' He gave her the ghost of a smile. 'It is sometimes easier to face difficult situations on your feet!'

Lavender smiled back a little tremulously. Lewis's gaze searched her face. 'Would you care for a drink? Something reviving?'

Lavender shook her head. 'No, thank you, Lewis. What did Mr Hammond have to say?'

Lewis grimaced. 'Arthur Hammond tells me—and indeed the whole household!—that there are rumours circulating in Abbot Quincey. Rumours that link you with his son. No doubt you heard most of what he had to say.' Lewis drove his hands into his pockets. 'Apparently you were seen at Steepwood Pool yesterday, Lavender, in a somewhat...intimate situation—'

He broke off as Lavender blushed bright red and pressed both her palms to her cheeks. She took an involuntary step back.

'Oh, no! There was someone there! I wondered at the time—'

Lewis raised his brows. He looked ever so slightly taken aback. 'Are you telling me that the rumour is true, then?'

Lavender met his eyes and looked quickly away. 'Yes... No! I suppose,' she looked away, 'it must have looked bad...'

Lewis walked back to the centre of the room. 'Would you consider your reputation to be compromised?' he asked in measured tones. 'Forgive me, Lavender, I have no wish to cause you further distress, but—'

Lavender burst into tears. 'Oh, I suppose so! Yes, I can see that people might consider it so... He said that he had nothing to offer me, and I know he was only trying to be noble but I love him...'

Lewis did not say another word, but came across and took her in his arms. Lavender cried into his shoulder.

'Oh Lewis, it is not *fair*—'

'I know,' her brother stroked her hair gently. 'But Lavender, he is right—'

'I don't care!' Lavender wept harder. 'I would marry him tomorrow—'

Lewis was shaking his head, but he did not say anything further and in a little Lavender's sobs quietened. Her heart felt weighted with lead. She knew that from any worldly point of view, both Lewis and

Barney were right. He did not have anything to offer her and the match would be the most unequal imaginable. Yet that did not matter to her, not when she wanted to spend the rest of her life with him. And now that everyone was talking…

'What happens now?' she asked forlornly, reaching for her handkerchief to try to mop her face.

Lewis passed her his. 'I think we need to hear what Mr Hammond has to say. He may well feel that he cannot marry you, but he has damaged your reputation—'

Lavender's eyes filled with tears again.

'It is not his fault!'

'But he must take that responsibility!' Lewis moved a little away. 'Lavender—'

There was a sharp rat-a-tat at the front door. 'If that is Arthur Hammond back with his latest set of demands, I shall have him horsewhipped from the house!' Lewis said feelingly.

Lavender, for all her misery, stifled a giggle. 'Oh dear, to contemplate such a father-in-law…'

Lewis looked bleak. 'Let us not contemplate any such thing until we have considered all possibilities! Now—'

'Begging your pardon, sir.' Kimber, even more expressionless than before, was in the doorway. 'Mr Barnabas Hammond is here and asking for an immediate interview.'

'How timely!' Lewis said dryly. 'Show him in, Kimber!'

Chapter Eight

Lavender had no particular desire for Barney to see her in such a state of dishevelment and tried to edge out of the study before he came in, but Lewis prevented her from doing so by catching hold of her hand and refusing to let go.

'You will have to face him at some point,' he said in an undertone. 'See what the poor fellow has to say first before you run away!'

Lavender gave him a shaky smile. 'I am no coward—I will not run away! But Lewis, I need time to think—'

Her brother nodded. 'You will have all the time you need, Lavender, but hear Mr Hammond out first—'

He broke off as Barney came in and though he let go of Lavender's hand he did not move far away. Lavender found this comforting. It seemed that no

matter how deep her disgrace, neither Lewis nor
Caroline was going to abandon her.

Barney came into the room with a firm tread but
his confidence was belied by the distraught look on
his face. He was white and strained and he addressed
himself directly to Lewis.

'I beg your pardon for intruding in this manner,
Captain Brabant! I know it must seem most singular,
but my business is urgent!' His gaze flickered to
Lavender for the first time. 'If I could see you
alone—'

'Certainly,' Lewis said, with suspicious alacrity. 'I
imagine that you will then wish to speak with my
sister, Mr Hammond?'

'I…yes…' Barney's gaze went back to Lavender
again and she could have sworn that it softened as it
rested on her. 'Miss Brabant, I beg your pardon…'

'There is nothing to apologise for, sir,' Lavender
said tremulously, and saw him smile a little, a smile
edged with sadness. She turned to Lewis. 'I shall wait
in the library.'

Lewis nodded, giving her an encouraging smile of
his own, and she went out of the room and closed
the door gently behind her.

The house was quiet. Caroline had evidently managed to keep Julia locked away somewhere and the
servants had all retreated behind the green baize
door. Lavender went into the library and curled up
in a window-seat.

She could feel all the happiness of the day before slipping away, oozing out of her like the stuffing from a cushion. She wondered if perhaps she had imagined that she and Barney could have a chance of happiness, and had been deluding herself that she could persuade him to overlook the inequalities of their relative social positions. Now that matters had come to a head, it seemed that that was all anyone could think of.

Lavender sighed. Whilst it might be an accepted thing for a man to marry beneath him, particularly for fortune, the same could not be said of a lady. She understood what Lewis had been implying, knew that in the eyes of the world she would be making a deplorable *mésalliance*. And yesterday Barney had been adamant that he would never ask her to do so. Now, however, his hand had been forced…

She was not sure how long she had been sitting there when the door opened and Barney came in. He was still very pale under his tan and his expression was set. Lavender got to her feet, suddenly nervous. Barney came across to her and took one of her cold hands in his.

'Miss Brabant. Yesterday I explained why I could not offer for you despite the esteem in which I hold you. It now seems, however, that I have compromised your reputation and I accept that that is true and that I must take the blame for it. I therefore have your brother's permission to ask for your hand in marriage.' He stepped back punctiliously, releasing her.

'You would do me great honour—the greatest honour—in accepting my offer.'

Lavender took a deep breath. His words had hurt her, for he made no bones about the fact that he was only proposing out of necessity. This was not how she had wanted it, and it seemed so cruel that she had had no time to talk him round, to change his mind…

She tried to smile.

'Pray, sir, may we not sit down and discuss this in a comfortable way? I fear that all this emotion so soon after breakfast will overpower me!'

Barney gave her a slight smile, but he sat down beside her on the window-seat and she saw him relax a little. He took her hand again, this time more naturally.

'Lavender, I am sorry that this is not as you would have wished it! God knows, I hold you in the highest esteem and could wish for nothing more than that you would be my wife! But,' he shook his head, 'I must ask you to also to consider the change in your circumstances, were you to marry me.' He got to his feet again restlessly, as though he was unable to stand the thoughts that crowded in on him, and took a few agitated paces away from her before turning back with a gesture of despair.

'I feel sick at heart to be asking this of you! How

long would it be before you regretted so hasty a marriage? You might become bitter and resentful, longing for what you had given up!'

He saw her instinctive gesture of denial and hurried on. 'Oh, you say now that you would never feel like that, but what can I offer you? I do not even have a profession! What, are you to live above the draper's shop? You, a lady brought up here at the Manor? Are you to help me serve behind the counter, dealing with the customers, at my father's beck and call?' He turned violently away from her. 'It is intolerable! And yet that is what I am asking of you, because now I am obliged to offer you the protection of my name—and that is all I can offer you! No home, no profession, nothing of my own!'

Lavender put her hands over her ears. 'Barney, I shall not listen! It need not be like that—'

'That is precisely how it is!' Barney's eyes were black with fury now. Lavender dimly realised that his anger was not for her, but for the frustration and cruelty of their situation. She stood up, moved across to him.

'Barney, listen. It is not as you suggest—'

'In fact it is even worse than I am suggesting!' Barney's face was tight with self-loathing. 'You may not know that I am no son of Hammond's, only his bastard nephew! I hold the little that I do have from his charity! I do not even have a name of my own to offer you! And you—' He closed his eyes briefly,

to open them again and focus intensely on her face.
'You have a considerable fortune of your own, not a
penny of which would I touch if we married—'

'Barney, stop!' Lavender came close to him, compelling his attention with her eyes. She put both her
hands on his arms, holding him still.

'I would feel my fortune had been put to a noble
use if it enabled you to pursue your ambition—'

Barney broke away from her. 'No! It is all wrong!'

'That is just foolish pride talking—' Lavender
took a deep breath and spoke more calmly. 'You
have done *me* the honour to ask me to be your wife.
I am fully aware of the…disadvantages you perceive
in our situation, but…' she kept her eyes fixed on his
face '…I love you.'

She slid her hands up to his shoulders and stood
on tiptoe to kiss him. After a moment she felt his
arms go round her and he bent his head to hers. The
kiss was deep and sweet, but there was an edge of
desperation to it and after a moment Barney freed
himself. There was despair in his face.

'Lavender, I love you too, but it is not enough…'

Lavender stood back out of the circle of his arms.
She felt suddenly cold. Her gaze scoured his face and
a part of her withered at what she saw there. She
spoke slowly.

'Very well, then, Mr Hammond. If that is the case,
I cannot marry you. You give with one hand, then
take away. You offer me marriage, then tell me all

the reasons why I should not accept! I love you and you say that you love me too, yet that is not enough for you. Well, I am braver than you. It would have been enough for me. But have no fear. I will not accept you. I thank you for the honour that you have done me, but I fear I must decline your offer.'

It was when she saw the relief in his face, fleeting as it was, that her heart truly broke. She was not sure how she kept her composure long enough to dismiss him, but her voice did not even shake.

'There is nothing more to say. Good day, Mr Hammond.'

When she heard the door close behind him, she threw herself down on the window-seat again and cried and cried.

'It is very difficult,' Caroline said, with what her sister-in-law thought was huge understatement. 'On the one hand, Mr Hammond is in the right of it, for there is no doubt that it would be a very unequal match in worldly terms!'

Lavender took a turn about her bedroom. She had locked herself away earlier, wanting to see no one, but Caroline had persuaded her to let her in and was now sitting curled up on the end of Lavender's bed.

'Why does everyone have to think in such a way?' Lavender demanded. Her head ached from the misery of it all. 'Barney is in every way my equal—he is clever and compassionate and kind, yet no one rates

those qualities and everyone thinks only of money
and position—'

'Here's a pother!' Caroline said, eyes twinkling.
'You have no need to defend him to me, Lavender!
I like Barney Hammond immensely and it has not
escaped my notice that he is all the things you say
and a very attractive man into the bargain! But—'
the light died from her eyes '—there is no doubt that
if you marry him you will be making what the world
views to be a huge mistake. Further, there is a prac-
tical point. You may think now that you could tolerate any circumstance for love, but in practice I
think you would find it difficult. Leaving aside the
slights and sneers of your fellow men, you would
have that pushing Arthur Hammond as a father-in-
law and a husband who was obliged to work in a
shop. Surely you can see that your circumstances
would not be enviable!'

Lavender went over to the window and stared out
into the dusk. Suddenly she wanted to escape the
house, escape the intolerable problem of her future.
The picture that Caroline had painted was bleak indeed and she could not deny it. It would have taken
a great deal of love and tenacity to overcome it. She
had been prepared to take a risk on that love, but
Barney had not—and that was the end of it. So perhaps, after all, there was no debate.

Briefly Lavender thought of Barney's secret plans
to study to become a pharmacist. She could have

funded his studies if he had been prepared to swallow his pride and accept her money. They could have been free of Hammond's influence, they could have been happy…

But Barney had shown himself too stubborn to agree to live off his wife's charity, even for love. Lavender pressed her head against the cool window-panes and closed her eyes for a moment.

She turned back restlessly to Caroline.

'There is another alternative, although we have not yet spoken of it. I have refused Barney and I will keep to my decision. It is not because I did not feel I could live with all the disadvantages you have out-lined, dearest Caro. It is because *he* does not feel that he loves me enough to do so. So I shall take my fortune and move away from the gossips and live on my own and never marry!'

It was said defiantly, but there was an ache in her heart. In the first place she loved Hewly and the Abbey villages, and hated the thought of living away. Secondly, she loved Barney even more, but if he could not see a way clear to marrying her for love, she would not compromise. It was a bleak future but it was at least an independent one.

Caroline was looking thoughtful. 'I understand your principles, Lavender, but there is a problem. You are but three and twenty and do not come into your fortune for another two years. What is to happen in the meantime? Are you to stay here and suffer the scandal-mongering? And wherever you go, your reputation will be in shreds—'

Lavender tried to shrug it off. 'It is of no consequence. I cannot care for the petty attitudes of small-minded people…'

As if in response to her comment, the door opened and Julia Chessford entered. She smiled limpidly at Lavender.

'Good evening, Cos! Are you well? And am I to wish you happy? Judging from all the gossip, I would hope so!'

Lavender gritted her teeth. 'No, you are not, Julia! It is all a big misunderstanding…'

'Really…' Julia breathed. She plumped herself down on the opposite side of the bed to Caroline. 'Lud, how unfortunate! If you could hear what they are saying in the village—'

'Thank you, Julia,' Caroline interposed crisply. 'We have no need of your gossip. No doubt the whole will blow over shortly.'

Julia smoothed her skirts. 'I wish I had your confidence, Caro. I think Lavender is very sensible to hide herself away! You know what the villages can be like—petty, small-minded, but with long memories!'

'I know precisely,' Caroline said, looking at her pointedly, 'as I am sure you do too, Julia!'

'Still,' Julia continued, with a blithe smile at Lavender, 'I confess it is a relief to know that there will not be such a low connection in the family! For all that Barney Hammond is a prodigiously good-looking young man, he and his fortune reek of the shop! It is preferable to climb the social scale rather than slide down it!' She gave Lavender a little, cat-like smile. 'Though I do not suppose you understand the niceties of such things, cousin Lavender!'

'Was not your own father in trade, Julia?' Lavender asked crossly.

Julia waved one white hand, not a whit discomposed. 'Lud, yes! But that is precisely what I mean! I married a gentleman, and soon...' she leant forward, eyes gleaming '...I shall attach a lord!'

Lavender sighed, glad in part that the conversation had moved on from her own romantic tribulations. One could always rely on Julia to talk about herself. She found it far more interesting a subject than talking of anyone else.

'I collect that you mean to marry Lord Leverstoke,' Caroline said calmly. 'Are you so certain of him, then, Julia? And had you forgotten that Leverstoke still has a wife?'

Julia shrugged uncomfortably. 'Poor Lavinia Leverstoke is very ill, you know, and not long for this world! And everyone knows that Charles has nursed her devotedly! I am sure that no one would grudge him some happiness when she is gone...'

'So that is why you are here!' Caroline said cheerfully, winking at Lavender. 'We had all wondered why you were hiding yourself away! How discreet of you, Julia! Whilst Lady Leverstoke is dying—'

Even Julia had the grace to blush. 'You are too unkind, Caro! Why should I not have some happiness—'

'I imagine those petty and small-minded people you referred to a moment ago might have something to say about the way in which you pursue your happiness,' Caroline said, getting up and smoothing down Lavender's counterpane with an irritable hand. 'How long will dinner be, I wonder? Come, Julia, let us leave Lavender in peace! She has had a trying day and I am sure would appreciate some quiet!'

Julia was impervious to hints. She turned her huge blue eyes back on Lavender.

'Did you know, dearest Lavender, that Arthur Hammond is not really Barnabas's father? That was a polite fiction put about to save his sister's name, though I often wondered why they bothered, since the silly creature died a week after the birth!' Julia wrinkled up her nose. 'Eliza Hammond was in service somewhere over Northampton way—it could even have been Riding Park now I think of it—and came back in disgrace! Nanny Pryor knows all the tales!'

Lavender gritted her teeth. 'I have heard the gossip, Julia. It really is irrelevant—'

Julia ignored her. Her eyes lit up and she gave a little shriek. She had clearly just had a scurrilous thought. 'Oh, how piquant! I do believe it *was* Riding Park! How if the father of Eliza's child was Lord Freddie Covingham himself, and when the Covinghams showed favour to Barney recently it was on account of the irregular connection!'

'What a deal of nonsense you do talk, Julia,' Caroline said disgustedly, resting one hand on the bedpost. 'In the first place I believe that Lord Freddie and Lady Anne were but recently married at the time twenty-five years ago—'

Julia opened her eyes very wide. 'Lud, Caro, I know that you have led a sheltered life, but even you must know that there is nothing to stop a man newly-wed fathering a child on the maid!'

'I pity you your cynicism!' Caroline snapped.

Lavender wished they would cease their brangling, and if they did have to quarrel that they might do so outside her bedroom. Julia was enough to try the patience of a saint and Caroline, who was normally so placid, seemed surprisingly quick to react. Lavender went over to her. She could see tears in Caroline's hazel eyes and realised suddenly how much of a trial it must be for her sister-in-law at five months pregnant having to tolerate Julia, who was forever planting her spiteful barbs.

'Come, Caro, you must be tired,' she said gently. 'I shall go down to the kitchens and arrange for you to have dinner in your room. You must not exhaust yourself before the Covinghams get here!'

Caroline gave her a grateful look. 'Thank you, Lavender. I confess I do feel a little low in spirits.' She took the hand Lavender proffered to help her to the door. 'Oof! That's better! I declare I am growing apace—in all directions!'

Julia looked as though she was about to make some malicious observation on this, but Lavender glared pointedly at her.

'Cousin Julia, do you wish to take your supper here? Though it is my room, I am happy to lend it to you!'

Even Julia got the message this time. She got up. 'Very well! I can see I am not wanted! I shall leave the two of you together and hunt up Lewis! It will be so delightful to talk to him of old times—just the pair of us!'

'Silly piece!' Lavender said stringently as she gave Caroline her arm along the landing to the bedroom. 'Lewis will not thank her for inflicting her company on him! How much longer must she stay, Caro? Can we not find a way to persuade her to go?'

'I shall spend my evening thinking on it!' Caroline agreed, sinking down into a fireside chair with a sigh of relief. 'She must be made to go or we shall all run mad!' She patted Lavender's hand. 'I have not forgot, my love, that you are the one who has a dilemma to deal with now! If you wish to speak to me—' She broke off, a twinkle in her eye. 'Oh dear, does that stubborn look mean that you have made up your mind? The times I have seen Lewis look just the same…'

Lavender laughed. 'I fear so, Caro. I am still of the same mind. I shall not marry Mr Hammond.'

Caroline shrugged. 'So be it. We shall see what comes. I hope that Julia's ill-bred remarks about his parentage did not offend you?'

Lavender shook her head. 'To tell the truth, I ought to thank her for it!' She saw Caroline's look of surprise and smiled. 'She reminded me of the book you see— With all the other events, I had quite forgot to ask Mr Hammond where he had obtained it from! Yet if it were amongst his mother's effects and she had been in service, she might well have taken it from Kenton Hall—'

'Julia said that she was in service at Riding Park, not at Kenton,' Caroline said slowly. She looked up at Lavender. 'Still, it is a good thought! We shall ask Lady Anne when she comes, for I do not for a minute believe Julia's scandalous assertion that Barney Hammond is Lord Freddie's son!'

'I should think not!' Lavender made her way to the door. 'The Covinghams are far too unfashionably fond of each other for such a tale to ring true!'

'Besides,' Caroline said with a smile, 'Barney does not have the Covingham nose! One might as well suggest that he was Sir Thomas Kenton's by-blow!' Her smile faded. 'Now there is a thought…'

Lavender was laughing to think of the unworldly

baronet siring an illegitimate son. 'How your mind
does run on, Caro! I fear that if Barney is the natural
child of any nobleman, the Marquis of Sywell must
still be the prime candidate!' She sighed. 'Do you
have any rose water that I might borrow? I fear that
Julia has left me with the most dreadful headache!'

'I had hoped to find you in better spirits, my dearest Lavender,' Frances Covingham said plaintively,
holding her friend at arm's length and eyeing her
closely. 'You look as wan as December! Now, what
is all this gossip I hear about you? To think I always
found the country slow!'

Frances slipped her hand through Lavender's arm
and steered her away up the stairs. 'Take me to your
room so that we can have a coze together! I hear that
Mrs Chessford is staying with you? What bad luck!'

It was the following day and the Covinghams had
arrived a half hour previously for a stay of a few
days. It seemed that the atmosphere in the house had
lightened immediately. Caroline was delighted to see
Anne again and Lewis had immediately taken Lord
Freddie off to have a look at the estate.

'We shall soon have you in plump currant again,'
Frances continued as they reached the top of the
stairs and went along the landing. 'Lady Perceval,
whom we called upon on our way here, said that she
never listens to village gossip and that you were not

to regard it. But *before* we disregard it, dearest Lavender, I want to hear all about it!'

Lavender laughed despite herself. 'It is not a matter for funning, you know, Frances!' she said wryly. 'I am not at all sure that your mama should let you associate with me, for I am in the most horrible disgrace!'

'Stuff!' Frances said staunchly. 'Mama is not such a high stickler to cut up rough about such silly rumours! She was more concerned to be trapped under the same roof as your cousin!'

Lavender smothered a giggle. There was something about Frances that was very reviving to her spirits. The younger girl was irrepressibly cheerful, and now her curious gaze was taking in Lavender's bedroom and she was nodding appreciatively.

'Oh, what a charming room! You are so fortunate, Lavender! And the view! I declare it is as fine as any in Northamptonshire!' She spun round and settled at the foot of the bed where Caroline had sat the night before, leaning her arms against the wooden rest. Lavender sat down opposite.

'So tell me what has been happening,' Frances wheedled. 'I hear it involves that delightful Mr Hammond! Do you think you might marry him, Lavender? Oh, lucky you—'

'Frances!' Lavender said, trying to sound strict but failing utterly. She smiled. 'I tell you, this is no matter for amusement—'

'I know! I am a hoyden!' Frances leant her chin
on her hand. 'But truly I thought him such a very
charming gentleman!' She shivered pleasurably. 'It
seems to me that most gentlemen are all surface and
no substance, but with Mr Hammond it is deeper than
that! In fact I would have quite a *tendre* for him
myself, and no doubt would bore you rigid with the
repetition of his name were it not that I am still hope-
lessly in love with Mr Oliver!'

'Have you seen Mr Oliver since the night of the
ball?' Lavender enquired.

Frances's face fell. 'No indeed, for Mama has been
odiously strict, you know! He did call, but she would
not allow me to see him so I was not able to tell him
that we would be in London from next week and he
should contrive to meet me there—'

'Oh, Frances!'

'Well...' Miss Covingham looked defensive '...I
must see him again, Lavender, positively I must! In
fact I am hoping that as he is such a good friend of
your Mr Hammond, he might be in this very neighbourhood! Who knows! But—' she frowned '—I
know you are trying to distract me! Now tell me the
whole story!'

Lavender told her, not the whole story, but most
of it, and Frances nodded and prompted and made
sympathetic noises. At the end of it she said with a
sigh, 'I can see that you feel you must refuse him,
Lavender dearest, but now you are prey to these

wretched gossips! You should face them out, you know!' Her eyes brightened. 'Oh, the very thing! The Percevals sent a card with us, you know, inviting us all to dinner—'

'Oh no!' Lavender knew she looked horrified. Ever since the gossip had broken, she had been possessed of a cowardly fear to step outside the house. She had certainly no intention of going into Abbot Quincey, or even going out into company. Yet if she was going to stay at Hewly until she came into her fortune she would have to go outside at some point. She could hardly skulk about the house for another two years.

'Well—' Frances put her head on one side '—perhaps we could start with a walk! I have no intention of allowing any friend of mine to become a recluse!'

She picked up the botany book, which Lavender had been keeping on her bedside table. 'Is this the book you mentioned just now, Lavender? The keepsake from Mr Hammond?' She bent her head over it, chestnut curls brushing the pages. 'It is so romantic of him…'

'The book has a mysterious history, if not a romantic one,' Lavender commented, smiling, 'and one that may involve Riding Park!' She told Frances briefly of their visit from Sir Thomas Kenton and of Julia's reminisces about Eliza.

'Of course, it is all very tenuous,' she said at the

end. 'Though Mr Hammond had the book from his mother, I have no idea how she came by it! For it was certainly Sir Thomas's book originally—' She broke off, shaking her head.

'Perhaps Mr Hammond has inherited other things from his mother!' Frances interposed, eyes huge with excitement. 'Maybe he has a whole chest of her effects locked away—books, clothes, a lock of her hair…'

'How Gothic!' Lavender tried not to laugh. Frances looked offended.

'Pray do not make fun of me, I am trying to solve the mystery!'

'I do not wish to discourage you,' Lavender said, 'but it is unlikely that Eliza Hammond would have been able to read a book of botany written in Latin!'

Frances looked cross. 'She might have borrowed it—'

'You mean stolen it—from her employer's library?'

'I mean borrowed…or had it given to her by someone!' Frances wriggled with excitement. 'Yes, I have it! The book was given to her by her lover!'

Lavender frowned. 'Then that would have been Sir Thomas Kenton, and that is foolish—'

'Why so? Was Sir Thomas above a dalliance with a maid?'

'Frances—'

'I wonder if Mama and Papa have any connections

with the Kentons,' Frances swept on. 'Perhaps they will remember Eliza Hammond. If she had been in service at Riding Park it would have been just after they were married, I suppose. Lord, what a sad tale. The poor girl, pregnant and abandoned by her lover, then dying so soon after giving birth!' The ready tears stood out in her eyes. 'And poor Mr Hammond, forever deprived of the knowledge of his father's identity!'

'I daresay that sometimes it is better not to know.' Lavender got up and moved over to the window. A dark cloud was edging across the sun.

'Oh but surely… A foundling is never sure of his place in the world…' Frances, with all the wealth and position of the Covingham family behind her, could only pity someone with no such certain place.

'Then one must carve a place for oneself, I suppose.' Lavender watched as the sky darkened and the rain started to fall. That was what Barney had been trying to do, she knew, with his studies and his ambitions to be a pharmacist. It was admirable and she knew that many a lesser man would have crumbled sooner, accepted his place on Hammond's charity and not sought more. She sighed. Her money would have enabled Barney to achieve his ambitions so much more quickly, allowing him to achieve his profession and support a wife. If only he would have taken that chance! They could have moved away— away from Abbot Quincey with its gossiping tongues that would never let them forget the forced and foolish match. She knew they could have been happy.

She sighed again. 'This is just idle speculation, and confusing at that! It gets us nowhere—'

'Then we must ask Mr Hammond!' Frances jumped up. 'Let us go at once! I shall fetch my bonnet—'

'It is raining,' Lavender said, watching with some relief as the drops tumbled from the dark sky. 'Perhaps later. Frances—' she put out a hand to the younger girl '—pray do not tell anyone of this! I do not like to gossip about Mr Hammond and we have only been imagining—'

Frances looked offended. 'Tell anyone? Why, Lavender, as though I would! You know I am the soul of discretion! I swear I shall not say a word!'

Chapter Nine

'Mama,' Frances said later that evening, sitting beside her mother on the sofa in the drawing-room, 'do you remember a housemaid by the name of Eliza Hammond? She would have been at Riding Park…oh, some six and twenty years ago!'

Lavender, who had been sitting across from her, discussing painting with Lord Freddie, looked up sharply. She should have known that Frances's ideas of discretion and her own were vastly different. Frances returned her suspicious look with one of bland innocence.

'Eliza Hammond?' Lady Anne said vaguely. 'I do not believe so, my love, but then I have so tiresomely poor a memory! And maids do come and go, you know… Why do you ask?'

Lavender started to speak at random, but Frances ploughed on doggedly. 'It is just that it seems she was our Mr Hammond's mother and was once in service with you. Oh, Mama—' she fixed Lady Anne with a pleading glance '—it is particularly important that you remember—'

Lady Anne frowned, pushing her *pince nez* further up her nose. 'Hmm. Twenty-six years, you say? I would have been a new bride then!' She smiled fondly. 'Wait... There was a girl—dark, very lady-like, quiet-spoken... Would that have been Matilda?'

'Eliza!' Frances corrected. 'Really, Mama!'

'Yes—' Lady Anne ignored her '—I recall her now, because she was so genteel that the Duchess—your grandmother, Frances—used to comment that people would think her better bred than her employers! And she probably was, for the Covinghams were all rogues a few generations back, and—'

'Yes, Mama,' Frances pleaded, 'but Eliza Hammond?'

'She left to get married shortly after I went to Riding Park,' Lady Anne said placidly. 'Is that what you wished to know, my love?'

Lavender and Frances exchanged a look. 'Left to get married, ma'am?' Lavender queried. 'Are you certain that she was not—' She broke off, blushing.

'What Lavender means, Mama,' Frances said impatiently, 'is that we thought Eliza Hammond had been turned off because she was *enceinte!* Are you certain this is the same girl?'

Their discussion was now drawing attention. Lavender saw Julia, who had been discussing mutual friends with Caroline, tilt her head in their direction, scenting gossip like a fox scenting prey. Lady Anne leaned forward to address her husband.

'Freddie, do you recall—'

'Eliza Hammond?' Lord Freddie nodded. 'Not that I am in the way of remembering such things, but I do remember her! Because of the scandal, my dear! Do you not recollect?'

This time Lavender saw Julia smile with satisfied malice. She felt increasingly desperate. It seemed quite improper to be discussing Barney Hammond's mother with such freedom in public. The poor woman could scarce defend her reputation and Barney himself would no doubt have been furious and mortified to think her the centre of such attention. Lavender was about to beg a change of subject when something Lord Freddie was saying caught her attention.

'...Left the Park to marry John Kenton,' he said cheerfully. 'Of course, we all thought him a fool, for his family were as poor as sparrows and his father most particularly insisted on him marrying a fortune, and what should the poor fool do but fall in love with a maid! Still, there was no arguing with him and the last I heard of it he was travelling home to get his father's blessing on the proposed match!'

There was a silence followed by chatter as everyone talked at once.

'Of course! I remember the whole now!' Lady Anne said triumphantly.

'Married the maid? How piquant!' This was Julia, looking torn between excitement and disappointment that Eliza Hammond appeared to have been respectably married after all.

'John Kenton? But surely that must be Sir Thomas's son...' Lavender was saying hesitantly to Caroline, whilst Frances said jubilantly, 'Then that is how she came by the book!'

Lewis raised his voice sharply to demand quiet. Everyone looked at him expectantly.

'My apologies,' Lewis said easily, smiling at their startled faces, 'if my appeal sounds more at home on a quarterdeck than in a drawing-room! I feel, however, that this may be rather important! Lord Freddie, can you tell us a little about John Kenton himself?'

Lord Freddie looked mildly surprised. 'Why, of course, old chap! Kenton was a bookish fellow who was forever off on mad trips about the world. Lord, it must be a matter of twenty-five years since he died! Disappeared in the South Americas somewhere, I heard, and his servants swore he was eaten!' He shook his head. 'Pity! He was a good fellow!'

'But what became of his wife?' Caroline asked. 'If he had married Eliza Hammond, where was she whilst he was abroad? And if John was the son of our Sir Thomas Kenton, why does Sir Thomas know nothing of his grandson?'

Lavender's shoulders slumped. 'Perhaps is just a coincidence and there is no family connection, Caro?'

'Perhaps so.' Caroline looked round the assembled group. 'Before we speculate further can I pour more tea for anyone? I find it helps the mental processes marvellously!'

'Sir Thomas mentioned that his sons had both died,' Lewis put in, when all the cups had been replenished. 'Perhaps one of them was John Kenton—'

'He was!' Lavender said suddenly. 'Do you not remember, Lewis? Sir Thomas said that he had lent the botanical volume to his son John—'

'Could be another family, all the same,' Lewis opined. 'John is a common enough name.'

'Was he a friend of yours, Lord Frederick?' Lavender asked carefully.

Lord Freddie nodded. 'One of my closest friends at Oxford, Miss Brabant! He was a bookish fellow, much cleverer than I! He always had an interest in odd fauna and flora, particularly the flora! That was why he was forever travelling, to collect specimens. On one trip he discovered that the bark of a particular tree was most efficacious against pain. Poor fellow!' He laughed. 'He was so excited and we were all so uninterested! And his parents!' Lord Freddie's laughter faded away. 'His father threatened to cut him off without a penny if he did not stay at home and act the gentleman, and his mother worried herself into

her grave over him, for she knew he would come to
a bad end!'

'Where was his home, Papa?' Frances asked, sitting forward and fixing him with a look. 'That would
surely help us tell whether the family is the same
one—'

'Kenton? Why just down the road, I believe!' Lord
Freddie scratched his head. 'Is not the village of that
name some ten miles distant? I know the Kentons
held the Manor there since the Domesday, but
whether they are still there... As I say, John was the
younger son, and his mother died when I still knew
him. What became of his father and brother, I cannot
say.'

Lavender's heart was beating very fast. 'Oh
surely—this must be the same family! There are too
many coincidences otherwise! But I do not understand...' She frowned. How had Eliza Hammond,
who had apparently left Riding Park to marry, ended
up pregnant and alone, throwing herself on her
brother's mercy?

'Why all the interest, my love?' Lord Freddie was
asking his daughter. 'I had not thought of John
Kenton for nigh on twenty years!'

Frances indicated Lavender's botany book.

'It is just that Miss Brabant has been given this
book,' Frances said, gesturing towards it, 'and wondered to whom it had originally belonged. It has the
Kenton coat of arms at the front, you see, and was

originally in the possession of Mr Hammond. Apparently he had inherited it from his mother.'

'Botany, eh?' Lord Freddie was flicking through the pages. 'Yes, this would be John's book, all right and tight. Just his sort of thing! And you say it was given to Mr Hammond by his mother?' He looked at Lavender. 'That is very suggestive, is it not, Miss Brabant?'

Lavender's throat was suddenly dry. It was indeed suggestive that Eliza had married John Kenton and had had the book of botany from him, handing it on to her own child, Sir Thomas's grandson.

'But I do not understand!' she burst out. 'If Miss Hammond and Mr Kenton were married then why was she obliged to return to her brother's house for the birth of her child? And why did she never tell anyone of the wedding—'

She broke off in confusion at the looks of sympathy on the faces of the others, all except for Julia who looked maliciously speculative. Caroline put her teacup down gently. 'I think we must consider, dearest Lavender, the possibility that the wedding did not take place. Lord Freddie has indicated that Sir Thomas wanted his son to marry a fortune. How if John Kenton had failed to gain his father's permission to the match and regretted his plan to marry Eliza—'

'And abandoned her, pregnant and penniless!'

Julia finished, clapping her hands. 'Oh yes, I like that idea!'

Everyone looked at her with unconcealed dislike.

'It does seem the most likely solution,' Frances said despondently. 'Poor Eliza! And poor Mr Hammond! It is not fair!'

Caroline fixed Lavender with a kindly look. 'I do feel that it would be best to speak to Mr Hammond about this, Lavender! Possibly Sir Thomas might hold the answer, but I do not feel that you should approach him behind Mr Hammond's back!' She took a sip of tea. 'When Sir Thomas first laid claim to the book I thought it most odd, and now we appear to have filled in the whole background to the tale without the slightest notion of whether or not we are in the right of it! Ten to one there is another explanation that Mr Hammond will furnish if only he is asked!'

'There is a picture of John Kenton at Riding Park,' Lord Freddie said suddenly. 'In the gallery, by the one of you as a girl, my love…' He smiled at Lady Anne. 'It is only small, but a good likeness—'

'Of course!' Lavender exclaimed. 'I was looking at it on the night of the ball! A dark gentleman with striking features—'

'Did he look like Mr Hammond?' Frances asked eagerly.

Lavender shook her head, smiling. 'I cannot really be sure. Nanny Pryor, my old nurse, says that Mr

Hammond's looks come from his mother's side of the family...'

Frances looked cast down.

'All the more reason,' Caroline said briskly, 'to speak to Mr Hammond about the book as soon as you can, Lavender. I am sure this mystery can be solved without any further speculation on our part!'

The conversation became general once more, but Lavender sat quietly drinking her tea and did not join in. The prospect of seeing Barney again was daunting enough, without trying to explain to him how she came to be expressing such a curious interest in his family history. Judging by his pride on previous occasions, she was sure it was not an interest that he would welcome. It would be much easier to approach Sir Thomas Kenton and ask him to provide the information on John's history, but she knew Caroline was right. Barney had to be made aware of the situation first and Lavender's heart sank at the thought of it.

Despite all Lavender's prayers for rain, the following morning was dry. Frances was adamant that they were to walk into Abbot Quincey and quiz Barney Hammond on the origin of his book, and although Lavender hung back from the proposed trip, she thought it only fair to acquaint him with his possible connection with the Kenton family.

It was a lovely day. The sun was bright and warm

and the hedgerows were full of birds, but for once Lavender did not wish to stop and enjoy the sights and sounds of the country. The roads were a little muddy, and after a mile Frances was already complaining that it was an unconscionable distance. To Lavender it seemed all too short. In no time they were in Abbot Quincey and walking up the main street, and she was glad of the moral support of Frances and Lady Anne.

'Back straight, chin up!' She could imagine the Admiral admonishing her as she walked past the curious stares of the passers-by. 'Nothing to be ashamed of, girl!'

Lavender straightened her back and looked directly ahead of her, yet even as she was walking past the Angel inn and the bakers and the milliners she was wondering which of these people had seen her with Barney at the pool and had hurried to spread their gossip.

The draper's shop was busy and it seemed that all conversation ceased as they crossed the threshold. Lavender's gaze had gone immediately to the counter, where Arthur Hammond was serving a customer. Of Barney himself there was no sign. Lavender did not know whether to be glad or sorry, and part of her simply wanted to turn and run.

Arthur Hammond looked up and his florid face registered indecision. It was the first occasion on which Lavender had ever seen him display hesitation when confronted by customers from the nobility. Clearly her own position was now equivocal since she had refused to marry his adoptive son, and no doubt he was still smarting over the way that Lewis had summarily evicted him from Hewly. On the other hand, Lady Anne and Miss Covingham were too important to be ignored. He hovered, came forward, fell back again, and finally brought himself to address them.

'Ladies,' he pointedly refused to look directly at Lavender, 'how may I help you?'

Lady Anne and Frances both looked at Lavender, who was hoping that she might quietly sink through the floor.

'I would like… I had hoped…to see Mr Barnabas Hammond…'

A whisper ran through the other customers, who had edged closer to listen, pretending an interest in the bolts of material that were closest to where Lavender stood. Arthur Hammond's face hardened with dislike.

'My son is from home! Beg pardon, Miss Brabant, but I have work to attend to and no time for idle chatter!'

Lady Anne looked down her nose at him and swept the two girls out of the shop without further ado.

'That man is so unpleasantly pushing and rag-mannered,' she observed crossly. 'Remind me not to patronise his shops again, Frances!'

'Yes, Mama.' Frances seemed quite cast down for once. 'You might at least have made a push to discover where Mr Hammond had gone, Lavender!' she whispered under her breath. 'Now we shall never solve the mystery!'

Lavender did not reply. She was feeling so miserable that she would happily have left the mystery of Barney's parentage where it belonged—in the past. First she had bolstered herself up to see him, then her hopes had been dashed by Hammond, and the whole experience had been so unpleasant that she thought she would never set foot in the draper's shop again. It was fortunate that she had already bought herself so many hats and gloves—now she need not go shopping for several years.

'I am to call on Lady Perceval,' Lady Anne said as they reached the gates of the Hall. 'Do you girls wish to accompany me?'

'No, thank you, Mama,' Frances said listlessly, after a glance at Lavender's face. 'We shall go back to Hewly.'

'Very well. Make sure that you return directly and do not wander—'

'No, Mama...'

'And do not take a short cut through the woods and become lost—'

'No, Mama...'

'And I shall see you shortly. No doubt I shall take the carriage back...'

'Yes, Mama...'

They walked on in silence and Lavender was glad that Frances had the delicacy not to chatter. For once her irrepressible friend seemed as cast down as she.

It was the sound of hooves upon the road that drew them both from their respective apathy. Frances caught Lavender's arm and pulled her on to the grass verge and almost into the hedge.

'Lavender, be careful!' Her voice lifted. 'Well, upon my word! It is Mr Hammond—and Mr Oliver!'

Lavender had never seen Barney riding before and had not even known he could. The thought brought a slight smile to her lips, for was it not just another of his secrets? He sat the black hunter with ease and competence, and beside him James Oliver brought his grey under control with a slight touch on the rein. He raised his hat.

'Miss Covingham! Miss Brabant! This is the most delightful surprise!'

Casting a fleeting glance at Barney's face, Lavender felt that his surprise was not of the delightful sort. His dark gaze was resting on her, but with none of the warmth or pleasure that she would have hoped to see. This was decidedly awkward. She had wondered what her reception would be and now she knew. He had reluctantly proposed and she had refused and now there was nothing left but cold pride.

James Oliver dismounted with alacrity, to loop his reins over his arm and walk alongside Frances with a touchingly eager pleasure. Barney on the other hand looked as though he might ride straight past with only the slightest of acknowledgements. Then, evidently succumbing to his own innate courtesy, he swung down from the saddle and came to stand beside her.

'Miss Brabant. You are well?'

'Yes, I thank you, sir...' Lavender could feel the colour coming into her face, the embarrassment that made it almost impossible to look at him. She made an effort. 'And you? I hope... That is... I hope you are well also?'

'Yes, thank you.'

There was a silence, in marked contrast to the chatter of Frances and Mr Oliver, who were strolling ahead. It was evidently Mr Oliver's intention to walk with them back to Hewly, and suddenly it seemed to Lavender a very long way to be filled with silences. She was going to have to broach the matter of the book, if only to pass the time. She cleared her throat.

'Mr Hammond, it is timely that we should meet, for there was something that I wished to ask you.'

'Yes, Miss Brabant?'

Lavender thought that Barney sounded ever-so-slightly bored.

'It is about the book that you gave me. I wondered about it because I remember you telling me that you

inherited it from your mother, yet it has the arms of
Kenton inside the cover. Do you know anything
more of its history?'

Barney looked blank. Worse, Lavender thought, he
looked totally uninterested. 'I fear not, Miss
Brabant.'

Lavender sighed. It was going to be even more
difficult than she had anticipated if he was going to
answer her in monosyllables.

'Are you certain? It could be very important! You
see—' She took a deep breath. 'Sir Thomas Kenton
saw the book when he called at Hewly, and claimed
that it had once been in his library. He had given it
to his son John. Yet the book was left to you by your
mother and there must be some mystery here—'

'I do not imagine so.' Barney glanced down at her,
his dark eyes indifferent. 'No doubt this John Kenton
left the book somewhere and my mother picked it up
from curiosity—or perhaps tidiness! She was a
housemaid, after all!' Now Lavender heard some
feeling in his voice, the anger of a man who was
tired of being reminded of the scandal and mystery
of his birth. No doubt Arthur Hammond had never
ceased to remind him of his mother's disgrace and
his own charity. She hesitated, on the verge of giving
up, but something made her persist.

'I am sorry if my interest seems ill-bred—'

'It does!' Barney sounded plainly angry now. 'In

fact, Miss Brabant, it seems damnably impertinent! Can you not just leave well alone?'

He had not raised his voice, but the hard edge to it made Lavender's eyes smart. She had already been upset by Arthur Hammond's rudeness and now Barney's contempt and lack of interest caught her on the raw.

'There is no cause for such discourtesy! I am only trying to help you, for it seems that John Kenton may have been your father!'

Barney dropped the horse's reins and spun round on her. He caught her wrist in a grip that felt bruising.

'And how will being the bastard son of this John Kenton help me, Miss Brabant? Do you know how many times I have tortured myself with thoughts of my father—doubt, speculation enough to drive a man to madness? How many times do you think that my uncle has spoken of my mother's shame and the fact that she did not—could not—name her lover? I am sick with the thought of it all!' His furious gaze pinned Lavender to the spot. 'Do you think that knowing the name of the man who dishonoured her would make me one whit more acceptable as the suitor of an Admiral's daughter? I think not! So cease your investigations, I beg, and do not pry into my history!'

Lavender stared at him. Wrapped up in her own unhappiness, it had not occurred to her that Barney might still be feeling bitter that he had nothing to offer her. She had thought herself so much better and braver than he for being prepared to dare all for his love. Now she saw that his torment sprung from the fact that he loved her just as much as she loved him but he would not relent until he felt he had something better to give her. The problem of his parentage just seemed to make matters more intractable. She put a hand on his arm.

'Barney, you know that I—'

'No!' He shook her off furiously. 'Lavender, I mean what I say! Do not interfere! And do not speak to me about this again!'

'He seemed very angry,' Frances said, awed, as they strolled in the Hewly Manor gardens that afternoon. 'To think I had imagined Mr Hammond as the most placid gentleman in the world!' She gave a giggle. 'When he mounted his horse and took off across country like that I wondered what could possibly have happened! And all James could do was lament that the horse was one of the best in his stables, and like as not it would break a leg!'

Lavender gave a wan smile. 'Well, I suppose I am well served for prying into Mr Hammond's business! What man would care to have his antecedents picked over in such a way? I knew it yet still I persisted! It will be best to leave well alone now!'

Frances looked horrified. 'Oh, no, you cannot do

that! Why, ten to one we shall find that Eliza and John Kenton were married and that Mr Hammond is heir to a fortune! Oh, Lavender, do not give up now!'

Lavender shook her head. She pushed open the gate into the lavender walk and the two girls strolled up the stone path to the house. The heads of lavender were dead and grey, their scent faint now in the autumn. Lavender tried to lift her spirits.

'You seemed to be getting on marvellously well with Mr Oliver, Frances—until your mama came along in the Perceval carriage!'

Frances smiled mischievously. 'Yes, was that not bad luck! Mama looked quite put out! Still, I had the chance to tell Mr Oliver of our address in London, and he assures me he will contrive a meeting during the Little Season!' She frowned a little. 'I think him quite sincere, you know, and for all Mama's concerns I am no silly miss to throw my bonnet over a windmill!'

Lavender thought that she was probably right. Frances was bright and insouciant but she was no fool, and no doubt Lady Anne would come round to the merits of the match. James Oliver might not have a title but he was as well connected as the Covinghams themselves and had a very tidy estate in Hertfordshire.

'Now, Lavender,' Frances was saying briskly, 'there is only one more day before we leave for London and I must, positively must, get to the bottom of the Kenton mystery! So I have decided that there is only one thing for it!'

Lavender felt her heart sinking. Frances was a dear girl and a great friend, but she was also totally incorrigible.

'Sir Thomas Kenton must hold the key to all this!' Frances was saying. 'And as he has already invited you to call, dearest Lavender, we may take him up on his offer tomorrow! It is decided! We are going to Kenton!'

Chapter Ten

Not surprisingly, Frances's plan to visit Kenton the following day was greeted with disapproval. She was already in her mother's bad books for having been found in conversation with Mr Oliver, and Lady Anne expressed the strong conviction that Frances should cease to behave like a hoyden and spend the day quietly resting before their journey.

During the late morning, whilst the ladies were taking a gentle stroll in the gardens, Frances grabbed Lavender's arm and pulled her through the doorway into one of the walled orchards.

'Lavender, I am resolved that we should go to Kenton in spite of everything!' she whispered. 'It is the only way! If we visit Sir Thomas he may be able to throw some light on the matter!'

'Your mama—' Lavender began.

'Oh fie! We need not tell her!' Frances's eyes were bright. 'Mrs Brabant always rests in the afternoons and like as not the other ladies will retire to their rooms! Mama certainly will if Mrs Chessford is about! I heard the gentlemen say that they plan to go out riding so they will not be back before dinner... It is ideal! We may ride over to Kenton in an hour and be back before nightfall!'

Lavender swallowed hard. 'I do not believe I have quite your spirit of adventure, dear Frances! But I am happy to take the carriage!'

Frances looked disappointed. Clearly a staid carriage drive did not fit with her ideas of romantic adventure.

'Oh, very well! I suppose that is better than nothing! Be sure to be ready directly after luncheon— pretend that you are taking a rest, then creep out to join me in the stable yard!'

That the plan worked at all was largely due to the fact that Caroline's rooms faced west, away from the courtyard, and that she and Lady Anne were enjoying a chat in privacy. Julia, meanwhile, had driven into Abbot Quincey on an errand and the gentlemen were away across the other side of the estate. Lavender was tolerably certain that no one had seen them go.

'Mama will be up on her high ropes when she finds out!' Frances said gleefully, as the countryside rolled past. 'But by then we may have solved the mystery of Mr Hammond's ancestry! Oh, Lavender, it is so exciting!'

Lavender was not so sure. She was aware that she

was behaving in an irresponsible manner ill-suited to a lady of three and twenty, and that she could be considered to be leading Miss Covingham astray. The fact that it had been Frances's idea to take the secret journey to Kenton was beside the point, for she could hardly blame her friend when the recriminations started. She clenched her hands on her reticule. Then there was the fact that she was going against Barney's expressed wishes, and that they might come away with no more idea of what had happened than they had had before... Lavender sat on the edge of her seat and wished for a more resilient spirit.

It was only ten miles to Kenton, and Lavender was still having serious misgivings by the time that the carriage drove through the trim village around the green, past the small stone church, and in at the gates of Kenton Hall. The stone wall was tumbledown and the deer park beyond was a mass of grass and wild flowers. Evidently Sir Thomas had neglected his grounds for his books, for the whole estate had about it an air of charming neglect.

The house came into view at the end of the drive, a compact building with golden stone and a red roof, much of it covered in ivy. The carriage sweep was thick with weeds. The girls got out and stood on the gravel. The first thing that struck Lavender was that it was quite silent; the house was shuttered and there was no sound but for the harsh cry of a peacock from the gardens.

Frances, whose yearning for adventure seemed suddenly to have deserted her, was looking about her a little apprehensively.

'Perhaps Sir Thomas is from home? Lavender, shall we go back, now, at once—'

'We cannot turn round and go tamely home now!' Lavender walked up to the oak front door and reached out decisively to pull the bell. She heard it jangle away in the depths of the house but there was no response. Sir Thomas, it seemed, was not at home.

'Oh, there is someone down in the gardens!' Frances was clutching her arm rather in the manner of someone about to run away. 'Perhaps... Do you think...'

'It is Sir Thomas!' Lavender caught sight of the figure of Sir Thomas Kenton as he crossed the terrace and strolled down a grassy walk towards the lake. He was carrying a book, his head was bent, and he had evidently not noticed his visitors at all.

'Sir Thomas!' Lavender turned away from the door and hurried across the drive to the small path that led through a gateway into the formal gardens. Around this, the east wing of the house, the gardens were more neatly kept, with box hedges and clipped lawns. Now that she was closer, Lavender could hear Sir Thomas reading aloud in Latin as he walked. He looked a little startled to be accosted from a great distance, but then his face broke into a broad smile.

'Miss Brabant! What a delightful surprise, my dear! How do you do?'

'Sir Thomas—' Lavender hurried forward to shake his hand. 'How are you, sir?' She drew Frances forward. 'This is Miss Covingham. Pray excuse us for arriving without warning—'

'Not at all, my dear!' Sir Thomas beamed at them. He tucked his book away under his arm. 'I am enchanted to have some company for afternoon tea! There are late strawberries from the hot houses, you know, in sore need of eating!'

He shepherded them up a straight path between tall hedges, up a wide sweep of stone steps and on to the terrace.

'Have you driven over from Hewly?' Sir Thomas asked, as he gestured for them to precede him through the long door leading into the library. 'It is a pleasant journey, is it not—at least in the sunshine!' He laughed. 'I cannot believe that I was so unlucky to have become marooned so close to home—'

'But indeed your poor luck was our good fortune, sir,' Lavender said quickly, 'and it also explains our intrusion here, for we have something very particular to ask of you!'

Sir Thomas looked intrigued. 'Then have a seat and acquaint me with it, my dear!' he said comfortably. 'But first I shall send for tea!'

He rang the bell for the maid and asked for afternoon tea and strawberries, whilst Lavender and Frances looked about them with ill-concealed curiosity. The library was a long, rectangular room with huge, high bookshelves and piles of volumes stacked up on the floor. There were windows at either end, but it was a dark room, made darker by heavy old furniture and gloomy hangings.

Sir Thomas returned his book to the top of one pile and fussed around, making sure that his unexpected guests were comfortable on the gold and gilt sofas.

'I so seldom have guests,' he murmured. 'It is about time that the house heard some voices and laughter again.'

'Oh, Lavender, look!'

Lavender had caught sight of the picture at the same time as Frances spoke. It was hanging to the right of the fireplace, a portrait of a man in the dress of the mid-eighteenth century. He was very dark, with hair so brown it was almost black, and deep brown eyes.

'Why,' Frances sounded quite amazed, 'it is the image of Mr Hammond!'

Sir Thomas looked to see what had attracted their attention.

'The portrait of Sir Barnabas Kenton? He was my father...'

'Sir Barnabas!' Frances said excitedly. 'Lavender, tell Sir Thomas the story at once!'

Sir Thomas turned his gentle blue gaze on her. 'Dear me, Miss Brabant, you both seem most perplexed by some matter. How may I help? Oh, but wait—tea first, tales later!'

The maid had returned with the tea, served in delicate china cups, and a huge bowl of strawberries and cream. Frances helped herself eagerly, but Lavender found that apprehension had blunted her appetite. She pressed her hands together to prevent their trembling.

'Now,' Sir Thomas said to Lavender, once they were all settled. 'What is this tale you have to tell, my dear? I am quite agog!'

'Well.' Lavender took a sustaining draught of tea. 'I wanted to ask about your son, Sir Thomas. Your younger son, I believe—Mr John Kenton? Was he ever married?' She saw Sir Thomas's look of blank puzzlement and hurried on. 'Forgive me, the question must seem most impertinent, and indeed it would be, but—'

Frances lost patience with Lavender's circumspection at this point. 'What Miss Brabant is trying to tell you, Sir Thomas, is that she—we—believe that your son John was married to a Miss Eliza Hammond of Abbot Quincey! We wondered if you could help us—confirm whether or not the story is true?'

Sir Thomas had turned quite pale, so pale that

Lavender put down her cup quickly and went across to his side. She felt a pang of concern, for the baronet was old and frail and Frances had sprung the news rather suddenly.

'Sir Thomas? Are you quite well, sir?'

'Good heavens, good heavens….' Sir Thomas was murmuring. 'I tried to find her, but there was no trace… And you say that she was in Abbot Quincey all the time? But how could that be, and Knottingley not know?'

Lavender put a hand on his. She was shaking with a mixture of hope and fear. 'Then is it true, sir? For there is something else you should know. Eliza had a son—'

There came the sound of a bell jangling throughout the house. Lavender and Frances exchanged a look, but Sir Thomas did not appear to even notice. He looked old and confused, and Lavender was suddenly afraid that their news had been too much for him.

'A son?' He spoke in a whisper. 'A son of John's? But how—'

The door opened. A butler, who looked as ancient and dusty as his master, stood in the doorway.

'I beg your pardon, Sir Thomas, but you have some visitors.' He sounded vaguely surprised at such an unusual circumstance. 'Lord Frederick Covingham, Lady Anne Covingham, Mr and Mrs Lewis Brabant.'

Frances's face was the picture of guilt. She put down the bowl of strawberries and stood up hastily. Lewis and Caroline were greeting Sir Thomas warmly, and Lord Freddie was shaking the baronet by the hand and explaining that he had once been a friend of John's. Lavender was glad to see that Sir Thomas was less frail than he looked, for he greeted the new arrivals with some animation and hastily ordered more tea. She was less pleased that the new arrivals had appeared before she and Frances had got to the root of the mystery, for now it seemed they might be summarily marched home, strawberries notwithstanding.

'Really, Lavender, this mad start is very unlike you!' Caroline complained once they were all settled again and the tea served. Her glance slid to Frances and she tried not to smile. 'We knew at once where you must have gone, for with Frances's insistence that you visit Kenton today, there could be no doubt! What has come over the pair of you? This escapade does credit to neither of you!'

Lavender, reflecting that Caroline must have been an authoritative governess, tried to apologise.

'I am sorry if we gave you cause for concern, Caro, but we both wished to find out about the history of John and Eliza—'

'The two of you are obsessed with this business,' Caroline commented. She smiled at Sir Thomas. 'I do hope, Sir Thomas, that the girls have not troubled you—'

Lavender grimaced at Frances. She felt about twelve and still in the schoolroom.

'Not at all, dear ma'am,' Sir Thomas was smiling gently. 'We had, however, reached a critical point in our discussions, for Miss Brabant had just asked me if my son John had ever been married, and suggested that he had a son!'

'Lavender,' Caroline said in a failing voice, 'I cannot believe you had so little delicacy—'

'I am sorry, but we cannot regard all that now, Caro!' Lavender leant forward urgently. 'Sir Thomas was about to tell us what he knew...'

Sir Thomas sighed. 'Yes, I knew of John's marriage, for he came to tell me when he had already been wed a twelvemonth. It would have been twenty-six, twenty-seven years ago, for John has been dead these four and twenty years past. Anyway, I was not well pleased, for the Kentons have never been rich and I had hoped he would make an advantageous match.'

'Did you meet John's bride, Sir Thomas?' Frances asked eagerly. She seemed to have recovered her spirits and had picked up her bowl of strawberries again.

Sir Thomas smiled at her. 'No, my dear, I did not. I did not even know her name! I quarrelled with John when he told me of the marriage. To my shame, I admit I threatened to cut him off without a penny! Mere bravado on my part, for I would never have borne such a grudge. Yet I was well served for my anger and pride, for John stormed out of the house and I never saw him again! I later heard that he had gone abroad and died in the Americas, and I wondered what had happened to his bride. I had Knottingley, my man of business, institute a search in Oxford, where John had lodgings, and they said that a lady had left there some months before, but no one knew her direction. She appeared to have no relatives or friends to support her, and the landlady had worried that she was sickly—' He broke off, shaking his head. 'At any rate, we could find no trace of her. I wondered if she would come to us here at Kenton, but she never did so. Often I wondered what had become of her, alone in the world and with John dead. I hoped that she had had family to go to.'

There was a silence.

'I do not understand,' Frances said plaintively. 'If Eliza Hammond had been married for a twelvemonth, why did she not tell her family?'

There was another silence.

'I think perhaps I understand,' Lavender said hesitantly. 'Mr Kenton had married beneath him in choosing a bride who was a maid in your house, Lord Frederick. Neither he nor his wife told their family. I believe they married secretly in Northampton, then moved to Mr Kenton's lodgings in Oxford. It was only when Mrs Kenton discovered that she was expecting a child that her husband decided to approach his family, knowing full well that he had been intended to make an advantageous match.'

Sir Thomas nodded. 'I doubt John could have supported two on his allowance, certainly.' His face fell. 'I fear his worst fears were realised—he came to Kenton and was repudiated. After which he must have hatched a plan to travel abroad and make his fortune.'

'I suppose that Eliza would not have been able to travel with him since she was *enceinte*,' Caroline said thoughtfully, 'but when she was near her time and sickly to boot, she decided to go home to the only place she could, which was Abbot Quincey. I dare say she would not have had the courage to come here—forgive me, Sir Thomas—but she had grown up a mere seven miles away, and so...' Caroline shrugged.

'Then Mr Hammond is your grandson, Sir Thomas,' Frances said after a moment. 'How delightful! He is the most charming young man, and so like your portrait there—' She nodded to Sir Barnabas beside the fireplace.

'Well,' Lewis said, after a pause, 'I suppose that someone should acquaint Mr Hammond of his situation, for surely he is in ignorance of all this—'

'Not precisely...' Lavender shifted uncomfortably in her chair. 'I tried to broach the matter with Mr

Hammond yesterday, but he… I am not sure that he…' She looked around at all the puzzled faces. 'Oh dear. In short, I am not at all sure that he will be pleased by our interference—'

The door opened to admit the same po-faced butler as before. He cleared his throat. 'Sir Thomas, you have two further visitors. Mr James Oliver and Mr Barnabas Hammond.'

'Oh dear,' Lavender said.

It was later, and the Brabants' carriage was rolling homeward in the dusk, carrying Caroline, Lewis and Lavender. The Covinghams' travelling coach was behind and Lavender could well imagine the scenes inside as Lady Anne and Lord Freddie ticked off their recalcitrant daughter. Lewis and Caroline's reproofs had been more measured, but then they probably thought that Lavender had suffered enough. She thought so too.

The look on Barney Hammond's face when he had found them all sitting there in Sir Thomas's library would stay with Lavender for a long time. He had looked directly at her only once, when he had first come in, and there had been such a flash of fury deep in his eyes that Lavender had looked away. Of course she had known that he did not want her to pry any further into his history, but she had thought…hoped…that once he had discovered that his parents had been married and he had a grandfather still living, he would come to her in gratitude. It had not happened and now Lavender was feeling slightly indignant, for surely Barney must see that he would still be just the adopted son of the draper if it were not for her.

Barney had clearly been ill at ease at Kenton and had explained to Sir Thomas that he had only called because he had gone to Hewly and had been told that the whole family and visitors were at Kenton on some urgent errand. Knowing that Miss Brabant had mentioned something of Kenton in connection with his ancestry—here his gaze had touched Lavender's face again, very briefly—he had come there himself to try to resolve the mystery.

At that point, Lavender had been sure that the whole matter was about to be resolved and Barney's love and gratitude pour down on her head. Unfortunately, the Brabants, Covinghams and James Oliver had collectively remembered their manners and decided to withdraw and leave Barney and his grandfather to discuss matters in private. It was all highly unsatisfactory.

Lavender sighed as she watched the darkening country flow past. It seemed she could not do right for doing wrong. She was in trouble with Lewis and Caroline for disappearing without a word and embarrassing them by involving Frances Covingham, and she was in trouble with Barney for delving into his past and digging up a secret for which he did not

seem particularly grateful. As far as she was concerned she would devote herself to her botany in future and leave everyone else to their own devices.

'At the least you could have taken me with you!'
Julia's voice was a petulant wail. 'The whole county
is talking of Sir Thomas Kenton's long-lost grandson, and I could have been there when it happened!
Of all the shabby tricks—to leave me behind!'

Lavender stoically ignored her cousin. She was sitting by the window in the library, trying to catch the
last of the daylight. Unusually, she was sewing an
embroidered shirt for Caroline's baby—a sort of
peace-offering for causing her brother and sister-in-
law so many problems recently. Lavender looked at
the shirt and sighed—she knew she had no talent for
needlework and the collar was distinctly lopsided.

'To think that Mr Hammond is Sir Thomas's heir,'
Julia was saying now, utterly unstoppable once she
had started. 'Heir to Kenton Hall—'

'And to the baronetcy!' Caroline put in slyly.

Julia's face worked like a pan of boiling milk.
'Well, upon my word, fate can be so very unfair! An
estate and a title for the adopted son of a draper!'
She turned on Lavender. 'I'll wager you will be re-
considering your refusal of his suit now, cousin! Lud,
to be Lady Kenton and mistress of the Hall!'

Lavender folded the tiny shirt neatly away. She did

not wish to stay and be the butt of Julia's bad temper, for she knew she would snap at her.

'He still has no money,' she said sharply. 'I thought that that was one of your prerequisites, Julia?'

Julia shrugged. 'Well, he may not be Hammond's heir since he is his nephew rather than his son, but the man is as rich as a nabob and might well do the pretty by him. Besides, with your fortune, Lavender, and Mr Hammond's prospects—'

'It would suddenly become a good bargain?' Lavender snapped. 'I thank you, cousin, but some of us look for more in a match than that! I am scarce likely to forget that a week ago everyone was telling me that it would be the most unequal marriage imaginable!'

Caroline sighed and Julia opened her big blue eyes very wide. 'Well, a week ago that would have been true! Lud, cousin, I do not see your point!'

Lavender slammed out of the library. She could not believe that she was the only one to see the hypocrisy of the situation. Suddenly all those who had put the match down as beneath her were praising it to the skies. It made her furious. Worse was the fact that Barney had not called at Hewly, either to thank her for her help or to repeat those offers he had made to her so recently. So the matter of a wedding was an academic one now anyway, since he had not proposed.

Lavender was in such a thoroughly bad mood by the time that she went out for a walk, that not even the beautiful evening could soothe her. The moon was rising above the forest and a breeze was rustling the autumn leaves. There was the scent of grass and smoke and the river rippled in the moonlight, secret and silver. Lavender paused to watch it eddy and flow and tried to find some peace in her heart.

She sat for a long time on a large flat stone on the bank, listening to the rustle of mice in the grass and the plop of fish in the river, and when she heard a step on the path behind her she did not need to turn her head to know who was there.

'Mr Hammond! How is it that you are forever skulking in the woods, sir!'

'I am sorry,' Barney's voice came out of the semi-darkness, not sounding particularly apologetic. 'In point of fact, I was not skulking but coming to Hewly to see you, Miss Brabant!'

'At this time of night?' Lavender knew she sounded sulky but she could not help herself. She had waited for days for him to call and now that he was finally there she had a perverse desire to be horrid to him.

'May I sit down?' Barney did not wait for her permission but settled himself on the rock beside her. 'I wanted to speak to you—'

'Did you?' Lavender snapped. 'I have grown tired of the waiting, sir!'

'Perhaps you thought I should come to thank you ere now?' Barney asked. He sounded amused. His arm brushed hers and Lavender moved pointedly away. She could feel his warmth, feel herself relaxing and leaning towards him. His presence undermined her defences.

'A show of gratitude would have been appreciated—'

'Ah, but you see I was very angry with you!' Barney still sounded amused. 'I had asked you most particularly not to interfere in my case and then I find that not only have you discussed me with your family and friends, but you have also taken it upon yourself to go to Kenton and to see Sir Thomas! First you ignore my express wishes and then I find I am beholden to you yet again—'

Lavender felt the indignant colour rush into her face then rush away again. This was not at all what she had expected. To be reprimanded when surely he owed her the biggest debt of gratitude imaginable! 'Well, upon my word! And I was expecting your thanks rather than your reproaches! You and your foolish pride! Are you not pleased to have found your grandfather and an estate and title into the bargain?'

It was not at all what was important to her, but she was so cross with him that she wanted to hit back. And having seen some evidence of his temper before, she knew that it was possible to provoke him.

It did not seem to work this time, however, for Barney laughed.

'Oh, I am most happy to meet my grandfather, for I like him prodigiously and I think—hope—that he likes me too! As for the rest, well, I have had plenty of people tell me over the past week that I should be grateful for my prospects, but I did not expect you to be one of them, Miss Brabant! I seem to recall that you swore you loved me even when I had nothing to offer you! It is strange to see you value worldly possessions so highly now!'

Lavender jumped up, stung. She did not want to be reminded of declarations of love when she felt so out of charity with him. 'Oh, I do not care two pins for your fortune, but I think you should acknowledge that it is as a result of my persistence that you are in this situation! If I had heeded your strictures and left well alone you would never have known of your parentage or your inheritance! And under the circumstances it seems to me ungrateful that you cannot give me that credit!'

Barney had also stood up now and was moving towards her with a deliberation that made Lavender suddenly nervous. She took a hasty step back, stumbled and would have fallen in the river had Barney not caught her arm.

'Careful, Miss Brabant! You will tumble into the water in a minute and then I shall be put to the trouble of fishing you out!'

'Oh!' Lavender stamped her foot. 'Let go, you odious man! I do not want you, nor your estate, nor your title, and I am sorry I ever interfered to find your family for you! I wish I had left you to struggle in the shop!'

Barney pulled her into his arms and before she could protest her lips were crushed beneath his in a kiss that drove all the remaining breath from her body. If her comment had been outrageous then she considered his behaviour to be no less so. When he let her go she wanted to berate him, but found that instead she needed to hold on to him to steady herself whilst the ground settled beneath her feet again and the stars stopped swinging in their courses. Barney did not seem to mind. He held her close and pressed his lips to her hair.

'Come, Lavender, let us put this foolish quarrelling behind us! Say that you will marry me, now that I do at least have something to offer you...'

Lavender could hear the smile in his voice. The press of his body against hers was infinitely distracting. She tried to clear her mind.

'You may remember, sir, that when you asked me to marry you before, I was willing—happy—to do so, and no consideration of rank or station entered into the matter. So I would not wish to be influenced by them, now that your circumstances have changed. No, I am sorry, I will not marry you.'

She felt Barney go still, then his arms loosened

and he stepped back from her. The chill evening air wrapped round her, filling the space where his warmth had been.

'Lavender, you know that my reluctance had nothing to do with my feelings and stemmed only from an awareness of the inequality of our situation—'

Lavender backed away. 'I know it. Yet I did not share your reluctance. I would have been happy to marry you and live on nothing in a cottage! I loved you enough to do so!'

Barney grimaced. 'Lavender, that is not fair! I was thinking only of you—the wretchedness of asking you to give everything up to marry me! Now I have so much more to offer—'

'And I do not want it!' Lavender said. 'All I wanted was you, but that was not good enough for you! So now that you have so much more the answer is still no!'

The tears came into her eyes and she dashed them away. 'I understand your pride and your reluctance. You did not want to offer for me before, when you felt you had nothing. I even understand that you might feel angry to be indebted to me for finding your link to the Kentons, although truly I consider that the greatest thanklessness!' Her voice was husky and she cleared her throat. 'What you forget, sir, is that I too have my pride! All that I have ever done has been to help you, and I do not see why I should fall in with your plans now, just because it suits your purpose! So—no—I shall not marry you!'

And once again she ran from him and did not look back.

Chapter Eleven

'This is most unfortunate!' Caroline sighed. It was the following morning and Lavender had just confessed to Caroline and Lewis that Barney had proposed again and she had still refused him.

'You are an unconscionably stubborn girl, Lavender!' Lewis said irritably. 'I cannot think where you get it from! Surely you must see that Mr Hammond is trying to do what is right and has been doing so since the very beginning!'

'I don't care!' Lavender knew she sounded petulant. 'I wanted to marry Barney when he had nothing to his name, but he did not wish it then! Just because he will one day be Sir Barnabas—well, a fine fortune-hunter I shall appear if I suddenly turn around and say that I will take him after all!'

'Well, that may be what people will say,' Caroline said fairly, 'but what does that matter? Surely the point is that you are in love with him, and that he loves you, and as such you would be foolish not to make a match of it!'

Lavender turned her face away. 'I do not wish to talk of it! I shall take my paints out and do some sketches for my book! I have no wish to stay here for your chiding, or to hear Julia going on about how the carriages are lined up outside Kenton Hall with all the eligible girls in the neighbourhood angling to be the next Lady Kenton!'

Lewis laughed and Lavender thought him quite heartless. 'I hear that Julia is to leave us soon, at any rate!' he said cheerfully. 'Poor Lady Leverstoke has passed away and I'll wager Julia is coming out of her seclusion to snap up Charles Leverstoke before anyone else gets there first!'

Caroline laughed. She put down the letter she was reading. 'And Anne Covingham writes that she and Sir Freddie have relented of their opposition to Frances's attachment to James Oliver, so matters there seem set fair! Now Lavender, if only you could settle your differences with Mr Hammond we may all be comfortable!'

'I think you are both disgusting!' Lavender snapped. 'I am shocked that you seek to encourage me to marry just for material gain! I am going out!'

And she stormed out of the room, leaving Lewis and Caroline looking at each other in amused resignation.

* * *

Lavender did not feel much better when she returned to Hewly for luncheon to find that the house was empty and Lewis and Caroline were away visiting. The morning had not been at all as she had planned: She had been stung by nettles and had dropped her sketching book in a stream so that her carefully illustrated pictures of Herb Robert had run all over the page. Feeling cross-grained and irritable, she took luncheon alone and was just silently chewing a cold collation when there was a knock at the door and Rosie came in. She bobbed a curtsey.

'Begging your pardon, Miss Lavender, but the carriage is here from Kenton Hall. There is a man with a message from Sir Thomas. He asks that you join him there immediately. It is a matter of extreme urgency, he says.'

Lavender put down her fork. 'A matter of urgency?'

'So Sir Thomas's servant says, ma'am. And he has sent the carriage especially—'

Lavender frowned. After her last escapade she had no inclination to go travelling on a whim and letting herself open to Lewis and Caroline's condemnation as a result. On the other hand, Sir Thomas was asking for her and the matter was evidently important enough that he had sent his carriage specially. She went over to the window and pulled back the drapes. Sure enough, a coach with the Kenton arms was standing beside the door and an ostler was holding the horses' heads and talking to one of the Hewly grooms. Lavender let the curtain fall back into place.

'Oh, very well. Tell the man I shall be ready in ten minutes.'

She scribbled a quick note for Caroline and Lewis, making it crystal clear that the invitation had come from Sir Thomas and was no mad start of her own, then ran upstairs to wash her hands and fetch a fresh bonnet. Her lavender blue dress had a stain on it where she had knelt down to rescue her sketchbook from the stream, but she did not feel she had the time to change. As it was, the horses were scraping the gravel when she went outside, and they set off without further ado.

It was only as they neared Kenton that Lavender was suddenly struck by the impropriety of her own actions. Last time she had been accompanied by Frances, which had been bad enough in its own way, but this time she had not even brought a maid with her. She was so accustomed to wandering about Hewly and Steep Wood at will that she seldom gave any thought to the danger she might be in, but now she wondered with a little stab of despair whether she would ever learn to go on as she ought. Her overwrought nerves prompted her to believe that the invitation might have been part of a kidnap plot, and she was just imagining all kinds of Gothic horrors when the carriage turned in at the gates of Kenton Hall and started up the drive.

It was immediately clear that some kind of transformation had already begun to take place. Men had been working in the deer park, cutting the grass beneath the trees and weeding the drive, but on this drowsy afternoon the gardens were as silent as they had been the previous week. The carriage pulled up outside the main entrance and the groom respectfully held the door for Lavender to dismount. She looked around for Sir Thomas, but it was his grandson whom she saw coming forward from the stables, the sleeves of his shirt rolled up to show that he had been working when she arrived. Lavender stared.

'You! But I thought—'

The coach rolled off into the yard and Barney came forward to take Lavender's hand.

'Thank you for responding to my invitation so promptly, Miss Brabant!'

Lavender blinked. 'I beg your pardon, sir. I thought it was Sir Thomas who had sent the message—'

Barney shrugged gracefully. 'I fear my grandfather is from home at present and it was I who sent the summons in his name! An unchivalrous deception, but I feared you might refuse if you knew the invitation was from me!'

He held the door for her and after a moment, Lavender followed him into the hall. Here, as outside, there were remarkable changes. The windows were open, letting in the cool autumn air, the furniture had been polished to a high gloss and all the curtains and carpets cleaned.

'My grandfather felt it appropriate to have the house spring-cleaned, for all that it is autumn!' Barney said, a little awkwardly.

Lavender smiled. 'Perhaps he felt that, despite the turning of the year, it was time for a fresh start?'

'Yes, perhaps.' Barney smiled back. 'Would you like to see more?'

Lavender agreed, a little hesitantly. She was curious as to why Barney had lured her to Kenton, but she found to her surprise that she did not resent it. Rather, a strange feeling of warmth had stolen over her when she had seen him coming forward to greet her. She was pleased to see him and she could not deny it. Everything had seemed wrong after their last quarrel, the balance of things quite upset, and she had had no idea how it could ever be put right again. She had been cross and bad-tempered without him but she did not want him to know that—at least, not quite yet.

They admired the library, where the portraits were in the process of being cleaned, then strolled out through the terrace doors into the gardens. It was even quieter than before.

'So your grandfather is away—but where are all the servants?' Lavender asked, looking round. 'There has been so much activity here that I quite expected to see them hard at their tasks!'

Barney laughed. 'I have given everyone the afternoon off! As you say, they have been working so hard that they deserve it!'

'And you have been working hard too, by the looks of things!' Lavender smiled. 'Have you been staying here at Kenton?'

'Yes, I have been staying with my grandfather—' Barney still brought the phrase out hesitantly '—these three days past, and he has suggested that I move to Kenton Hall as soon as may be convenient. There is much for me to learn of the estate and the farms and—' Barney broke off, shaking his head. 'It still seems quite extraordinary!'

'Do you like Sir Thomas?' Lavender asked hesitantly. 'When we met before you said that you did!'

Barney gave her his sudden smile. 'Oh, prodigiously! To tell the truth, I was not entirely happy about the discovery of my new situation—' he slanted a look down at her '—which was one of the reasons why I was so ungrateful when you sprang the surprise of my inheritance on me! I had so many plans relating to my study of pharmacology and no wish to give them up... Anyway, Sir Thomas feels that need not signify and that I may continue my work at Kenton, so perhaps I shall achieve my ambition eventually and join the Royal Pharmaceutical Society! I confess it is a relief to think that it will not all be gentlemanly pursuits and that my work may feature somewhere!'

Lavender laughed. 'To think that so many people might envy you, sir, and that you secretly hanker for your experiments and your studies!'

Barney pulled a face. 'Disgraceful ingratitude, I know! But I had worked so hard and always wished to achieve success through my own merit!'

'Which is admirable,' Lavender conceded, 'but it will not make you turn your back on your inheritance, I hope?'

'No,' Barney was smiling. 'I would be foolish indeed not to see the benefits that that entails, and there is no point in struggling unnecessarily! Besides, Sir Thomas deserves better than that—having found a grandson so late in life he does not deserve to lose him twice!'

Lavender blinked a little, ashamed of the tears that prickled her eyes. 'I am so glad, for he is such a nice man!' She smiled. 'How has your uncle taken your good fortune?'

Barney grinned. 'Oh, he is well pleased! In fact I do believe he wishes it had all occurred sooner, and then he would have been on calling terms with Kenton Hall these five and twenty years past!'

Lavender smiled to think how happy the social climbing Arthur Hammond would be now. To have a nephew connected with the landed gentry was more than he could ever have imagined.

Barney took her hand. 'Lavender, forgive me for bringing you here under false pretences, but I needed

to speak to you in private. I have proposed to you
on two occasions and have no intention of making a
third declaration! I should tell you that I rode over
to Hewly this morning and obtained your brother's
permission—a second time—to marry you, and that
he and Mrs Brabant wished me the best of good luck
against your stubborn nature! So I do not intend to
beat about the bush! You are to marry me three
weeks hence. Sir Thomas has arranged for the banns
to be read here at Kenton and is delighted that there
is to be a family wedding after so long a time. All it
requires is your consent!'

Lavender stared at him, affronted. She was not
sure what rankled more, Lewis and Caroline's per-
fidious betrayal or Barney's high-handedness when
she had expected a pretty proposal. She freed her
hand from his and stepped back.

'You presume a great deal, sir! How if I do not
wish to be married?'

'It makes no odds,' Barney said implacably. 'In
the first place, you told me several weeks ago that
you were in love with me, so I am no coxcomb to
remind you of it! Secondly I do not believe that you
wish to remain a spinster! That may well suit others,
but it will not do for you! Come, Lavender, why do
you not consent? You could live here at Kenton and
still study your botany... You know you would like
it...'

Lavender did like the idea of it and it rankled with

her to have to admit it. She turned her back on him and started to walk down the path towards the court-yard. She had no clear idea of where she was going but she hoped that Barney might come after her and follow his proposal up with a sweeter persuasion. She knew she was being stubborn and she was even more annoyed when Barney did not follow her to press ardent words of love on her, but sauntered along at some distance behind, whistling.

Lavender began to feel a little foolish. She reached the stableyard, hoping that the carriage might be waiting and she could prevail upon one of the grooms to take her back to Hewly. However, there was no one about. She peered into a barn stacked high with hay, and turned to see Barney standing in the doorway and laughing at her.

'Lavender, when will you stop running away? I told you that you are here at Kenton alone with me!'

Lavender raised her eyebrows. 'Oh surely, sir, you cannot mean to suggest that my reputation is in danger! It is lost already, if you recall—'

'Ah yes...' Barney smiled, moving closer. 'So you are implying that you are already irreparably compromised by me and cannot fall any further! I think that a mistake—'

Before Lavender could read his intention, he had taken hold of her wrist and pulled her down into the hay.

'You suggested before that I had spent my time

tumbling village girls in haystacks,' Barney said. 'Well, it was not true, but I am happy to remedy the situation now!' He rolled Lavender over on to her back and pinned her down in the hay.

'Let me up!' Lavender cried, sneezing as the hay tickled her nose. 'This is absurd, sir—'

'Then agree to marry me!'

Lavender struggled, threshing around in the straw and succeeding in doing nothing other than lose her bonnet. 'There must be any number of women who would wish to be Lady Kenton of Kenton Hall!'

'I daresay, but I want this one! Lavender, I love you! Must you be so difficult?'

Lavender lay still and looked up into the dark eyes so very close to her own. She put out a hand to touch his cheek. 'I am not sure...' she murmured.

Barney took her hand in his, turned it over and kissed the palm. 'Then I must make you sure,' he said huskily. 'Where had we got to, that day at Steepwood Pool? Ah, I remember... Your hair was tumbled all about you...' He paused to look at her, 'just as it is now. And your dress...' His fingers moved to the buttons at her neck.

Lavender slapped his hand aside. 'Barney! What are you doing—'

Barney looked at her expressively. He was shrugging off his jacket and untying his stock. 'I would have thought that that is obvious! I am seducing you in order to force you to marry me!' He pulled his shirt over his head with an impatient gesture. 'Oh, and also because I wish to do so!'

Lavender sat up abruptly, just as he leant over her again. The movement brought her palms up against the smooth brown skin of his chest and she lay back with a little gasp.

'Oh! Surely you cannot be serious! There is no need to seduce me!'

'You disappoint me.' Barney's breath stirred a tendril of hair as his lips drifted across the soft skin below her ear. They moved on to brush her mouth, lightly, teasingly, before withdrawing. 'So you will marry me?'

'Yes,' Lavender whispered, pinned to the spot by the heat in his eyes. 'Oh yes, I will…'

'Good,' Barney sounded brisk, but he lowered his mouth to hers again with lazy sensuality. 'We shall seal our bargain,' he said, against her mouth.

His lips teased hers apart, deepening the kiss until Lavender's head spun and the blood burned hot in her veins. When Barney's fingers returned to the neck of her gown and started to undo the row of buttons at her throat, she did not resist but tried to help, clumsy in her eagerness. The material parted, and as Barney bent to kiss the hollow of her throat, Lavender ran her hands over his shoulders, pulling him closer, revelling in the velvet hardness of the muscles beneath his skin.

It was not long before they were exactly as they

had been beside Steepwood Pool, Lavender in her shift, speechless with desire as Barney unlaced the bodice to slip his hands inside and cup her breasts. The yielding hay surrounded her, filling her senses with the hazy, fruitful smell of summer, a scent that mingled with her desire and made her light-headed with need. She wriggled the shift down to her waist, arching against Barney so that her breasts were pressed against his chest as she raised her mouth for his kiss again. He drank deep of her and she could sense his need, barely held in check. Her questing fingers stole down to his waist and tugged at his breeches, seeking the fastening.

'A moment—' His impatience matched hers. She could hear it in his voice, feel it in the tension of his body. Lavender closed her eyes as he moved to pull the trousers off, then opened them wide again as he followed his own divesting with hers. A belated modesty made her clutch the shift and drawers to her nakedness, but Barney prised them from her fingers, covering the coolness of her bare skin with the warmth of his own at the same time as his mouth covered hers. She felt his hand on her thigh, and shifted to accommodate his body with her own. There was the most intolerable ache within her and she longed for him to appease it with his body on hers, and even as she thought it, he was inside her and the pleasure filled her and she cried aloud.

They lay still for a long time afterwards, clasped

in each other's arms, half-hidden in the hay. Eventually Barney stirred, pushed the tumbled hair back from Lavender's face and kissed her slowly, drawing out the pleasure. He allowed his hands to travel over her in triumphant possession, sliding over her hips, tracing the curve of her breasts. Lavender made a little noise of contentment, pulling him back into her arms.

'Who would have thought it would be so pleasurable,' she murmured.

'Not I, certainly.' Barney's face was pressed against her neck and she could feel him smiling against her skin. 'Is it better than painting?'

'Oh, far better!'

'Or botany?'

Lavender stretched, raising her arms above her head. Barney let go of her a little, but only so that he could bend over her and kiss her again. Lavender squirmed.

'Barney—'

'You were flaunting your exquisite body and how could I resist?'

'Exquisite…' Lavender thought, warmed suddenly by pride and something else. Suddenly Barney's hands were on her waist again, pulling her close to him again. The tide of passion swept over them.

'Barney—' Lavender gasped, spun up in the sensations of the moment.

'I said that you would prefer to be married,'

Barney said later, lazily. They were lying entwined in the hay again, unable to move far away from each other. 'Unless, of course—' his mouth brushed hers '—you do not wish to marry me now?'

In response, Lavender snuggled closer and they lay quiet again until the clock on the stables chimed the hour. Barney stirred and said:

'I imagine my grandfather may be back soon, and the servants are returning this evening so perhaps we should get up—'

Lavender let out a little shriek and sat bolt upright, casting around desperately for her clothes. 'Oh no! If Sir Thomas finds me here, he will scarce consider me a suitable bride for his grandson!'

Barney pulled her back down into his arms. 'I think you suitable, and that is what matters. So, are we to make our unequal match?'

Lavender smiled into his eyes. 'With all my heart,' she said.

*   *   *   *   *

The drama continues!

Look out for the final volume of Regency drama,
intrigue, mischief…and marriage in

The Steepwood Scandals Volume 8

featuring
An Inescapable Match *by Sylvia Andrew*
& The Marrying Marchioness *by Paula Marshall.*

Available next month, from all good booksellers.

THE STEEPWOOD

Scandals

Regency drama, intrigue, mischief...
and marriage

VOLUME EIGHT

An Inescapable Match by Sylvia Andrew

When Deborah Staunton finds herself destitute, she
is thrown on the Percival family's mercy.
Help presents itself in the highly eligible shape
of Hugo Percival...

The Missing Marchioness by Paula Marshall

Since the murder of the Marquis of Sywell,
Madame Félice has been careful to conceal her true
identity. Now, she senses danger and, for the first
time in her life, feels the lure of a man's attraction.

On sale 1st June 2007

www.millsandboon.co.uk

A young woman disappears.
A husband is suspected of murder.
Stirring times for all the neighbourhood in

THE STEEPWOOD

Scandals

Volume 1 – November 2006
Lord Ravensden's Marriage by Anne Herries
An Innocent Miss by Elizabeth Bailey

Volume 2 – December 2006
The Reluctant Bride by Meg Alexander
A Companion of Quality by Nicola Cornick

Volume 3 – January 2007
A Most Improper Proposal by Gail Whitiker
A Noble Man by Anne Ashley

Volume 4 – February 2007
An Unreasonable Match by Sylvia Andrew
An Unconventional Duenna by Paula Marshall

A young woman disappears.
A husband is suspected of murder.
Stirring times for all the neighbourhood in

THE STEEPWOOD
Scandals

Volume 5 – March 2007
Counterfeit Earl by Anne Herries
The Captain's Return by Elizabeth Bailey

Volume 6 – April 2007
The Guardian's Dilemma by Gail Whitiker
Lord Exmouth's Intentions by Anne Ashley

Volume 7 – May 2007
Mr Rushford's Honour by Meg Alexander
An Unlikely Suitor by Nicola Cornick

Volume 8 – June 2007
An Inescapable Match by Sylvia Andrew
The Missing Marchioness by Paula Marshall

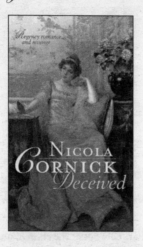

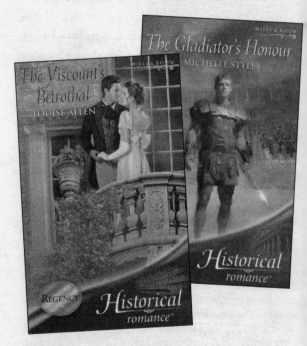

**In 1875, a row
of tiny cottages
stands by the
tracks of the
newly built
York – Doncaster
railway…**

Railwayman Tom Swales, with his wife and five
daughters, takes the end cottage. But with no room to
spare in the loving Swales household, eldest daughter
Mary accepts a position as housemaid to the nearby
stationmaster. There she battles the daily grime from
the passing trains – and the stationmaster's brutal, lustful
nature. In the end, it's a fight she cannot win.

In shame and despair, Mary flees to York. But the pious
couple who take her in know nothing of true Christian
charity. They work Mary like a slave – despite her heavy
pregnancy. Can she find the strength to return home to
her family? Will they accept her? And what of her first
love, farmer's son Nathaniel? Mary hopes with all her
heart that he will still be waiting…

Available 16th March 2007